Moments with the MASTER

WISDOM FOR THE JOURNEY

JOHN THIELENHAUS

TATE PUBLISHING
AND ENTERPRISES, LLC

Published by Tate Publishing & Enterprises, LLC
127 E. Trade Center Terrace | Mustang, Oklahoma 73064 USA
1.888.361.9473 | www.tatepublishing.com

Tate Publishing is committed to excellence in the publishing industry. The company reflects the philosophy established by the founders, based on Psalm 68:11,
"The Lord gave the word and great was the company of those who published it."

Book design copyright © 2014 by Tate Publishing, LLC. All rights reserved.
Cover design by Ivan Charlem Igot
Interior design by Mary Jean Archival

Published in the United States of America

ISBN: 978-1-63367-574-2
Religion / Christian Life / Devotional
14.10.16

Now glory be to God! By his mighty power
at work within us, he is able to accomplish
infinitely more than we would ever dare to ask or hope.
May he be given glory in the church and in
Christ Jesus forever and ever through
endless ages.

—Ephesians 3:20-21

This book is dedicated to my wife Jane, who has been my friend for more than fifty-two years. She is the most precious gift the Lord has ever given to me. If given the chance, I'd marry her all over again!

To our son, Douglas, and his wife, Brenda, and to our daughter, Susan, and her husband, Eric, your presence and love has brought so much joy to our hearts and our home. And in honor of our grandchildren, Monica, Melinda, Zeke, Stephanie, Chris and Joshua who have filled our lives with laughter and hope for the future.

Thanks and Acknowledgments

I am filled with thanks and gratitude to God for allowing me to experience the incredible blessings of this project. I have never worked so hard nor felt God's presence with such clarity. Thanks to my dear wife Jane for her suggestions, help, and skill in this project. I would like to acknowledge my parents whose lives of devotion to Jesus Christ was the guiding light of my life. God placed in their hands the chisel that shaped every aspect of my life.

Furthermore, I would like to thank dedicated professors, mentors, coworkers, and congregations whom I have served for five decades of ministry. My deep thanks for so many people who, through their writings, sermons, and wise counsel, have greatly affected my life. I'm grateful for family and friends whose love and prayers have sustained me in my journey and been a constant source of strength and encouragement.

Finally, I thank the people who have passed through my life, who have become the fabric of God's great plan for my life. May the blessings of God rest upon each of you! Thanks for your love and grace—I will be forever indebted to you!

Thanks to Tate Publishing for believing in me and making my dream come true.

Introduction

Welcome to this exciting book, *Moments with the Master*—a collection of daily meditations from God's word that can facilitate your spiritual journey as you are equipped to live with God's perspective. Many of the devotionals are reflective of my "growing up" years spent on our Kansas farm and later from my pastoral ministry.

After you read each Scripture and the corresponding devotional, take a moment to reflect on what God is saying to you. Ask God to help you make the changes necessary to become the person God wants you to be. Do not allow your past to control your future. *Moments with the Master* will deepen your relationship with the Lord, giving you courage to face the challenges of each new day!

May God strengthen your walk with him! He cares deeply about you and wants to bless you more than you could possibly hope or imagine. Have a great year exploring his truth! When you follow God's instructions, you can be assured that the best is yet to come! *Moments with the Master* is a great way to discover the purposeful, joyful, and abundant life God created you to enjoy!

> And now just as you accepted Christ Jesus
> as your Lord, you must continue to
> live in obedience to him. Let your roots grow down into
> him and draw up nourishment from him, so you will grow
> in faith, strong and vigorous in the truth you were taught.
> Let your lives overflow with thanksgiving
> for all he has done.
>
> —Colossians 2:6-7

Life Is a Parade

January 1
Joshua 1:1-9

America celebrates New Year's Day with the fabulous Tournament of Roses Parade from Pasadena. Every float is covered with flowers, about a hundred thousand blossoms! While admiring beautiful floats, we know life is not a "tournament of roses!" God never promised us a tournament of roses, but he turns mornings out of evenings and brings roses from thorns. It has been a real joy to trust him in last year's journey!

Despite troubles and challenges, we've been blessed throughout last year's journey. But today we are "on the other side of the Jordan"—a New Year! Each year sets new paths for our feet, new experiences, challenges, new joys and sorrows. We have not passed this way before, but confidently travel with faith in this New Year. The New Year may mean changes in our plans, some refocusing, retirement, a move, or a new job. But with Christ before us and his Spirit in us, we can travel with hope and genuine excitement. He who led in the past will be our abiding portion—the Eternal "I AM"—the One who is the same yesterday, today, and forever!

With confidence we move forward in the grace of a New Year. In 365 days, we need to be ready for the next "Tournament of Roses" Parade. That means, in every day ahead, followers of Jesus must help "build and decorate the float" whatever the cost, to the praise and glory of our Great God. Let's make the most of this year by living our lives as Godly disciples, redeeming the time until he returns and judges our "float!"

My moment of reflection…

Faith 101

January 2
Matthew 14:22-32

Facing a New Year is like the wild ride Peter faced one stormy night on the Sea of Galilee. The disciples thought it would be a routine commute to the other side, but Jesus knew it was going to be a pop quiz in "Faith 101!" My generation has grown up singing Andrae Crouch's song, "Through it all...I've learned to trust in Jesus, I've learned to trust in God." But have we? Is that really true? When bright skies turn black and waves are high and we don't see any help on the horizon, do we really trust him? That's what Peter had to do. That's what we must do throughout the year!

When Peter stepped out of the boat that unforgettable night, he was leading the way by faith. It wasn't John or Philip who climbed out of the boat. It was Peter, with eyes fixed on Jesus, who attempted the impossible! In that turbulent moment, Peter learned that he did have faith, but had so much further to go. There's nothing wrong with getting wet when we seek to walk on water or go "under" for a couple of seconds when the Lord is there to pull us up!

The "good news" is Peter reached a new level of faith that night. The only way you are going to grow and mature in faith is to reach your hand toward the Lord's outstretched hand and take one step while keeping your eyes on Jesus. It is with that kind of faith we get "out of the boat" and walk with him, joyfully accepting the challenges he places before us!

My moment of reflection...

I Won't Let You Fall

January 3
Psalm 90:1-17

A fire swept through the home of a couple with small children. They all managed to get out of the roaring inferno safely. Without warning, one of the boys dashed into the burning home to look for his dog. In his search for his dog, the boy found his way to an upstairs window when he heard his father yell, "Son, jump! I can catch you! Jump now!"

Filled with terror, the boy cried, "But daddy, I can't see you." Trusting his daddy's voice, the boy jumped blindly into the smoke and safely into his father's arms!

Many times we find ourselves on a dead-end street, full of hesitation and doubt. At a fork in the road, we don't know which way to turn. We are afraid because we can't see the hand of the Lord. We know he's there, somewhere, but it's so dark and we feel so alone! But listen to the Lord: "What really matters is I see you. I know what I'm doing! You can jump into my purposes for your life and I won't let you fall. Trust me!"

When you step out of your comfort zone and get out of a sinking boat, you will find the Father's arms strong enough to catch you and his grip firm enough to guide you wherever your path may lead. God gives us what we need and guides us with his grace. He will "...provide good things to eat when you are in the desert...You will be like a garden that has plenty of water or like a stream that never runs dry" (Isaiah 58:11, CEV).

My moment of reflection...

Your Finest Hour!

January 4
Proverbs 3:1-12

Preparing for Christian ministry, I chose Proverbs 3:5-6 as my life's verses: "With all your heart you must trust the Lord and not your own judgment. Always let him lead you, and he will clear the road for you to follow" (CEV). Solomon teaches there are three commitments in life that prepare one for the decisions of life—commitments that build a lifestyle that enjoys God's daily direction, no matter "what!" This is his instruction:

- Determine your Director—"Trust in the Lord with all your heart!"
- Detect your Detractor—"Lean not on your own understanding!"
- Declare your Delight—"In all your ways acknowledge him!"

It's simple: "Acknowledge him!" And the promise is, "God will direct your paths." Not that he might or should or could—but will! In this age of aimlessness, how can I experience God's will for my life today? When I come to the inevitable fork in the road, how can I know what decision God would have me make? Here is the wisdom: If you work on determining and detecting and declaring, God will direct!

Reflecting on my spiritual journey of more than fifty years, I have found that the Eternal God was present at every juncture of life. We make countless mistakes and our lives are haunted by past failures. But as sons of God, we have been redeemed and forgiven and Christ has become our spiritual identity. Today can be your "finest hour" as you determine to trust in the Lord with all your heart! Look forward with great anticipation today to see what God is going to do with you. It could be your "finest hour!"

My moment of reflection…

Standing Strong

January 5
Matthew 7:21-29

Jesus was a great story teller!

> Anyone who hears and obeys these teachings of mine is like a wise person who built a house on solid rock. Rain poured down, rivers flooded, and winds beat against that house. But it did not fall, because it was built on solid rock. Anyone who hears my teaching and doesn't obey them is like a foolish person who built a house on sand. The rain poured down, the rivers flooded, and the winds blew and beat against that house. Finally, it fell with a crash. (Mt 7:24-27, CEV)

Everyone has experienced storms in their life! Maybe you are in the middle of a storm today—a storm of sickness, depression, financial stress, or strife in a relationship. While storms can take many forms, they all share a common tendency: they tend to inhibit or stop progress toward God's wonderful plan for your life! Trouble comes, not because God is punishing you or trying to teach you a lesson, but because we live in a fallen world. Some storms are the result of pure disobedience, like Jonah, who ran from the presence of God.

As an obedient "doer" of the word, your house will not fall when a storm comes. However, failure to hear and "do the word" will leave you open to storms. But as a doer of the word, you will be in a position to walk in blessings, prosperity and success. So in the calm or in the storm, listen carefully to the words of the Master who says, "Be of good cheer...peace be still" (John 16:33; Mark 4:39, KJV).

My moment of reflection...

In His Time...

January 6
Ecclesiastes 3:1-22

The years seem to fly by, don't they? Years, months, weeks, hours, minutes, and seconds whip by—almost faster than you can see. We are cautioned in the word of God that our lives on earth are very short! Moses reminds us that our lives are like "tender grass" that is green in the morning and dried up by evening (Psalm 90:5-6), and James tells us our lives are short, like "a vapor" (James 4:14). Not only does God do all things in his time, Solomon writes that "God has made everything beautiful in its time" (Ecclesiastes 3:11, NIV).

Let these verses remind and encourage you that your time is in God's hands:

- "But as for me, I trust in Thee, O Lord, I say, "Thou art my God." My times are in Thy hand" (Psalm 31:14-15, NASB).
- "There is an appointed time for everything. And there is a time for every event under heaven" (Ecclesiastes 3:1, NASB).
- "Let us not lose heart in doing good, for in due time we will reap if we do not grow weary" (Galatians 6:9, NASB).
- "Therefore, be careful how you walk, not as unwise men, but as wise, making the most of your time" (Ephesians 5:15-16, NASB).

Your gift today is time—be careful how you spend it! Make the most of every opportunity to share God's grace with everyone you know. The next time you see a timer counting down, remember God's counter is running too. The time is short between this moment and when we shall see him face to face. Until then, continue to serve him with your whole being, with all that you are!

My moment of reflection...

Encouragement

January 7
Jeremiah 1:1-19

You can be or do or say anything God calls you to be or do or say! God came to Jeremiah and said, "Before you were born, I chose you to speak for me to the nations...I promise to be with you... so don't be afraid" (Jeremiah 1:5, 8, CEV). God had great plans for Jeremiah, and he has great plans for you—he has not changed! God knew what Jeremiah really needed at that moment was a word of encouragement, a word from someone who really believed in him! Many of us need someone who will say to us, "I believe in you!" Believers have such an encourager—the Lord! He sees possibilities within us we never dreamed possible. If we believe in him and his dream for our lives, we can accomplish more than we ever dreamed possible. A little girl was working with plasticine, a clay-like substance that can be used over and over because it does not harden. She formed a beautiful angel-like creature with wings but quickly molded the angel into a clay ball.

"What's this?" she asked.

"A ball," someone said.

"Nope," said the girl, "it's a hiding angel."

Some of us have within us "hiding angels," just waiting, longing to be released. You are released when you discover that you are a child of God! Before you were formed in the womb and before you were born, you were set apart for something good and beautiful. To believe that about ourselves is to unleash powers and possibilities beyond our imagination. Let God touch your lips and encourage you to release the "hiding angel" today!

My moment of reflection...

In the Presence of the All-Powerful

January 8
Luke 5:1-11

Peter had been fishing all night and caught nothing! Jesus tells Peter to fish in the deep waters. Soon their nets were so full their nets were breaking, and they needed help! Then it dawned on Peter: This Nazarene carpenter is more than a man! Peter reacts, "Lord, don't come near me! I am a sinner" (Luke 5:8, CEV). Some people don't know how to behave in God's presence because they haven't had much experience with God!
Remember Isaiah? He had the most notable confrontation with God in history! When King Uzziah died, he came to the temple and saw the Lord exalted, seated on a throne. Then he heard these words, "Holy, Holy, Holy, Lord All-powerful! The earth is filled with your glory." Isaiah cries out, "I'm doomed...I have seen the King, the Lord All-Powerful" (Isaiah 6:3-6, CEV). Sometimes, like Isaiah, we may not maintain a proper decorum in God's presence. We don't know how to act!

In the presence of the Divine, Isaiah and Peter realized they needed help. Both discovered they had a mission in life—to live the Jesus life. Isaiah said, "Here am I, send me." And Peter heard Jesus say, "Don't be afraid; from now on you will catch men." Their mission was to take Christ's love to folks who wouldn't know how to behave in church!

But here is the good news: God is here, right where you are this very moment! He is seeking to make his presence known to each of us. So how do you act in his presence? It's simple: don't be afraid, confess your need, and find your mission!

My moment of reflection...

Abundant Living

January 9
Jeremiah 17:1-18

We live in a world of opportunity but often fail to see or use our potential. A struggling farmer living in the dusty panhandle of Texas was asked by an oil company for the right to drill for oil on his land. After many requests, he reluctantly gave permission to drill for oil—and instantly became a millionaire! He had been sitting on a reservoir of wealth while struggling to make a living. How sad and tragic—yet so common!

God's will for his children is not to live in poverty or ignorance, but to be happy and at peace with themselves. That's God's plan for your life! If you are not at peace with yourself, it may be because you are sitting on some gift, opportunity, or potential blessing.

Many times our dreams are doomed not by outside forces, but forces within. We focus on our limitations, not the possibilities. God has so uniquely constructed the world that there is a niche for every one of us. That's why each of us is wonderfully gifted with so many abilities and talents.

The critical ingredient in achieving our potential and success is confidence. Trust in God! God said through Jeremiah: "I will bless those who trust me. They will be like trees growing beside a stream—trees with roots that reach down to the water...they are always green...they bear fruit every year" (Jeremiah 17:7-8, CEV). If you want to achieve your hopes and dreams, trust God to supply your every need; he will give you all you need to be happy, fruitful, and successful.

My moment of reflection...

Life...at the Crossroads

January 10
Exodus 3:1-15

We all encounter crossroads from time to time. It's just part of life! Although crossroads may seem to be exciting ventures, they are risky, sometimes even dangerous. These intersections offer the possibility of both pain and pleasure and usually require conviction. Remember Abraham? The Lord told his friend to leave his country, family, and relatives and go to the land that God would show him. No guarantees except the presence and blessing of God. Moses encountered God in the burning bush, sending him into hostile territory on a rescue mission. Jesus, our Lord, faced a terrible crossroad called Gethsemane and said, "My Father, if there is no other way, and I must suffer, I will still do what you want" (Matthew 26:42).

In our crossroads experiences, we want to know how best to fulfill God's purpose for our lives. In our "direction choice," we experience ambivalence and confusion. But in the end, as we labor in prayer and seek Godly counsel, we sense clarity about our future and begin our journey.

While everyone comes to crossroads in life from time to time, it is comforting to know there are fellow pilgrims who are upholding us with the gift of prayer. With a dedicated prayer life for ourselves and for others, I am convinced that God will pour out his blessing on our lives and we will discover the "mind of Christ," enabling us to take the right turn at every crossroad in our lives. A crossroad can become the highest treasure in life—and you can go on your way rejoicing, knowing you have made the right choice!

My moment of reflection...

Tomorrow

January 11
John 16:16-33

In Deuteronomy Moses presents a view of the future to fellow pilgrim travelers. He was not clairvoyant, but he possessed insight and faith. Moses knew the future would be different from anything they had known in the past—that's the nature of tomorrow! Change will be part of our agenda. Living in a world of change, we must find keys to unlock doors of new opportunities. That's both exciting and scary!

Every tomorrow brings new responsibilities and possibilities. Life tomorrow will have hills and deep valleys. Tomorrow will involve hardship and challenge. No detours from tough duty are available for anyone. While we may love and hug the past, you will never get it back. We will only get tomorrow, not yesterday. Hills are made for climbing and we are made for climbing too! Jesus said, "While you are in the world, you will...suffer" (John 16:33, CEV). Our tomorrows will include pressure, obligation, urgency, "But cheer up," says the Lord. That's what makes valleys so fruitful and our tomorrows so exciting!

What we really need and long for in our uncertain journey of tomorrow is security, and assurance! We need to know God cares, that he is present in all our tomorrows. To help us understand his presence in our tomorrows, Christ tells us he is our Shepherd who leaves the ninety and nine to care for the one who is lost (John 10). God's steadfast care and his dependable love and wisdom are his gifts to us in all of our tomorrows. So as you journey into an unknown tomorrow, put your hand into the hand of God. It's the only safe way to go!

My moment of reflection...

Midnight...I Can't Sleep

January 12
Acts 16:16-40

Recently I spent most of a night awake, unable to sleep. Lying in the darkness, the thought hit me: *Every man has his midnight!* Your "midnight" is that time when your eyes can't penetrate the darkness, when the oil in your lamp is low, or when you're lonely and scared, not knowing what the future holds—or if there will be a future! You wonder, "Where is God in my struggle? Doesn't God care?" We've all had our "midnight" hour—probably more than once! So how does one recover from "midnight" darkness?

The beauty of Christianity is seldom witnessed by those who have been sheltered from the storms and battles of life. Furthermore, the value of faith is not captured in a worship service when singing "Great is Thy Faithfulness" or enjoying rich fellowship. The truth is, the real beauty of Christianity is not felt when all is well!

To fully understand the beauty of Christianity, we must view it at the midnight hour! Midnight comes when tragedy strikes, when grief shatters all hope, when your cherished dream is dashed, when you want to give up and can't. Somehow, in that moment, your faith overcomes the midnight darkness and despair.

Peter was delivered miraculously from his "midnight" by an angel. Paul and Silas found deliverance in their "midnight" through prayer and praise. For some of us, it is 11:59 p.m. and midnight is just sixty seconds away. Midnight comes...every day...every week...year after year! In those moments, when we desperately need light, go to the source, "The Light of the World," the one who never disappoints and never fails to show up!

My moment of reflection...

Ingredients for Success

January 13
Genesis 45:1-15

Often we obey God intermittently—just long enough to straighten out the last mess we created in our life. We allow momentary desire and popular opinion to replace personal conviction. Joseph was one of the most successful men in history, inspiring millions to do the "right thing" always!

Since Joseph was his father's favorite, his brothers plotted how to get rid of this arrogant dreamer. But in divine providence, Joseph was sold to Potiphar, who soon recognized that Joseph was a man of character, someone he could trust with everything he owned, including his wife. Things went south and Joseph found himself in prison, but even in prison his character and commitment to God kept shining through adversity. Joseph's life took strange twists and turns until Pharaoh made Joseph the second most powerful man in the land. Through famine, Joseph "saves" Egypt but also "saves" his mischievous brothers and family by providing needed assistance. Overcome with emotion, Joseph reveals his identity, telling his family that this whole event was orchestrated by Jehovah God!

Against enormous odds, Joseph never lost confidence in the goodness of God. What was his secret? It was not his intelligence or his talent or some special leadership skills. It was his character, his commitment, his confidence in God—he was a man who could be trusted! This story is included in the Bible to help us understand we too can live successful lives. Be true to your values. Trust in the goodness of God! No matter what twists or turns your life takes, if you will pattern your life after Joseph, you too will be successful.

My moment of reflection...

Encouragers Needed!

January 14
Hebrews 10:19-25

One great quality of a "Christ follower" is their ability to encourage others. Barnabas was called the "Son of Encouragement" (Acts 4:36) because every time you see him, he is bringing encouragement and hope to someone in need. When Paul needed support, Barnabas was there to support his acceptance into the church, which he had formerly persecuted. Barnabas was not an apostle or preacher—just a man full of faith who responded to needs with encouragement!

The word *encourage* comes from the same root as "comforter" used in reference to the Holy Spirit (John 14). The Holy Spirit comes to help, to give a spiritual boost, to encourage us in our journey, to comfort us in times of need. That is what Barnabas did: he was generous with encouraging words, with actions, and with his pocketbook.

In the cold days of winter, we often find our car battery too weak to start the engine. We need a boost to get our car running. The ministry of encouragement is like a car that comes alongside ours and gives us a jump start. The strength of one is transferred into the weakness of another. When we see people who are discouraged, burdened by the hardships of life, and plain ready to give up, we need to come alongside and give them a spiritual jump start. What about those among us who have failed and are ready to walk away from life? They need another chance! Aren't you glad someone gave you a chance after you failed? God gives us the ministry of encouragement! As we encourage others, we ourselves are energized by him!

My moment of reflection...

When Life Seems Unfair

January 15
Job 1:1-2:10

One of the most puzzling and unpopular biblical messages is the story of Job! This ancient book is filled with treasures waiting for discovery. Job was a moral, wealthy, and godly man who lived during the patriarchal period. As the story unfolds, we see Job in sorrow, loss, and extreme suffering. This righteous man of antiquity is a profile of courage in the face of adversity. Never did he give up or compromise his integrity. Even when his wife and friends brought charges against him, Job claimed his innocence.

Job was tenacious when afflicted, but proclaimed his innocence, which infuriated his friends. He didn't give in to suffering but demonstrated remarkable courage and passed the school of hard knocks with flying colors, graduating with honors. Even when he was under intense accusation, he was thankful. Tested like no other, God gave him this compliment: "No one on earth is like him—he is a truly good person who respects me and refuses to do evil" (Job 1:8, CEV).

Job didn't serve God because God had put a hedge around him and sheltered him from harm. No. Job loved God, not for fame or reward, but for better or worse! When everything seems to be out of your hands and when life seems unfair, we still have choices. We are not just bystanders! God is faithful and he will not allow you to be tempted beyond your limitations. All through his struggles, Job was alone to the human eye, but carefully guarded by God's watchful eye. So when life seems unfair, remember this: "God is near. You are not alone!"

My moment of reflection…

Drawing Near to God

January 16
James 4:1-10

God expects growth in our walk with Jesus. James challenges believers to "draw close to God, and God will draw close to you" (James 4:8). Jonah reacted to the call to come closer by running away in the opposite direction; and when we, like Jonah, start running away, we find ourselves in big trouble. But it doesn't need to be that way!

God called Moses to draw closer to him and come into his presence. After their bondage, the children of Israel settled at Mount Sinai. While at Sinai, Moses went up the mountain to hear the voice of God. The mountain shook, the sky grew dark, lightning flashed, thunder rolled. It was a frightening sight to the disobedient Israelites as God revealed his power and glory. They were afraid to come closer to God because of his holiness and their sinfulness.

Jesus said when we gather together in his name he would be with us. As we spend time in his presence, God reveals his grace, mercy, compassion, and love. When we deliberately spend time in his presence, the virtues of his character begin to come alive in our lives.

Alone with God on the mountain, God gave Moses the Ten Commandments so Israel would know what God expected, so they could grow closer to him. We need to hear from God today because we are in trouble! When we climb the mountain and enter his presence, there is no limit what God can do in us. We can never be "too close!" It is true: If we draw close to God, he will draw close to us!

My moment of reflection...

Enoch…Walking with God

January 17
Psalm 119:97-105

God passionately wants a close, intimate relationship with his creation. Micah the prophet tells us what God requires from his people: "The Lord has already told you what is good, and this is what he requires: to do what is right, to love mercy, and to walk humbly with your God" (Micah 6:8).

Enoch was a saint! We know little about Enoch except that he lived a godly life and had a glorious exit! The Bible tells us that Enoch was the father of Methuselah and walked with God for three hundred years (Genesis 5:21-24). Enoch started his walk with God at age sixty-five, so for three hundred years he enjoyed close communion with God. There was never a cloud between them. God was a pleasure to Enoch and Enoch pleased God. Walking with God implies progress. He did not walk for a while and stand still. Each day Enoch found himself nearer the goal. He didn't attempt to walk alone…he walked with God. And finally, "God took him," which means that he did not taste death. Among the millions of men, only two never died—Enoch and Elijah! At age 365, God took Enoch directly to heaven!

At age sixty-five, Enoch made a choice to walk with God! Hopefully, you have made the decision to walk with God—it's a choice you must make and it's never too late to make that choice. Enoch made his choice at age sixty-five, when many retire. You may think all your choices have been made. Enoch teaches us any person, at any stage of life, can decide to "draw near to God!"

My moment of reflection…

Walking in Obedience

January 18
Genesis 6:1-22

Noah, the obedient boat builder, appeared in history when he was five hundred years old. We don't know much about Noah, but this we know: he lived in a time when mankind was very corrupt and so evil that God said he would destroy the human race. But in the midst of this godless culture, Noah walked with God. The Bible says: "Noah was a righteous man, the only blameless man living on earth at the time. He consistently followed God's will and enjoyed a close relationship with him" (Genesis 6:9).

Following God's instructions, Noah built a vessel large enough to shelter his family and a pair of all the birds and beasts. Enduring godless ridicule, he followed God's directions and built the ark. When the waters of judgment covered the earth, Noah and his family survived. But Noah walked in obedience to every command!

If you have tried to walk a cat on a leash, you know it doesn't work! Cats have no intention of walking with their master. Often our walk with God is like a cat on a leash: we take off in our own direction, pulling with all our might against his plan. But like Noah, when you take God's hand, you need to know that he sets the pace and chooses the direction of your walk. Pulling against God won't do any good at all! When you are obedient to God's commands, you may not know the dangers of the future; but you will be safe as long as you follow God's lead. Noah teaches us obedience is the key to "drawing near to God."

My moment of reflection…

Abraham...Walking by Faith

January 19
Hebrews 11:8-10

Abraham stands out as a landmark in world history! He was chosen by God to be the "father of the faithful." Abraham was ninety-nine years old when the Lord appeared to him and said, "I am God Almighty; serve me faithfully and live a blameless life" (Genesis 17:1). Abraham was a sheep rancher; he gave no prophecy or wrote any laws! Yet he stands out as one of the most important men in Bible history. Why? Because he was a man of faith and he "walked with God by faith!"

"By faith Abraham obeyed when God called him to leave home and go to another land that God would give him as his inheritance. He went without knowing where he was going" (Hebrews 11:8). Noah had specific instructions, but not Abraham. When Abraham started walking with God, he had no idea where he was headed— no map that outlined the future. He was subject to failures and pain. He was renowned for his active, working, living faith—that's how we remember this man of faith!

Abraham's story is written in blood and tears, but it was his obedience that earned him the honor of being "God's friend." Walking with God is a "walk of faith." If you are going to walk with God, there will be rough roads and steep climbs. Sometimes you have to grit your teeth and step out in faith. But we can always count on God to give us enough light to see the next step to take. Abraham teaches us that to "draw near to God" we must walk by faith!

My moment of reflection...

David...Walking with All Your Heart

January 20
Psalm 42:1-11

David was Israel's greatest king, an eloquent poet and prominent figure in religious history. Trained as a shepherd, David was a soldier and champion warrior. As a musician, he was a poetic genius as seen in his majestic psalms. But David's character was stained by his grievous sin against God and Uriah. However, he was known as a man after God's own heart! Perhaps it was David's heartfelt confession as he cried for forgiveness that makes him one of our favorite characters.

One thing becomes obvious about David: When he walked with God, he put his whole heart into it. God said this about David: "David...is the kind of person who pleases me most. He does everything I want him to do" (Acts 13:22, CEV). He valued his time with God and had a compelling hunger and thirst for God's word. For David, time with God was as necessary as food and drink. He wrote, "Your teachings are sweeter than honey" (Psalm 119:103, CEV).

If we gorge on worldly junk, we lose our taste for the sweetness of God's word. It is imperative that we develop a taste for God! David awoke before dawn and stayed up through the night watches. He meditated on God's promises and took time to praise God. Isaiah reminds us some people "remove their heart far from God." But not David! His goal was clear: "But as for me, how good it is to be near God" (Psalm 73:28). David shouts to every believer: "If there was ever a time to get near to God, it is now!"

My moment of reflection...

It's Just a Small Thing!

January 21
Matthew 6:19-34

We have grown up with the philosophy that "bigger is better." That is especially the message portrayed on television—but that's not necessarily true. Zechariah warns us not to despise small beginnings (Zechariah 4:10). In effect, Zechariah is saying, "Small is also beautiful!"

A large crowd gathered in a stadium to honor men and women who had faithfully served their country. The master of ceremonies told the gathering that some folks think their job isn't important because it's such a little job. But he said, "You are wrong!" He ordered all the lights turned off. There was total darkness! Then he struck a match. In the darkness, the entire crowd could see the flickering light. The darkness had been penetrated by one little light.

Get the message? You are important…you count…you're needed! Our world will be better or worse because of you. True, you can't do everything, but you can do something! To help us understand our importance and value, Jesus said, "Look at the birds. They don't need to plant or harvest or put food in barns because your heavenly Father feeds them. And you are far more valuable to him than they are" (Matthew 6:26).

The work you do may seem unimportant. But if it is humbly offered to the Lord in love, God has promised to mightily bless your small work. Today, whatever talent or gifting you may possess, regardless of how small or insignificant you think it may be, use it for the Lord and it will become great! Remember, "There's no such thing as a small thing!"

My moment of reflection…

The Law of Echoes

January 22
Luke 6:20-42

A boy lived with his grandfather in the high mountains of the Swiss Alps. Sometimes, just to hear his voice, he would go outside and shout, "Hello." To his amazement, from the canyons beyond reverberated over and over, "Hello...hello." He yelled again, "I love you," and immediately the response, "I love you!" One day, because the boy misbehaved, the grandfather disciplined him severely. The child reacted by screaming at his grandfather, "I hate you!" To his surprise, the rocks and boulders across the mountainside responded in the same tone, "I hate you!"

That's life! We get in return exactly what we give; it all comes back, sometimes in greater measure than we gave. Jesus taught his disciples: "Don't judge others, and God won't judge you. Don't be hard on others and God won't be hard on you. Forgive others, and God will forgive you. If you give to others, you will be given a full amount in return...the way you treat others is the way you will be treated" (Luke 6:37-39, cev). This "law of echoes" applies to all of life. If our conversation is negative, sour, and demanding, the echo reflects those same characteristics, almost without exception!

If you want others to judge and condemn you, you start it. If you want them to be understanding, broad-minded, allowing you room to be you, then begin by being that way yourself. Like begets like, smiles breeds smiles, laughter is contagious. But, unfortunately, so are frowns and hard, abrasive words. The law of echoes is eternally true: "Whatever you deposit you draw out in return...and sometimes more!"

My moment of reflection...

Remember...Don't Forget

January 23
1 Thessalonians 5:12-22

To remain faithful to our calling, we must develop the habit of thankfulness! One of the most grievous sins is the sin of thanklessness. Thankfulness is a spiritual discipline, critical for every maturing believer. St. Paul reminds us that a mark of the depraved nature is "they knew God, but they wouldn't worship him as God or even give him thanks" (Romans 1:21). Israel often was guilty of murmuring. Moses said, "Be careful not to forget the Lord, who rescued you from slavery in the land of Egypt" (Deuteronomy 6:12). The root of their problem was ingratitude and failure to remember! Remember what?

- Remember from where you came! They had been slaves, in Egypt, but God brought them out of bondage.
- Remember and never forget the goodness of the Lord.
- Remember the Lord's commands and obey them.

We are so like our forefathers! We are guilty of thanklessness on many occasions. Despite our financial difficulties, we enjoy prosperity. But in this prosperity, we must always remember we are totally dependent upon God. In his final advice to some friends, Paul told them: "Always be joyful. Keep on praying. No matter what happens, always be thankful, for this is God's will for you who belong to Jesus Christ" (1 Thessalonians 5:16-18).

My moment of reflection...

I Will Tomorrow...

January 24
Proverbs 27:1-22

I love it! A popular restaurant had this sign in the window: "Free pizza tomorrow!" After dining, some clients returned the following day for their "free" pizza. But when they arrived, the sign said, "Free pizza tomorrow!"

Tomorrow is the busiest day of the year. We plan many things, but not today! Days turn into weeks and months and the year passes without doing what we had intended. We plan to share Christ with a friend, but before tomorrow comes, he dies. We desire to read the Bible, but not today. We say, "When I get caught up with work, I will have added time." In the meantime, the Bible gathers dust. We plan to help those in need, to visit someone in the nursing home. But... not today! We plan to send a note of appreciation to those who have helped us. However, time passes and we find ourselves visiting the funeral home to pay our "respects." We wait for tomorrow...but find the door closed!

Successful people have a plan and follow through with their plans. They not only plan to serve God, they serve him and live for him today! Last year, thousands of people became highway statistics. They had plans for tomorrow, but tomorrow never came. Solomon warns: "Don't brag about tomorrow! Each day brings its own surprises" (Proverbs 27:1, CEV). For some, this will be their last year or month or day! There is no assurance of tomorrow! Today is the only sure day you have. Christ could come today or you could go out into eternity. Love and live every day as if it were your last!

My moment of reflection...

Until He Comes

January 25
Mark 16:14-20

These precious words fell from our Savior's lips: "I am going to prepare a place for you...when everything is ready, I will come and get you, so that you will always be with me" (John 14:2-3). As Christians, we base our faith on Christ's words and work. We believe he will return as he promised. But what do we do between now and then?

"I will return" encourages readiness! Peter reminds us the Lord will return "as a thief in the night." Jesus insisted upon readiness—there will be no other opportunity for redemption. Destiny will be decided when the Lord Jesus returns. His return encourages believers to be ready with personal growth and spiritual maturity. Peter also stresses godliness—since all things will pass away, our conversation ought to be holy, filled with godliness. We ought to be living the best life possible. What a challenge!

"I will return" encourages service! Nearly on every mention of the Lord's return there is mention of service. Since much needs to be done before the Lord's return, Christians should work with zeal and dedication.

Christ comes to us in many ways: at conversion, in worship, in obedience, and some day in victory! On that day, living saints will rise to be with him and saints who have already died will be resurrected. The battle with sin will be over, death will be defeated and sent into exile, and we will worship God without limitation. What a day...until he returns!

My moment of reflection...

Without Vision...We All Lose

January 26
Habakkuk 2:1-4

Solomon told the leaders of Israel "where there is no vision the people perish" (Proverbs 29:18, KJV). Our vision shapes and controls us and becomes the determining factor who we become and what we do. Our vision determines how we look, our relationships, and what our marriage will become. Visions also shape nations and movements. Our vision determines our interests, our finances, and the totality of the human experience. In fact, no part of our life is untouched by its influence, including our spiritual focus.

Those believers in Acts were amazing! They became "world changers" because a few devout people empowered by vision claimed the world for Christ. We cannot live in the past or live off memories. We are people of faith who light candles daily to defy the darkness. Can you imagine what your life would be like if Jesus had not come and you could not know him? Our limitation is not a lack of talent or brainpower. It's not money, not a lack of ability—but availability—putting ourselves at God's disposal.

We often miss "visions" that are right in front of our eyes, if we would only take time to really look. We not only need sight, but divine insight which only the Holy Spirit can give to us. Ask God today for a vision for your life—something to do, someone to love, someplace to go! As you look at your resources and the needs of our world, you're only reaction can be, "My God, what a fantastic time to be alive! What a time to be used by God for something great!"

My moment of reflection...

Monuments that Last

January 27
Matthew 6:19-34

Near my boyhood home in Western Kansas stands a group of gravestones. John Davis, a farmer and self-made man, had them erected. Beginning as a hired "farm hand," Davis managed to become wealthy in his lifetime, but he had few friends. When his wife died, he fashioned an elaborate statue in her memory. One thing led to another until he'd spent thousands on monuments honoring himself and his wife. John Davis died at ninety-two, a resident in the county poorhouse, having spent his resources on statues.

Today, the monuments are slowly sinking into the ground, becoming victims of time, vandalism, and neglect—a sad reminder of a self-centered life. Few people attended Davis's funeral. The only person moved by any sense of personal loss was the tombstone salesman!

Before we become too hard on Davis, let's take an honest look at the monuments that are being erected today. Monuments of fortune and power and pleasure are tailor-made for our time. But conspicuous by its absence is the philosophy of Jesus who taught one gets rich by giving rather than getting, by serving rather than looking out for number one, by surrendering rights rather than taking control. Christ's philosophy was wrapped up in one simple statement: "More than anything else put God's work first and do what he wants. Then the other things will be yours as well" (Matthew 6:33, CEV). When he died two thousand years ago, nobody understood because they were too busy building their own monuments…and we still are!

My moment of reflection…

Attractiveness through Christlikeness

January 28
Acts 4:1-22

Despite personality differences, people are attracted to one another. Some people possess a charisma that draws them to each other and become lifelong best friends. Sometimes the attraction is because of material success or social status. But if these are not backed up by an attractive person underneath, the chemistry will quickly fade and the interest is over. As followers of Christ, our personal goal is to become so "attractive" that our friends and family will be attracted to Jesus. If we are going to become attractive to Christians and non-Christians, we must develop Christlikeness in all of life.

Peter and John annoyed religious leaders of Jerusalem because of their teaching about Jesus. The council was amazed with their boldness in their presentation! The Bible says, "When they saw the boldness of Peter and John…they recognized them as men who had been with Jesus" (Acts 4:13). This is certain: We become like the person we spend the most time with. So as Christ-followers, when we spend time with him, we become like him, and people sense it. The aroma of Christ attracts people to us and the Savior.

So how do we become Christ-like? What are the building blocks of Christlikeness? They haven't changed in two thousand years: practicing the presence of God, loving obedience to his word, and fellowship with fellow Christians. When you live a Christ-like life, people will take note that you have been with Jesus, and like Peter and John, people will be amazed at your quality of life! The magnet of an attractive life is to become like Christ in every manner!

My moment of reflection…

Attractiveness through Honesty

January 29
Psalm 24:1-10

As Christians, our lives are being transformed into a magnet that draws people to you and to God. To be "attractive" to others, honesty is a character trait which must be evident in life. Solomon wrote: "Good people are guided by their honesty; treacherous people are destroyed by their dishonesty" (Proverbs 11:3). Jesus enforces honesty when he said, "If you cheat even a little, you won't be honest with greater responsibilities" (Luke 16:10). We are taught that honesty is the basis of successful relationships.

We live in a world where honesty often takes a back seat to opportunity and expediency. It is true that an honest person stands out above the crowd of blurred morals and standards. Jacob understood the value of honesty when he returned the money that was placed in bags of grain during a famine (Genesis 43). Underlying the Ten Commandments is the demand to be fair and honest in all relationships.

Success does not honor God if you cheat or damage others to get ahead! The way we speak and work and play makes an impression on people, both believers and nonbelievers. A Christian who refuses to stretch the truth or lie attracts notice. When you are honest, you not only have a clear conscience, but you earn the trust and respect of your friends and the blessing of God. If you want others to gravitate to you, make sure honesty marks all that you do and say. In the midst of a secular world, God grants us the heart and desire to be truthful because honesty stands the test of time!

My moment of reflection...

Attractiveness through Generosity

January 30
Mark 12:41-44

Our Father is so gracious and generous in his provision for his children. But we must never forget that we are responsible to God for how we use those provisions. It is not optional, but rather required that "we are found faithful." Jesus made it clear:

> You must each make up your own mind as to how much you should give. Don't give reluctantly...God loves the person who gives cheerfully. And God will generously provide all you need. Then you will always have everything you need and plenty leftover to share with others. (2 Cor 9:7-8)

We become attractive to others when we practice generosity!

One way of becoming attractive to others is to be generous, a character trait that should be evident in all Christ-followers. Generosity is another of those magnets that draw people to you. People love a generous person—giving time, money and help always attracts friends. We can remember people who were exceptionally kind and generous to us! It made us feel important, special, treasured! Because of our "me first" culture, we often neglect to live out generosity. God loves the generous heart!

When adopting a generous spirit, you will be rewarded with the pleasure of helping others as well as the satisfaction of drawing others to yourself. When our personality is under the control of Jesus Christ, he will lead us to those who need our attention. Jesus gave us the key: "In everything, do to others what you would have them do to you" (Matthew 7:12, NASB). Someone somewhere needs a generous heart. Be that person today!

My moment of reflection...

Attractiveness through Encouragement

January 31
Mark 14:2-9

Some qualities of life serve as magnets in drawing others to us! Two very important character traits in life are encouragement and affirmation. Often at funeral services, friends send floral arrangements to pay tribute to the memory of a loved one. Maybe, however, those flowers would have brought needed encouragement and joy while their friend was alive. My departed mother used to say, "If you are going to give me flowers, give them now!" Perhaps, the importance of encouragement is best captured by Solomon who said, "The right word at the right time is like precious gold set in silver" (Proverbs 25:11, cev).

The gift of affirmation is so important! To hear "I love you," "I'm so glad you are my friend," "I'm so proud of you" can make you successful when you are doomed for failure. We need encouragement when under stress or when we've finished a difficult task. You can encourage someone by a word of thanks or an expression of support in times of struggle.

God thought that encouragement was so important he made it a spiritual gift. Paul instructs believers that "if your gift is to encourage others, do it" (Romans 12:8). In Hebrews, Christians are told to encourage others daily (Hebrews 3:13). An example of encouragement is found in the woman anointing Jesus with expensive perfume. Whether by word or deed, encouragement promotes sensitivity and thoughtfulness. Like always, people are hungry for feeling wanted and appreciated. Encouragement is the foundation for lasting relationships. Today, someone somewhere needs a "pat on the back" and an encouraging word. Be that person!

My moment of reflection…

Enthusiasm

February 1
Colossians 3:1-17

Many things catch your eye, but only a few catch your heart—so pursue passion! The secret of a successful business, career, or life is enthusiasm and passion. People without enthusiasm tend not to be effective. Paul reminded his friend Timothy not to become discouraged but to fan the flame he had been given by God (2 Timothy 1).

A businessman was walking in New York when he heard a boy's voice. "Ninety-eight, ninety-nine, one hundred! Mister, that's you—you get a free shine." Soon the lad was "enthusiastically" polishing the man's shoes.

"What's this all about?" asked the businessman.

"It's my birthday and every hundredth person gets a free shine."

Grateful for the "free shine," the man gave the boy a big tip and walked on. Nearby, a policeman grinned and said, "Every day is his birthday. He does more business than the other shoe shine boys put together."

Sure enough, in the distance, the man could hear, "Ninety-eight, ninety-nine…"

The Bible endorses an enthusiastic spirit: "Whatever you say or do should be done in the name of the Lord Jesus, as you give thanks to God" (Colossians 3:17, CEV). Enthusiastic people inspire us. It is the single ingredient that is the difference between success and failure! People who want something badly enough to take a risk and willing to endure the sacrifice to accomplish their dreams are infectious world-changers! Listen! "Ninety-eight, ninety-nine, one hundred. Mister, you get the free shine!" May that positive, enthusiastic spirit mark your life in all you do. Life is exciting and worthwhile when passion governs your mission!

My moment of reflection…

Together, We Can...

February 2
1 Corinthians 12:12-31

There is an ancient story about a blind man and a crippled man who happened to stumble into each other in a forest. Both were lost! In their misery, they struck up a conversation sharing their stories.

The blind man said, "I cannot see to find my way out!"

The crippled man nodded, "I cannot get up to walk out!"

Sitting there, saddened by their situations, the crippled man suddenly cried, "I've got it! You hoist me up onto your shoulders and I will tell you where to walk." Together, they found their way out of the forest!

Paul said, "The eye can never say to the hand, 'I don't need you.' The head can't say to the feet, 'I don't need you'…If one part suffers, all the parts suffer with it, and if one part is honored, all the parts are glad. Now all of you together are Christ's body, and each one of you is a separate and necessary part of it" (1 Corinthians 12:21-26).

We are like the two men in the forest! We need help from time to time. The pressures of our culture and the discouragement of life get us down. We struggle to find our way back to the Light—back to the right way. We need help! That's why God gave us the church and friends. Each person has a gift to share to build up one another. Each of us can offer an encouraging word to a struggling friend. I can't do it by myself…and you can't do it by yourself! But we can make a difference together!

My moment of reflection…

Little Things "Are" Important

February 3
Mark 9:38-50

The Hyatt Regency in Kansas City was the site of a dance contest in July 1981. Hundreds were standing on a catwalk with glass sides that spanned the lobby below. People stood on the catwalk enjoying the festive atmosphere below. Suddenly, celebration turned to tragedy—without warning, the walkway collapsed on hundreds of people, killing 114, injuring 188!

Months of investigation revealed a flaw in the construction of the walkway: small washers that should have been used were omitted. Insignificant washers led to the worst disaster in the history of Kansas City.

Little things are important. A mustard seed, round stones, a little boy's lunch. These and other things point to a powerful lesson in life: Little things are important! God has always used insignificant things in life to accomplish the significant. He uses foolish things, weak things, despised things to accomplish his will!

No matter how successful we may become, we must remember that our role is that of a servant. Daily we are called to do "little things" that we may think worthless, forgetting that God uses little things to accomplish the significant. If you don't believe that, just read this well-known proverb: "For the want of a nail, a shoe was lost. For the want of a shoe, a horse was lost. For the want of a horse, a battle was lost. For the want of a battle, a war was lost. For the want of a war, a kingdom was lost! All for the want of a nail!" Still today, "little things" are important!

My moment of reflection...

The Greatest Is Love

February 4
Matthew 22:34-40

We are in the habit of speaking in superlatives: "This is the finest automobile ever built." "She is the sweetest girl in the world." "He's the richest man in town." It seems we are careless in giving top ranking to too many things. The word of God contains little of such speech. But when it is used, we must pay special attention to it. Jesus tells us about the greatest commandment: "You must love the Lord your God with all your heart, all your soul and all your mind. This is the first and greatest commandment" (Matthew 22:37).

In our "love conscious" culture, we love anything that brings fulfillment and satisfaction to the physical man. If possible, many people would buy affection and love as they go to the local delicatessen to buy food! But love is not available for purchase nor is love cheap; it is sacred and something beautiful.

Jesus said the greatest commandment was to love God with our entire being and personality. It seems that some place more affection on some tangible entity than upon a wise, loving Heavenly Father who cares for his creation. It is instructive that the scriptures teach we are able to love only because he first loved us. Having received this wonderful gift "to love," should we not love the Lord our God with all our heart and soul and strength? What is really most important to you? In time, all your loved possessions will pass away. But your love for God and his love for you is the greatest. It is eternal!

My moment of reflection...

What a Day!

February 5
Psalm 118:1-29

"What a day" is a common expression! These words describe an unusual day filled with surprises, or it may describe a frustrating day when everything seems to go wrong. Maybe those words are said with a sigh at the end of an exhausting day. Life is made up of a succession of many days, but only a few are really remembered—remembered because of some pleasure, catastrophe, or disappointment. Yet each day is a separate compartment in our allotted time.

The failure or success of life depends not so much on a few exciting red-letter days, but on all our days, seasoned with a positive attitude and choice. The psalmist said, "This is the day the Lord has made. We will rejoice and be glad in it" (Psalm 118:24).

We cannot control our days, but we can control our attitudes and choices that make the difference in the way each day affects our lives. Each day is God-made and God-planned! I'm glad life is broken up into segments—a morning and evening, a sunrise and sunset. We cannot relive a single day, but we can learn by the experiences it provides us.

I'm tempted to think I would be glad if I had a day free from problems, work, or pain. But when I think about my days, it seems my best feelings come at the end of those days when I faced up to responsibility and overcame. Then in the evening I can reflect and say, "What a day!" with great satisfaction. So friends, have a "good day" as you live your life for his glory!

My moment of reflection…

Living Stones

February 6
1 Peter 2:4-12

The stone that is shapeless is a useless stone. It will be cast aside and left unused! But the stone that undergoes the mason's chisel and hammer becomes useful and will be formed into something that will remain, something that men will long remember and use. Life is exactly like that!

Peter compares life to a "living stone" to be built into a spiritual house by God for God. Listen to Peter: "Now God is building you, as living stones, into his spiritual temple" (1 Peter 2:5). For every person in the world, there is a place for him to fill. This place Christians call the "plan of God." But no stone can fill a place or be useful if it is not shaped, but often this shaping is very painful!

Life shapes us. Parents, teachers, and friends shape us! While we allow many forces and experiences to mold us, many people will not allow the Master Sculptor Jesus to shape them, which is the greatest tragedy in life. Experience shows us man cannot shape himself. We just have too many problems and will remain useless by our own effort, and we become "castaways!" But thanks to God, who in his holiness and purity comes along, shapes us, and we become "living stones." To be useful in his world, we must allow God to shape us so that we can be used for his kingdom and in our world as we serve others. So willingly, let the Master Sculptor form and shape you into a "work of art" so you can be useful in his kingdom and in your world!

My moment of reflection…

Tragedy of Mediocrity

February 7
2 Chronicles 25:1-28

We live in the "get-by" age! Students capable of A's are satisfied to graduate with B's or C's. Workers in our businesses tend to be clock watchers instead of time watchers. We have Christians who are satisfied with casual worship instead of using every appropriate opportunity to grow and develop their spiritual lives. The scripture addresses this condition that plagues our "get-by" age. Amaziah, a young king in Judah, "did what was pleasing in the Lord's sight, but not wholeheartedly" (2 Chronicles 25:2). Jesus teaches us to "love the Lord your God with all your heart, all your soul and all your mind" (Matthew 22:37).

Do you know that when we wholeheartedly do a task, when we employ all of our faculties, it makes for strength of body, character, intellect, and spirit? Neglecting our ability leads to atrophy, wasting away. A wild goose joined domestic geese and was well-fed but unable to fly above the henhouse; some range cattle became accustomed to pen feeding yet died rather than go back to grazing on the range. The same principle is applicable to humans who prefer to exist on a diet of minimums. And this is especially true in the spiritual realm.

A majority of us live well below par on most levels. We gear much of our life to emergency living! History teaches that the majority of those who are successful in life refuse to be victims of mediocrity! Even in emergencies they find unexpected strength. Please join me in refusing to be victims of mediocrity! Live today with passion—you'll never regret it!

My moment of reflection...

Intimacy with God

February 8
1 Thessalonians 5:12-28

Prayer is one of the sacred privileges of being a Christian! We are made to worship God, to bring him pleasure. It is the will of God that his children pray! If prayer is vital to spiritual health, how would you describe your prayer life? Most believers are not happy with their prayer life! Genuine joy will escape us until prayer becomes a vital part of our spiritual diet.

Paul's final advice to his close friends was, "Keep on praying. No matter what happens, always be thankful, for this is God's will for you who belong to Christ Jesus" (1 Thessalonians 5:17-18). In calling us to prayer, Jesus sought to impress his disciples with the urgency and importance of prayer and gave them an example they should follow.

Prayer is not a meaningless function or duty crowded into the busy, weary ends of the day. We are not obeying our Lord's commands when we spend a few minutes on our knees in the morning rush or late at night, when our mind and faculties are tired with the day's activities. God is always within call and his ear is ever attentive to the call of his child, but we can never know him intimately by a few words of hurried communication.

The "ear of God" can only be reached by continuous waiting upon him. We can never know God by brief, fragmentary, unconsidered repetitions of intercessions that are requests for personal favors and nothing more. Prayer is intimacy with God! If you listen carefully, you may just hear him say, "Keep on praying...no matter what happens."

My moment of reflection...

Pressing On...

February 9
Hebrews 12:1-13

I like sports, especially "home teams" who are on the verge of a championship. We all like a winner! Why? It's because we appreciate the dedication and disciplines of great athletes...even when they lose. Remember Mary Decker? Mary was the American women's distance runner favored to win the gold in 1984! I still remember that race and what happened! She prepared for years to win the gold, even setting aside marriage for training. In one of the most memorable events of the '84 Olympics, another runner crossed lanes in front of Decker, causing Mary to break stride and stumble...and Mary's hopes of winning disappeared! My heart sank with sadness for this great athlete!

Life is a lot like that race! When we least expect it, we find ourselves stumbling over something. Sometimes it's an attitude, sometimes an action of others. But if we want to win, we press on despite life's hidden snares. Spiritually, what guarantees a "win?" To quote the Bible: "Pressing on" (Hebrews 12:1).

"To press on" means to stretch every fiber in our body to cross the finish line, to win the gold, to get the championship ring! We do not get to the finish line by taking the path of least resistance, by settling for good instead of the best! It means dedication and determination, to get up when we have fallen down, not quitting, which is the greatest failure of all.

Eric Liddell said in *Chariots of Fire* that when he ran, he felt the pleasure of God. What a thought: "bringing pleasure to God." Join me in "pressing on" with pleasure despite the occasional fall. You'll be glad you did!

My moment of reflection...

Contentment Brings Joy

February 10
Philippians 4:10-20

Whether it's the slick pages of a magazine or the compelling advertisements on our big screens, we are confronted with pictures that grab our attention. As you are bombarded by these enticing, full-color ads, the thought suddenly "hits" you, *I can't do without this* or *I need this to be happy!* Funny, you have just been convinced "you deserve the best"—something bigger, something better!

The ads of our culture are simple: they are designed to stimulate our curiosity, urging us to buy or use their services. They shape our habits, tastes, and purchases. But what these ads really do is subliminally send a message to our brain that says, "Without this, there is nothing but discontentment…what you need is something better and bigger!" The inner peace of contentment has just been mysteriously pushed away.

Paul said, "Religion does make your life rich, by making you content with what you have. We didn't bring anything into this world, and we won't take anything with us when we leave. So we should be satisfied just to have food and clothes" (1 Timothy 6:6-8, CEV). For Paul, contentment is simple: Something to eat and somewhere to live! That's all! It doesn't mean I can't have nice things or buy something new. But it does mean that Paul had learned to hold "things" loosely—he controlled things, things didn't control him!

Paul tells us he had learned this life-changing lesson: "To be content" (Philippians 4:11). His secret to contentment was he learned to relax and enjoy whatever circumstances came his way. Godliness with contentment is great gain (1 Timothy 6:6).

My moment of reflection…

Hallmark of a Hero

February 11
Joshua 1:1-9

Joshua, Moses's successor, should be an inspiration to everyone! The weary general looked across the wilderness of Lebanon and the Euphrates River in the setting sun. At that moment, human fear wrestled with faith. Never before had any man been given such a momentous task—leading God's people to the Promised Land.

Moses was dead! Israel's hero was gone and now Joshua contemplated the struggle he would face in the coming days. Would he succeed or fail? At that moment, God spoke to Joshua: "I promise you what I promised Moses…I will be with you…I will not fail you or abandon you. Be strong and courageous" (Joshua 1:3, 5). He remembered the word God gave to Moses before his death: "Do not be afraid or discouraged, for the Lord is the One who goes before you. He will be with you; he will neither fail you nor forsake you" (Deuteronomy 31:8).

God had carefully prepared Joshua for his destiny. He passed every test and was qualified to be Israel's new leader. Of all his tests and experiences, none was more important than the assurance of God's presence. It was the presence of God that made the difference! After a long and beautiful tenure of service, this faithful and courageous soldier died!

What's important in life? It wasn't the battles Joshua won or the walls that came tumbling down or the dividing of the Jordan River! Joshua stands out because he "did as he was told, carefully obeying all of the Lord's instructions" (Joshua 11:15). It's wholehearted obedience—always the "Hallmark of a Hero!"

My moment of reflection…

Joy of Friendship

February 12
John 15:1-17

One of the most comforting words in life is the word *friend*! But it's a word tossed about with various meanings. A friend is someone willing to spend himself eagerly on another; someone you can trust while never doubting their loyalty. Friends are the most valuable asset you have in this world!

Moses and God had a favorite place to meet: "The Tent of Meeting!" In that sacred space, surrounded by a cloud, God gave Moses instructions and a blueprint for leadership. The Bible says the Lord spoke to Moses "face to face, as a man speaks to his friend" (Exodus 33:10). The Patriarch Abraham is called "the friend of God" (Isaiah 41:8). Jesus was not ashamed to call his disciples "friends." He said: "You are my friends if you obey me. I no longer call you servants, because a master doesn't confide in his servants. Now you are my friends since I have told you everything the Father told me" (John 15:14-15). Now that's a friend!

Many people want friendships, but are not willing to pay the cost of that relationship. Friendship involves compassion, commitment, and communication to those who are your friends. To be that lasting friend, you must be loyal, kind, and forgiving, and if you are, your friend(s) will be there to the end. Today, someone somewhere is looking for a loyal, caring friend to demonstrate to them all the characteristics God has demonstrated to you. So the choice is clear: You can either build some walls or be a friend and build some bridges! The choice is yours!

My moment of reflection...

Life on God's Plan

February 13
Genesis 26:1-33

Isaac is not the commanding character like his father Abraham or his son Jacob. He did not have the daring faith of his father or the adventure of Jacob. Isaac was a passive guy whose life was largely controlled by other people.

But Isaac had another side! Unlike Abraham and Jacob, who are "uncommon" men, Isaac exhibits the qualities of average humanity. You will find a score of Isaacs for every Abraham. As a representative of average men, the great majority of us stand with him: neither rich nor poor, neither wise nor foolish, neither finished-saint or hopeless tramp!

This commonplace man did an uncommon thing, a really great thing! He erected an altar, built his home nearby, and dug a well in the immediate vicinity. "Then Isaac built an altar there and worshiped the Lord. He set up his camp at that place, and his servants dug a well" (Genesis 26:25). In his story, you find three indispensable threads to the fabric of character and nations—religion, home, and work!

While Isaac leaves much to be desired, he is listed among "God's Hall of Faith." Isaac did something refreshing when he reopened wells his father dug years earlier. We need to reaffirm the tremendous truths of previous generations—religion, home, and work! These virtues form the essentials of a happy and productive life. If we remain faithful in these essentials of life, we inherit true power and nobility. While we respect the faith of our fathers, we all have a career to map out and the glory of life is to do what God has planned for us!

My moment of reflection...

Valentine's Day

February 14
1 Corinthians 13

February reminds us of Valentine's Day. Valentine's Day is one of those fun times where tradition encourages us to send heart-shaped notes to friends and romantic thoughts of affection to our sweethearts. And yes, boxes of candy and flowers and gifts also do the trick!

Though the origin of Valentine's Day is lost in myth and legend, expressions of love have been exchanged for centuries. St. Valentine is the name given to two legendary martyrs who lost their lives in the third century. One was a Roman priest and the other a bishop in Italy. Legend holds that a saint fell in love with his jailer's daughter. Before his execution, the martyr sent a farewell letter to her, signed "Your Valentine."

Remember those special school days when we gave Valentines to classmates and received some in return? What delightful memories—memories that add warmth and color to the cold days of winter. Valentine's Day reminds us of the importance of putting feelings into words, telling your special "someone" they are loved!

I'm grateful God didn't just think about loving us. Instead, he wrote it for all to read and demonstrated it by sending Jesus. He said: "But Christ showed his great love for us by sending Christ to die for us while we were still sinners" (Romans 5:8). God sends heaven-sent valentines over and over that he loves us! He has made it so clear. But the final move is yours—loving God and others. Do you love someone? If so, have you said so? Don't put it off any longer—do it today! Happy Valentine's Day!

My moment of reflection…

Do You See What I See?

February 15
Isaiah 6:1-8

Most people during their lifetime have experiences which put them in the "spotlight." It might have been graduation from college or marriage or the first child! If you are a "Christ-follower," the highlight of your life was when you fell in love with Jesus. Nothing can compare to that highlight—you never forget!

For Moses, it happened at a burning bush in the desert. For Isaiah, it happened in the temple—and he was never the same! During a national crisis, King Uzziah died! Things were going well; great progress was made under his leadership. They had experienced prosperity and established a powerful army. Without warning, the king was afflicted with leprosy and isolated for the rest of his life. When he died, people felt their source of national strength had departed. In that moment, Isaiah discovered a nation's strength lies in Almighty God, not in some earthly king.

In his hour of need, Isaiah came to the temple with a sense of uncertainty concerning the future. His mind was disturbed as he was searching for meaning when he had a remarkable vision of God which changed him forever. An angelic chorus sang, "Holy, holy, holy, Lord All-Powerful! The earth is filled with your glory" (Isaiah 6:3, CEV). In that moment, alone with God, Isaiah is cleansed and volunteers for service. It was his "shining hour!"

God's plan includes all of us! Don't wait to be drafted; be sensitive to God and his work. Some people have to be drafted, while others volunteer! Just maybe God will put you in the "spotlight" today!

My moment of reflection…

Time Is Running Out!

February 16
Isaiah 38:1-8

The headlines read: "Hezekiah trusted in the Lord...There was never another king like him in the land of Judah, either before or after his time. He remained faithful to the Lord in everything" (2 Kings 18:5-6). Solomon was greater in wisdom and David in genius, but none trusted the Lord and followed him as faithfully as did Hezekiah. He was a good king, reigning between two bad kings. With Hezekiah's reign, he made sweeping reforms which changed the direction of the nation!

Even with great people, "some rain will fall!" Time is a gift which makes us look upon our years as a trust handed into our temporary keeping! Because of our humanness, death is in the back of our minds; but what if death becomes an immediate probability? Death is a friend of life because it is the knowledge that our years are limited which makes them so precious.

At the prime of life, with so many plans and future projects, the announcement comes: "Set your affairs in order, for you are going to die" (Isaiah 38:1). In sorrow, he reminds the Lord he had lived a pleasing life before the Lord. He asked the Lord for a few more years to complete his work. And God answered his prayer: "I will give you fifteen more years of life!" Healed and recovered, Hezekiah promises to "walk" carefully, but forgot his vow and manifested pride in those last years. Tragic ending!

Whether life is long or short, Hezekiah would tell us that the completeness depends on what it was lived for! Choose carefully!

My moment of reflection...

From Sunday to Saturday

February 17
Isaiah 40:25-31

Corporate worship is so refreshing—hearts are moved, vision lifted, and lives challenged. We feel close to God and each other in our fellowship. Instinctively, we wish that this state of spiritual ecstasy would continue every day. But we know from experience it won't last long due to the pressures of living. We soon descend the mountain into real life! So the driving question becomes, "Is there something we can do to stabilize a consistent spiritual level?" Isaiah encourages us by saying, "But those who wait on the Lord will find new strength. They will fly high on wings like eagles. They will run and not grow weary. They will walk and not faint" (Isaiah 40:31). His answer: "Soar…run…walk!"

It is natural for excitement at the beginning of a new task. But soon the "new wears off" and one settles down to a stable pattern of living. After soaring in the higher world of energy and enthusiasm, the believer finds himself running on common earth. Yet, very few of us run—we walk day by day! The main company of God's people neither "fly" or run…they walk. Most of God's work is accomplished by plodders—on Monday…Tuesday…Wednesday…the "blessed" walk!

Look what happens! Enthusiasm grows into spiritual determination; impulsiveness has been tempered with wisdom. The "walker" has learned how to "walk and not faint;" that he can "do all things through Christ who gives him strength." So from Sunday to Saturday, just walk with God knowing that he is your power and strength and, as such, "you can do all things," even on Monday!

My moment of reflection…

It's Family

February 18
Ephesians 3:14-19

On a raw winter night, an elderly lady confessed this was her first plane trip. A wise flight attendant, sensing she was uneasy and tense about her trip, introduced himself to her. It was hardly a night for a "first" flight, as rain and sleet was hammering on the plane as it taxied for takeoff. Breaking a strict rule, the attendant unfastened his seat belt and took the elderly lady's cold hand in his. She squeezed his hand tightly and held on. After they were aloft, she said, "Now, son, if you are afraid when we land, come back here and I'll hold your hand again!"

This story reminds me of our Heavenly Father—how he cares for his children, regardless of their need or who they are! He is deeply concerned over whatever concerns us. Paul shows his caring heart as he prays for his Ephesian friends. Thinking about the wisdom and scope of God's incredible plan, he says, "I fall to my knees and pray to the Father, the Creator of everything in heaven and on earth. I pray that from his glorious, unlimited resources he will give you mighty inner strength through his Holy Spirit" (Ephesians 3:14-16).

Paul reminds us that God is our Father, the Father of all! But there's more: He is the Father to whom we all have access whenever. God created the family, the basic unit in society. Created sinless, they sinned against God. But even sin did not cause God to cease being their Father. He loves the family and wants to hold hands today…whoever you are and wherever you are!

My moment of reflection…

Memories

February 19
1 Corinthians 11:23-30

God has given us the great gift of memory—the ability to remember and reflect! We appreciate memory even more when visiting family and friends who have lost this ability. Gathering his disciples together, Jesus took bread, offered thanks, and said, "This is my body, which is given for you. Do this in remembrance of me" (1 Corinthians 11:24). There are many ways of remembering people: words spoken or deeds performed. But the most common way of remembering someone is by a photograph. Most of us have in our possession or on display in our homes the photo of a friend or loved one.

Maybe you have a favorite photograph of your parents! Is this photo a snapshot taken without their awareness or is it a professional portrait? Photography preserves cherished memories. They recall pleasant moments that bring delight to the heart.

The Gospel can be studied as a picture album. It contains many visual pictures of God as he revealed himself in his son Jesus. A favorite Gospel photo of Jesus finds the Master seated near the crest of a mountain with his disciples near him (Matthew 5 and 6). He is teaching them principles and characteristics of becoming citizens of the kingdom—the Beatitudes.

Regardless of your favorite memory or photo of Jesus, we can be grateful that the Bible is a photo album showing who Jesus is and how he serves, cares for, and loves us. As you study and relive ministry of Jesus today, be thankful for your gift of memory, especially the memory of our Lord. He said, "Don't forget!"

My moment of reflection...

Digging for Treasure

February 20
Psalm 119:9-24

On his deathbed, a prosperous farmer called his sons, telling them he was giving his farm to them in equal parts. But before he died, he told them he had very little cash, but they would find the greater part of his wealth buried somewhere in the farm ground about twelve inches deep. As they were leaving his bedside, he added he had forgotten exactly where he had buried his wealth!

What a dilemma for the sons! Lost treasure, hidden wealth! So the sons did what most of us would have done...they started digging, searching for the treasure their father talked about in his will. In all their digging, they found nothing! But since they had the ground "dug up," they decided to plant a crop so they could reap a harvest. Each year after the harvest, the sons continued to dig in search of buried treasure. As a consequence, their farm land was turned over more thoroughly than any other farm. The result of their effort, they reaped abundant harvests year after year. Finally it dawned on them what their father meant when he said his wealth was buried in the ground!

Jesus told believers something about our treasure. He said, "I have given them your word" (John 17:14). The psalmist wrote, "I have hidden your word in my heart that I might not sin against you" (Psalm 119:11). The inheritance of our treasure is available to all on an equal basis in God's word. But the responsibility to begin digging belongs to each of us individually! Begin digging today... and you will find!

My moment of reflection...

The Unfinished You

February 21
Ephesians 4:1-16

Coaches were evaluating a prospective football player. He was very athletic, with all the assets of a future star. Someone made this observation, "He is a fine-looking lad, but he hasn't grown up yet!" What did he mean?

Often in our youth, we've heard the stern voice of a parent or teacher say, "What am I going to do with you? When are you going to grow up?" Paul wrote a letter to some friends, where he said, "Until we come to such unity in our faith and knowledge of God's Son that we will be mature and full grown...that we will no longer be like children" (Ephesians 4:13-14). Similarly, Peter said we should "grow in the special favor and knowledge of our Lord and Savior" (2 Peter 3:18). Both Peter and Paul were writing to adults, not children, and their challenge to them is "grow up!"

Only God can make a person what they ought to be! The only perfect man who ever lived was Jesus Christ, and only someone perfect can raise us up to the heights of character and maturity that God wills for us. Many folks are living stunted, dwarfed, and inferior lives because they refuse to reach higher, reaching to God. When Gladstone, the British statesman, was asked to name the sixty greatest men in history, out of those named, fifty-six were believers in Jesus Christ.

Appearance and physique does not equal "grown up" or mature! You are no longer children when you refuse to be pushed around, when you begin to stand for something and begin to work for someone! Press on!

My moment of reflection...

Hope in a World of Change

February 22
Matthew 24:1-36

The psalmist wrote: "In ages past you laid the foundation of the earth, and the heavens are the work of your hands. Even they will perish, but you remain forever...you are always the same; your years never end" (Psalm 102:25-27). The Hebrews must have been startled when they heard heaven and earth would one day pass away! In fact, the ancient world must have laughed at the thought that one day their nations would be no more. In our day, we think there will always be an America! Yet the Bible tells us the heavens and earth will pass away.

Change is everywhere! We cannot go back to old days and old ways, but we are bewildered about what tomorrow brings. Without change there is no hope for a better world; and yet change brings risk and uncertainty. Believers cannot deal with change properly until we get our focus on the unchanging! God doesn't change: "He is the same yesterday, today and forever!" That's the reason the psalmist tells us the earth will wear out like a garment but God remains the same. God does not change. He has never changed, nor will he!

Living in a changing world, the Christ-follower does not fear change. You can depend on God's faithfulness, which is the same from one generation to another. You can rely on his love that lasts for all eternity. Every promise he has ever breathed is rock solid. So when your world begins to spin out of control and fear grips your heart, cling to the One who never fails or never changes!

My moment of reflection...

Pressure

February 23
Mark 6:30-46

A great problem in our culture is pressure! From the classroom to the research lab, from the home to the office, we all experience pressure. No one is exempt! Without doubt pressure has become the most characteristic problem of our age. It is present in every endeavor and activity, and we are paying a high price for this stress.

We live in a fast moving world, bombarded by change. At the turn of the century, it took a month to go around the world, but in recent years, it took Colonel Glenn less than two hours. We're living in an age of tremendous advance, but are paying a high price—in tranquilizers and frayed tempers. Isaiah reminds us, "In quietness and confidence is your strength" (Isaiah 30:15).

Sometimes, we add more pressure to our lives by immature thinking. We overextend ourselves, taking on more than we can handle. That might have been Isaiah's experience when he instructed us to be quiet and "wait" for God. Jesus was no stranger to pressure. He constantly poured energy into helping people, healing and teaching them. I think he would say to us today, "Take one day at a time! Rest, pray, meditate. Find a quiet place!"

The psalmist was no fool! He didn't "dive" between blankets in order to shut out the harsh realities of the world. He simply learned the only way to cope with pressure was to wrap up each day and leave it with God, and the only way to face the future is to settle with the past! Then he could say, "In quietness and confidence is your strength!"

My moment of reflection…

Holy Living

February 24
1 Peter 1:3-16

The Bible has some stern words of warning to all people: "Come out from them and separate yourselves from them, says the Lord" (2 Corinthians 6:17). In this passage, our Lord was not asking, but telling us what to do—to be a separate people! Without losing the intent of his words, Jesus was saying, "Be Holy!"

Two words have done great damage to Christianity—*secularize* and *compromise*! Today, the sacred and religious have been so "secularized" that in many instances it has lost its real meaning. "Compromise" has also dealt a serious blow to faith when we allow the worldly to become religious and the religious worldly. Jesus was asked to compromise, but he did not. However, Israel compromised her religious ideas with the pagan philosophy of her neighbors and she was met with destruction.

We need men and women who heed and accept the challenge "to live holy lives." Peter calls believers to be holy in everything they do. He is concerned that no believer slips back into their old conduct of doing evil. In the light of your new dignity and destiny, be holy like Jesus is holy. This is the heart-cry of a man who knew all about personal failure.

To make his case, Peter reminds believers they are not ordinary people. He wrote, "You are a chosen people. You are a kingdom of priests, God's holy nation, his very own possession" (1 Peter 2:9). We live in times that try our faith. The need of the hour is for committed men and women who will accept the challenge of living holy lives!

My moment of reflection…

God's Word—Our Tool

February 25
Joshua 1:1-9

Joshua said, "Study this Book of the Law continually. Meditate on it day and night so you may be sure to obey all that is written in it" (Joshua 1:8). The Bible has been described as a mirror, as food, as gold, and as honey. These metaphors and others help clarify why the Bible is critical to personal success and holy living.

Our skeptical world rejects much of the biblical story as being the word of God. Because of the viewpoint of some, the Bible has been removed from the classroom because they claim it discriminates. Courts have affirmed their faulty thinking. Perhaps we are becoming like our biblical forefathers who "mocked the messengers of God and despised their words" (2 Chronicles 3:16). It takes a couple of dollars to put a Bible in the hands of our youth, but now that we take the Bible away from the school, we pay thousands of dollars to keep them in prison!

For the psalmist, the word of God is a lamp and a light to show the way. For millions, the Bible is a book of comfort, peace, courage, and forgiveness. It is the only book to meet the deepest needs of the human heart!

Jeremiah likens the word of God to a hammer that breaks a rock in pieces (Jeremiah 23:29). Sin hardens hearts as hard as flint, and only hammer blows can crush them. However, a hammer is useless unless it is used by a human hand. So today, use this tool God has given the world, lest we too fail!

My moment of reflection…

Putting God First

February 26
Philippians 2:1-11

The prophet Micah and the apostle Paul have something in common: both gave the formula for daily successful living! Micah testifies, "For me, I look to the Lord for his help. I wait confidently for God to save me, and my God will certainly hear me" (Micah 7:7). Micah tells us "to look to the Lord," which is faith; "I will wait," which is patience; and "My God will hear me," which is confidence. Paul uses similar words but with a different twist: "Your attitude should be the same that Christ Jesus had" (Philippians 2:5). Taken together, Micah and Paul give us a foolproof formula for a successful day!

Of the eve of his departure for college, a student was given some advice for success. With respect for their son, the father said, "Remember, my son, if you are to succeed in life, if your impact in the world will be significant, you must be willing to be third!" Arriving at the university, this wise student hung this motto above his desk, "I am willing to be third." When we are willing to put God first in our life and others second, we have already achieved success.

That's exactly what Jesus did—his Father's plan and will were always at the forefront of his agenda. The needs of others always occupied center stage. An amazing thing happens when you bury self in the interest of God and others—self will be exalted to a place of confidence and honor. So today, "Let his mind be in you" and your days will be marked by success!

My moment of reflection…

Surrendered

February 27
Genesis 32:1-32

Jacob had two great religious experiences! One was at Bethel, when he was driven from home by fear of his brother. In a dream, Jacob promises to give God a tenth of all he earned if God would be with him and protect him. His second life-changing experience was when he decided to return home. As Jacob approached the border of his own country, he heard his brother Esau was approaching with a large band of warriors. This news drove Jacob to his knees whereon God revealed himself in a most remarkable way.

There is nothing we need more these days than a vision of God. Coming face to face with the Living God can be a life-transforming and life-enriching experience. Such was the case with Jacob, whose name was changed from Jacob the deceiver to Israel, the "Prince of God." It is hard for us to understand how conquest can be achieved through surrender, but remember that God's ways are not our ways!

God never works on a "trial and error" basis! His word to Jacob was, "I will be with you…I will not leave you." When Jacob awoke from his dream, he said, "Surely the Lord is in this place, and I wasn't even aware of it" (Genesis 28:16). Literally, Jacob became a "changed" man. Originally, his name had meant "deceiver" or "thief," but God now says to Jacob, "Your name will no longer be Jacob…it is now Israel, a 'Prince of God'" (Genesis 32:28). It was when Jacob saw himself as he was that God enabled him to see himself as he could be! Conquered through surrender!

My moment of reflection…

Testing Time

February 28
Genesis 22:1-14

Few students look forward to a test! Even a "pop quiz" can produce agony of soul. Some discredit testing and say that the tension created is detrimental to the student. However, we have to admit that both teacher and student would be under some handicap if there was no testing. While testing can create tension, it reveals desired progress. Success indicates it's time to move on to a new plateau of investigation and achievement. Ours would be a confused world if there were no tests by which we could measure progress.

Did it ever occur to you our Heavenly Father might be interested in your spiritual progress? Does it not seem right and natural that our Lord would both test the genuineness of our discipleship and our progress toward spiritual maturity? He did so during his earthly ministry. Some failed and others made low grades, but there were those who "passed" with high marks and received his congratulations.

"God tested Abraham's faith and obedience" (Genesis 22:1). Satan tests us to destroy us, to bring out evil. But God puts us to the test to bring out the good in us. God asked his friend Abraham to sacrifice his beloved son Isaac on the altar. Abraham offered no excuses and did not delay doing what he knew he should do. Being a man of faith and obedience, with all diligence, he gave himself to the task—and he passed the test on Mt. Moriah! So when "tests" come your way, God isn't there to destroy you, but to note your achievement and to check on your spiritual progress!

My moment of reflection…

Victory

March 1
Genesis 45:1-15

The most faithful of God's children experience trouble, sickness, disappointment, and tragedy. Because you trust God and do right is no guarantee everything will turn out fine. Sometimes it does and sometimes it doesn't!

Few people face more trouble than Joseph! The apple of his father's eye, he cherished fond dreams of the position of privilege in his family. He enjoyed every opportunity life could provide. Seemingly, he had a safe and prosperous place in his family. But instead of receiving love from his family, his brothers envied and hated him with murderous thoughts. Instead of killing Joseph, they sold him into slavery and he ended up in Egypt. In Egypt, Joseph found himself favored in the house of Potiphar. Everything was fine until the immoral wife of Potiphar began to tempt him. When he refused to become a party to her lust, she plotted to falsely accuse him and he found himself in prison.

Joseph had every right to be bitter. Yet somehow through his ordeal, he remained in command of his emotions and faced the trials victoriously. He fulfilled God's plan for his life. In the end, Joseph was elevated to a position of prime minister, a position where he was the means of saving his family from starvation.

The absence of hatred and resentment is remarkable! There is only one answer for Joseph's victory and personal achievement! He was able to rise above the trials because of his genuine faith in God which is affirmed by the apostle John: "For every child of God defeats this evil world by trusting Christ to give the victory" (1 John 5:4).

My moment of reflection…

Consider your Ways

March 2
Haggai 1:1-15

Haggai was a prophet with strong convictions! The people of his day were religious but very materialistic. Because he knew what needed to be done and what the future held, he shares the concern of God for his people. Haggai reported: "This is what the Lord Almighty says: Consider how things are going for you" (Haggai 1:7). Several times in this small book, Haggai urges his people to "consider" their ways!

Often we are concerned about the ways of others and not about ourselves. Jesus talked about the folly of judging others while ignoring their own sinfulness (Matthew 7:3-5). Politicians place the troubles of the world on their opponents. Diplomats work overtime to outthink and outmaneuver potential enemies. We spend our time and energy in trying to blame others rather than taking responsibility for our mistakes.

Jeremiah spoke about the conditions of his day. He said after listening to the conversation of leaders, "What do I hear? Is anyone sorry for sin? Does anyone say what a terrible thing I have done? No! All are running down the path of sin as swiftly as a horse rushing into battle" (Jeremiah 8:6). Instead of blaming others for our problems, we need to take responsibility and ask, "What have I done?" or "Consider my ways!" Haggai declared at the root of their trouble was the fact they had left God out and postponed doing his will! May God grant us the wisdom to "consider our ways," making sure they are wise! Today, "consider your ways" and do what is right!

My moment of reflection...

Cheer Up...Could be Worse

March 3
Galatians 6:1-18

"Cheer up, things could be worse! So I cheered up...and sure enough, things got worse." We've heard these sayings: mother told me there would be days like this, from bad to worse, out of the frying pan and into the fire, between a rock and a hard place! Sometimes these "bad days" come in bunches. The only "good" thing about "bad days" is we all have them, no one is exempt!

Some days you honestly wonder why you got out of bed that morning. Even though people want to help us with our "tough days," tough days are usually solo flights. So what is the answer to these universal trying experiences? The enemy tries to persuade us on hard days that God doesn't care. But he does! Listen to this encouragement in Galatians:

- "Don't get tired of doing what is good" (Galatians 6:9). On tough days, have heart, don't quit, stand firm, persevere! Ask God to build a protective shield around your heart.
- "Do good to everyone" (Galatians 6:10). Our tendency is to do evil, to fight, to get irritated, to get even. Stay quiet and consciously turn it over to the Lord.
- "Don't let anyone trouble you" (Galatians 6:17). Refuse to let anyone or anything gain mastery over your soul.
- Let "the grace of our Lord Jesus Christ be with you" (Galatians 6:18). Let grace flow through your thoughts, attitudes, words...while you sit on the fence and relax!

Today, remember the strong teaching of Peter: "Give all your worries and cares to God, for he cares about what happens to you" (1 Peter 5:7).

My moment of reflection...

Contentment

March 4
1 Timothy 6:6-21

There is a great deal of restlessness in our world. It seems like everyone everywhere is so busy with many responsibilities and duties. To be sure, some degree of aggressiveness is needful and important for motivation. But it can get out of control so that instead of providing contentment and satisfaction, it brings worry and unhappiness. This is neither good for man's physical nature or his spiritual inner man.

Paul rates godliness as a high quality and commodity in a person's life, something that should be sought at all cost. The apostle tells us "true religion with contentment is great wealth" (1 Timothy 6:6). Paul contends that "godliness with contentment" is a great asset that brings happiness and peace in one's life. And yet, a minority has contentment as a goal in life!

Talking to some people, you get the impression they lack so much in their lives. And yet, we are so blessed. We have so much! For perspective, Paul reminds us we came into this world with nothing and we leave the same way. Then he adds, "So if we have enough food and clothing, let us be content" (1 Timothy 6:6-8).

The Children of Israel claimed to be grateful God had brought them out of captivity. But as you follow their journey, their thanksgiving, gratitude, and contentment vanish as they complain and murmur in their wanderings. They paid a heavy price for their complaining and murmuring! Let's be thankful to God for the things we have. And all of us need to remember that "Godliness with contentment is great gain!"

My moment of reflection…

Be Merciful

March 5
Luke 6:20-38

A key word of our day is *testing*. We encounter testing in most every areas of life. We test in education, give psychological tests, and test physical strength. In the spiritual realm, one's faith and character is often tested in daily living.

The depth of our spiritual life is measured by compassion that manifests itself through kindness and mercy to fellow human beings. As believers, we are to reflect the characteristics of our Father as a child carries the DNA of their parents. The character qualities of our Heavenly Father are reflected in our lifestyle: "You must be compassionate, just as your Father is compassionate" (Luke 6:36).

We live in a world that is without compassion! Left to his biological identity, men will fight like beasts for food and shelter. He is heartless and cruel! Education and culture may enlarge one's intellect and sophistication, but it does not increase his capacity to love and practice mercy. Mercy comes from the inner man and work of the Holy Spirit.

Many folks offer acts of charity to those in need, but this alone is not evidence of a merciful heart. The Bible insists mercy is a product of the heart, not the pocketbook! Our kindness and benevolent deeds are not limited to those who "deserve" them, but to everyone who has a need. Jesus gave the perfect expression of mercy as summed up in the Golden Rule: "Do for others as you would like them to do for you" (Luke 6:31). He also said, "God blesses those people who are merciful. They will be treated with mercy" (Matthew 5:7, CEV).

My moment of reflection...

Peace in His Presence

March 6
Mark 4:35-41

Some of life's greatest joys and challenges come with interruptions and unplanned crisis. Jesus and his disciples were boating on the sea. After an exhausting day of ministry, they started out for the quiet and solitude of isolated shores. They were looking forward to some deserved "quiet time." But their cruise was interrupted by a sudden storm!

The Sea of Galilee was notorious for storms which arose so quickly. Annoyed at first, then frightened, the panic-stricken disciples awoke Jesus, who was asleep in the back of the boat. They shouted, "Teacher, don't you even care that we are going to drown?" (Mark 4:38). Jesus used this occasion for a miracle and a pointed rebuke for the disciple's little faith.

It is easy to overlook the real meaning of this story. Jesus was teaching his disciples that wherever he is the storms of life become calm! It means in the presence of the Lord the most terrible tempest turns to peace at the sound of his voice. Traveling with Jesus is to travel in peace, even on a stormy day! He comes to us in the storms of fear and anxiety and says, "Peace, be still!"

The beauty of this story is not only that he calmed the winds and sea, but he can calm the storms arising in the lives of his disciples today. In panic we cry out, "God, don't you care? Do something!" He does care and he understands! Listen to his promise: "You will keep in perfect peace all who trust in you, whose thoughts are fixed on you" (Isaiah 26:3).

My moment of reflection…

The Magnetic Christ

March 7
John 12:20-36

I'm intrigued by the science of magnetism! Perhaps it interests me because there is an element of mystery involved, namely, how could an unseen force attract another object and hold it. Scientists teach us our world has two forces acting on it. It has one tendency to run off at a tangent from its orbit, but the sun draws it to itself, and so between these two forces, it is kept in a perpetual circle.

It is interesting to note there are two forces in the life of every person. There is the pull of the world trying to pull us out and there is the pull of the Son trying to pull us in! Jesus explicitly said, "And when I am lifted up on the cross, I will draw everyone to myself" (John 12:32).

The "pull" of Christ is not an academic or debatable question. For two thousand years, Jesus has drawn men unto himself. This "pull" does not come from natural sources but the Father draws us to Christ. Men are drawn by his everlasting love, his goodness, and because he is the embodiment of truth.

We are drawn for something! All of us have purpose in life. It is unthinkable God would draw men to his Son without a specific purpose. We are called for personal redemption, but beyond our salvation, we are called for service to mankind. But the overall purpose for being drawn to Jesus is to glorify our Heavenly Father. The magnetic pull of Jesus is a mystery, but it's real. Thank God he is still drawing people to himself to this very day!

My moment of reflection…

Difference a Day Makes

March 8
John 20:19-31

We've heard the statement made to someone who failed to come to a party: "You should have been there—you missed so much!" The implication is, we had so much fun and good times were had by all, except you! Thomas, where were you?

It was resurrection day and Jesus appeared to Mary who supposed him to be the gardener. But Jesus revealed to Mary he was the Lord. Mary's assignment was to tell the disciples Jesus was alive and he was going to ascend to his Father. That evening, the disciples were assembled in a room, doors were shut because of fear when Jesus suddenly stood in their presence and said, "Peace be with you" (John 20:21). How the disciples rejoiced to see their Lord. He who was dead is now alive! While they are delighted their Master is back, they are sad because Thomas is not there to share their joy.

Being together, especially in times of sorrow and loss, encourages us with hope and joy. By his absence, Thomas missed the gladness Jesus brought. After Jesus showed the disciples his hands and his side, "they were filled with joy" (John 20:20). After Jesus gave the disciples his peace and blessing, he said to them, "As the Father has sent me, so I send you" (John 20:21).

Because Thomas "missed the party," we call him the doubting disciple! But days later, Thomas was in the Upper Room when Jesus appeared again. One look was all that he needed, a touch wasn't required. All doubts were dispelled and Thomas cried out, "You are my Lord and my God" (John 20:28, CEV).

My moment of reflection…

Expressing Gratitude

March 9
Psalm 116:1-19

It's common to hear folks ask, "How can I make more money?" "How can I get a better job?" "How can I live longer and happier?" But it is rather unusual to hear a person ask, "How can I adequately express my gratitude to God?" The psalmist reflected on the beauty of God's goodness to him in the past. But now he is seeking a more adequate expression of thanksgiving for God's grace and kindness. Listen to him: "What can I offer the Lord for all he has done for me?" (Psalm 116:12). This is a question we must ask ourselves as we reflect on God's grace.

The psalmist had been very sick, even to the point of death. Now his health had been restored and he is well enough to go to the temple. So among the decisions he made was that of choosing to "walk in the Lord's presence as I live here on earth" (Psalm 116:9). We find many encouragements to walk with God throughout the scriptures. Noah and Abraham walked before the Lord. Paul challenged his friends to "walk in newness of life" (Romans 6:4).

God delights in our gratitude. Our enemy seeks to camouflage his presence. But God promised to walk among his people: "I will walk among you; I will be your God, and you will be my people" (Leviticus 26:12). The best expression of Godly gratitude is our daily walk. It is our walk that authenticates our talk and brings pleasure to God. So today, walk before the Lord—it's your gift to God!

My moment of reflection...

Giving Our Best

March 10
Hebrews 11:1-4

Giving is an honor and privilege! There are countless forms of giving. We give praise, a smile, and a kind word. We give time, money, and effort. It is not always easy. In fact, God calls us to sacrifice, to give until it hurts!

Giving in our culture is often done with "leftovers." If we have time or money left after our needs are met, then we consider giving. We give the best years of our lives and our best talents to the secular world. If we are not too tired or too broke, we scatter a few crumbs here and there.

Hebrews was written to encourage people in a time of stress and difficulty. Abel is listed in faith's hall of fame because he responded to God with genuine faith. In Hebrews 11, Abel offered his very best offering to God. Maybe it was his best because it was a blood sacrifice from his flock, but even more important is the fact Abel's gift represented the response of his heart to the greatness and generosity of God.

All that we possess is the result of God's grace! And our giving is an outward expression of an inward work of God's grace. What causes some to give to others miles away, to people they don't even know? Really, there is only one reason: the grace of God! God loves a cheerful giver, and a generous heart. So our challenge: "If you give you will receive…whatever measure you use in giving—large or small—it will be used to measure what is given back to you" (Luke 6:38).

My moment of reflection…

Discipleship

March 11
Matthew 16:21-28

Some people seem to be "out of their minds!" They do the most foolish things. For instance, four men had been fishermen all of their lives. They were raised with the smell of fish on their clothing. They were good at catching fish; in fact, two of them were so well off, they had hired servants and one had a "vacation" home!

But these fishermen went haywire—they changed jobs! No doubt the pay was better. No! Perhaps they got four weeks of vacation and overtime pay. No! Maybe they got health insurance, sick leave, and company transportation. No! In fact, these four received no salary; they worked around the clock, acquired no vacation or benefits, and walked everywhere they went.

Out of their minds? Maybe! You decide! Their names were Peter, Philip, James, and John. Their occupational change was from fishermen to disciples of Jesus Christ. They still maintained their trade as fishermen, but now becoming disciples of Christ came first in their lives. Their work, their time for pleasure, their family, eating, and sleeping were all secondary. Being a disciple of Jesus came first!

These first-century disciples knew what Jesus meant when he said, "If any of you wants to be my follower, you must put aside your selfish ambition, shoulder your cross, and follow me" (Matthew 16:24). Everything of value has its price! One can get almost anything and become anything if willing to pay the price. Becoming a Christ-follower involves giving up, giving in, and imitating Jesus. But remember this: Jesus never marks down his demands and there are no "sales" in discipleship!

My moment of reflection...

Light in the Darkness

March 12
Acts 16:25-34

Prayer and praise are powerful weapons in times of need. When it is darkest God shows up in remarkable ways to deliver his followers. Paul and Silas were in prison! Their backs were raw and bloody from an unjust beating. They were in physical pain, facing uncertainty. But in the darkness of the "midnight" hour, these two faithful servants were singing and praising God. They had no idea an earthquake was coming!

Suddenly, an earthquake shook the prison, opening doors and loosening prisoners' bonds. In charge of two important prisoners, the jailer woke up and discovered every door was open and every prisoner loosed. He did what any man would have done: He "called for lights and ran to the dungeon and fell down before Paul and Silas" (Acts 16:29). One minute the jailer was a potential suicide, and the next minute he was a child of God!

The "powers of darkness" are trying to extinguish the light of Christian faith. Things we hold dear are being shaken, leaving us with a sense of paralyzing helplessness. Sometimes all we see is darkness! Then we are reminded that even in the darkness, there is light. Overwhelmed by darkness, light was shining through two prisoners, Paul and Silas. The only way to turn "out the darkness" is to turn on the light, and that is our function. We are to be lights in the world, to let our light shine! Jesus said, "You are the light of the world...don't hide your light...let it shine for all...so that everyone will praise your heavenly Father" (Matthew 5:14-16).

My moment of reflection...

Climb Every Mountain

March 13
1 Kings 22:1-9

Mountains have always been inviting to people! In summer people flock to the mountains for vacations, in the winter for skiing. But mountains are not only for enjoyment, they are challenges made to conquer—to climb to the very summit!

In Old Testament days, there was a king in Israel who felt the impulse to "climb every mountain." He was irritated and embarrassed because some foreigners were occupying the city of Ramoth "and we haven't done a thing about it" (1 Kings 22:3). The word *Ramoth* means high places. Ramoth was a fortified mountain on the east side of the Jordan River, captured by the Syrians in one of many battles between Israel and Syria. The King of Syria had promised to give it back to Israel, but had broken his promise. Ramoth in Gilead was a high place with rocky and treacherous roads. The trip was dangerous, besides the conflict with the battle-wise Syrians. Yet, God's people were doing nothing about repossessing it.

This is a picture of some believers. As followers of Jesus, we are made for the heights. We should never be satisfied with the mediocrity of the valley when we can attain the breathtaking beauty of the heights. The pull of God is upward and the thrust of the cross is toward the skies. The adventure of the summit demands preparation, stamina, and discipline. But it's worth the effort! Those who have walked the heights are never satisfied with the lowlands, and those who have lived in the mountains will never be at home in the valley! Climb the mountain…and begin today!

My moment of reflection…

Shadows

March 14
Acts 5:12-16

None of us may be famous, but very likely we'll influence someone who will influence someone who will influence someone else! Like it or not, we leave our mark on others. We never know who is watching!

The apostles were held in "high regard" for their ministry among the multitudes. As a result of their miracles, sick people were brought into the streets so "Peter's shadow might fall across some of them as he went by" (Acts 5:15). The teaching from this passage is significant: our shadows or lives influence the lives of others and other people's shadows or lives influence us—some for good and some for evil! In the story of Ananias and Sapphira, we see the judgment of God as both died, the result of telling a lie. This event and other signs and wonders influenced people a great deal. They were so moved they wanted the "shadow of Peter" to fall upon them for healing. It is true a man's shadow is the symbol of his influence. None of us lives unto himself and none of us dies to himself!

Influence is never neutral, it is irrevocable. Once it's done, it's done! Influence is like fragrance: it depends on the flower! When we fraternize with sinners and compromise with sin, we lose our influence. Guard your lives constantly, maintaining uncompromising watchfulness against things that destroy your influence. Your shadow is very important! On a white stone that marks the grave of a little girl are these words: "It was easier to be good when she was with us!" Be careful of the shadow you cast today!

My moment of reflection...

Cornerstone

March 15
1 Corinthians 3:1-23

Of the lovely and descriptive titles for Jesus, the picture of Christ as cornerstone returns again and again to give strength, security, and stability. The song we sing says: "Rock of Ages, Cleft for Me." With the world tottering on shaky foundations, it is so reassuring that Jesus is the foundation stone from all eternity!

Fourteen miles out to sea on the East Coast is a rock called the Eddystone. During storms it is completely covered, but when the storm is over, there it stands immovable, the same from century to century. A rock that is perpetual and everlasting is used in scripture as an image of him who is from everlasting to everlasting.

The psalmist said, "Who is God except the Lord? Who but our God is a solid rock?" (Psalm 18:31). In the New Testament, the same simile is applied to Jesus. At the close of his Sermon on the Mount, our Lord describes building of two houses on different foundations. Both were assaulted with rain, wind, and floods. One washed away, while the other stood the storm because it was built on the Rock.

Jesus deliberately called himself the Foundation Stone as did Peter and Paul. Isaiah seemed to have a clear picture of the Messiah when he referred to him as a tried stone, a precious stone, and sure foundation. When all around us fails and crumbles, he endures! When David was pursued by Saul, he fortified himself in the rocks and said, "The Lord is my rock, my fortress, and my savior...He is my shield...and my stronghold" (Psalm 18:2). Praise God. He never changes!

My moment of reflection…

Joy in the Journey

March 16
1 Chronicles 29:10-20

In scripture, life is compared to a journey! David reminds us "we are here for only a moment, visitors and strangers in the land as our ancestors were before us. Our days on earth are like a shadow, gone so soon without a trace" (1 Chronicles 29:15).

Life is a matter of luggage! When a child begins to toddle, he displays a passion for carrying things. The little guy is often burdened by the load he is trying to carry. The same is true for the inexperienced traveler. The inexperienced traveler may be identified by too much luggage. A good rule to follow as to how much baggage one should take would be: reduce your baggage to the very minimum—and then cut it in half!

What we leave behind and what we take along on the journey is critical! We may travel too heavy or travel too light! So we are faced with a dilemma—what to take along. Spread life before you, all of it, and then see what is important to carry with you or leave behind. Leave behind anything that will hinder you from maximum speed and efficiency, like bitterness, spiteful memories, doubt, and any clutter. But make sure your luggage includes firm convictions, a sympathetic spirit, and a deep faith in God.

When packing your luggage, remember there is another trip which is even more important—for when you arrive at your destination you can't go back and get something you have forgotten, and your journey is over! With wisdom, begin packing today, making sure you have everything you need.

My moment of reflection…

In God's Hand

March 17
Psalm 31:1-24

Many people live in the grip of fear. Economic uncertainty, political instability, and the threat of a worldwide holocaust hold nations in constant fear. An old song entitled "He's Got the Whole World in His Hands" brought peace and comfort to many. But for some reason, even after we've put these words to memory and sing them, we don't believe what we sing.

Perhaps a majority of folks don't believe their lives are in God's hands, because if they did, it would be evident from the way they lived. Scholars in psychiatry suggest an alarming number of people live in worry, anxiety, and in the grip of fear. And some believe the explanation for this struggle is the current generation has lost their grip on God!

David had his share of problems! At times his situation seemed hopeless, gripped by despair. Yet, envisioning God as his fortress, David found grace to say, "My future is in your hands" (Psalm 31:15). Our lives are not in the hands of some unknown power. God controls life, not "fate." The events of life that come on us are controlled by Almighty God. Furthermore, the length of our life is known and determined by God. David's life was frequently in danger. He didn't know whom he could trust. But he sustained himself with the knowledge that the end of life would not come by chance.

After David described his fear, he declared his trust: "But I am trusting you, O Lord…You are my God! My future is in your hands" (Psalm 31:14-15). You can overcome fear when you are "in God's hand!"

My moment of reflection…

Found Faithful

March 18
Matthew 25:14-30

The Greek philosopher Diogenes went for a walk throughout the city at noonday with a lighted lantern searching for an honest man. Five centuries before Diogenes, Solomon was given credit for saying, "Many will say they are loyal friends, but who can find one who is really faithful?" (Proverbs 20:6). Diogenes doubted the existence of an honest man and Solomon wondered where a faithful man could be found.

Faithful can mean many things! It can mean firmness in maintaining one's promise or thoroughness in observing one's duty and devotion to another person. Being faithful can mean being bound by ties of honor or love to something apart from oneself, or it can mean moral steadfastness. Implied is consistency, an abiding loyalty, not subject to change or to the whim of a passing emotion.

It was not curiosity that prompted Solomon to ask, "Who can find a faithful man?" Nor was it just good advice that Jesus gave when he taught, "Unless you are faithful in small matters, you won't be faithful in large ones" (Luke 16:10).

The key requisite God is looking for in a Christ-follower is faithfulness! It is faithfulness that is the essence of God. A thoughtless person dumped a dog at the intersection of a busy highway. As a loyal pet, the dog refused to leave, waiting for his master to return. Finally after many days, the dog died waiting for his master to return. That's faithfulness and loyalty! Faithfulness must be the motto and badge of every believer. My prayer is that all of us will hear his words, "Well done, good and faithful servant!"

My moment of reflection...

Our Father...

March 19
Matthew 6:1-15

The prayer life of Jesus is most revealing! He lived in an atmosphere of prayer; his prayer life was never at the mercy of moods. Jesus did not permit prayer to be crowded out of his busy schedule. He prayed during and before all the great crises of his life. He prayed at the time of his baptism, before the selection of disciples, during his transfiguration, in Gethsemane, and while on the cross.

The prayer life of Jesus contains elements of communion, thanksgiving, petition, and intercession. There is a significant difference between Jesus's prayers and the prayers of the disciples. His prayers were short and real while theirs were weak and unsatisfying. Perhaps it was their weak, ineffective prayer-life that led them to Jesus with this request, "Lord, teach us to pray" (Matthew 6:1-15). So he gave them a model prayer, a pattern of prayer we should follow.

Jesus brought a unique revelation of God to his disciples when he told them to think of God as their Heavenly Father, One who is sovereign, majestic, and holy. As our Father, he has perfect knowledge of our past, present, and future. He knows where we have been, where we are, and where we will eventually be. He taught his disciples to pray like this: "Our Father in heaven" (Matthew 6:9).

Prayer is one of the wonderful privileges of being a Christ-follower! It is an awesome privilege to call God our Father—a privilege we must not take for granted. So as you approach the Father in prayer, remember he is the Almighty One who deserves your adoration, reverence, and wonder.

My moment of reflection...

Hallowed Be Your Name

March 20
Matthew 6:5-15

Many people who pray often feel the "wires are down," that God doesn't hear us! Christ-followers know they should pray and do, but nothing comes forth. The privilege of prayer often becomes commonplace to many Christians. Perhaps we would pray more adequately if we reverenced the name of God in our speech and lives. Jesus taught his disciples to pray, "May your name be honored" (Matthew 6:9b).

Our world is a profane world! It is not uncommon to hear our Lord's name profaned in many ways. Men treat God's world like it doesn't belong to him. We secularize life and simply ignore God. In light of the profane, Jesus instructed his disciples to pray "hallowed be your name." This plea for divine intervention is a request for God to reveal his character of holiness and to eliminate all that is profane from the mind and the heart.

When Jesus taught his name was "hallowed" or "honored," he was literally telling his disciples God's name should be treated differently from all other names. His name is absolutely unique, holy, and sacred, demanding our reverence in all we do and say.

During the construction of St. Paul's Cathedral in London, architect Sir Christopher Wren gave instructions that if any workmen were heard using profanity, they were to be dismissed without exception. Profanity is a verbal expression of an attitude which is opposite of the petition, "May your name be honored!" By this petition our Lord was teaching his disciples to enter into the presence of God on our face rather than trampling into his holy presence with muddy boots!

My moment of reflection...

Thy Kingdom Come

March 21
Matthew 6:5-15

Jesus became separated from his parents and when they found him, he was in the temple talking to scholars about his Father's business. About fifteen years later, he defined his "Father's business." One day he walked away from the carpenter's shop and shortly thereafter preached his first sermon. It was a short sermon: "Turn from your sins and turn to God, because the Kingdom of Heaven is near" (Matthew 4:17).

When Jesus taught his disciples to pray, "May your kingdom come soon" (Matthew 6:10), he used a phrase found throughout the New Testament. In the Old Testament, the Jewish people were waiting with hope for the Messianic Kingdom. "May your kingdom come" is really a prayer for the rule of Christ to be triumphant in all of life.

Two thousand years ago, Jesus taught his disciples to pray for the kingdom, for the extinction of tyranny and corruption. At the same time, he told his disciples to pray for righteousness and truth in all life—government, science, art, and social life. By offering this petition, we are asking God for help to do his will on earth even as it is done in heaven.

This prayer, "may your kingdom come soon," is no easygoing prayer that may be offered in an offhanded way. It is a demanding prayer that involves serious personal responsibilities. If offered sincerely, it is a prayer that the King of the kingdom will take complete possession of us and exercise kingly rule in our hearts. As you pray that his kingdom would come soon, remember the kingdom is a gift from God to you!

My moment of reflection...

Thy Will Be Done

March 22
Matthew 6:9-13

A graduate student was filling out a questionnaire, helping him locate his first job. One of the questions was, "Where would you like to locate?" The student said, "Anywhere the Lord leads—in the state of Georgia!"

The disciples asked Jesus to teach them how to pray. He told them to pray that God's kingdom would come soon and that "his will be done here on earth, just as it is in heaven" (Matthew 6:10). Jesus thought of the will of God as sovereign wisdom, justice, and goodness by which things are governed. This is in utter contrast to the attitude which considers the will of God to be cold and cruel fate. Our Father does not wish to suppress and crush our will and makes us slaves. Instead, he wants to eliminate the discord and destructive tensions of life, enabling us to live a life of harmony. To surrender to his will is to exalt and enrich our will, to bring out our very best!

This petition, "Your will be done," is the key to understanding prayer. When Jesus taught his disciples to pray "your will be done here on earth, just as it is in heaven," he was giving the divine blueprint by which they were to build a significant life of achievement that would bring complete satisfaction to their lives. If we would experience the delights of the heavenly life in the here and now, we need to pray sincerely, "Thy will be done here on earth, just as it is in heaven." May God's will be done in your life today!

My moment of reflection...

Our Daily Bread

March 23
Matthew 6:5-15

When Jesus taught his disciples to pray, he gave a comprehensive blueprint to follow for all time. He taught them about God's glory—his name, his kingdom, and his will! But then the focus changed to their needs: give us, forgive us, and lead us!

The God of the universe is not some vague absolute! He is a Living Spirit who expresses himself through the material of nature and the concrete history of man: "The Word became flesh" (John 1). God is interested in our bodies. He took a body, came to earth, and said during his wilderness temptations, "People need more than bread for their life" (Matthew 4:4). He offers not simply soul salvation, but whole salvation for the body, mind, and spirit.

When Jesus said, "Give us our food for today" (Matthew 6:11), he was saying it's okay and right to pray for daily needs, even bread! As our Father, he knows we need bread! After all, if we are to serve and do his will, we must have energy and strength.

By this petition, the Lord encourages us to trust our todays and tomorrows into the care of our Heavenly Father. He is capable of providing for all our needs. He wants us to ask him to meet those needs. This wonderful truth relieves our fears and anxieties about tomorrow. The psalmist understood God's provision: "Once I was young, and now I am old. Yet I have never seen the godly forsaken, nor seen their children begging for bread" (Psalm 37:25). Remember, we are all debtors to the generosity of God—don't forget to ask!

My moment of reflection...

Forgive Us Our Debts

March 24
Matthew 6:5-15

After asking our Heavenly Father for provision, we are to request pardon: "Forgive us our sins, just as we have forgiven those who have sinned against us" (Matthew 6:13). Jesus links the petition for daily bread to the confession of sin and plea for pardon. The suggestion seems to be as we go to him for daily bread, we need to go to him for daily forgiveness. As the body is nourished by food and needs to be renewed daily, even so the spiritual nature needs to be restored by confession and cleansing every day.

This petition, "Forgive us our sins, just as we have forgiven those who have sinned against us," is most frightening! Jesus, in the plainest language, is saying if we forgive others, God will forgive us, but if we refuse to forgive others, God will refuse to forgive us. So if we pray this petition with an unsettled quarrel in our lives, we are asking God not to forgive us!

Jesus lived a life without sin! But we have all sinned and fallen short of the divine standard. Guilty, we need forgiveness only Christ can provide by his death on the cross. When Jesus counseled the disciples that they must be willing to forgive until seventy times seven, he was pointing out the absolute necessity of forgiveness.

To sin is human but to forgive is divine! We are never closer to God's grace than when we admit our sin and cry for his forgiveness. And we are never more like God than when we extend forgiveness to "those who have sinned against us!"

My moment of reflection…

Temptation

March 25
Matthew 6:5-15

For many, prayer becomes "the last straw" to be used in the case of an emergency. Some pray when the doctor announces, "There is no hope." When disaster strikes or people experience tragedy, they pray! This petition of the Disciple's Prayer teaches that prayer is not just an escape hatch. Our Lord is teaching his disciples to pray for God's help even before they feel a need for his help: "And don't let us yield to temptation" (Matthew 6:13).

Temptation is a big deal! Jesus told his disciples that temptation and testing is a universal experience. Satan, the evil one, will seek to ambush us and catch us in his traps. But as Christ-followers, we need to recognize God has power to lead us past and "out of" the desires that spring up in us. Temptation will be part of our experience as long as we live because we live in a fallen, corrupt world. So the antidote to overcoming temptation is to seek after righteousness.

It's never "smart" to treat sin lightly, to be courteous to temptation or to be overly confident in the face of temptation. Peter's overconfidence (Matthew 26:33-35) is a powerful lesson to us all. Only God can keep us alert to temptations that surround us and deliver us from evil that promises us satisfaction and good times.

Part and parcel of our earthly weakness is meeting disappointment and some very unpleasant situations along the way. But as a believer, we have freedom and divine authority to pray, "Don't let me yield to temptation!"

My moment of reflection…

Deliver Us from Evil

March 26
Matthew 6:5-15

Jesus taught his disciples to pray, "Deliver us from the evil one" (Matthew 6:13). In this model prayer, Jesus instructed his followers to yearn for the kingdom and seek his will. Then he talks about man's needs—daily bread and forgiveness. Because evil corrupts and destroys that which is good, Jesus instructs us to pray that we will be delivered from evil.

This final petition, "Deliver us from the evil one," is a desperate cry for deliverance from all wickedness. Sin is anything contrary to God's will and by nature destructive to the happiness of mankind. God never condones or tolerates sin! No gimmicks will bring deliverance. Only Jesus can deliver us from sin and the evil one! God is a God of deliverance—a recurring theme throughout the Bible. Paul affirms the human dilemma, "Oh, what a miserable person I am! Who will free me from this life that is dominated by sin? Thank God! The answer is in Jesus Christ our Lord" (Romans 7:24-25). The day is coming when we will be delivered from the presence and practice of all evil. Until that day, we need to pray, "Deliver us from the evil one!"

This beloved prayer closes with an angelic chorus of praise: "For yours is the kingdom and the power and the glory forever. Amen." This affirmation, while not in the earliest manuscripts, is an appropriate doxology and fitting conclusion to the Lord's Prayer. The focus and concern of this prayer is all about God and his glory, wisdom, and power. No wonder we ask, "Lord, teach us to pray!"

My moment of reflection...

Growing Old—Staying Young

March 27
Isaiah 40:28-31

Remember the story about Ponce de Leon and his search for the fountain of youth? He felt if he could locate this fountain and drink its waters, no one would grow old but remain youthful. He never found such a fountain! That search was useless, because there is nothing to keep us from growing old. But we have found other "fountains" of youth: ways to cover gray hair, makeup for wrinkles, and other "helps." But we still grow old!

Isaiah wrote, "Even youths will become exhausted, and young men will give up. But those who wait on the Lord will find new strength. They will fly high on wings like eagles. They will run and not grow weary. They will walk and not faint" (Isaiah 40:30-31).

The father looks through the telescope of time and longs for the youth of his teenage son. But the son peers through the other end and covets the maturity of his father. Actually, the only old age to be dreaded is that of the heart. Physical frailty is inescapable, but spiritual frailty is preventable. We need to keep June in our hearts no matter how often December knocks at our door!

Fear and the temptation to glorify the past must be avoided! However, we need to accept our years gladly, keep interested in life, and learn to wait upon the Lord. There is no substitute for "waiting upon the Lord." Maturity celebrates harvest while youth champions planting. The years we enjoy now are but the reflection of all the years that have gone before. Enjoy today. It is a gift of God!

My moment of reflection...

Point of No Return

March 28
Luke 9:57-62

Recently a crisis occurred on an airliner over the Pacific when the navigator informed the pilot they had reached the "point of no return." They arrived at that particular place in the journey where it would be impossible, because of fuel supply, to return to home base. It was mandatory they continue to go forward!

There are times in life when we reach the "point of no return!" There is a window, a time when we can turn around, a time when we can return. But then we arrive at a certain place from which it is impossible to go back and we must go on. As much as we would like to go back to the comfort of our origin, to the familiarity of home base, or to the complacency of noninvolvement, it is impossible to do so without disastrous results. We are forces of forward motion! In the words of Columbus: "Sail on, sail on!"

For Jesus, "as the time drew near for his return to heaven, Jesus resolutely set out for Jerusalem" (Luke 9:51). Jesus knew his ultimate destination: sorrow, injustice, pain, rejection, death! No one is exempted from crossroads, and neither was Jesus! As Jesus faced his future, the "point of no return," he said, "Anyone who puts a hand to the plow and then looks back is not fit for the Kingdom of God" (Luke 9:62).

Dedication is for life. There is no turning back, ever! Jesus plowed his life "furrow" with no thought of turning back. His vision was clear. Now he encourages every believer to tread faithfully in his steps.

My moment of reflection…

Dedication Is Expensive

March 29
Luke 19:28-44

After a short but productive ministry, Jesus is nearing the end of his earthly journey. Luke says, "As the time drew near for his return to heaven, Jesus resolutely set out for Jerusalem" (Luke 9:51).

Imagine a loaded truck coming down the highway at a high rate of speed. Suddenly the driver realizes there is danger of a crash. He applies the brakes but the truck plunges out of control. Its mass and speed carry it beyond control of the driver, resulting in tragedy. We are all familiar with this kind of mechanical momentum.

Palm Sunday and the following week give us a portrait of spiritual momentum. Palm Sunday differs from any other day of Passion Week—there is joy and exultation, yet overtones of sadness and tragedy. This did not cause Jesus to shun his divine responsibility. He was completely dedicated to his Father's will, and that dedication was expensive because it ended in his death. In the crowds, we see and hear the momentum of ignorance and hate: "Crucify Him, crucify Him" (Luke 23:21). But there is another momentum that gives us hope! It is the momentum of love—a love nothing can stop, but it means an innocent man will die! Love is expensive because Jesus went to the cross as the Savior of the world.

In Irving Stone's novel, *The Agony and the Ecstasy*, the master sculptor speaks to young aspiring Michelangelo. "Dedication is expensive," he says, "and it will cost you your life."

Michelangelo, with great insight, replies, "What else is life for?"

"Blessed is he who comes in the name of the Lord!"

My moment of reflection…

Defective Discipleship

March 30
1 Corinthians 3:1-23

Evangelist Dwight L. Moody said, "A Christian is the world's Bible and some of them need revising." This statement reveals the situation which existed with some of Paul's friends at Corinth. They were followers of Jesus but their spirituality was very shallow. Paul calls them "infants in the Christian life" (1 Corinthians 3:1). Defective discipleship is true of the modern church! We want to be disciples and yet be "balcony Christians" looking on at the same time. We want a tune-up, not an overhaul job!

The behavior of Paul's friends was marked by pride, bitterness, and resentment. They were adult in years but still acting like children in their relationship with one another. As infant Christians, they had not learned the discipline of separation. That is, they were still participating in immoral practices of pagans. Finally, they had lost their sense of priorities. They had many gifts with which to serve God and one another. Instead of serving one another with love and kindness, they used their gifts as weapons.

The result was painful for Paul! He wanted them on the cutting edge of their spiritual maturity and walk with the Lord. But what he found was a group of infants who were controlled and led by their own desires. Instead of being a church illuminating the way so others could find Christ, they were sadly lacking in obedience. As believers in a fallen world, God is calling us to be an open epistle, not defective disciples! So by the grace of God, let's determine to be the world's Bible in our discipleship!

My moment of reflection…

Make a Wish

March 31
John 15:1-11

The short story, "Aladdin and the Wonderful Lamp," is a fable about a poor family and their son, Aladdin, who possessed a magical lamp. He received anything he asked for from the genie. It's a fascinating story, but untrue! Let's suppose you had a magical lamp and could make several wishes! What might your wishes include? Riches? Health? Power? Fame? As a Christian, I don't need a magical lamp—but I have several promises which I have already been given.

I need cleansing! Jesus made this promise: "You are already clean because of what I have said to you" (John 15:3, CEV). A universal need confirmed by experience is that all men are sinners and by his death Christ provided for our cleaning. I wish for joy! Again, Jesus promised, "You will be filled with my joy" (John 15:11). The natural result of cleansing is we are filled with joy. Finally, I would wish my prayers be answered. Jesus promised, "If you stay joined to me and my words remain in you, you may ask any request you like, and it will be granted" (John 15:7). Prayer will not be answered by the magic genie but according to the perfect will of God! As you abide in Christ, ask what you will and it shall be done. Can't get any better than that!

It's a nice story—but it's only a fable! Take your magic lamp, I don't need it! All I need is provided by the Savior to any disciple anywhere, anytime! So "make a wish" for cleansing, joy, and answered prayer and it shall be done!

My moment of reflection…

Neutrality

April 1
Matthew 9:27-38

Our Lord spent his entire life "going about doing good" deeds. One day, after Jesus healed a blind demoniac, the Pharisees said he did it by the power of Satan. Explaining a kingdom divided against itself cannot stand, Jesus said, "Anyone who isn't helping me opposes me, and anyone who isn't working with me is actually working against me" (Matthew 12:30). In plain words, Jesus said you cannot be neutral!

Neutrality is defined as "not taking part in either side; in a middle position between two extremes; indifferent." Spiritual neutrality is impossible and forbidden by Jesus, who said, "No one can serve two masters. For you will hate one and love the other, or be devoted to one and despise the other. You cannot serve both God and money" (Luke 16:13). The message of the Bible is you cannot be neutral regarding Jesus Christ!

When Da Vinci finished his great work *The Last Supper*, a friend came to see his masterpiece and commented on the lustrous beauty of the silver cup. That was not the response sought by the artist. Da Vinci grabbed a brush and obliterated the cup because he wanted nothing in his picture that would draw attention from the Lord Jesus!

As you consider the role Jesus plays in your life, remember it is impossible to be neutral or to serve two masters! The attitude of the crowds was one of amazement and wonder as Jesus healed the blind demoniac while the Pharisees were prejudiced by the truth, blinded by their own sin. The message of Jesus is very clear: "You cannot be neutral about me!"

My moment of reflection…

Those Awful Debts

April 2
Matthew 20:20-28

Some of us are "in debt" or have been sometime in our life. If you are in debt, you know how difficult it is to get out of debt. Sometimes you feel like all you do with your money is owe it to someone! The world was hopelessly in debt because of sin. And sin, in God's economy, required death of the sinner! That's what Easter is all about—paying the debt!

Easter reminds us Christ did something about the world's debt: "He paid it!" The Bible tells us that Christ gave himself "a ransom for all" (Matthew 20:28). *Ransom* means to pay a debt for someone and includes the idea of payment through exchange. So by Christ's death all of us have been ransomed and released from the debt of sin.

In 1829, George Wilson was sentenced to be hanged for murder. President Andrew Jackson pardoned him, but Wilson refused it and insisted it was not a pardon unless he accepted it. The case went to the Supreme Court and Chief Justice Marshall gave the following decision: "A pardon is paper, the value of which depends upon its acceptance by the person implicated." George Wilson was hanged because he refused to accept the president's pardon.

Christ secured a pardon for all of us! He secured it by giving himself as a "ransom for all." Jesus paid every sinner's debt, yet only those who accept the ransom will be saved. So this Easter season, give thanks for Christ's death, the resurrection, and for your faith in him. He has canceled the debt and now you are free! Happy Easter!

My moment of reflection…

Death Notice

April 3
Gospels

Jesus of Nazareth was born 4 or 5 AD in Bethlehem and died at the young age of thirty-three. His mother and earthly father were Mary and Joseph. Early in life he was dedicated in the temple by a family friend, Priest Simeon. His boyhood years were spent in Nazareth, playing with his brothers and sisters and working in his father's carpenter's shop.

Following his baptism, Jesus began his teaching ministry, traveling throughout Palestine. He had no formal education but easily held his own debating temple scholars. In contrast to others, he lived a perfect life, sinless and beyond reproach. His winsome personality caused many to follow him, becoming his disciples. He was a master teacher who loved boating and fishing and dinner parties. He loved people, especially those who were sick, lonely, and disadvantaged. He was accused of spending too much time with sinners. His whole life was spent in loving and caring for others, which in the end cost him his life! His life's purpose was to "do the will of his Father."

Knowing difficult times lay ahead, he went to Jerusalem and was arrested early this week and a kangaroo court quickly found him guilty on trumped up charges. He was condemned to death by crucifixion. His death occurred at 3:00 p.m. this afternoon and was later buried in a garden tomb in a private ceremony. He leaves to mourn his mother Mary, several brothers and sisters, eleven disciples, and many friends who believed in him and loved him. In lieu of flowers, his Father suggests gifts to his Church.

My moment of reflection...

God's Kind of Love

April 4
1 John 3:1-11

There is no more overworked word in modern life than the word *love*! You see it everywhere: on billboards and television, in magazines every day. It is used to sell everything from denture cleaners to false eyelashes. Love is mentioned in much of the music that floods culture. But real love cannot be splashed around like that!

Our world is a wonderful place to live with all its modern conveniences and fantastic achievements. At the same time, we live in a universe where countries can't get along with each other and families are ravished by struggle. Neighbors can't live peacefully together and relationships are falling apart! People don't like others, let alone love them! It is obvious the greatest need of humanity is love.

God chose the beloved disciple John who knew Jesus more intimately than anyone else to write about love. He exhorted God's people to live as children of God by loving one another! John wrote, "Think how much the Father loves us. He loves us so much that he lets us be called his children" (1 John 3:1, CEV). It was agape love that sent Jesus to die for the sins of the world and gave us the privilege of "sonship!" It is a love that loves the unlovely, a love that never stops loving!

God's kind of love is superior to any other kind of love. Yet, amazingly, God's kind of love can be demonstrated through the life of every believer. All a believer is or has or ever hopes to be is the result of God's agape love. Praise the Lord!

My moment of reflection...

Good News from a Graveyard

April 5
Matthew 28:1-20

The Easter message is "good news" from a cemetery! Graveyards have always been melancholy places because they are associated with sadness and separation from loved ones. The cemetery is the last place one would expect to receive good news! Yet this is the origin of the Easter message.

From the beginning, man raised the question Job asked, "Will we humans live again?" (Job 14:14, CEV). Century after century, wise and foolish, rich and poor, young and old have marched into the clammy chambers of death. Men have stood in fear of death but could do nothing about it. It remained for Jesus Christ, the God-man, to come with an authentic answer to Job's painful, perplexing question.

It is no accident that every resurrection story ends up with a foot race. The disciples ran to see the evidence of the empty tomb, Mary leaves the scene with haste and joy, and the women abandon their carefully prepared spices to share the resurrection news! Christ's victory over the grave is an exciting truth—a story that must be told. The resurrection is the basic truth of Christianity. No other religion or sect can claim the same!

The angelic announcement of his resurrection is the greatest announcement ever given: "He isn't here! He has been raised from the dead…come…see where his body was lying…go quickly and tell his disciples he has been raised from the dead" (Matthew 28:6-7). The Easter message is not an argument, it is a divine proclamation. Not only is Easter the greatest event in human history—it is "Good News from a Graveyard!" Rejoice!

My moment of reflection…

Resurrection Light

April 6
Luke 24:13-34

Anyone who has known the loss of a friend knows the utter depression and sorrow of two men who plodded along the Emmaus Road after the crucifixion of Jesus. Their Master died and was buried. Their hope was gone! Our hearts go out to them in their sorrow and loss and yet beat with joy at the revelation they were about to receive—Jesus is alive!

Coming alongside these sorrowing disciples, Jesus by his presence is ready to help them find their way. Many questions flood their troubled minds! Why? Still today thousands of people are looking for hope and a new road to carry them to happiness, but tragically the pursuit is futile.

Suddenly, as the Emmaus travelers walked along sharing their story, Jesus came beside them! Still unrecognized, he quoted from the scripture to show them how all the things that they bemoaned were written beforehand. Still they didn't know who he was! Only as they sat down to break bread did the "light" shine for them and "their eyes were opened and they recognized him" (Luke 20:31). And at that moment Jesus disappeared!

Within the hour they were on their way to Jerusalem and were greeted with the report, "The Lord has really risen" (Luke 20:34). Now centuries later, Resurrection Light still shines and he speaks to us as he did to his disciples on the Emmaus Road. During this Easter season, let each of us seek him and allow him to lead us by his "light." May the joy and peace and hope of Easter flood your heart and mind! Resurrection light still shines!

My moment of reflection...

He's Alive!

April 7
John 20:1-29

Easter proclaims Jesus Christ arose the third day following his crucifixion! But his resurrection affirms much more—he was alive on the fourth and fifth days! He was alive during the forty days before the Ascension and at Pentecost when he poured his Spirit on the church. He was alive that notable yesterday when he appeared to Paul on the Damascus Road. He is alive today, confronting sinner and saint alike. He is alive forever! That's the insistent message of every believer.

The message of Christmas is that Jesus stepped into history from eternity to be the Savior of the world. After living a perfect life, he was crucified and buried in a borrowed tomb. But three days later, he arose from the dead! Later when he ascended to his Father, he did so not as an alien or a wandering pilgrim, but as a resident returning to his permanent home.

Easter affirms the news that Jesus is the Christ, the Son of the Living God. No doubt about it, Easter is the greatest event in history! The resurrection destroys fear of death and replaces it with hope and the promise of eternal life. Seeing that the tomb is empty, those trusting him have the responsibility of telling everyone they know that "He's Alive!" When doubt surrounds you, remember the tomb is empty: "Christ has risen just as he said!"

Too many Christians are living in the grave and that is no place for a child of God. Tombs are for the dead. Because he lives, we can live in confidence, assurance, and hope! He's alive!

My moment of reflection...

He Tarries among Us

April 8
Acts 1:1-5

Following his crucifixion and resurrection, Jesus "appeared to the apostles from time to time and proved to them in many ways that he was actually alive. On these occasions he talked to them about the Kingdom of God" (Acts 1:3).

The forty days between the resurrection and ascension must have been wonderful days for the apostles. There was joy in their hearts that the crucified Lord was alive. There was the hope every morning that Christ might appear to them and become another proof that he was alive. Most of all, there was the anticipation of his teaching and promises.

If Jesus had appeared to them on one occasion only, they may have doubted the resurrection, thinking it was just an illusion or their imagination. For that reason, Jesus "piled up proofs" of his resurrection by tarring among them. After all, dead men don't rise, but this one did! Jesus used this period of time to school his disciples in their future responsibilities, to nurture their independence and individual judgment.

Later, when a cloud received Jesus out of their sight, the apostles knew quite definitely that his physical departure would make no difference to them. He was close to them though unseen. He gave them the promise, "I am with you always!" There is an old Greek myth where a statue comes to life, steps down from the pedestal, and becomes a living person. After his crucifixion, Jesus stepped out of the tomb and by many proofs demonstrated he was really alive! Centuries later, the resurrected Lord still "tarries among us" and declares, "I'm Alive!"

My moment of reflection...

Every Christian—A Witness

April 9
Acts 8:26-40

A newly hired deckhand was being shown the various compartments of a great ocean freighter on which he would be working. After the tour, he asked the captain where the passengers stay. The old seaman replied, "There are no passengers on this ship, every person who sails with us works!" Jesus taught every believer is a witness, a worker (Acts 1:8).

The entire world would be thrown into an immediate religious revolution if Christians everywhere accepted the fact that there are no passengers on the ship of Christianity, that all believers belong to the crew. Sadly, many Christians consider themselves as passengers drifting along toward a heavenly destiny, while being cared for and comforted by the crew. When they hear the words of the captain, "Tell people about me everywhere" (Acts 1:8), they think it means to enter Christian ministry. But rather, it is a command to every believer to witness to the lost around him.

As children of God, we have been given a full inheritance of the kingdom to enjoy and cherish! But it's more than that! As members of the crew we are called to bear fruit, which means reproduction! An apple tree is judged to be a successful apple tree when it produces apples. Within each apple is the seed and potential of another apple. It may be a long process of planting and growing but in the end the tree produces apples.

Nothing pleases Jesus more than seeing Christians bear fruit! Remember, there are no passengers on this ship. Every believer is called to be a fruiting-bearing worker, a witness in the kingdom!

My moment of reflection...

A Major in Minors

April 10
Matthew 23:1-36

In graduate school, I had the responsibility of counseling students in the selection of their major. I spent hours listening to students agonizing over what major they were going to choose. I remember one student in particular. This young man had accumulated enough credits to be a junior at the university, but each semester he would become fascinated by a new subject and determine he would like to complete a minor in that discipline. The last time we talked, he had chosen five minors but "no" major! Jokingly, I thought, *He ought to major in minors!*

It occurs to me that much of what we do in our spiritual lives falls into the same category—majoring in minors! We go from one spiritual high to the next, from one religious fad to another, from one current teacher to whoever is next on the "best sellers" list. Like the young university student, there is a serious need for us to ask if all this activity is taking us where we want to be when we get through. Are we majoring in the areas that are the first concerns of Jesus Christ?

Jesus had some harsh words to those who "majored in minors." Listen to him: "You Pharisees and teachers are show-offs...You give God a tenth of the spices from your garden...yet you neglect the more important matters of the Law, such as justice, mercy and faithfulness. These are the important things you should have done" (Matthew 23:23, CEV).

Mercy. Justice. Faithfulness. Make that the major of your spiritual life and the minors will take their proper place.

My moment of reflection...

Pressure

April 11
James 1:12-18

Believers are faced with unbelievable pressures these days. Living in a "pressure-packed" age, we ask the question, "How ought a believer to live in such times?" James tells us that "whenever trouble comes your way, let it be an opportunity for joy" (James 1:2).

You've heard the saying that a "Christian is like a tea bag; he isn't worth much until he has been through some hot water!" All of us having been through pressure know one thing: "Pressure can be profitable!" James instructs us that God tests us, not to destroy us but to demonstrate us. It is the pressed flower that releases aroma, the hot furnace that yields the best steel, and the pressure and heat of the earth's elements that create costly diamonds.

As you face pressure, remember that pressure produces! The God-allowed pressures in our lives are to develop character and dependability. God never promised an easy journey, but he did promise a safe and triumphant landing. God allows pressures in our lives to bring us to completeness and maturity. We must remember no one is immune to pressure, that pressures are temporary and are great opportunities to learn!

So when pressures and trials come, face them joyfully and confidently for real victory in life. Meet life's challenges and pressures, not with dull resignation, but with a positive, enthusiastic spirit of trust and cooperation with the plan of God! And never forget that God tests us not to destroy us but to demonstrate us! Finally, James reminds us that God "in his goodness chose to make us his own children...his choice possession" (James 1:18). So rejoice!

My moment of reflection...

Delays

April 12
Galatians 5:16-26

On a trip from Florida to Ohio, we were delayed several hours because of heavy traffic. In our delay, I was reminded Americans don't like to wait—it makes us unhappy and upset! I think we would agree delays are irritating and aggravating. Perhaps it's because we are very demanding—we want what we want when we want it. None find delays easy to accept!

You are at the grocery store with a busy evening ahead. Lines are long and only two checkout lanes are open. The clerk is new on the job and as she gets to you her cash register tape runs out. You're delayed! You're having dinner out. Everyone is hungry, the diner is very busy and two waitresses short. So you sit there with a glass of water and a menu to chew on. You're delayed! How do you respond?

The rubber of Christianity meets the road at just such intersections in life. Our faith is not tested by the quietness of our life, but in long grocery lines and busy restaurants. That's where the real tests are! Paul wrote, "When the Holy Spirit controls our lives, he will produce this kind of fruit in us: love, joy, peace" (Galatians 5:22). This fruit is the necessary style and buttons and zipper of the garment. The remaining fruit give color and beauty to life: "patience, kindness, goodness, faithfulness, gentleness, self-control" (Galatians 5:22). All of us need to accept delay, to smile and respond with a pleasant, understanding spirit. Ask God to keep you calm, cheerful, and relaxed. No pills, no booze, no hocus-pocus. Just resting in Christ!

My moment of reflection…

It's Contagious

April 13
Hebrews 10:19-25

When someone has the flu, a bad cold, or other common sickness, it's quite common to ask, "Is it contagious?" Because none of us enjoy being sick, we tend to stay away from those who may be carriers of any contagious illness.

I believe there is something even more contagious than common illnesses—our daily attitudes! Most of us have been in a gathering with pessimists and people with negative attitudes. As you know, it is easy to "catch" that same negative spirit in your conversation and behavior. But similarly, when a person with a positive attitude and demeanor enters the room, our conversations tend to shift to a more positive tone. All this seems to indicate that attitudes are highly contagious, and each one of us is a carrier!

How's your attitude as a Christian? Jesus says we are the "light of the world." That means our attitudes are to glorify and reflect Jesus in all we do! Do others see our enthusiasm and zest for life? The Bible commands us to love one another! Are the attitudes we reflect toward others loving and kind? God's word says to "think of ways to encourage one another to outbursts of love and good deeds" (Hebrews 10:24-25). We all have the potential to stimulate each other to love and good deeds by displaying Godly attitudes—good, positive attitudes! We encourage others through our positive spirit which allows our friends to see Jesus through our loving spirit. We need to be aware that every attitude we reflect is contagious to so many people! Today is your opportunity to encourage someone!

My moment of reflection...

A Helping Hand

April 14
2 Kings 5:1-23

Recently I saw a man carrying a pail of water in his yard. His little boy was on the other side of the pail trying to help carry the bucket. I don't think the little guy really helped that much, but he seemed happy and proud. By his face, I could see the father was pleased and proud as well. A father is glad when his children try to help!

What is true of our earthly father is true of our Heavenly Father. He likes us to help him! It may seem strange for you to think of helping God, because God is God—and he can do anything that needs to be done alone! While that is a fact, it is also true there are many things that God needs our help if he is to do them.

Remember the Old Testament story of how God cured the Syrian captain Naaman of his leprosy? God healed the captain but not without the help of a little Hebrew maid in Damascus. Because of her love and concern for her master's health, she said "I wish my master would go to see the prophet in Samaria. He would heal him" (2 Kings 5:3). Naaman was obedient to Elisha's instructions and was healed.

There are many things God wants to do and is ready to do, but he can't do them until someone steps up to the plate to help him. God needs all of us to help him so something that needs to be done gets done! What can you do? Lend a helping hand—be available today!

My moment of reflection...

Christ's Return

April 15
Titus 2:1-15

On the very day Jesus ascended to his Father, the Bible says that "someday...he will return" (Acts 1:11). Christ's return needs to be continually on our minds! When the "blessed hope" becomes ingrained in our minds, a transformation is apt to take place in our living. Titus tells us to "look forward to that wonderful event when the glory of our great God and Savior, Jesus Christ, will be revealed" (Titus 2:13).

For many people, the only time they contemplate the Lord's return is at funerals or near-death experiences. Reason is most of us are here-and-now thinkers much more than then-and-there people. Critics have denied it, cynics have laughed at it, and scholars have ignored it! But his return stands solid as stone, soon to be fulfilled and offers believers great hope and encouragement. No wonder the Bible tells us to comfort one another with the truth that Jesus is coming again!

What should you do until he returns? You don't sit around listening for some bugle call or staring up into the sky looking for the rapture cloud! Rather, you get your act together and live every day as if it's your last for his glory. You work diligently at your job to shake salt out every chance you get and to shine brightly where you are planted! Tickets for the event are free, but don't wait. About the time you finally make up your mind, the whole thing could have happened, leaving you looking back instead of looking up! After all, what good is a ticket if the promised event is over?

My moment of reflection...

When Life Comes Apart

April 16
Colossians 1:15-23

We live in a "fragmented" world where every man is for himself. It seems there is no unifying purpose among people and nations of the world. When a nation extends friendship beyond its borders, it is often interpreted as "butting in" rather than helping out! Individuals too are falling apart. Prisons are overcrowded, psychiatrists are overworked, and marriage counselors are exhausted. Instead of man being looked upon as a whole, he is often treated as a conglomeration of parts. That's the problem: we can never understand any part of anything unless we see meaning of the whole!

Jesus posed a powerful question, "Doesn't life consist of more than food and clothing?" (Matthew 6:25). Many have never learned that truth! They want answers to life's questions but there seems to be none, especially if God is left out of the picture. Christ is the only one who gives balance and harmony to life. When he is left out there is no balance—thus no peace!

If our fragmented world is to become whole, we must not only deal with the outer shell but with man's total person. Paul reminds us that God "existed before everything else began, and he holds all creation together" (Colossians 1:17). Life hands us a series of seemingly unrelated, haphazard experiences. To the cynic this makes no sense, but Jesus takes this fragmented mess and brings healing. The glory of anything lies in its wholeness! A symphony is composed of individual sounds, but when the sounds are blended, noise becomes harmony and pleasing to the ear. Jesus wants to take a fragmented world and make it whole!

My moment of reflection...

Don't Give Up!

April 17
Isaiah 40:27-31

Army recruits were being drilled on a hot, sultry day. An officer was displeased to see one of the rookies drop his rifle. He ordered the offender out of formation and asked the recruit, "How long have you been in the Army?"

The less-than-enthusiastic rookie looked at the officer and replied, "All day, sir!"

We all have days when we feel like intentionally dropping our "rifle!" We are fed up with the way things are going and feel like "giving up." The Bible is no stranger to those feelings. Paul spoke of Demas, his fellow worker who gave up: "Demas has deserted me because he loves the things of this life" (2 Timothy 4:10).

Like some baseball teams, we can get our runners on base, but we can't get them home! We get a good start but we "die on third." To be able to fail and get up and go on requires faith in the conviction that there is meaning in living, that God has a design and plan for our life.

Paul asked his friends, "You were getting along so well. Who has interfered with you to hold you back from following the truth?" (Galatians 5:7). We start well, but something hinders us—lack of faith, courage, or perseverance, which soon fizzle out! The key to "keep on keeping on" is given by Isaiah: "Those who wait on the Lord will find new strength. They will fly high on wings like eagles. They will run and not grow weary. They will walk and not faint" (Isaiah 40:31). Tempted to give up? Don't. There's so much yet to do!

My moment of reflection…

I Can't—I Can

April 18
Philippians 4:10-20

Einstein could not speak until he was four years old and did not read until he was seven. Beethoven's music teacher said that as a composer he was hopeless. Thomas Edison's teachers said he was so stupid he could never learn anything. Walt Disney was fired by a newspaper editor because he was thought to have "no good ideas." These are examples of individuals who achieved recognition and success in their lives despite the negativism and criticism of others. They simply refused to say, "I can't!"

When a person's life is characterized by a negative and defeatist attitude, there are predictable results. Failure is assured resulting in unhappiness, disappointment, and depression. Nothing of value is accomplished by a person who approaches a task with the feeling that he would not succeed. And if a negative, defeatist attitude dominates a Christian's life, demonstration is made to the world that Christ has not made a difference in his life. As a result, the world will never be drawn to nor seek to emulate a life which does not radiate the confidence and joy of personal faith.

Paul reminds us, "I can do everything with the help of Christ who gives me the strength I need" (Philippians 4:13). The choice is yours—no one can make it for you! Jesus is waiting to help you succeed to the highest level of your potential if you will trust him. With him, "you can if you will" develop a confident and positive approach to life that promises success in your journey. So when you feel like "you can't," remember Beethoven!

My moment of reflection…

Trust and Trustworthiness

April 19
Jeremiah 9:17-24

America is longing for competent leadership! The public has lost confidence in the great institutions that determine our future—our educational system, our political personnel, and those who oversee our economy. When honesty and trust are in question, it naturally leads to genuine concern.

Comparable situations existed in the history of Israel. Jeremiah brought some serious charges against religious and political leaders of his day. He charged leaders with injustice and walking after things that did not profit (Jeremiah 7:7). As society maintained a proper relationship to God and humanity, justice was common. When it wasn't, then humanity was gravely affected and turned sour!

America's problems are based upon her rejection of God and his laws. And as faith in God degenerates, we can expect conditions to worsen. When the moral and ethical fiber of our society is weak, we can expect weak leadership and days of crisis. Courageous, trustworthy, and moral leaders are the need of the hour!

Moral standards have one origin—God himself! History has proved that civilizations have prospered or suffered in direct relationship to alignment with divine law. History does repeat itself! The God of history still honors those who honor him. Jeremiah gives the answer to our dilemma: "Let not the wise man gloat in his wisdom, or the mighty man in his might or the rich man in his riches. Let them boast in this alone: that they truly know me and understand that I am the Lord who is just and righteous, whose love is unfailing, and that I delight in these things" (Jeremiah 9:23, 24).

My moment of reflection…

Called to Greatness

April 20
John 3:22-36

We are living in a day when there seems to be a famine of great men and women—an absence of heroes! Historically, there have been numerous men and women we can easily identify as heroes, giants who have made great contributions to their generation in every field of endeavor.

Speaking about "greatness," the Bible says that John the Baptist "will be great in the eyes of the Lord" (Luke 1:15). Ever wonder why? When you carefully review John's life, you will find two predominant characteristics which thrust him into the circle of greatness—humility and courage!

Jesus taught "whoever is the least among you is the greatest" (Luke 9:48). John described himself as "a voice crying in the wilderness." Just a voice, but what a voice! When Jesus came to be baptized by John, he tried to excuse himself by saying he was not worthy even to untie his shoelaces. He also said, "He must increase, but I must decrease!" The philosophy of our age is "sell yourself... blow your own horn...look out for number one!" Ultimate greatness will never be found in money or muscle, but in the heart of one who walks humbly with the Lord.

John was courageous and unafraid to speak the truth. True courage is scarce today! Today is the age of the comfortable pew and pleasing truth! John, however, called religious leaders "on the carpet" when they broke the law. No wonder John is remembered as "a great man." I pray that God will ignite the spark of greatness in your life and that you will be willing to pay the cost!

My moment of reflection...

Brokenness

April 21
Mark 14:1-9

Jesus was having dinner with Simon in Bethany when a woman interrupted their party. Uninvited, this lady came into the room and broke a bottle of expensive perfume and poured it on Jesus. Immediately, the whole house was filled with fragrance. It was an electric, never-to-be-forgotten moment for all the guests, but some were indignant at the waste! Imagine the emotions of that event!

Being broken and "smelling up" the whole place is what the Christian life is all about. Most of the time we get together in "separate alabaster vases"—contained, self-sufficient, emitting no fragrance at all! But Mary, when she came to Jesus, broke her vase and the contents were forever released. Most of us have Jesus inside us and we keep him contained. Our great need is to smash the vase—we have to let the life out! Our world is crying for the fragrance of hope and love and forgiveness.

Of course, it's scary to be broken, and what's more, it's costly! It was costly for Mary and it will cost you as well. But the way to up is down for Jesus—brokenness is critical for wholeness. The Holy One lives among broken lives. So when we break the vase and fragrance fills the room, it isn't long until the whole world is filled with the fragrance of Jesus.

When Jeremiah shattered a bottle it was a warning of coming judgment. But when Mary broke the alabaster box and fragrance filled the room, it was her way of proclaiming God's love and forgiveness. While costly and usually painful, brokenness is the only way to glory!

My moment of reflection...

Traveling Light

April 22
Matthew 11:25-30

Unpacking from our last vacation, I was amazed at how much "stuff" we did not use or need on our trip! It reminded me that many of us are carrying excess baggage through life. We carry guilt, doubt, grief, loneliness, and fear, all of which drains us of energy and the joy of living. Our call is to travel light, trusting God with burdens we were never intended to bear.

Jesus issued this invitation, "Come to me, all of you who are weary and carry heavy burdens, and I will give you rest" (Matthew 11:28). If we let him, God will lighten our load and give us joy in the process. In Psalm 23, David is concerned that we build trust in the true God, not a god of our own making who could never supply our needs on the journey!

David said his God was Yahweh—the God who was uncaused and unchanging! Relationships change, health changes, weather changes! While most everything changes, David's God Yahweh, who ruled the world last night, is the God who rules it today. He has the same love, same plan, and the same power he had from the beginning! Remember the old music professor who tapped his tuning fork and said, "That's middle C! It was middle C yesterday, it will be middle C tomorrow, and it will be middle C a thousand years from now"? In life's journey, we need a middle C! Yahweh is the only One we need, the One who will give us rest! Why carry excess baggage when you have a shepherd who meets your every need and gives you rest?

My moment of reflection...

Strive for Excellence

April 23
2 Chronicles 2:5-9

We need disciplined workers and energetic leaders who are committed to great ideas! Solomon was preparing to build the Temple and he wanted it to be great because he was serving a great God. Since this was God's Temple, no shortcuts in materials or labor was allowed. His motive was not just to make it good—it must be the best! Solomon was grateful for the privilege of building the temple but humbled that God should choose him for such an awesome task. Whatever we are called to do, we must strive for excellence by doing our very best!

Solomon looked for people who were gifted, skilled, and experienced craftsmen for the project. He wanted workers who were committed to do their very best and materials of highest quality. Paul affirms Solomon's attitude and pursuit of excellence in his challenge to all Christians: "Work with enthusiasm, as though you were working for the Lord rather than for people" (Ephesians 6:7).

Excellence is never easy! It always costs time, energy, and resources. But as we raise the standard of what we do for the kingdom, unbelievers will be more likely to take note if our goal is the pursuit of excellence. They will be more attracted to us, to what we have to say and to what we are doing. Thus our witness for Christ becomes more effective as we attract others to the body of Christ. So our challenge is always to do our very best with what we have, trying to be exceptional rather than just good enough for his glory!

My moment of reflection...

You are Rich!

April 24
Isaiah 26:1-19

Rich! You are rich! You are very rich! While you may not be wealthy and rich in material goods, you are so very rich in the blessings of God. You can be rich because you are happy in what you are doing and joyful in what God is doing for you.

You are rich because you are loved and Christ died for you, giving you the promise of eternal life. You are rich because God has chosen you to be a partner in his creation, managing a phenomenal world as his steward. You are rich because you have the sacred privilege of going to him with every problem, especially on those occasions when you feel inadequate and unsure of yourself.

You are rich if you are content with what you have. Paul reminded Timothy that he came into the world with nothing and that his attitude should be contentment (1 Timothy 6:6). If you keep the right attitude, God will supply you with the grace and strength for every circumstance. God wants to develop your character and make you into a beautiful person. Never give in to self-pity simply because your resources seem inadequate or you think that God won't meet your every need! He's already said that he would supply all your needs—just trust him!

And one thing more! Never forget the promise that God "will keep in perfect peace all who trust in you, whose thoughts are fixed on you" (Isaiah 26:3). You are rich when your trust in God brings you the ultimate gift—God's perfect Peace!

My moment of reflection...

Unity

April 25
John 17:1-26

One of the highest priorities Jesus has for his people is unity! Jesus prayed that oneness and unity would flourish among believers as a testimony to his ministry. When you enter the family of God through faith in Christ, you become "one" with all of God's people—people from every nation, race, kindred, language, and tribe. But the fact that all are human does not automatically make them "one." Even the claim to know Christ does not necessarily make them "one." Merely being human and professing faith in Christ does not automatically produce unity—at least not as Jesus defined unity!

On the other hand, unity is possible despite barriers that usually divide—race, origin, religion, language, etc. Only as his supernatural grace transforms hearts and gives new purpose for life can unity really be realized. Let me illustrate unity! Here is a pile of bricks. All the bricks have uniformity. They appear similar but they lack unity. But when those same bricks are cemented together into a well-structured house, they have unity in purpose, oneness in design.

God calls his people to be "living stones" and he builds them into a "holy temple." Do you ever feel like a loose brick? Would anyone miss you if you were out of place? God notices loose bricks and holes in brick piles. It is important our unity be based on our oneness in Jesus Christ. That determines how we treat one another and causes us to do what we do. Only then will there be unity and purpose in the family and the world will know that Jesus is Lord!

My moment of reflection…

Our Task

April 26
Mark 6:30-44

I am fascinated and intrigued by the story of the feeding of the five thousand in Mark 6. To feed the multitude with five loaves and a two fishes and have twelve baskets of leftovers is truly a lesson of miraculous multiplication. In this story, Christ shows himself as being the same Jehovah who miraculously fed Israel with manna for years in the desert.

The disciples had been taught to "seek the kingdom of God and his righteousness." Now it was time for his followers to see him as the divine "Bread of Life" and source of all blessing. His command to "make disciples of all nations" was an unbelievable task considering their weaknesses, resources, and number. But the Lord called them and calls us to do his work in bold reliance on him as the divine supplier of all our needs.

Our troubled world needs a reason for living, truth to believe, and goodness to live by—things our bankrupt society cannot offer! The Child of God has been entrusted with special ability to meet these needs. So where do you fit in the picture? It is important for every Christian to see themselves not as one of the five thousand comfortably seated on the hillside waiting to be served, but as servants who are giving bread to those who are hungry! It is so easy to see the problem instead of the potential or to measure our resources rather than trust in God's provision. Whatever we give to him he will bless! As a conduit of his grace, our task is to be a distributor of the bread—a servant in residence!

My moment of reflection...

Be an Encourager

April 27
1 Thessalonians 5:9-18

Life can be hard and often we encounter difficulties that were not in our plan! Encouragement helps to take the sting out of life and gives hope to the hurting, the lonely and forgotten. As believers, how can we lift up, affirm, and help others in their need?

- Be observant! Sometimes it's the small things in life that we miss because we are too occupied thinking about ourselves.
- Cultivate a positive spirit! Encouragement cannot thrive in a negative atmosphere.
- Be supportive to someone who may be hurting! Cookies or, making a call will always be appreciated by someone who is discouraged.
- Write a note not just for special occasions, but at unexpected times! Written notes seem to be a lost art but are always appreciated. These notes give feelings of worth and honor.
- Make a phone call! Just letting people know you are thinking of them and praying for them can give them a needed lift.

Children need five positives for every negative. It is imperative that we develop a spirit of personal encouragement with no thought of being paid back. A well-timed expression is never forgotten. Paul's teaching is still appropriate: "So encourage each other and build each other up, just as you are already doing" (1 Thessalonians 5:11).

My moment of reflection...

My Body—God's Temple

April 28
1 Corinthians 6:18-20

Listening to a heated debate recently, I heard a sophisticated "know it all" make the politically correct statement, "It's my body...I can do with it whatever I want!" That's quite a statement to make, but is it really true?

Yes, it's your body and you probably will do with it just as you please. You have to live your own life as no one else can live it for you. Parents, teachers, and friends may encourage you to act in a certain way, but it's really your life and your body! But here's the rub: you must take responsibility for the way you use your body. According to the "operations manual," you have no right to take unnecessary risks that might cause someone else or yourself to suffer by your abuse! If you make a choice and things don't turn out the way you expected, don't blame someone else!

When you became a believer, you gave yourself to the Lord—your body, mind, and soul. That means, God owns you—all of you! Paul declared that since the body is the temple of the Holy Spirit, we are to give our "bodies to God...a living and holy sacrifice" (Romans 12:1-2). That means no one has the right to abuse or misuse their body because their body is "God's house!" If you have given your life to God, then your body is not yours to do with just as you please. You are a steward of your body and obligated to do with it what would please the Owner!

My moment of reflection...

Pray First, Plan Later

April 29
Psalm 25:4-14

Making plans is a huge part of life! We often approach planning with something that sounds really good in our own mind. However, unless our plans are born out of prayer and seeking the mind of Christ, the likelihood of success is in question. Prayer becomes the foundation of our plans and prepares the way for certain success. Solomon had it right when he said, "Seek his will in all you do, and he will direct your paths" (Proverbs 3:6).

God will give us vision for what he calls us to do. But we must continually seek him on how he wants us to proceed and how to carry out each step. When we remain connected to the source of power, we will be successful carrying out his perfect plan. Also sharing our plan with our colleagues will add wisdom and confirmation as well as checking our own motives and ambitions.

David learned this lesson when he asked God when he should attack the Philistines. The Lord's answer was clear: "When you hear a sound like marching feet in the tops of the balsam trees, attack! That will be the signal that the Lord is moving ahead of you to strike down the Philistines" (2 Samuel 5:24).

James confirms the role of prayer in the planning process: "If you need wisdom—if you want to know what God wants you to do—ask him, and he will gladly tell you" (James 1:5). So pray first, then plan, and you will be surprised at the amazing things God will do through you!

My moment of reflection...

Walking on Water

April 30
Matthew 14:22-33

In the mid-West, we know what it's like to "see" the wind! When you begin a new job or a new relationship, you begin with hope. You start the new venture with faith, no wind, and blue skies, then reality sets in! Storms, opposition, financial challenges, and a host of troubles blindside you. The truth is because of the "wind," some folks never get out of the boat. There is no guarantee life in the boat will be safer—everything is risky! If you stay in the boat, you'll eventually die in the boat and end up wondering what life might have been if only you'd stepped over the side!

Besides Jesus, Peter is the only man who ever walked on water! Only Peter knew the joy of being empowered by God to do what humanly couldn't be done. Walking on water changes you forever! Because Peter got out of the boat he had an experience with Christ others didn't have. Failure isn't sinking in the waves—it's never getting out of the boat!

I like the way the story ends: "Then the disciples worshiped him" (Matthew 14:33). Reflecting on what God has done, the only proper response is worship. When you remember what God has brought you through, your heart will become tender and your lips declare, "I will always praise the Lord. With all my heart, I will praise the Lord" (Psalm 34:1, CEV). If you get out of the boat and keep your eyes on Jesus, there is no limit to what you can do for God and what he wants to do for you and through you!

My moment of reflection...

From Sand to Rock

May 1
Matthew 16:13-28

Peter closely resembles many of us: he was impetuous, impatient, quick to speak, and fearful in times of danger! Yet this man with all his failings was destined to be one of the great leaders of the church. Jesus gave Peter great honor when he said, "You are Peter, and upon this rock I will build my church" (Matthew 16:18).

It is unfortunate our first thoughts about Peter focus on his mistakes rather than on his ministry following the resurrection. How would you like to be remembered for your mistakes rather than on your achievements before you reached maturity? Peter made mistakes, but let those of us who are without sin cast the first stone!

Peter was an amazing person, but the importance of his life is not that he denied Christ but that Christ changed him! It is significant that after the resurrection Christ's loving and forgiving message was "go tell the disciples and Peter." Peter became a rock against which the storms of adversity, misunderstanding, and persecution could not break! In the end, Peter was willing to die for Jesus.

It is true Peter denied Jesus after he confessed him as the Christ. The road from sand to rock is not an easy road—it is straight and narrow and filled with struggle. But Simon Peter moved from "sand to rock" as affirmed by Jesus when he called his disciple "Peter!" God is in the business of changing people, no matter their past. Peter went from "sifting sand to solid rock!" Thank God change is still possible today...if we just "let go and let God!"

My moment of reflection...

Conformity

May 2
Romans 12:1-8

One of the loudest voices of our generation is conformity! Jesus knew it would be like this—it always has been. God chose Paul to warn believers about the dangers of conformity: "Don't copy the behavior and customs of this world" (Romans 12:2). While the Gospel is a positive message, there are times when we need admonition that carries a negative tone. So Paul challenges believers to a life of nonconformity, refusing to accept the pattern of this age as the standard for life!

Believers are faced with great pressure to conform to the standards of their age. The moral standards of the world are false and sinful and give no consideration to the spiritual nature of life. After a plea for deliberate and joyful commitment of the body to the will and work of the Lord, Paul says to "stop being fashioned" to evil and sinful ways of life. Like a fatal disease, evil is contagious, aggressive, and will destroy if we give consent.

Spiritual progress must be made despite handicaps. The world will not congratulate us because of our devotion. There must be something in our attitudes, actions, and ambitions that distinguishes a believer. If we would serve God, we must refuse to let the world squeeze us into its mold. This is not a plea for purity or tolerance but an affirmation that there is a negative side to the life of complete dedication to the will of God. So with grace, Paul urges us to stop being fashioned according to "the pattern of this world" and be conformed to the image of his Son (Romans 12:2).

My moment of reflection...

Unexplainable Power

May 3
1 Samuel 17:45-51

How long has it been since something happened in your life that could only be explained as God's doing? Often we go long periods without seeing God "at work" in unexplainable ways. That may mean we are not trusting God or failed to take that step of faith that seemed risky and uncertain so God could reveal his miraculous power.

The pioneers in the early church changed the world because of what was happening around them and happening in them. It was the unexplainable power of God that was changing lives, not just what they heard from teaching. Many unbelievers see Christians as living wholesome, moral, and successful lives, not any different than what they could achieve by themselves. How sad!

Do we notice the small miracles that come our way like praying for a parking spot close by and its right there? Recently we made hotel reservations without being promised we would get our request for a first floor room. When we arrived, our room assignment was perfect: first floor, close to the pool, exercise room and breakfast bar just around the corner. God had supplied again—beyond our dreams!

It's the unexplainable events in our lives that cause others to notice and investigate the great God we serve. Paul understood God's power when he wrote, "Now glory be to God! By his mighty power at work within us, he is able to accomplish infinitely more than we would ever dare to ask or hope. May he be given glory...forever and ever" (Ephesians 3:20-21). Today, look for his unexplainable power!

My moment of reflection...

Taking God Seriously

May 4
Genesis 19:1-29

Sodom and Gomorrah, cities of the Old Testament, were absolutely degenerate, populated with professionals in the world of wickedness. God had this to say about their conduct: their lifestyle is "extremely evil, and everything they do is wicked" (Genesis 18:20). This was God's evaluation of their conduct and God never "winks" at sin!

Lot and his family were drawn to Sodom and became accustomed to their lifestyle, possibly viewing it as acceptable. Then God stepped in and gave Lot an evacuation plan: "Run for your lives…do not stop anywhere…and don't look back! Escape to the mountains, or you will die" (Genesis 19:17). What a gracious act! On the verge of a holocaust, Sodom and Gomorrah were about to be destroyed with fire and brimstone. God destroyed these wicked cities and they sank in the salty waters of the Dead Sea.

God cared enough for Lot and his family to map out a plan that would lead them to safety. Lot and his daughters ran for their lives but Mrs. Lot didn't make it. Apparently she couldn't bring herself to believe God meant what he said and "she became a pillar of salt." Why? Who knows for sure, but I'd suggest she was too attached to that lifestyle and simply refused to cut off her ties. It was too extreme, unrealistic. Her philosophy was "there's no need to take God seriously!" But God really means what he says!

The philosophy of our day is the same: "No need to take God seriously!" But the message of God and the Bible is he means what he says: "Take God Seriously!"

My moment of reflection…

Called to Daily Worship

May 5
Psalm 99:1-9

The Bible challenges us to "go right into the presence of God, with true hearts fully trusting him" (Hebrews 10:22). God wants us to worship him every day! In Genesis, we read that God walked with Adam and Eve in the cool of the day. God cherishes communion with his creation—every day!

God hasn't changed! He made us to glorify him forever and he cherishes our daily fellowship and seeks our company. Unfortunately, we have often confined worship to an hour on Sundays. Every day we are called to contemplate the holiness of God in praise and worship. The psalmist said, "Exalt the Lord our God! Bow low before his feet, for he is holy" (Psalm 99:5). Let your mind soak in his perfection, his completeness, and glory. Rejoice in his creative genius and majestic power. Give thanks for the rising sun and the falling rain. Praise him for life. Thank him for his changeless love.

Begin each day with joy knowing that you are not bound to a visible altar where you practice devotion as a mechanical obligation. God waits for you at every dawn. He listens for your word of praise, your humble adoration, and heartfelt thanks! Whether in a stained glass chapel or in the quiet closet of your mind, it doesn't matter. Any place you worship God in spirit and in truth will become a hallowed place. There you will find strength and peace for the needs of every day. So friends, God longs for your worship every day— don't forget this sacred appointment!

My moment of reflection…

Down, but Not Out

May 6
Psalm 46:1-11

Sports announcers were discussing great running backs in professional football. Among other greats, Walter Payton of the Chicago Bears was mentioned as one of the greatest running backs in the NFL, maybe of "all time." One commentator said, "Do you realize that Walter Payton has gained over nine miles of offense in his running career?" The other sportscaster thought for a moment and responded, "Yeah, and to think that every 4.6 yards of the way someone was knocking him down!"

Ever feel like that? Just as you were making progress, significant headway, someone or something comes along and tries to knock you down. You know the feeling—we all do! Well, friends, take heart. Jesus told us there would be experiences that storm in on us like violent rain, like floods that rise over us. All of us have felt the winds relentlessly beat against us which shake the very foundations of our existence. Yet through it all, Christ speaks of a "rock" that can withstand every storm.

In the midst of the storm, the psalmist speaks of a sure foundation when he wrote, "God is our mighty fortress, always ready to help in times of trouble" (Psalm 46:1, CEV). For those of us who have been running the race, we know with confidence that God is our Rock, our Fortress, and our Deliverer! It's been a long haul. At times we've been knocked "down, but not out!" When the forces of nature have done everything to oppose and destroy us, God stands victorious. He cannot be defeated; and if God is for us, who can be against us?

My moment of reflection…

No Black Outs!

May 7
Luke 24:35-52

You are enjoying a relaxing evening at home! Without any warning, the lights go out! It's an eerie feeling—complete darkness except the flickering light from a candle. Immediately you go to the window and peek outside, and all you see is darkness. You hear sirens of fire trucks or police cars! You think maybe an accident knocked out a utility transformer and probably very soon the power would be restored and lights back on!

You instinctively turn on the light switch, but no power. You grab the television remote and then you remember, no power. Sitting in the flickering light you think how good a cup of coffee would taste. But then it dawns on you, no power to heat water! The furnace fan is off and the house is getting colder! No power!

Thankfully, when you awake the next morning, the power is on! The electric power we have learned to trust and expect will fail from time to time; but God's power never fails. We remember the Lord taught us that "glory and power belong to him alone" (Revelation 19:1). As I remember his teachings, I'm so grateful for his power to forgive, to save, to remold our lives. Aren't you? I'm so dependent on him and recognize his power is so readily available to strengthen me each day in my journey with power—endless power with no "blackouts!"

As we journey through the awesome possibilities of each day, let's make sure that we are living our lives in his power and not our own. Be thankful for his gift of power that never fails!

My moment of reflection…

Stress

May 8
Matthew 11:25-30

Like potatoes in a pressure cooker, we are under a "ton" of stress and pressure. Every day we are bombarded by many pressures. They may be as simple as making lunches for our kids before 7:00 a.m. or as severe as a collision with another car...or another person. Death in a family, a divorce, losing a job or celebration of a holiday—all contribute to stress of daily living.

How do you cope with stress? Many folks try to cope on their own, with no hope on the horizon! If you are struggling with major issues, you are in the danger zone, a sitting duck for the adversary. Satan is taking aim at you with both barrels, hoping to open fire while you are vulnerable.

Hear what Jesus says: "Come to me, all of you who are weary and carry heavy burdens, and I will give you rest...and you will find rest for your souls" (Matthew 11:28, 29). Wow! Nothing complicated, no fanfare or special password—just come! Allow Jesus to take your stress as you take his rest. It's just that simple! You ask, does he really know what trauma is all about? He sure does! Remember, he's the one whose sweat became like drops of blood in the agony of Gethsemane just before his crucifixion. If anyone understands stress, he does! Just remember that he's a master at turning devastation into restoration! Trust him today for all your needs—because he cares for you!

My moment of reflection...

Harvest Time

May 9
2 Corinthians 9:1-15

Springtime is the season for life and growth! The anticipation of spring brings hope and excitement that harvest cannot be far behind. Soon we will be harvesting beautiful flowers and the fruit from our gardens. Raised on the Kansas plains, I always looked forward to harvest time—a most wonderful time of the year!

My father taught me this biblical principle: "Remember this—a farmer who plants only a few seeds will get a small crop. But the one who plants generously will get a generous crop" (2 Corinthians 9:6). We reap the consequences of our investment—sow little, reap little; sow generously, reap generously. All creation shares in the blessings of God's kindness and grace. We enjoy the earth that God created—the sunshine, rain, growth and more, much more. We are undeserving and unworthy, but God in his goodness gives us more than we sow—every time!

We never reap in the same season as we sow. We plant wheat in the fall, but harvest the next summer! Amazing! In our impatient culture, it's hard to wait for a different season. Since God is in control, he will bring the harvest in "his own time!" While we cannot do anything to change last year's harvest, we have time to influence the next harvest. Start today to sow seeds of generosity and encouragement and you will insure a bountiful harvest. The choice is yours: plant little, reap little; plant generously, reap generously!

My moment of reflection…

Honor... Your Mother

May 10
Proverbs 31:10-31

Mother's Day is one of the busiest days of the year for restaurants, telephone companies, and florists! While society encourages us to remember our mothers, the Bible honors many famous mothers who have left us with lasting legacies—women like Eve, Sarah, Hannah, and Mary!

Mothers are crucial for home and family success! God chose Mary to be the mother of his Son. Mary was a young girl when Gabriel announced that she would become pregnant by the Holy Spirit and become the mother of Jesus. Available and obedient, she gave birth to the Savior, dedicated him at the temple, and supported him throughout his ministry, even at the cross.

We honor Godly mothers because of the divine sanctity of the home. Home is the earth's primary institution established by God. Mothers by their sincere faith and sensitive spirit, model for us a life that is pleasing to God. In formative years, our mothers taught us about love, care, and faith. We remember their prayers, their songs, and their love. Abraham Lincoln said, "I remember my mother's prayers and they have followed me; they have clung to me all my life. All that I am and hope to be I owe to my angel mother." Mothers are partners with God in producing those whom he can use to be "salt of the earth." Flowers bring temporary gratitude to our mothers, but that which brings abiding joy to a godly mother is the honor she is due!

My moment of reflection...

Attitude Check

May 11
Philippians 2:1-11

You've heard about the little boy who was being disciplined and was told to sit down in the chair. Reluctantly, he sat down but said, "Mommy, I'm sitting down on the outside, but I'm standing up on the inside!" This little boy expressed what he felt, but often, without saying anything, what we are feeling on the inside shows up on the outside! It's true that our attitude is the primary force that will determine whether we succeed or fail—even spirituality!

Out attitude determines our approach to life and the success in our endeavors. Scripture reminds us that "you will always reap what you sow" (Galatians 6:7). All of life is impacted by how we react toward our work and how successful we are in relationships. Our attitude can make us or break us. Beginning a task with a positive attitude will affect its outcome. Teachers often not only look at a child's IQ, but their AQ, or attitude quotient, as well. Studies have shown that success or failure in any undertaking is determined more by mental attitude than by mere mental capacities.

When we face difficulties, we need to look at both the obstacles and the opportunities. Every opportunity has a difficulty and every difficulty has an opportunity. Life can be likened to a grindstone: whether it grinds you down or polishes you depend upon what you are made of! So let's do an attitude check by making sure we are living positively and expressing the "mind of Christ!"

My moment of reflection...

…on the Positive Side

May 12
John 8:1-12

Time just seems to go "faster and faster!" Recently, I read a very interesting and challenging statement regarding how we use our time: Positive anything is better than negative nothing! I like that quote—it would be a great motto for living. We are surrounded by a world of negatives and "negators" who have a major impact on so many. The affirmative can be equally contagious. Positive motivates and inspires us while the negative neutralizes and discourages. Considering the contrast, it is hard to realize why anyone would ever choose anything less than the positive—but they do!

Billy Sunday was a great evangelist, who by his life and words led many folks to Christ. On one occasion, a lady confronted and criticized the evangelist for his bold approach in sharing Christ. When Mr. Sunday asked her how she shared her faith, she replied that she didn't participate in such forwardness. Billy's reply was so revealing: "Well, I like the way I do it better than the way you don't do it!" You see, her nothing produced nothing! Wow!

I choose to surround myself with positive people. They seem to propel me to greater performance. Folks who do nothing are generally content to sit on the sidelines and criticize. My advice to anyone whose life is built around the negative and criticism, "go bury your talent quickly!" Since every day is filled with opportunities, let's focus on the positive because "positive anything beats negative nothing" hands down!

My moment of reflection…

Higher Power

May 13
Proverbs 3:1-12

Two television personalities were debating their understanding of God, whom they called their "higher power," and how this "power" worked in their lives. One of the celebrities said she could best explain the working of her "higher power" by telling a story she heard in her last therapy session. Here's the story!

A man was talking to a priest and said, "Hey, Father, you got it all wrong about this God stuff. He doesn't exist! I ought to know!"

"Why's that, my son?"

"Well, when I was ice fishing in the Arctic, far from the nearest village, a blizzard blew in with strong winds and blinding snow. I was a goner. So I got down on my knees and prayed real hard, begging God for help!"

"And did he help?"

"No way! God didn't lift a finger. Some Eskimo appeared out of nowhere and showed me the way home!"

We smile at this funny but sad story! God is not dead—he is real and he is powerful, able to do more than we could imagine and is always present in our times of need. While you may not recognize him at first, God has a way of "showing up" and leading us through the most difficult situation. Isn't that what he promised? He said: "Trust in the Lord with all your heart; do not depend on your own understanding. Seek his will in all you do, and he will direct your paths" (Proverbs 3:5-6).

My moment of reflection...

Character

May 14
Matthew 5:13-16

Character is critical for success! Character is not who you are when others can see you—it is who you are when you are all alone, when it's just you and God! In our fast-paced culture, we are so busy and overscheduled that sometimes it is easy to overlook the small things in life, but someone is watching!

A pastor went to a grocery store to pick up some needed items. He paid for the items, grabbed the receipt and change, and went to his car. As he was getting into his car, he noticed that the checkout person had given him too much change! What should he do? Running behind for an appointment, he decided to go back and "make it right." He said to the checkout girl, "It appears you gave me too much change by accident."

The girl looked at him and said, "No, sir. I did it on purpose. Your sermon last Sunday was on honesty and how important it is to be honest as a Christian. I gave you too much change so I could see if you really meant it!"

The unsaved are watching us all the time. They listen to the words that come out of our mouth, they look at our actions to see if they match our words. The world is hungry for something real, and you may be the only one who lets them see the purity of Jesus! If I'm not mistaken, they still call this quality *character*!

My moment of reflection…

Starting Over

May 15
Joel 2:18-32

Starting over, to get somewhere else, you got to know where you are! Very seldom does anybody "just happen" to wind up on the right road. The process of "starting over" involves redirecting our lives and that is often painful, slow, and can be very confusing.

Take Jonah for example! This guy was prejudiced, stubborn, and openly rebellious. While other prophets ran *to* the Lord, he ran *from* the Lord. Somehow Jonah got his directions crossed up and he wound up on a ship bound for Tarshish, but God told him to go to Ninevah. Through a divine chain of events, Jonah found himself in the digestive tract of a gigantic fish. What a place to "start over!" In the belly of a fish Jonah prayed—he yelled for mercy and promised to get back "on target!"

Jonah was starting over, changing directions—now on his way to Ninevah! Perhaps you can identify with the prophet. You've dodged and ducked the will of God, going your own way! You are tired and ready to give up—plus the enemy says you're through, useless, finished! But that's not what God says. The Lord says, "I will give you back what you lost to the stripping locusts" (Joel 2:25). God is a specialist in making things new, turning something beautiful and good out of something broken. Start where you are! Freely admit your need, don't hide a thing, and God will "make all things new." Praise God for a "second chance!"

My moment of reflection...

Plugged In

May 16
1 Samuel 3:1-21

A study was conducted to determine the most challenging needs of the church. Leaders from Europe and America provided input regarding their most important concerns. Of all the issues submitted, prayer and discipleship were most critical.

Ernest Hemingway once lamented, "I live in a vacuum that is as lonely as a radio tube when the batteries are dead and there is no current to plug into." How sad! Fortunately for the Christian that is not true. As believers, we have a mission and a message. God has placed us on earth for a brief time to do an urgent work. Our lives have a purpose and all our days are scheduled in his perfect plan. We travel on an "appointed and anointed" way! What does God want you to do? Like Samuel, say, "Your servant is listening" (1 Samuel 3:10). Find something to do and begin doing it now! Find a need and fill it—"Get plugged in!"

Prayer is meant to be preventative more than remedial! Like many, we pray when there is a need or when we're in trouble. Jesus looked at prayer differently. He said at all times we "ought to pray… and not lose heart." In other words, prayer isn't the last thought—it is the first thought. Instead of praying when we are tempted, Jesus said we should pray that we "enter not into temptation." Get "plugged in" so that you are ready when the pressures come—because they will!

My moment of reflection…

In All Things Charity

May 17
Mark 9:38-50

It's funny but tragic! Neighbors from the same church family were arguing about the proper way to recite the Lord's Prayer. One neighbor wanted "forgive us our trespasses" while the other demanded "forgive us our debts." Unable to come to some agreement or compromise, fellowship between the two neighbors was permanently broken! Tragic!

Most of us remember similar disagreements. Such silly skirmishes would be hilarious if they weren't so prevalent and damaging. It is one thing to stand firm on major issues clearly set forth in Scripture. But it's quite another thing to pick fights over "jots and tittle."

On one occasion, the disciples "nailed" a guy for casting out demons in the name of Jesus because "he isn't one of our group" (Mark 9:38). Jesus chastised them for such an attitude. He really wanted them to get rid of the idea that they had a monopoly on miracles. He wouldn't tolerate their bigoted spirit. Simply put, our Lord never "nit-picked!"

So how do we handle such "petty" differences when they occur? A wise principle to follow is this: As long as our knowledge is imperfect and our preferences vary and our opinions differ, let's leave a lot of room in the areas that really don't matter. Diversity and variety provides us with a beautiful blend of balance, but a severe spirit is a killer, strangling its victims in a noose of criticism. Here's the key: "In all things charity"—it always works!

My moment of reflection...

Help!

May 18
Exodus 18:13-27

Recently I read a prayer that makes lots of sense. It's time to pray when "the world has gotten you down, you feel rotten, you're to doggone tired to pray and you're in a big hurry; besides you're mad at everybody...cry help!" This prayer admonishes us to "slow down...cool it...and admit our need!" It's a real struggle for us to cry out for assistance. Asking for help is smart. At the heart of our drive is pride, plain unwillingness to admit our need. The result of our failure to seek help is impatience, anger, and long hours with little laughter.

We are not the messiah! There is no way you can keep going at "full speed" and stay effective. Because you are human and nothing more, stop trying to cover all the bases and learn to relax! Jethro watched Moses his father-in-law tackle one problem after another, eating on the run and neck-deep in activities from morning till night. Jethro wasn't impressed with his boundless drive and neither was God!

Jethro reproved Moses with some strong words: "Why are you trying to do all this alone?" (Exodus 18:14). In simple words, Jethro told Moses to "call for help!" The benefits of sharing the load are fantastic. It will be easier for you...and you will be able to endure. But most of us are too proud. A seventy-hour work week is not a mark of efficiency or spirituality! Our efficiency is enhanced not by what we accomplish but more often by what we relinquish. Help!

My moment of reflection...

Rejoice in the Lord

May 19
Psalm 5

George Green was sleeping soundly as his boat glided up the river in 1906 as the first missionary assigned to Nigeria. At the sound of war drums and the advice of the captain, Dr. Green was warned of grave danger should he embark. The doctor thought for a moment and said, "I have hundreds of friends in America praying for me. God has called me to this place; I have planned and prayed for many years. I will proceed!" God preserved the life of Dr. Green! Over the years, he founded a hospital in Nigeria, trained medical personnel, and led thousands to Christ.

What can I learn from this story? Just this: Just as God had a Noah to build an ark, a Moses to lead a group of slaves from Egypt, a Jonah for Nineveh, a Paul to build a church, God has you to…! What a privilege to think that God has chosen you for this time and place—to serve and help the body of Christ just like Dr. Green.

And so we pray, "Lord, grant us the power to use our minds to think and extend our hands as we serve the body and share your heart with our world!" We see many needs but God has many people and I cannot help believe that you are one of many that God would like to use in his Kingdom. So, listen for his call today, and respond with your heart! "Rejoice in the goodness of the Lord!"

My moment of reflection…

Change

May 20
Psalm 55

During the winter, we dream about going to some sunny "faraway place" like the Caribbean instead of being fenced in by snow. If only the doctor would say, "You need a change," and then provide the "change" for the change! Because of boredom and listlessness, a change of scenery and weather can be very beneficial.

David said this about change: "My enemies refuse to change their ways; they do not fear God" (Psalm 55:19). When there are no changes in our lives, chances are we are coasting along, indifferent to spiritual reality. We have no time for God, divine wisdom, or his awareness. The cutting edge of a mature person is adventure and we can never be content in a rut. As believers, we need to be very careful lest we become comfortable and contented!

There's a Canadian road sign which reads, "Choose your rut... you'll be in it for the next twenty miles!" I remind you that a "rut" is a grave with both ends knocked out! Like it or not, God has placed us in a world where stagnation is a deadly sin—and who wants to rot?

To see life as an adventure and not just coasting along, we must keep an open mind and not look over our shoulders at our accomplishments. Keep a mental wastebasket nearby to throw away the bad and cling to the good. And most important to change, stay close to God, who is forever making all things new and who enables growth!

My moment of reflection...

Keep On Keeping On

May 21
2 Corinthians 4:16-18

Some mornings we wake up and feel like we've been hit by a truck. And getting out of bed is a major accomplishment! It is on those days that we really have "to press on" to get started for the day. Despite times of struggle and disappointment, Paul told us to "press on." He was working toward the goal of being all that God had intended him to be—and to leave the past behind!

Keeping our goal in sight might mean that we have to put an actual picture in front of us to remind us of the end product. Sometimes we put up a chart so that we can visually be reminded of the goal. Then we chart our step-by-step progress so we can see just how far we've come. That encourages us to "keep on keeping on!"

Sometimes we get weary, take our eyes off the goal, and just want to "give up!" But life is a journey filled with many goal-setting adventures. A very wise writer said to "keep our eyes on Jesus, on whom our faith depends from start to finish" (Hebrews 12:2). Keeping focused on Christ and leaning on his strength within us helps make our goals and ambitions come true. It is his power within us that will empower us to be our best and accomplish great things for the kingdom. So let's set big goals—because we have a "big" God! Then "keep on keeping on!"

My moment of reflection...

Encourager or Discourager

May 22
1 Thessalonians 3:1-8

Discouragement is the occupational hazard of living today! It is so easy to become down in the dumps, stuck in the blues, or carrying the weight of the world. The wind goes out of our sails, it rains on our parade, and our bubble bursts. There are many ways to categorize people—we do it all the time without even realizing what we are doing. But looking at Christians, there seems to be two distinct camps: the encouragers and the chronic discouragers!

In the discouraging camp, you hear things like "Is that the best you can do?" "Meatloaf? Again?" "When you washed the windows, you missed a spot!" If you want to leave people discouraged and depressed, major on minors, overlook the 90 percent they did right and concentrate on the 10 percent they did wrong! It seems like those who major on discouragement seem to enjoy and flock to each other. The psalmist said that his enemies "encourage each other to do evil" (Psalm 64:5). These "birds of a feather" seem to "stick" together!

As believers, encouragement is part of our job description. Isaiah, the Old Testament prophet, is remembered for the consolation, comfort, and hope that he gave to his nation. If your goal is to encourage others like Isaiah, you'll find you are never out of work. Your "encouraging pilgrimage" can begin today. So as my mother used to say, "If you can't say something good about someone, don't say anything at all!"

My moment of reflection...

Unopened Gifts

May 23
1 Peter 4:7-11

Remember the excitement you felt as a child when you anticipated opening gifts at Christmas or at your birthday party? I hope you are still thrilled whenever you open a special gift. Can you imagine receiving a gift and not opening it? Failure to open a special present from a friend could be called "the tragedy of the unopened gift!" Our "unopened gifts" conceal our unrealized potential—and every person alive has unrealized potential!

Every member of the Body of Christ has been gifted by the Spirit. Peter instructs us that "God has given gifts to each of you… manage them well so that God's generosity can flow through you" (1 Peter 4:10). That's a clear call to all believers. Got a gift? Then use it! God expects us to contribute to the well-being of everyone, especially fellow believers. He wants us to look for opportunities to bless the world and serve one another! Paul said that every time "we have the opportunity, we should do good to everyone, especially to our Christian brothers and sisters" (Galatians 6:10).

What do you do well? What are you complimented on? Maybe the only thing you need to do is start using your gifting! One thing is true: you will never be happier than when you start serving and using your God-given abilities! Nurture your own gifts and when you meet people who don't think they have any gifts, encourage them to look deeper and help them "open their unopened gifts!"

My moment of reflection…

The Winning Attitude

May 24
Matthew 6:25-34

John is the kind of guy you'd love to hate! He's always in a good mood and has something positive to say. He is a natural motivator. One day an employee asked him, "I don't get it! How can you be such a positive person all the time?"

He replied, "Each morning, I have two choices as to how I will live today. You can choose to be in a good mood…or you can choose to be in a lousy mood. I choose to be in a good mood!" Life is all about choices!

Several years later, John fell sixty feet from a communications tower. After much surgery and months of rehabilitation, John survived. As he lay on the ground, realizing his critical injuries, he remembered he had two choices: "I could choose to live…or I could choose to die! I choose to live!" In the operating room, he yelled at the doctors, "I am choosing to live. Operate on me as if I am alive, not dead!"

He lived, thanks to the skill of his doctors, but also because of his amazing attitude. From him, I've learned that every day we have a choice—and attitude is everything! It was our Master who said, "Don't worry about tomorrow, for tomorrow will bring its own worries. Today's trouble is enough for today" (Matthew 6:34). Remember: "Today is the tomorrow you worried about yesterday!" At every turn in your journey, you have two choices! Choose carefully today!

My moment of reflection…

Pattern for Growth

May 25
2 Timothy 2:1-13

A widely acclaimed surgeon told his television audience the story and reason for his success. After many years of schooling, constant reading, and talking to leading surgeons, "becoming the best surgeon possible" was his consuming goal. Growth is demanding! Whether we want to grow professionally or spiritually, there is a price to be paid. Before Paul was executed for his faith, he wrote a letter to young Timothy. He issued a strong challenge to Timothy to discipline himself in every way possible to become effective in service and ministry. He said, "Be strong...endure suffering... follow the rules...work hard" (2 Timothy 2).

Growth demands overcoming fear! Apparently Timothy was timid because Paul explained that God did not intend this trait to keep him from success. Facing dangers become easier when we know we have inner resources like love, power, and self-control to keep us from fleeing in times of danger. Discipline is also critical for maximum growth! A soldier never looks for suffering. He does not want it, but he accepts it when it comes without complaint. Soldiers give themselves in single-minded dedication. Distractions must be avoided at any cost!

Spring is alive with growth—you see it everywhere you look! God intends every believer to grow, to become spiritually mature so that the problems of daily living can be faced with purpose. We must accept the challenge of personal growth but also encourage others in their journey to spiritual maturity. May spiritual growth be your "consuming" goal!

My moment of reflection...

Precious Memories

May 26
Joshua 4:1-24

Memorial Day is typically marked by a parade and marching bands. While some consider the celebration of this day as sentimental or nostalgic, Memorial Day has always been precious to me. I am always moved as the flag is raised and then lowered to half-mast and the presentation of wreaths to the war dead. Singing "God Bless America" and listening to the bugler's taps echo through the cemetery brings a lump in my throat. I pray that God will keep America free and that Americanism will flourish in the centuries to come.

Reflecting on Memorial Day, I remember the words of General Joshua in the days of a great event in Israel's history. He said that when your children ask, "What do these stones mean to you? Then you can tell them, 'They remind us that the Jordan River stopped flowing when the Ark of the Lord's covenant went across.' These stones will stand as a permanent memorial among the people of Israel" (Joshua 4:6-7).

Joshua was instructed to erect memorial stones as a reminder to Israel and succeeding generations of the blessings and power of God in delivering them from bondage and wanderings. Israel was soon to forget—and we too forget his power and deliverance. Memories are crowded out with the pressing duties and plans of today and tomorrow. May precious memories flood your soul today, causing you to be thankful for our great heritage and gratitude to men and women who died to make us free!

My moment of reflection...

Side Trips

May 27
Matthew 6:19-34

Remember the story about the farmer who hitched his horse to a wagon for a trip to town to get supplies? His old hound dog followed, running here and there—chasing rabbits and anything else he could sniff out.

When the farmer arrived in town a friend remarked about the apparent difference in the condition of the horse and his old dog. Although it was the horse that pulled the loaded wagon, he seemed relatively unaffected by the trip. However, the hound dog was panting feverishly, thoroughly exhausted, and resting under a shade tree. The farmer's explanation was simple: "It wasn't the trip that got my dog all tired out. It was all them side trips!"

The same thing can happen to us! It's so easy to get distracted and sidetracked on our "trip to town." There is certainly no shortage of rabbits to chase and there are plenty of brush fires begging for attention. Each of us must decide what is most important and then pare away all the "stuff" that would steal our time and sap our strength.

Jesus said, "Make the Kingdom of God your primary concern" (Matthew 6:33). Only then can we be assured that all the necessary other things will be taken care of for us. We must never forget that "vision always precedes effective service." Let's make sure that we put "first things first" in all we do so that none of our effort will be wasted or misguided!

My moment of reflection...

Satisfaction in Serving

May 28
John 13:1-17

As a child I'm sure you had some big ideas about what you wanted to be someday: a policeman, a fireman, a professional athlete! If the boy Jesus had been asked what he wanted to be when he grew up, he probably would have startled his interrogators by saying, "A Servant!" The other kids probably laughed. "Who would ever want to grow up to be someone's servant?" But in God's sovereign plan, that is exactly what Jesus grew up to be.

The disciples were arguing about who would be the greatest in the kingdom. There was a lot of pride in being one of the chosen twelve, but they needed a leader! Which one of them would become the leader? Jesus did an amazing thing! He removed his tunic, leaving only the inner garment, the obvious mark of a slave. Then Jesus—God's Son, Creator, Redeemer, King—began washing the disciples' feet! By his actions, Jesus was saying to his disciples, "If you want to follow me, please me, work for me…then learn what it means to be a slave." What a powerful picture!

That's not an easy lesson to learn! It's much easier to tell a person where the nearest bathhouse is than to wash his feet. But anyone who would follow Jesus must learn this lesson. Servanthood and serving is meaningful and gives great satisfaction because we serve a Living Savior! As Jesus said, "You know these things—now do them! That is the path of blessing" (John 13:17).

My moment of reflection…

Quietness

May 29
Psalm 46

The sign "Quiet Please" is a sign that you often see posted on the walls of hospital corridors. This sign indicates the need for soft voices and noiseless motion in the presence of sick people. Quiet and rest from noisy activity have great healing power! Quietness includes stillness, peace, confidence, and thoughtfulness.

Moses, Israel's great leader, found greatness in the quiet solitude of the plains of Midian. Joseph, the prime minister of Egypt, emerged from the dark quiet of a prison to a position of power and leadership. The apostle Paul spent three years in quiet obscurity in Asia following his conversion. Our Lord grew up in the quiet village of Nazareth. He often invited his disciples to come away into a desert to rest and renew their physical and spiritual strength. St. Augustine said in a prayer, "Thou hast made us for Thyself, O God, and our souls are restless until they rest in Thee."

The psalmist said, "Be silent, and know that I am God" (Psalm 46:10). Daily we are surrounded with noise and confusion and other interruptions! But God never asks us to do more than we can. He programmed us with promises for survival! He said, "As your day, so shall be your strength." If you need inward quietness today, make a little chapel in your imagination and know that God is there to give peace. Then say to yourself, "The Lord gives perfect peace to those whose faith is firm" (Isaiah 26:3, CEV).

My moment of reflection…

Perfectionism

May 30
Philippians 3:12-21

Many of us start the day thinking we will be perfect, or at least try! But it isn't long until we realize our humanness —we are not perfect! A common ailment of our day is "perfectionitis." There is a big difference between wanting to improve myself and wanting to be absolutely perfect. While wanting to improve is natural and human, "perfectionitis" is an example of playing god—but only God is perfect!

Authors work at polishing their writings so the real message will shine through their work. Some people, however, miss the delights of life because of their exaggerated sense of perfection. Driven and possessed by their obsession, they become miserable rather than enjoying life. Perfectionists are so self-critical that they are afraid to venture forth facing new horizons; they are afraid of failure!

One of life's paradoxes is that in order to win, one must learn to lose! We must learn the difference between a single inning and a whole game. Moses never entered the Promised Land. He died at the mountaintop, looking at the beauty and glory of Canaan. We don't think of Moses as a failure, but rather as an overwhelming success.

We cannot achieve everything that we set out to do, but we can get closer to it. With God on our side, he can help us to fail gracefully and then aspire to greater improvement. No wonder he said, "Be perfect even as your Father in heaven is perfect" (Matthew 5:48).

My moment of reflection...

I'll Do It My Way

May 31
Psalm 23

Golf reveals a lot about a person. In the 1997 British Open, golfer Jean VandeVelde had a seven-stroke lead with one hole to go. All he needed was a six on a par-four hole—he got a seven and eventually lost the match in a playoff. His caddy said, "I think he and I, we wanted too much show."

We all desire to live life our way. Instead of giving our struggles to God, we try to fix it ourselves. Our problem is we want "too much show." We are stubborn, independent, and have too much self-reliance. We don't need advice and think we can handle issues without outside help. Forget God's way—we want to do things our way!

According to the Bible, that is precisely our problem. "All of us have strayed away like sheep. We have left God's paths to follow our own" (Isaiah 53:6). The Bible compares us in many places to sheep. Sheep are dumb, cannot care for themselves, and when left alone they die. They are defenseless—they have no fangs or claws, can't bite you, or outrun you. And they are dirty, unable to clean themselves.

Everyone notices the warrior or the singer, but who notices sheep? Only one person notices the sheep—the Good Shepherd who cares and protects the sheep! Because we are always in need, we need to "do it God's way!" The Good Shepherd says, "Trust me…Do it my way!"

My moment of reflection…

Our Cornerstone

June 1
Ephesians 2:19-22

Limestone fence posts, called stone posts, were the homesteader's answer to the shortage of wooden fence posts on the treeless prairies of Kansas. Stone posts are still used on Kansas farms today. They were first used to mark property lines and keep animals in designated areas. Because of their strength and durability, they were used as foundation and cornerstones for various structures.

Isaiah prophesied that he would place a foundation stone in Jerusalem. "Look! I am placing a foundation stone in Jerusalem. It is firm, a tested and precious cornerstone that is safe to build on" (Isaiah 28:16). Many years later, Jesus identified himself as this stone that had been rejected by the builders (Matthew 21:42). The cornerstone of any building represents the starting place of construction. It becomes the foundation upon which all the rest of the building is built. In similar fashion, the salvation that Jesus provided for us is the foundation of our faith—durable throughout the ages!

With Jesus as our rock—our cornerstone—we can safely and confidently build our lives on this solid rock. The scriptures tell us that God has a designed plan for our lives and we can trust him to work out that plan as we choose to build our lives on him. Jesus is our Cornerstone and God is the architect. We just need to follow his blueprint, building our lives with his divine guidance and living for his glory. Thank God for our precious and eternal Cornerstone!

My moment of reflection...

A Night of Tears

June 2
Numbers 14:1-10

The ability to laugh and cry is a distinct characteristic of man, not shared by any other creature. Israel wept all night because they opposed the decision of Moses and Aaron to dwell in a new land promised by God. They wished to die or at least return to Egypt despite the appeal of Joshua and Caleb. "All the people began weeping aloud, and they cried all night" (Numbers 14:1) is one of the most tragic nights in Israel's history.

Despair causes people to weep! Problems paint a gloomy picture of our future. Seeing ourselves as "grasshoppers" in the face of giants, we approach our challenge based on misinformation. Lack of courage blinds us to the answer of our problem and we murmur against God. Often those who suffer from despair turn on those they love like a wounded animal. How sad!

Difficulty causes people to weep! Though it would be challenging, Joshua and Caleb believed Israel could conquer the Promised Land—they were so near! But because of their spiritual rebellion and failure to accept the promise of God, they rejected the challenge. We find Moses and Aaron weeping over Israel's choice!

We all have moments when we feel like "grasshoppers" in a giant's world! We weep in our struggles and setbacks to the immediate conquering of our "promised land." We sense God's miraculous deliverance and our hearts are filled with tears of joy. In our sorrow and despair, God is rich in mercy and his kindness never fails. Whatever difficulty you're facing, trust God for your "Promised Land" and wipe away those tears!

My moment of reflection…

A Night of Fear

June 3
Matthew 14:22-33

Students of behavior suggest fear is a universal emotion. Peter nearly drowned one night because his focus was misplaced. Instead of relying on the power and promises of God, he allowed winds of adversity to take control of the moment. In his panic-stricken moment, controlled by his feelings, the vision of angry waves blocked his vision of Jesus…and "down" he went!

Fear arises in the midst of life's storms! For the disciples, as long as Christ was "in sight," there was no fear. But when they were "on their own" in the storm, they were overwhelmed with fear. Storms are often tools God uses to strengthen us and prepare us for future ministries.

Fear also arises because of our failure to perceive the presence of Christ. It was "about three o'clock in the morning when Jesus came to them, walking on the water" (Matthew 14:25). His unexpected presence does not always conform to expectation. When the disciples saw Jesus walking on the water, they were paralyzed with fear.

Since we are all plagued with this contagious emotion, how can we dispel fear? The words of Jesus are classic: "It's all right…I am here! Don't be afraid" (Matthew 14:27). In their paralyzing fear, they hear Jesus say, "Take courage—be of good cheer!" The wind stopped, the storm was over, and the disciples worshipped him! Like Peter, if you take your eyes off of the Savior, you will become fearful. Trust the Lord and he will meet your needs and you will never hear the words of rebuke, "You don't have much faith…why did you doubt me?"

My moment of reflection…

A Night of Denial

June 4
Matthew 26:30-35, 69-75

The disciples are in a boat on a stormy lake, filled with fear. But Jesus saves the day and Peter is rescued from drowning. Days later, after the disciples experienced the goodness and compassion of God, Simon Peter denies the one who reached out to pull him to safety. Unbelievable! Incredible!

Jesus was fair with Peter—he warned him a moment of denial would soon appear. But Peter would not believe he could ever be guilty of such an act. Peter's response to our Lord's warning was "No…I will never deny you" (Matthew 26:35).

Weeks earlier, Peter made a marvelous confession about Jesus: "You are the Messiah, the son of the Living God" (Matthew 16:16). But later when invited to spend time in prayer with the Lord before his arrest, Peter fell asleep. Jesus said his spirit was willing but his flesh was weak! Because of his indifference and lack of alertness to Satan's subtle approach, Peter's self-confidence led to his denial. Jesus warned Peter before the rooster crows he would deny the Lord three times, and he did! But the story doesn't end there! Thank God for Peter's repentance. Sincere repentance is always met by loving forgiveness on the part of the Savior.

On the other side of his denial, Peter emerges as a man of courage, faith, and loyalty. There may be times we too are guilty of denial. As we daily depend on the Lord for strength and courage in our journey, the greater the probability we will achieve victory over denial. Our call is clear—"watch and pray!"

My moment of reflection…

A Night of Accounting

June 5
Luke 12:13-21

Accountability is part of life! Jesus tells the story of a farmer who was successful and apparently wealthy. His barns were full, overflowing with grain, so he planned to build additional storage. Proud of his accomplishments, he announces to himself, "You have enough stored away for years to come. Now take it easy! Eat, drink and be merry" (Luke 12:19). But Jesus said to him, "You fool! You will die this very night. Then who will get it all" (Luke 12:20).

In this story, Jesus asserts "all creation" is accountable for all of life's blessings, however great or small. Life's blessings come from God and we are indebted to God. The farmer in this parable is not a bad man. He prospers but without a thought of obligation to God. Sometimes we see life's blessings as a result of our abilities or evidence of our personal merit. As a result, this man felt he owed God nothing and planned to use his wealth for himself and his pleasure.

Life's decisions may make a fool of us! The world acclaimed this successful farmer as wise and thrifty but God called him a "fool." In our blind obsession for material gain, we forget there will be an accounting. The farmer made adequate preparation for this life but none for the life to come. He prepared for old age, famine, drought, everything but death which would strip him of all he earned that very night. One day we will give an account to God. As you prepare for this eternal accounting, lay up treasures in heaven and be rich toward God!

My moment of reflection…

A Night of Unprofitable Toil

June 6
John 21:1-14

King Jehoshaphat ruled in Judah for twenty-five years. In his search for wealth, he built a fleet of ships to explore the world for gold. The night before the ships sailed, a storm arose and the ships were destroyed (1 Kings 22). Sometimes life is like that—we give great effort to an endeavor but it ends in futility.

Simon Peter and several disciples decided to go fishing. They fished all night "but they caught nothing" (John 21:3). Exhausted after a night of toil, their nets were empty! From the shore, Jesus calls out to them, "Friends, have you caught any fish?" Responding no, they were soon to discover Christ was their solution to their night of unprofitable toil. Jesus gives them a command: "Throw out your net on the right-hand side of the boat, and you will get plenty of fish" (John 21:6). They did and their nets were overflowing with 153 large fish! And to top it off, Jesus invited the weary fishermen to a delicious breakfast of grilled fish and bread.

The lesson is clear: We need divine guidance in our labor. We may know the sea well and have the finest nets and years of experience, but we still need divine guidance. When Christ's commands are obeyed, life's accomplishments begin to be realized. There is always time to learn "without Christ we can do nothing." When Jesus is invited to join in our endeavors, we discover he does over and above what we could think or ask! Thank God he still stands on the shore and calls out, "Come and dine!"

My moment of reflection...

A Night of Mystery

June 7
John 3:1-16

No matter how brilliant or educated, there are some things beyond our understanding. We call them mysteries! The Bible is filled with mysteries, events that baffle the most sophisticated mind— the mystery of providence or the prosperity of the wicked or the mystery of salvation!

Nicodemus was a religious and moral man who obeyed all the laws of the Jewish nation. While his religious life was beyond reproach, Nicodemus was a sinner accountable to God. He recognized his need for inner peace and knew forgiveness could not be met by his own efforts. Culture or regulations could not meet his deepest need. But he was aware of "a teacher sent from God" who could deal with the emptiness of his heart. Talking to Jesus about his need, Jesus told him "unless you are born again, you can never see the Kingdom of God" (John 3:3).

Jesus told Nicodemus the mystery of the "new birth" is like the wind—you can feel the wind and see its effects but cannot see the wind itself. Likewise, you can feel God's presence and see the effects of the "new birth," but you cannot see the agent of salvation. The "new birth" is mysterious and incomprehensible to human reason but it's real!

The "mystery" of life is that God loves sinful men who deserve judgment rather than acceptance. God's love is not sentimental, but sacrificial and costly. The mystery of God's love moves Jesus to unbelievable acts and imparts eternal life. Though we may never comprehend the mystery, thank God that when we accept his forgiveness we have eternal life!

My moment of reflection...

A Night of Eternal Darkness

June 8
John 13:18-39

Darkness brings a level of uncertainty and anxiety! Buried in the heart of every man is something of the nature of Judas. This sad story reminds us that for every person who rejects Christ, the act of death is followed by the night of eternal darkness!

Judas Iscariot, one of the disciples, betrayed the Lord Jesus. Midnight seldom comes unannounced! The setting of the sun, the appearance of stars, and darkening of the sky warn that the midnight hour is approaching. Jesus with love and sincere concern warned Judas of the danger ahead: "The truth is, one of you will betray me" (John 13:21). Even the long list of "wrongs" in Judas's life warned him of the coming "midnight hour!" But sadly, he failed to listen!

The one living in darkness is responsible for eternal darkness. We can't blame anyone else. Judas chose to live in the darkness of unbelief. At any moment he could have turned to the light of salvation in Christ but he would not!

Moments after Judas left to complete his deed, Jesus told his disciples, "I am the way, the truth and the life" (John 14:6, CEV). Only the cross and confession is the way out of eternal darkness. There are five suicides recorded in the Bible. These men had two things in common: they entered a night of eternal darkness and they rejected the light of God's grace. In life's darkest moments, when we think there is no way out, Christ offers hope. "Those the Father has given me will come to me, and I will never reject them" (John 6:37).

My moment of reflection…

Ask...Seek...Knock

June 9
Matthew 7:7-11

"Ask...seek...knock!" What a tremendous declaration followed by a staggering promise! Jesus was a continuous source of amazement to those who walked with him. He was the most thrilling personality this world has ever seen. Over and over again men were astonished at his ministry. Those who knew and followed him had ordinary days changed into days of unbelievable surprises.

The disciples marveled at his preaching! But never did they ask him to teach them how to preach. But one day they came upon him in prayer and a holy hush fell over them—deep reverence filled their hearts. Though they had been accustomed to hearing prayers all of their lives, they had never witnessed real prayer before. When Jesus had finished his prayer, they came to him and said, "Lord, teach us to pray!"

Jesus was an expert on prayer! From experience, Jesus knew the worth and power of prayer. As one with authority, he told the disciples to "keep on asking...looking...knocking. For everyone who asks receives. Everyone who seeks, finds. And the door is opened to everyone who knocks" (Matthew 7:7-8). What a staggering promise!

Yet many do not pray! Some fail to pray because of ignorance, sin, or lack of faith. The tragedy of many people is they want so little and are satisfied with almost nothing. They have no big dreams and lofty hopes, no great ambitions and burning desires. Wanting nothing, they pray for nothing. They are satisfied with life as it is until a big need comes into their life. So the advice from the Master: "Keep on asking...keep on seeking...keep on knocking!"

My moment of reflection...

The Golden Rule

June 10
Ephesians 4:25-32

A basic law of the universe holding the solution for all relationships came from the lips of Jesus. He told his disciples to "do for others what you would like them to do for you" (Matthew 7:12). Because God has dealt so graciously with us we should follow his example and practice generosity and kindness to one another.

Stand at the seashore and watch the tide go out and come in. There is no power on earth great enough to stop the tide; that principle operates all through life—what goes out comes back. Send out love and love comes back. Send out hate and hate comes back; mercy and mercy comes back. What we give we get!

A basic law of physics is for every action there is a corresponding reaction. That is also a law of life! We want people to like us, to take a real interest in us. We want people to overlook our faults and forgive us. People long for appreciation—it is a longing of every heart. Of the ten lepers who were healed, only one took the time to say thanks for the healing. The "Golden Rule" says "to get appreciation, give it and to be forgiven, forgive!"

No one can live the "Golden Rule" without God in his heart and life. The "Golden Rule" is old but it is as good as ever! We cannot expect to receive God's gifts if we do not treat one another as we desire to be treated by our Heavenly Father. So today, "do for others what you want them to do for you!"

My moment of reflection...

Living Life Over

June 11
Matthew 7:22-34

If you had life to live over—what would you do differently? An eighty-five-year-old lady said she would make these changes: "I would make more mistakes...I would relax and take fewer things seriously...I would take more chances, climb more mountains, and swim more rivers...I would pick more daisies and I would eat more ice cream."

Immediately, my mind skipped to Jesus and his interest in lilies and sparrows and children. Remember what he said? "Look at the lilies and how they grow" and "foxes have dens to live in and birds have nests" (Matthew 6:28; 8:20). He had time for things that most people overlooked, even little children. I thought about my "bucket list" and wondered how many things I overlooked because "I just didn't have time!" Maybe because of my workaholic nature I gave up hunting and fishing and my golf game fell apart!

If I could live life over, I would eat more vanilla-flavored ice cream with a lot of wonderful friends, punctuated by the memory of times when what I did was important to somebody or gave a cup of cold water to someone! In retrospect, the best thing about the way life worked for me was that I didn't worry about tomorrow. God's grace was so great in my yesterdays that I felt absolutely confident about the future. I hope that your life has been very satisfying, but make sure it's not outside the sovereign grace and mercy of God!

My moment of reflection...

Welcome Home

June 12
Luke 15:11-32

One of the mysteries of nature is the return of salmon to the headwaters of the river where they were hatched. Often this journey is hundreds, even thousands of miles with the latter stages, an endless struggle against strong currents and steep rapids. But unless it is caught by man or suffers accident en route, this powerful fish never gives up until it reaches the source of its being!

Our journey has some comparisons! At birth we are close to our Creator, but many grow further and further away from God as we become more preoccupied with our material wants and the means of satisfying them. Christ and the meaning of his life grow dimmer with the passing of years. Yet we have the testimony of those who become restless with a discontent they cannot explain.

The "Lost Son" had everything he wanted while at home but became dissatisfied and left home. When his money and friends were gone, he realized his hopeless condition and decided to return to his father. There he was graciously received by his waiting father. The voice of God can never be completely stilled in the human spirit. Greater than the instinct which compels the salmon back to the very pool of its birth is the mystery of the all-inclusive perfect love that God has for us—even those who have wandered far away! Regardless of where you are today, the welcome mat is always out and you are always "welcome home!"

My moment of reflection…

At the Movies

June 13
Psalm 19:1-14

I attended the "movies" last night and saw such a marvelous, breathtaking spectacle that it made me gasp in wonder and praise! No, I didn't attend the local theater or watch television. Rather, I had a "box seat" on my patio watching an approaching storm! As I sat facing west, the sun was beginning to set and storm clouds were brewing. Majestic thunderheads were boiling, moving swiftly into the sunlight until they finally blotted it out. I watched the clouds form all kinds of figures—there was the form of a man, the face of a horse, a cathedral! While I used a lot of imagination it was still a "great show" which magnificently displayed the power and glory of our Creator.

Spellbound by the beauty of the moment, I remembered the words of David, "The heavens tell of the glory of God. The skies display his marvelous craftsmanship...night after night they make him known" (Psalm 19:1-2). In reverence, I bowed my head and said, "Thanks, Lord, for letting me see your glory!"

What a great movie! Wish you could have been there too. Talk about variety—no two scenes alike. There were no murders, no anger, no hatred, no sex, and no commercials—just the rumble of thunder! The storm broke, but I just sat there filled with wonder and praise. As the sun fell beyond the western horizon and the curtain of darkness descended, I heard my heart sing, "My God, how great Thou art!"

My moment of reflection...

Just One More Step

June 14
Isaiah 40:25-31

Noel was seventy-two years old and in bad shape physically! He had abused his body with bad habits, was forty pounds overweight, and had some serious heart issues. Because of health problems, his life insurance was cancelled and his physician warned him not to attempt anything strenuous. Realizing that his dad wouldn't live much longer, his son challenged him to start walking.

Noel accepted the challenge against his doctor's warnings. Soon long walks developed into runs and the next thing you know, this seventy-two-year-old decided to run the New York Marathon. Now having run the marathon several times, his personal goal is to be the first person to run the marathon at the age of one hundred!

What a challenge! Sometimes it's all I can do to put one foot in front of the other and simply take one more step. Know the feeling? Then I remember that the Bible says, "Even youths will become exhausted, and young men will give up. But those who wait on the Lord will find new strength. They will fly high on wings like eagles. They will run and not grow weary. They will walk and not faint" (Isaiah 40:30-31).

To all walkers, runners, and sprinters: Never underestimate the power of just one more step...especially if you are walking with God! With all the challenges we face, never take your eyes off the Father, because with his strength, one more step may lead you to a marathon victory!

My moment of reflection...

A Night of Anxiety

June 15
Genesis 32:24-30

We are faced with issues in life that cause us to be anxious! The good thing about most problems is they are temporary or never come to pass. Jacob was not an admirable character! He deceived his father and swindled his brother out of his inheritance. He was a shrewd conspirator and at times a contemptible trickster. But the story of his all-night wrestling match at brook Jabbok gives us a glimpse of his true nature. In his struggle, Jacob learned that anxiety does not rid tomorrow of its sorrow—it robs today of its strength.

One of the chief causes of anxiety is loneliness! Loneliness is contrary to God's intention and provides fertile soil for anxiety. Being alone removes us from sources of strength and encouragement. Solomon tells us "people who are alone when they fall are in real trouble" (Ecclesiastes 4:10). Sometimes past transgressions or fear of the unknown can cause sleepless nights.

For Jacob, the events of the next day proved worry was needless as the worst did not come to pass. Worry and anxiety is unbecoming to a believer. David wrote we should give our "burdens to the Lord, and he will take care of you; He will not permit the godly to slip and fall" (Psalm 55:22). Jacob teaches we must hold on no matter how tough the battle becomes. The end of the story is good news: Jacob emerges from his struggles with a brighter tomorrow because of his persistent faith in God's protective power. We too can know victory over anxiety when we cast our care upon the Lord!

My moment of reflection...

Coasting

June 16
Ephesians 4:14-16

I read a little "gem" that raised a red flag! After a long day, I was tired, a bit testy, and out of energy. I was in a perfect "coasting attitude," if you know what I mean. I was at the point of exhaustion and then I read "the only way to coast is downhill." It was the exact word of counsel and encouragement I needed!

Remember bike rides when you coasted down a long hill? No work, no effort! The coasting part was exhilarating—it's the ride back up the hill that's the killer! Most of us work hard, spending incredible energy in the uphill climb. The uphill climb is demanding and exhaustive, punctuated by welcomed periods of rest and refreshment. Plateaus are necessary and important...but fatal if prolonged.

You can never stay in one place—you are either growing or in decline. Any dead fish can float downstream, but it takes a healthy, vibrant fish to swim against the current! There is no such thing as static sainthood. You are growing or in decline! Peter had some powerful words for anyone thinking about coasting: "Grow in the special favor and knowledge of our Lord and Savior Jesus Christ" (2 Peter 3:18). You will never become like Jesus by coasting. Real growth comes when we face the winds of difficulty and experience the grace of his sufficiency. So spread the word—coasting is out for growing Christians. We are marching to Zion, not sleeping in some Hilton!

My moment of reflection...

Honesty

June 17
Philippians 4:6-9

I saw this sign in a department store: "Shoplifters will be prosecuted to the full extent of the law!" Managers report "they are getting ripped off" by all kinds of people. Recently a woman who seemed very pregnant was stopped by store personnel as she walked out of a grocery store. After being stopped, she "gave birth" to a chuck roast, pancake syrup, toothpaste, several bars of candy, and a pound of butter.

Even with our sophisticated alarm systems, the problem of theft grows larger each year. Humanity is filled with dishonesty: cheating on exams, taking a hotel towel, not working a full eight hours, bold-faced lies and half-truths. What's the answer? Simple, return to honesty and integrity! External punishment may hurt, but it doesn't solve anything. In some cultures, when a thief is caught, they cut off his hand. While that may deter, it doesn't stop stealing! Cutting off the hand to stop stealing misses the "heart" of the problem by about twenty-four inches. Dishonesty doesn't start in the hand any more than greed starts in the eye. It is an internal disease!

Any hope? Absolutely! To cure that "internal disease" Christ offers you his life, his honesty, his integrity! Not a lot of rules and don'ts but power to counteract your dishonest bent—a new nature! You don't have to cut off your hand to become an honest person. Allow Jesus to be the honored presence in your life and you will find "honesty is the best policy!"

My moment of reflection...

Trophies

June 18
Hebrews 11:1-6

He was brilliant! At age five he wrote a concerto and by ten he was playing the best of Bach and Handel. Before his brief life ended, he had composed over six hundred works. His name was Mozart! He died at the age of thirty-five—lived in poverty and died in obscurity! Only a few friends came to his funeral. There is no granite shrine to mark his grave. He is gone...or is he? Somehow I believe the "Mozart touch" is a timeless trophy that brings delight for endless generations. In his music, Mozart lives on!

Recently I walked through a cemetery, stopping at several markers to read the markers. I knew none of the deceased...it was like I was stepping on sacred soil, a gripping encounter with the past. Quietness swept my soul!

I learned that life is very short! For Mozart it was 1756-1791—that's it! That "walk" taught me opportunity is now, not later. And I learned that death is sure. You can't dodge it...it's coming! You may not be a Mozart but your trophy is your contribution, whatever that may be. Known or unknown, it is your investment, your gifted touch that will live far beyond the grave. God displays these trophies forever. It is said of Abel: "Even though Abel is now dead, his faith still speaks for him" (Hebrews 11:4, CEV). You are important and the investment of your time, talent, and treasure in the Lord's work will be the only trophy you leave behind. Such trophies never tarnish!

My moment of reflection...

Be Fruitful

June 19
Psalm 1:1-6

A wealthy businessman, known for his unethical ways, told a friend that on his "bucket list" was a pilgrimage to the Holy Land. He said he wanted to climb Mount Sinai and read the Ten Commandments aloud where Moses read them, as if that would make him more spiritual. His friend said, "I have a better idea. Stay in Chicago and keep them!"

I think that Jesus would have preferred he stay in Chicago and "keep" the commandments as well. But we prefer some great religious experience to the routine of obedience. We would like some mountaintop "highlight" rather than actually showing evidence of a changed life. For Jesus, the proof of a person's encounter with God was whether or not there was fruit in their life. If there is no fruit of a transformed life and corresponding character change, our words carry little value.

The apostle Paul spoke of the fruit of the Spirit, which he said was "love, joy, peace, patience, kindness, goodness, faithfulness, gentleness, and self-control" (Galatians 5:22-23). For Jesus, it doesn't matter how many times you have been to Mt. Sinai or how many deeds you have performed, but whether or not your life has shown the fruit of a life yielded to God. The psalmist captured the perfect imagery of fruitfulness. He said a fruitful person is one who bears "fruit each season without fail. Their leaves never wither, and in all they do, they prosper" (Psalm 1:3). Fruitful—you be the judge!

My moment of reflection...

Living by the Rule

June 20
Matthew 7:12

The J. C. Penney store used to be called the "Golden Rule Store" and those who worked for him were called "associates." Mr. Penney treated them just as well as he would like to be treated—with love, respect, and kindness! In 1902, he took his general store and built it into a multibillion dollar business because he lived by the Golden Rule.

How do you treat people? Jesus didn't say, "Treat people with the same respect that they treat you." He said, "Do for others what you would like them to do for you" (Matthew 7:12). The "Golden Rule" is the most well-known thing Jesus ever said. It is the summit of ethics and behavior! It tells us that God has done for us exactly as he wants us to do to him. It reveals the heart of God and shows us how God's heart longs for us to live and act.

Jesus's whole ministry was seeking the blessing of his Father. Then he said that we have to live in right standing with him, but also in right standing with other people. We are evaluated by God and rewarded in direct proportion to the way we treat and feel about other people. That's scary—but we are responsible for our own conclusion. Want to be forgiven? Forgive! Need affirmation? Affirm! Enjoy a compliment? Compliment others! I'd like to be like that, wouldn't you? Sound impossible? It is without the grace of God!

My moment of reflection…

Man of the Hour

June 21
Deuteronomy 6:1-25

Father's Day is one of the highlights of the year. The day draws families together to honor the father of each home. History demonstrates that fathers have tremendous influence on their children for good or evil. Fathers are heroes to their offspring and children are enthralled with the expression "My Dad!" God has placed fathers in homes to help mold children in the ways of the Lord and to teach them the great truths of God's word.

God is looking for fathers to meet today's challenges! In the history of Israel, the record says that "in those days messages from the Lord were very rare" (1 Samuel 3:1). Samuel became God's voice against the wickedness of his day. Morality is essential to life and no father or parent can be great without it. Equally important, God needs men who will speak his counsel to the family. Even though the instruction and counsel may not be pleasant, men are to teach the "whole counsel of God" to their family. When we do what God commands, he blesses!

In a time when the foundations of our homes are shaky, God needs men to give wisdom and shepherd their families. Whether it's an Abraham or Job or Joshua, God needs men who will see their responsibility clearly and then do it in complete obedience. God bless our fathers as they encourage their children to love and follow Jesus in days of wicked expediency and compromise. Happy Father's Day!

My moment of reflection...

Waiting

June 22
Hebrews 6:13-15

Waiting is an event all of us experience every day of our lives! Waiting—waiting for the coffee to perk, waiting at the stop light, waiting your turn at the bank, waiting to be served at your favorite restaurant! Waiting is not one of our favorite pastimes! Observing people who are waiting, it is one of the more unpleasant experiences of life, evoking various emotions. But it is a part of life—and no matter what your age, we are never finished waiting. There will always be something to wait for!

More than a dozen words are used for "wait" in the scriptures. We are called to wait upon the Lord, to wait with full confidence, to wait with hope, to wait patiently, to wait with confidence, to wait for a long time! Waiting is deliberate and purposeful in God's plan and timing. Waiting is God's way of refining us, developing our character. It also seems that waiting is God's plan for providing his best for us.

Waiting is hard. It was especially hard for Abraham. God made a promise to Abraham: "I will certainly bless you richly, and I will multiply your descendants into countless millions. Then Abraham waited patiently, and he received what God had promised" (Hebrews 6:14-15). Abraham received God's blessing and in the process his character was sharpened. Waiting is foreign to our culture—but a tool in God's plans for our spiritual maturity! By patiently waiting, God has promised to renew your strength!

My moment of reflection…

Responsibility

June 23
Psalm 31:1-24

Success and responsibility go hand in hand! There can be no success without responsibility. Responsibility inevitably precedes a successful venture. In a successful life or marriage or business, someone must take responsibility. The quality of one's work and life indicates the quality of one's sense of responsibility.

Who is responsible for your life, for your personal growth, for your success or failure? Some people find excuses and some take personal responsibility. There is an old adage that everyone wants to harvest but nobody wants to plow! When it comes to responsibility, some people opt out for convenience or they are crippled by compromise—they really don't contribute toward the success of the project or plan.

When it comes to taking responsibility, none of us know how much sadness or happiness life holds for each of us. However, with the psalmist, we can say to God, "My life is in your hands" (Psalm 31:15, cev). When God gives the gift of time we are made personally responsible for how we use it. Time is a resource and we become stewards of how we use that time. Life is like a paratrooper school—we share the responsibility but we also exercise accountability. One successful jump does not make a paratrooper! The process must be repeated again and again! Yesterday's victories are history and every day is filled with new ventures and new responsibilities. In success, you experience great joy because you have learned responsibility. God is faithful—we must be responsible!

My moment of reflection...

Being Hospitable

June 24
Hebrews 13:1-3

There is an interesting story about four people whose names were Everybody, Somebody, Anybody, and Nobody! There was an important job to be done. Everybody was sure that Somebody would do it. Anybody could have done it, but Nobody did it! That's often the way it is with ministry, especially hospitality. Hospitality is Anybody's job and Everyone can do it, but Nobody does it because we think Somebody else will!

If everyone can do it—what is hospitality? It's so simple! Hospitality is being friendly, sharing love and concern, being receptive and open wherever you are. It means welcoming a stranger, listening or weeping or sharing food and our home with someone like Abraham (Genesis 18). When the Patriarch Abraham invited three strangers into his tent, he had no idea he would learn that he would become a father. When we invite people or even strangers to our home, it often turns out to be very rewarding and the blessings in return are more than expected.

Everyone can show hospitality! Instead of catching up with our friends, staying in our own little group or running around doing errands, we need to be looking with "visitor" eyes. Everyone must look for those who are new or alone, friendless, hurting, lonely, or needing a meaningful relationship. Even a smile or hello or sitting with someone who is alone can go a long way in showing you really care. Next time you are at church—be hospitable. Show someone you care!

My moment of reflection…

Investments

June 25
Malachi 3:1-12

Jesus is interested in your investments—especially your investments in the kingdom! On one occasion while in the temple, Jesus sat near the treasury and was watching people give their gifts. He is interested in the gifts of rich folks and poor widows and continues to be profoundly interested in our gifts. Money still talks!

In the days of Malachi the prophet, people were indicted with robbing God, a rather serious charge. Even though our names have not been entered on police ledgers, failure to honor God is still robbery! Some rob God because of their failure to recognize God's ownership while others fail to exercise faith. Failure to honor God with our gifts, we forfeit the smile of God's approval and blessings are withheld. In addition, we miss the joy of partnership with God in worldwide ministry and service.

We have been blessed to enjoy material success beyond what we deserve! We can selfishly hoard our "full barns," but in so doing, we will lose them. We can waste them or we can intelligently spend them freely for our own pleasure. But the wise man acknowledges God's ownership and understands that all material things are temporary! Jesus still sits over by the treasury and looks over our shoulder to observe our investments as he did centuries ago. Our gifts are simply visible symbols of God's sovereignty over all that we are and have! It hasn't changed: "It's still more blessed to give than to receive!" Try it!

My moment of reflection...

The "Write" Encouragement

June 26
Philippians 1:3-11

Letter writing is nearly a lost art! There are so many ways of sending "instant" messages these days that it doesn't seem necessary or important to write a letter anymore. In New Testament days, letter writing and delivery was not an easy task. In Paul's case, it was especially difficult because he was often traveling or in jail. But the letters he did write survived the ages and comprise a very important part of our Bible.

God valued the written word and gave us the Bible as a permanent record of holy history. The scriptures embrace God's love for the world, his concern and encouragement for his creation. Written words, even if they are a scribbled note, can be read, saved, reread, and can be an encouragement for years to come. Letters are personal and lasting—proof of an enduring relationship from someone who cares!

There is great value in writing a word of encouragement to a friend, colleague, or family member. Your letter is an investment of time and energy, and says, "I value you…you are important." Often we forget to say thanks for a gift or work performed. Writing a note expresses our thanks and affirms a relationship that may be kept for years. Think of someone who could use a note of encouragement today and write it. It could change their life! Pastor David Jeremiah said that "written encouragement is one of the most effective tools God has given to his children." Bless someone today!

My moment of reflection…

Not Knowing

June 27
Acts 20:22-38

There is a statement in scripture that flashes like a bright neon sign! Paul made it while saying good-bye to a group of friends at Miletus. It was one of those moments charged with great emotion. Most of those present were choking back tears, realizing that they would never see Paul again. Looking across the Mediterranean Sea, the aging apostle said, "Now I am going to Jerusalem, drawn there irresistibly by the Holy Spirit, not knowing what awaits me" (Acts 20:22).

What an honest admission! "I am going…not knowing what will happen!" In a nutshell, that's the Christian life! Going… not knowing! As followers of Jesus, we believe he is leading us in a certain direction with a divine plan in place—leading that is unmistakably clear. It may not be logical or explainable, but clear, at least to us! So out of sheer obedience, we go—pack our bags, bid farewell to friends, and strike out, facing a future that is as uncertain as the leading is sure. As believers, we have all walked that path. For sure, we remember Abraham who pulled roots from his hometown to go to "somewhere!"

Most often, when asked why, the best answer we can give is "God!" God calls us strangers and pilgrims—people on the move, living in tents, ready to roll whenever and wherever he leads! So "not knowing" is no big deal if you are available and obedient to the call of God!

My moment of reflection…

Worship

June 28
Psalm 147:1-20

Many Christians lack a proper understanding and practice of worship and the role it plays in their personal lives. Private and personal worship receives little attention, and as such it often becomes a sporadic, haphazard experience. We seldom prayerfully consider the function of music in our spiritual journey and have allowed it to follow the pattern of tradition or the path of least resistance. Music is so important, not just as an art or entertainment, but as a tool in our spiritual maturity. Paul instructs us to "sing psalms and hymns and spiritual songs to God with thankful hearts" (Colossians 3:16).

We spend the overwhelming part of our time and energy in fellowship and outreach but little time in thoughtful, creative worship preparation. We are coming to meet the king—the Master of the universe! What an awesome experience to be in communion with the Father!

God calls us to come "face to face" with the God of scripture. The disciples were "glad when they saw Jesus!" There must be daily quiet times when we move all things aside in life and meet with Jesus—alone! We are driven to him because of our fear, our uncertainties and our need for fellowship. In those moments of personal worship we receive his peace, his comfort and power. God looks forward to meeting with you every day—in private! Psalmist says, "Bow down and worship the Lord our Creator" (Psalm 95:6, CEV). God is worthy of your worship today—make daily worship your priority!

My moment of reflection…

Pleasing God—Loving People

June 29
1 Thessalonians 2:1-20

Ten o'clock every morning was a special time for the old town hound! As the train rushed through the village, the old dog would do his best to catch it. As two men watched the daily chase, one remarked, "I wonder what that dog would do with the train if he ever caught it." Like the dog chasing the train, Christians often chase material things—we all do it! We spend our efforts getting a new car, bigger house, better job, more money, the list goes on. But like the old dog, what will we do with these things when we "catch them?"

Paul's ministry in Thessalonica was not easy. Persecution became so intense that he was sent away for his own safety. But under his watchful care, they grew in their walk with the Lord. Paul was proud of these believers. He said: "What gives us hope and joy and what is our proud reward and crown? It is you! Yes, you will bring us much joy" (1 Thessalonians 2:19)

The only thing we can take with us to heaven is a friend! Your "crown of rejoicing" is not things you pursue in the material realm. It's people—those who are indebted to you for how God has used you in their coming to faith and growth in grace! Let's join Paul in "pleasing God and loving people" by pursuing the things which will not go up in smoke—people!

My moment of reflection...

If I Should Die...

June 30
Psalm 19:1-14

Most of us have thought about our death and leaving this world and the friends we love. Some of us read the obituaries in our papers to see if someone died that we knew. In fact, many of us have even made some preparation for our death such as our last will and testament. Faced with her untimely, imminent death, a college girl wrote in her journal these thoughts:

> If I had only a short time to live, I would immediately contact all the people I have ever loved and make sure they knew I loved them. I would play all my favorite music and sing my favorite songs...and I would dance, I would dance all night! I would look at the blue skies and feel the warm sunshine. I would tell the stars and moon how lovely and beautiful they are. I would say "good-bye" to all the things I own—my stuff. Then I would thank God for the great gift of life and then I would die in His arms! Wow!

Much of our life is lived in a hurry! We never take time to see the beauty and loveliness of our universe. The essential sadness of our human family is that very few of us even approach the realization of our full potential. For me, the real tragedy of life is to have lived and died without ever really having lived or loved! Today, live life to its fullest and really love!

My moment of reflection...

God Bless America

July 1
Matthew 5:13-16

As we celebrate our freedom and liberty in a few days, it is evident that as followers of Jesus Christ, we are engaged in a cultural battle—a battle for the soul of America! In the Gospels, Jesus talked about hiding our light under a bushel. Our "light" is our faith-driven compulsion to influence the world for God and for good as we see to push back the darkness and illuminate evil.

For too long, believers have allowed ungodly and liberal forces to shut us up and put us down. Currently, the heart of this culture battle is over the definition of marriage. We have self-appointed "experts" who think they know more than God; their accomplices fill our courtrooms and city halls all over America. Christians must allow our faith and his Spirit to influence all areas of our culture. If people of faith are reluctant to exercise their rights, our nation will pay a heavy price!

In the early history of our nation we are told that it was the men and women of God who made the difference between freedom and slavery. Today, people of faith must come off the sidelines and get into the battle. The stakes are high—survival is at stake! Jesus said it clearly, "You are like light for the whole world" (Matthew 5:14, CEV). As people of faith, we run the risk of being pushed to the sidelines of culture if we sit idly by and exhibit little or no godly concern. God bless America!

My moment of reflection...

Investing in Heaven

July 2
Revelation 7:9-17

The goal of every believer is to get to heaven and see Jesus face to face! Isaiah gives a preview of glory: "They will neither hunger nor thirst. The searing sun and scorching desert winds will not reach them anymore. The Lord in his mercy will lead them beside cool waters" (Isaiah 49:10). Jesus spoke about "many mansions" and Peter indicates that heaven is an "inheritance" for believers. Inspiration opened a door that allowed John to give us a picture of heaven—a place that should motivate all Christians to invest there!

John paints an unforgettable portrait of heaven. Heaven is like a garden! In this beautiful garden, all necessities are provided. There is plenty of water and vegetation. Everything we need is provided. Heaven is not only a tabernacle where we have perfect fellowship with God and a city where we have perfect protection, it is a garden where we have perfect provision. There is no darkness because God himself is the light! We cannot walk through the gates on our own merit—heaven is only accessible through the life and death of Jesus!

As Christians, heaven is ours! How are we investing in our future home? A wealthy oilman said, "The best way I know to lay up treasures in heaven is to invest my money in people who are going there!" Heaven is a "heaven-going" business. So "store your treasures in heaven…wherever your treasure is there your heart…will be also" (Matthew 6:20-21).

My moment of reflection…

God's Constitutional Government

July 3
Isaiah 33:17-24

This week, Americans will celebrate the birth of our great nation. Independence Day 1776 was the beginning of the greatest republic ever to exist. Independence does not mean anarchy—the complete absence of government and law—but rather a carefully planned constitutional government. Three distinct branches of government guide our democracy—the judicial, the legislative, and the executive branch. This American system of government has served as a workable formula for centuries!

The prophet Isaiah seems to have special insight into the governmental process. He spoke of a kingdom where God reigns supreme—a theocracy! Isaiah wrote, "The Lord is our judge, our lawgiver, and our king. He will care for us and save us" (Isaiah 33:22). While the Lord is our sovereign judge, the child of God is a citizen of two kingdoms and submits to the laws of our land, but God is the ultimate Judge. We follow the laws of the state but recognize that God is the ultimate and perfect Lawgiver. Finally, the Lord is our ultimate king. As citizens, we respect and follow the laws of our land.

As citizens of this great nation, we are greatly privileged and wonderfully blessed! But we are aware that history's highways are filled with wreckage of nations that forgot God. Isaiah was right when he said that God was our Judge, Lawgiver, and our King. Let's give thanks to the Sovereign King for the liberty and freedom we enjoy! God bless America!

My moment of reflection…

Pray for America

July 4
2 Chronicles 7:14

No doubt about it—our nation is at a "crossroads!" Problems galore: war, economic issues, foreclosures, a very liberal media, attacks on family values, dishonesty in "high" places, and soon another election season in which politicians are trying to impress us with their agendas. In the meantime, one thing every believer ought to be doing is praying that God will move among us.

As Christians we must lift America before the Lord at this critical juncture in history. The welfare of our beloved land hangs in the balance; so it is imperative that believers unite in fervent and consistent prayer. In speaking about prayer Paul said that we should plead for God's mercy and pray for those "who are in authority, so that we can live in peace and quietness, in godliness and dignity" (1 Timothy 2:2). God wants us to pray for our leaders even though they do not reflect Godly principles. Nonetheless, we are instructed to pray.

Our suspicious hearts get bogged down and we start thinking that our nation has fallen away so far that God himself can't return it to its former greatness. But he can! "If my people…will humble themselves and pray and seek my face and turn from their wicked ways, I will hear from heaven and will forgive their sins and heal their land" (2 Chronicles 7:14). God has given us his word that he will bless our land. Our responsibility is to pray for our beloved America!

My moment of reflection…

Heroes

July 5
Hebrews 11:1-40

All of us admire a hero! On Independence Day, we remember all those heroes who sacrificed for our freedom. Like you, I am moved to tears when I see our soldiers return from conflict to be reunited with their families. Today, we salute every person who served and paid the ultimate price for our freedom.

When we were children, we all had heroes—someone who did the daring deed! And we dreamed about being a hero ourselves. But as we grew to adulthood, we often let our dreams slip away and we settled down to a very ordinary life. Being heroic never comes naturally and it always involves paying a price. There is simply no shortcuts to heroism! All of life involves risk and fear of failure. Without faith and not taking the risk, you guarantee failure, especially if you are not willing to pay the price!

Perhaps the reason why so many enjoy reading Hebrews 11 is because they enjoy seeing portraits of real heroes! Abel, Enoch, Noah, Abraham, Sarah—all heroes because of their faith! The difference between ordinary people and heroes is their faith. Heroes commit themselves to a task and exhibit a willingness to endure the sacrifice and pain to accomplish the dream.

In New York Harbor stands the Statue of Liberty which invites the weary traveler and the tired immigrant to the land of freedom. With arm upraised, grasping the flaming torch, she symbolizes our treasured freedom. Thanks to our service persons for their gift of heroism, for liberty, and freedom! Isn't liberty beautiful?

My moment of reflection...

Jury Duty

July 6
Matthew 7:1-5

Most of us have had "jury duty!" And for sure, all of us have been asked to make a judgment about a matter sometime. However, there are some folks who seem to feel they are on "permanent jury duty" as they go through life. So Jesus gives us a word about judging: "Don't condemn others, and God won't condemn you" (Matthew 7:1, CEV).

A reporter was doing a story on laziness! He saw a man in the field sitting in a chair and hoeing weeds. This had to be the ultimate in laziness, or so he thought. Rushing back to his car to start his story, he looked back a second time and what he saw changed his entire outlook. He saw that the pant legs on the farmer hung down loose—the man had no legs. What seemed at first to be a story of laziness turned into a story of great courage!

Jesus wasn't saying that we should never assess people with some discrimination, but rather that we should not have a harsh, judgmental spirit. When we make judgments, we often do it on the basis of what we have seen and that's not always enough to provide the whole picture. God made the point that man looks at the outward appearance, but the Lord looks at the heart (1 Samuel 16:7). So "look before you leap"—look at yourself before leaping into a quick judgment and you just might see the "log" in your own eye!

My moment of reflection…

Pathway to Blessing

July 7
Luke 18:1-8

Our Lord invites us to ask, seek, and knock for that which we need! George Muller was born in Prussia in 1805. When Muller was converted to Christ, he was impressed with recurring statements of Jesus to "ask" for what we need. Believing God and without a salary, he and his wife set out to establish an orphan home to care for homeless children of England. Muller expected God's blessing on the work in direct proportion to the time he spent in prayer!

George Muller not only counted on God to provide but that he would provide abundantly! For over sixty years he prayed, caring for 9,500 orphans during his lifetime. These children never missed a meal. He never asked for help from anyone but God—over 7.5 million dollars came to him over the course of his life which he vowed was all in answer to believing prayer!

The cornerstone of prayer is the character of God and is powered by our persistence. Persistence means that you keep at something, you don't give up. You have patience as you continue to believe that God is going to answer the prayer you have prayed. You believe! The pathway to blessing is simple—ask, seek, knock continuously! God wants to show other people the love and kindness that he has shown you—and he does through your faithful and persistent prayer life! God's track record of the past supports his promises for the future! So keep asking...it's the pathway to blessing!

My moment of reflection...

Time

July 8
Ephesians 5:10-20

Time is a mysterious thing! All men are subject to the restrictions and privileges of time. We regulate life by the clock. We eat, sleep, work, and play with one eye on the clock. Benjamin Franklin said, "Time is money," but it cannot be replaced—once it's gone, it's gone forever. And yet, so many do not find time for the truly important things in life. We are in a big hurry to hear and see nature, to spread a little kindness, or to listen to beautiful music. We are too busy, hurrying aimlessly to somewhere to do something!

Time is God's time—time belongs to God! Paul exhorts us to "make the most of every opportunity for doing good" (Ephesians 5:16). The glory of life is that we can use time to attach ourselves to values that are timeless and not worry about running out of time. As God's gift to us, we must use time with great appreciation.

The brevity of life constantly reminds every creature that we only have so much time. When it is finished, we cannot get any more. While we make plans for tomorrow, Solomon teaches us that we "Each day brings its own surprises" (Proverbs 27:1, CEV). If there is someone to love or thank or encourage, do it now! God promises that your strength "match the length of your days" (Deuteronomy 33:25). Paul cautions every Christian to walk as wise men making the most of every opportunity!

My moment of reflection…

Despair

July 9
Hebrews 2:1-18

As a farm boy, I learned there is only one way to plow a straight furrow—pick out some object at the other end of the field and fasten your eyes to that object! If a rabbit popped out of a nearby bush you must not watch him dash away. To plow a straight furrow you had to keep your eye focused on the object which had become your guide point!

The writer of Hebrews had this in mind when he warns us against drifting away from the words of Christ: "We must listen very carefully to the truth...or we may drift away from it" (Hebrews 2:1). We have many daily pressures and problems but as long as we see Jesus in the same picture we're all right. It's when we omit him from the total picture that we begin to drift!

Life is made up of anxieties and unplanned events. To enjoy the fruits of a garden, we weed, water, and care for the plants. If weeds take over, it remains a garden but it doesn't bear the intended fruit. Our journey with God is his gift to us but we are responsible for the attention we give to it and the fruit that comes from it. You cannot neglect your spiritual life and at the same time experience victory in your daily life. Today, anchor your soul to his promises and fasten your eyes upon Jesus—because he is the answer to life's problems.

My moment of reflection...

Resting in God

July 10
Hebrews 4:1-16

A great promise that fell from the lips of our Lord was "Come to me, all of you who are weary and carry heavy burdens, and I will give you rest" (Matthew 11:28). This same thought is imparted in Hebrews 4! The "rest" spoken of in the Bible has nothing to do with inactivity or a slow rocking-chair approach to life.

My father helped me understand the biblical concept of rest. When we were building a fence, we would dig holes, place the posts in the hole, and tamp the dirt tightly; then he would say, "Now while we are resting, let's stretch the barbed wire and staple the wire to the posts." God rested from creation but in no way did he cease to carry out his divine will and purpose for creation. With the entrance of sin came a curse and man possessed great unrest of soul. But Jesus died for that sin and made it possible for us to enjoy the "rest" only God could provide.

God still speaks and admonishes us to come to him and enter into his rest, a rest that is accessible only by faith. The "rest" offered can only be received as a gift, a yoke that fits perfectly. His rest makes the burdens light and the journey meaningful. Some final words of Stonewall Jackson were, "Let us cross the river and rest under the shade." However, Jesus brings "rest" to our lives before we cross the river!

My moment of reflection…

Stunted Christians

July 11
Hebrews 5:1-6:1

Returning veterans from war indicate sometimes it is impossible to tell who the enemy is! A man may be an ally in the daytime but an enemy at night. A big problem in Christendom is spiritual immaturity—believers whose identity is in question.

Stunted Christians are "dull of hearing"—that is, they want just enough commitment to be a Christian but no more; they are sluggish and indifferent. Evidently these folks had been believers for a long time but possessed little spiritual growth. They had not learned obedience, refused to make a sacrifice, or tied down by responsibilities. In fact, they "dropped back" which indicated a total lack of spiritual progress. They were like babies who were still dependent on others for their nurture and growth.

Stunted Christians are promoters of stagnation—they forfeit the joy of progress. There is little excitement for those who packed up for a summer expedition into the wilderness but stayed at the base camp. The truth is believers who are unhappy in their faith are Christians but have never discovered that Christ intends life to be an exciting adventure.

When Columbus began his historic voyage, Spanish coins had a motto which meant "nothing else beyond." After the new world was discovered, the motto was changed to "more beyond." That's our call: "To go on to perfection!" In our journey to perfection, we need to surrender to the Holy Spirit and proceed to the goal of our high calling—to maturity!

My moment of reflection...

Hope

July 12
Hebrews 6:13-20

One of the great words of life is hope. The power and force of hope cannot be measured! It is one word that "keeps us going." Some people are optimistic by nature and others pessimistic. One man sees a rose bush in terms of thorns; another sees only roses. Any man whose hope is based on temperament is clutching a hope that is deaf, dumb, and blind. Hope is not daydreaming—it is desire with expectation of obtaining what is desired.

The Bible is filled with references about hope. Hope enabled Abraham to become the "father of the faithful." Hope abides forever, inspires clean living, and is an anchor of the soul! The anchor is a symbol of hope. From the moment men built ships and sailed the seas, the anchor meant hope and safety. Pythagoras said that wealth is a weak anchor but wisdom and courage are anchors which no storm can shake.

The Bible rises above pagan wisdom, declaring that Christian hope is both sure and steadfast (Hebrews 6:19). Our anchor cannot be dislodged because it is grounded in heaven! Jesus is our living hope because he was raised from the dead as our ever living Lord. When he ascended to the Father, our hope was firmly planted in heaven. This hope is God's gift to you—you must claim it! In a world that is growing old like a tattered garment, our confidence is anchored in Jesus who is our eternal hope!

My moment of reflection…

Giving Your Best

July 13
Hebrews 11:32-12:2

"Why should I knock myself out?" "No one cares...why should I?" "If you do a good job, no one appreciates it." How many times have you heard such statements or said them yourself? It is easy for this kind of attitude to creep into our spiritual outlook. Concerning the great men of faith included in God's honor roll, it states that "they were too good for this world" (Hebrews 11:38). If one expects earthly praise for faithfulness, we will be disappointed! Be assured of this: the world will not see your worth and even Christians fail to express appreciation for your ministry!

Against insurmountable odds, God brought victory to these faithful servants. To be part of God's blueprint for the ages is a thrilling experience. These servants believed in God's promise of redemption, but did not live to see its fullness. We should give our very best because a sacred trust has been handed to us and we must be faithful! We "knock ourselves out" because Jesus is the author and finisher of our faith—we want to please him!

Mozart's life ended like a torch burning in the wind! In the year of his death at age thirty-six, he spent his last days working on the Requiem, the song of death. While Vienna was ringing with his fame, Mozart died consumed with his labors. And so must we! Each of us is writing his own Requiem. We will never regret "knocking ourselves out" for Jesus!

My moment of reflection...

Joy—and the Place I'm In

July 14
Philippians 1:12-26

There are a lot of miserable people in this world, many of whom attribute their misery to the place they live or job they have. True, we have financial struggles and tough neighbors and jobs we don't like which rob us of our joy, happiness, and desired satisfaction.

We think because we are in a "hard place" we are justified in ceasing to rejoice. Paul experienced many hardships in life; and now he was in prison. His prison stay wasn't a soft place or life on a downhill drag. Right in the middle of his trial, he wrote, "I rejoice… and I will continue to rejoice" (Philippians 1:18). Amazing!

When you are in a difficult place it is easy to become bitter and discouraged. I have never met a bitter person who was happy and filled with joy. Bitterness and joy don't blend! Paul did nothing worthy of prison; in fact, his imprisonment was branded with injustice. Perhaps in the back of his mind, Paul was wondering, "Where is God in my struggle and doesn't he care?"

But God was working out his plan! God was about to use Paul's momentary struggles to bless, encourage, and strengthen others in their difficulty. When all is well, we find it delightful to sing, but when hardships come and the rain falls, we have no song and a smile is replaced with a frown. As you struggle with mountains or valleys in your life, realize that as you rely on the grace of God's control you will be able to say "I rejoice…and I will continue to rejoice" wherever!

My moment of reflection…

Joy—and the People I'm With

July 15
Philippians 1:27-2:30

People are essential to a life of joy! What often takes away the melody from our hearts and keeps us from living the life of joy is not living in right relationship with people. Like a dislocated bone, as long as relationships remain dislocated, there is no happiness, no joy, and little fulfillment.

Satan desires to destroy our fellowship with other believers. Sometimes opposition comes from without; but often the struggles we face come from within! Paul warns us: "Don't be selfish; don't live to make a good impression on others. Be humble, thinking of others as better than yourself...be interested in others too and what they are doing" (Philippians 2:3-4).

The presence of Godly conduct and conversation in relationships produces joy and fulfillment. Paul pleads to let the "mind of Christ" be the filter of all conduct and conversation. The unwillingness to forgive destroys the joy that cements relationships. Few things disrupt friendships and destroy harmony than an unforgiving attitude. The moment one refuses to forgive is the moment you die within and the life of joy fades from the scene.

Joy is dependent on unselfish concern from your friends. Timothy was preoccupied with concern for his friends. It brought him genuine joy! The life of joy is dependent on having a right relationship with people. Rejoicing is impossible as long as you have a dislocation, whether it's in your elbow, your finger, or in your heart. You will never be able to sing until you get right with others. And when you do, you too will know "the life of Christian joy!"

My moment of reflection...

Joy—and the Person I Am

July 16
Philippians 3:1-21

God loves you and has a wonderful plan for your life! God's intention for his creation is they live a life of joy and fulfillment. If you are not a joyful Christian you are something less than God designed you to be.

A prerequisite for personal joy is to understand our spiritual history. Our past may be rich in traditions and characterized by wonderful service. However, rich heritage and sterling character can leave us empty and unfulfilled. It doesn't make us joyful! Paul's word is forget the past and "look forward to what lies ahead" (Philippians 3:13). A danger for us is relying on past victories to satisfy us today—and we go stale. We strive to get fun and sparkle in life by living on stale grace, like old stale bread. God's call for us is to walk in "newness of life" every day!

To be full of joy, my spiritual attitude must be characterized by intimacy—intimacy of the heart! The intimacy called for is to know Christ in such a way that Jesus becomes the preeminent passion of my life. Passion and intimacy is experienced when you are forgiving, learning to be thankful, and allowing God's word to dwell richly in our hearts.

Paul, the joyful apostle, was driven by expectancy. For him there was always a tomorrow, always something new and exciting. His high calling in Christ gave him his ultimate fulfillment and joy in life. Like parents who have a dream for their children, Christ's plan for you is to be joyful with the person you are becoming. Enjoy life today!

My moment of reflection...

Joy—and the Good It Does

July 17
Philippians 4:1-23

A child was eating lunch when a ray of sunshine focused on her spoon. As the little one brought the food to her mouth, she exclaimed with a happy laugh, "Look, I've swallowed a spoonful of sunshine." Those who have been indwelt by the Spirit of God should not have to be told to be happy. Yet, many Christians are gloomy and mournful! For that reason our Lord admonished us to be happy and joyful.

Your life of joy makes Christ attractive to others! Nothing makes Jesus less appealing and attractive to others than sour-puss, hostile believers. Paul gives pointed instruction: "Always be full of joy in the Lord...Let everyone see that you are considerate in all you do. Remember, the Lord is coming soon" (Philippians 4:4-5). We make Christ attractive by thinking thoughts that are honorable, right, pure, lovely, excellent, and worthy of praise (Philippians 4:8). What you think will be expressed in making Christ attractive or unattractive. It's that serious!

Many do not have the grace to cope with life's problems! When confronted with mountains, they fall apart at the seams, get mad at God, and crumble beneath the load. We cannot bear burdens alone, we need each other to draw encouragement and grace in the difficult moments of life. I suspect that someone needs you today!

For Christian joy to do any good, it must be shared. There is a world "out there" that wonders if Christ really makes any difference. It is your life of joy that can convince the world that Jesus makes the difference! It really does!

My moment of reflection...

Change

July 18
Psalm 102:21-28

Change is everywhere! It is part of our world—medicine, church, politics, technology, the list could go on and on! Few people enjoy change. We like our comfort zone and really don't want to leave them. One humorist said, "Nobody likes change except a baby with a wet diaper." That may be true, but we deal with change every day!

Dealing with change causes anxiety! Sometimes change is so fast it's like we're on a runaway train and we can't keep up. Despite changes we must remember to turn to the One who never changes. He has been likened to a rock on who we can plant our feet while the torrents of change surround us or like a ship's anchor that holds us strong in a storm. Jesus told his disciples they are not to be troubled or afraid because his peace will be with them (John 14).

We must not despair—things that really matter have not changed. Malachi gives us a beautiful picture of the Lord: "For I am the Lord, I do not change" (Malachi 3:6). Hebrews 13:8 reminds us that "Jesus is the same yesterday and today and forever." So when everything seems to be different, remember what's important has not changed—he has not changed! He will not fail us and we can rely on him forever! The hymn writer put it well: "O thou who changes not, abide with me." Remember—he always will!

My moment of reflection...

The Lord Is Good

July 19
Psalm 34:1-22

David had been in great danger. He prayed and his prayer was answered. In response to answered prayer, David said, "Taste and see that the Lord is good" (Psalm 34:8). The old proverb is still true: "The proof of the pudding is in the eating!" You couldn't possibly explain to a person how a tomato tastes if he never tasted one. We can't explain to a person the joy of salvation if you have not experienced salvation!

David is right, the Lord is good! We need to look on the bright side of things like Caleb who gave a positive report about taking the land of promise. It is a real joy to be part of the answer rather than part of the problem. Not much joy is derived by being on a demolition team. It takes little skill to tear down but great skill to construct a beautiful building. When we look on the bright side and seek to be an answer to problems, we begin to see the joy of being on the "building" team—and that tastes good!

A little boy was carrying a pail of honey! He was asked how sweet honey is. Unable to explain how sweet "sweet" is, in desperation he said, "Taste it and see for yourself!" You have tried some things and they haven't worked. So when we look on the bright side and seek to be an answer to problems, we discover that "the Lord is good!"

My moment of reflection...

Wisdom

July 20
Matthew 5:38-48

A truck driver was eating his lunch at a crowded roadside diner when gang members demanded his table. Disrupting his meal, the driver calmly paid for his meal and left. The bikers laughed and said, "Ain't much of a man, is he?"

The waitress responds, "He's not much of a driver, either. He just backed his rig over your motorcycles."

How do you react to people who make life difficult for you? We all encounter people who are hard to live with. How do you treat the "jerks" in your life?

Jesus gave helpful instructions to those who followed him. He said, "Don't resist an evil person, don't try to get even and turn the other cheek!" He was really saying his followers should respond differently than the world responds. This is hard and really impossible unless we are energized by the power of the Holy Spirit.

We all have people who have authority over us and they can make life miserable. Our natural instinct is to resist. But Jesus raises the standard: turn the other cheek, don't go just a mile, go two miles! It's amazing how much better we feel about ourselves when we go the extra mile and how quickly relationships are smoothed over when we do more than expected. What a testimony to the work of Christ in our lives when we perform the extra-mile service with a smile. Wisdom for today: Do not be overcome by evil, but overcome evil with good!

My moment of reflection...

Integrity

July 21
Numbers 30:1-2

Paul Harvey told the story of four young men who were late to class. They told their teacher the reason was a flat tire. Because they missed a test, the teacher said they would pass if they would answer just one question: "Which tire was flat?" We are living in times when there is such a lack of integrity and character. Looking for people of integrity in our generation is like searching for a needle in a haystack.

Men and women of integrity are rare! Jesus taught we should be as good as our word. Children used to be taught that reputation was extremely important. Abraham Lincoln said that for a man to train a child in the way he/she should go, he must walk that way himself. Jesus said that "your word is enough" (Matthew 5:37). As believers whose citizenship is in heaven, we must show integrity in our words and deeds. Moses said that a man shall not violate his word—he should do according to all that proceeds out of his mouth (Numbers 30:2).

Integrity is doing what you said you would do. It means keeping your promises. If you promised to return a call, integrity means you return the call! A promise is a holy thing, whether made to a chairman of the board or to a child. Horace Greeley said, "Fame is a vapor, popularity an accident, riches take wings, those who cheer today may curse tomorrow, only one thing endures—character!"

My moment of reflection...

Fasting

July 22
Luke 18:10-14

We live in a culture where food dominates America's favorite pastime! The Golden Arches and other eateries capture our daily attention. Like you, I like food and love all those delicious goodies. But there are times when God calls us to deny ourselves and voluntarily abstain from food for spiritual reasons.

In the 1870s, Minnesota was plagued with grasshoppers that destroyed their crops. The following year, the governor called for a day of prayer and fasting so everyone could go before God and ask for his protection for the new crop. God heard the prayers of his people and sent unusually extreme subzero temperatures that destroyed the larvae. God answered their prayers!

Fasting is laying aside any pleasurable or vital activity for a period of time to intensely pursue God with the intent of obeying his will. Fasting is appropriate in times of crisis and mourning and in times of repentance. Fasting doesn't guarantee spiritual blessing, but puts us in the position to experience blessing as God moves. It increases our sense of humility and dependence upon God and raises the level of our spiritual awareness. Jesus cautioned not to fast like the hypocrites who wanted publicity to gain public approval. As God leads you to fast in secret, be ready to meet God on a whole new level. Jeremiah said, "If you look for me in earnest, you will find me when you seek me. I will be found by you, says the Lord" (Jeremiah 29:13-14).

My moment of reflection…

Motives

July 23
Matthew 6:1-4

What you do matters to God! God expects you to be kind and do "good" in the world—to help others through personal involvement and through giving generously and sacrificially. But there is something else that God expects: God expects us to have the right motive! Why a man does "good" and shows kindness matter greatly to God.

People give for recognition and prestige—to get the applause of men. Some give for self-satisfaction and self-admiration. Others give out of obligation, to fulfill a sense of duty. And there are some who give to secure the recognition of God, to feel God is pleased and favors him because he has done "good." God is not pleased when you "sound the trumpet" or seek the praise of men! Self-promotion never pleases God!

True giving—giving which pleases the Father—is a response of love. Jesus says, "Don't dwell on how much you are giving and don't call attention to your giving!" Looking at our world and seeing the pain and suffering, there is only one motive and that is love, a desire on behalf of Christ to help those in need. Any person immersed in God and sees the needs of the world does not get entangled with the worldly affairs and the applause of men. He quietly and diligently goes about pouring himself into helping others. Why? Because he covets God's approval! What you do matters greatly to God. Look for ways to be kind and generous today!

My moment of reflection…

Forgiveness

July 24
Genesis 50:1-22

One of the greatest gifts you can give is the gift of forgiveness to someone who has mistreated you. At the same time you give the gift of forgiveness to others, you give yourself the gift of a heart that is free from hate, anger, and hostility. Forgiveness is foundational to Christian living, yet one of the very things that hold people in bondage today. Jesus taught, "Forgive us our sins, just as we have forgiven those who have sinned against us" (Matthew 6:12).

Forgiveness is a command and spiritual principle, not a suggestion. As such there is no limit to forgiveness—it is limitless! Forgiveness is hard and it runs deep. It is not easy to give up our right to be hurt, to be angry to get back, to hate others for what they have done. You may have lost a great deal because of someone's actions. Joseph had every "right" to be angry, but instead, he embraced his brothers and forgave them. So did Esau, Stephen, and Peter! And you must too!

Clara Barton, founder of the American Red Cross, was reminded of a vicious deed that someone had done to her years before. But she acted as if she had never even heard of the incident.

"Don't you remember it?" her friend asked.

"No," was Barton's reply, "I distinctly remember forgetting it!"

We learn to forgive because we are people seeking to be like God! Forgiveness will transform your relationship with God, with others, and with yourself!

My moment of reflection...

Worship

July 25
Hebrews 10:19-25

In a remote mountain village in Europe several centuries ago, a wealthy nobleman wondered what legacy he should leave his neighbors and friends. After much thought, he decided to build them a beautiful church.

No one saw the complete plans for the church until it was finished. After all the construction was completed, the townspeople gathered and marveled at its beauty and completeness. Touring the beautiful new sanctuary, suddenly someone asked, "But where are the lamps?" How will it be lighted?

Quickly, the nobleman pointed to some brackets that he had installed in the wall. Then he gave each family a decorative lamp which they were to bring with them each time they came to worship. He said, "Each time you are here the area where you are seated will be lighted. And each time you are not here, that area will be dark. This is to remind you that whenever you fail to come to church, some part of God's house will be dark. Please bring your 'lamp' each Sunday so no part of God's house is ever dark!"

On numerous occasions, the Bible instructs us to love and serve one another. Part of our service is coming together as a body in corporate worship. This is our challenge: "And let us not neglect our meeting together, as some people do, but encourage and warn each other, especially now that the day of his coming back again is drawing near" (Hebrews 10:25).

My moment of reflection…

Peace

July 26
John 14:1-31

In the Florence Gallery is a painting named *Peace*. It pictures the sea tossed by a raging storm with darkening clouds, wild waves, and fierce lightening. Waves are beating against a large rock. In the cleft of the rock is a little vegetation surrounded by beautiful flowers. Nestled among the greenery is a dove sitting calmly on her nest, undisturbed by the fury of the storm! That's peace!

Jesus spoke about his gift of peace: "I am leaving you with a gift—peace of mind and heart...so don't be troubled or afraid" (John 14:27). Peace is the universal desire of humanity. The biblical concept of peace is serenity, perfect contentment which is a result of complete happiness and complete security. Isaiah, with keen anticipation, says that Christ is the peace "bringer" and that his name is "the Prince of Peace." Before peace can come, there must be a revolution of character which Jesus termed the "new birth" because you don't put new wine in old skins or new cloth on old garments.

After Jesus went to his Father he sent the Holy Spirit to give us victory and produce peace within us—that is, to bring about a perfection of relationships, both with God and man! So now we can live at peace with ourselves, peace with others, and most of all peace with God! Thank God for the gift of his peace that gives every Christian serenity and perfect contentment in the fury of raging storms!

My moment of reflection…

Stability

July 27
Hebrews 13:1-25

When God's final shaking destroys the temporary and reveals the eternal, there will be only one source of stability—Jesus Christ! Through Christ we shall transcend the limits of time and cross over the golden span to eternity. There is only one source of stability: Jesus Christ! "I am the Lord, and I do not change" (Malachi 3:6).

The ethic and outlook established by Jesus is always current. Despite technological and cultural progress, human nature remains the same—sin continues to wreck lives, producing selfishness and hatred. But in this environment, the believer is called to "continue to love each other (Hebrews 13:1). A vital part of this ethic is to show hospitality, let fellowship abound, and be content with what you have! In difficult times, "don't run" but stand together! Because "Jesus is the same yesterday, today and forever" (Hebrews 13:8), we must be loyal to this changeless Christ. We are like actors on the stage who play our part, coming and going. But the director is forever, his preeminence is permanent, his leadership is forever, and his kingdom is eternal.

The word *Hebrew* means "one who has crossed over." God called Abraham to cross the Euphrates by faith. He called Moses to lead the Hebrews across the Red Sea to freedom. He called Joshua to lead his people across the Jordan River into the Promised Land. This same "changeless" Christ calls us to follow him wherever! "Let us go on."

My moment of reflection...

Almost Perfect

July 28
Psalm 31:1-24

Stradivarius is synonymous with fine violins! Antonius Stradivarius insisted no instrument made in his shop be sold until it was as near to perfection as human skill could make it. His philosophy was simple: "Other men make other violins, but no man shall make a better one!" God said that Noah was righteous and blameless, but even Noah made mistakes (Genesis 6).

We are in the process of becoming all God wants us to become! As believers, we still make mistakes—mistakes because we are in a hurry, afraid something is going to happen so we take control. In our panic we make mistakes. Sometimes mistakes happen because of our neglect. We become so busy that we neglect our spiritual life which may lead to disobedience. Unrestrained curiosity and "blind spots" lead to failure because we are unable to see ourselves for who we really are. It's easy to see the mistakes of others and so hard to see our own!

God says, "Put on my shoes, walk in my steps, strive to be like me...Be holy!" There's a mountain in the Northeast that looks like the face of an old man. It is reported that a man spent so much time looking at the face of the mountain that his face eventually began to resemble the old man of the mountain. Lesson: The more time we spend trying to be like him, the more we'll begin to look like him to others! "Be holy even as I am Holy!"

My moment of reflection...

Kindness

July 29
Ephesians 4:1-6

The first biblical concept most children memorize is "Be ye kind!" However, it's one thing to parrot these words but another to really be kind. Our world desperately needs the virtue of kindness. Jesus came to do more than die for our sins and to save us from hell. He came to help us break with attitudes, ambitions, and actions that are self-destructive and hurtful to others. He came to give us a new pattern of thinking and action that leads to abundant living now!

Jesus is loved for his kindness—to a leper, to Zacchaeus, to hungry crowds, to an adulterous woman, to a thief, to his mother, the list goes on! Kindness is a language the dumb can speak and the deaf can hear. It is the oil that takes friction out of life. Kindness is not instinctive but must be developed and cultivated. When Paul spoke to his Colossian friends, he encouraged them to clothe themselves with kindness. So the command is clear: "be kind and merciful" (Ephesians 4:32, CEV).

Kindness is an expression of greatness! In the story of the Good Samaritan, it was the Samaritan who was moved with compassion and kindness to a person in need. Kindness is availability, usefulness and benevolence—it is giving oneself to others! There is urgency for his Spirit to develop kindness in our life. Today, make time for kindness! Abraham Lincoln demanded "malice toward none and charity for all." Be kind to someone today!

My moment of reflection…

The Ascension

July 30
Acts 1:1-11

At the height of the space program, the launching of the manned spacecraft was a popular attraction. People traveled to Cape Kennedy to see the spectacular launch and millions watched the event on television—countdown to liftoff! There was an exceptional thrill about that event!

The most spectacular "liftoff" was witnessed by eleven men! The risen Lord remained on earth forty days after his resurrection. He remained so he might establish resurrection proof, give encouragement to fearful disciples, and impart closing instructions to his disciples. Then on the Mount of Olives, Jesus ascended: "While he was blessing them, he left them and was taken up to heaven" (Luke 24:51).

The ascension of Jesus was no optical illusion, no subjective vision, but a literal objective fact. It occupies an important and essential place in the completion of our Lord's ministry. The ascension of Jesus assures us of his finished work. The One who identified with us now is identified in heaven and is crowned with glory and honor. But the big question of the disciples: "Is he coming back to earth again? Will we see him again?" The scriptures tell us that "someday, just as you saw him go, he will return" (Acts 1:11). The marvel of his ministry on earth amazes us; the thrill of his ascension challenges us to trust him. In the meantime and until he returns, we follow the king who reigns. If we do, we will reign with him forever!

My moment of reflection...

Grace

July 31
Ephesians 2:8-10

One of the cherished words among believers is the word "grace!"
We speak freely of the "grace of God" and being "saved by grace."
We can sing four stanzas of "Amazing Grace" without looking at
the hymnal. A few years ago, a theologian with tongue-in-cheek,
wrote a book entitled *Grace Is Not a Blue-eyed Blonde* to shock us
into realizing that we throw around theological words without
understanding what they mean.

"Grace" appears nearly two hundred times in the Bible. In
Genesis, we're told "Noah found favor in the eyes of the Lord"
(Genesis 6:8). The final reference is a benediction: "The grace of the
Lord Jesus be with you all" (Revelation 22:21). Initially, Greeks used
grace to describe favor shown to a friend. This places a limitation
upon grace. But when Jesus came, he removed all limitations and
boundaries from the word. When Christ died on the cross, grace
leaped from confinement as an expression to friends and included
enemies as well.

We must understand that grace goes beyond salvation—grace
becomes the spring and source from which all blessings come. In
other words, he who saves us by his grace also brings us into the
sphere of grace and endows us with all the blessings and favors that
are expressed by his love. God abounds in grace! All of God's dealings
with his people are filtered through the lens of his marvelous grace.
What a joy to be recipients of God's wonderful grace!

My moment of reflection...

Happiness Is…

August 1
Matthew 5:1-12

At the conclusion of the Beatitudes Jesus said, "Be happy…be very glad! For a great reward awaits you in heaven" (Matthew 5:12). The Beatitudes paint the picture of a self-contained individual who has achieved happiness. According to Jesus, happiness is what happens "in" us, not what happens "to" us! Happiness is not caused by outward circumstances—it's a matter of the heart!

Our world has dedicated itself to the pursuit of happiness! The Declaration of Independence declares "we are endowed with certain rights—life, liberty and the pursuit of happiness." However, we live in an unhappy world. Many folks seek happiness in ways that produces misery—drugs, alcohol, pleasure, etc. Let's face it, happiness has not been found for the world's majority.

Happiness is a state of the mind, a condition of the heart! Jesus said the truly happy and blessed people are those who are poor in Spirit, mourners, meek, righteous, merciful, pure, peacemakers and the persecuted. No reference is made to what we consider the prime essentials of happiness—health, work, money, security, home, friends and love. While these good things may accompany happiness, they don't produce it. The beggar on the street may be more contented than the rich man in his palace.

God's formula for happiness is a relationship with Jesus! In the Upper Room Jesus bequeathed the most astonishing gift to his disciples: "I have told you this so that you will be filled with my joy. Yes, your joy will over-flow" (John 15:11). Happiness is God's gift to every believer and the Beatitudes become a character reflection of his grace in our lives.

My moment of reflection…

Happiness—Through Humility

August 2
Psalm 32:1-11

Many are blind to the meaning of happiness; multitudes pursue happiness in things and with people to learn they are not really happy. For most, the genesis of happiness is to grab all the money you can get, avoid suffering, don't let people get in your way, assert yourself and live it up while you have the chance! The beatitudes so contradict our conventional ideas of happiness that we find them hard to believe, much less accept.

Jesus taught that "God blesses those who realize their need for him, for the Kingdom of Heaven is given to them" (Matthew 5:3). When Jesus uttered this beatitude he was speaking about realizing our utter helplessness and at the same time, our dependence upon God. Until we see ourselves helpless and destitute, God is unable to help us! But when we see ourselves at the end of our rope, then God says, "Blessed are the poor in spirit!" Pride and self-sufficiency which consumes so many is the opposite of this beatitude. Poverty of spirit leads to happiness because it qualifies us to serve in the kingdom!

The result of poverty of spirit and humility is the birth of hope! Our Father takes us just as we are with all our shortcomings. The only requirement is we come with an empty vessel. Our extremity becomes God's opportunity and our place of despair becomes the scene of Christ's victory in our lives. When we let go of the rope we make an amazing discovery: "Underneath are the everlasting arms." And so the pathway to happiness is to become "poor in spirit!"

My moment of reflection…

Happiness—Through Sorrow

August 3
Psalm 51:1-19

A modern rendition of this beatitude might read "blessed are the rich, happy are the successful, fortunate are they who have no troubles; for them life is a bed of roses!" This is not what Jesus said at all. He does not appeal to those who are at the top, but those who carry burdens. He feels their hurt and is touched by their needs, driven to do something about it. He speaks to the unfortunate, the sorrowful and tells them "God blesses those who mourn, for they will be comforted" (Matthew 5:4).

"Laugh and the world laughs with you; cry and you cry alone" is our philosophy. The last thing anyone wants to do is to cry or mourn. But Jesus drops a bombshell when he tells us there is happiness in sorrow, comfort in crying and gladness in grief! What does he mean? The sorrow Jesus has in mind is sorrow over sin. When we repent, not only are we forgiven but "we shall be comforted." The ultimate gift God gives is the "blessed hope" of heaven, deliverance from the very presence of sin!

In the Upper Room the disciples mourned the impending loss of Jesus. But he told them to look beyond their sorrow, because he would see them again. Our call is to repent, to mourn over sin and allow Jesus to mold us to be a polished instrument fit for the Master's use. Out of the spirit of heaviness the new man emerges, clad in the garment of praise. What a promise: "Blessed are those who mourn, for they will be comforted!"

My moment of reflection...

Happiness—Through Meekness

August 4
Psalm 37:1-11

Jesus instructed his disciples he would "bless those who are gentle and lowly, for the whole earth will belong to them" (Matthew 5:5). This beatitude is not popular because those who are meek are considered weak, spineless and unable to stand up for themselves. Meekness is not considered an asset but a liability!

Our culture believes in the survival of the fittest; in order to succeed and survive one must be aggressive and heavy-handed. Yet Jesus comes to us in the hustle of modern life with confidence and says, "Blessed are the meek!"

As a fruit of the spirit, meekness denotes "being molded" by God! It's not a natural grace but God-given and signifies both strength and gentleness. As we allow God to control our lives, he begins to train us. The meek are eager to listen to the teacher and learn—they have a teachable attitude!

Look at the promise: "They shall inherit the earth!" The word "inherit" means to enter into possession of something which has been promised by God. When Jesus declared the meek will inherit the earth, he was saying they will possess all that God has planned for them from eternity; they will be filled with all the fullness of God. We possess the earnest of our inheritance now, but the day is coming when the meek will shine forth as the sun in the kingdom of their Father. Jesus invites us to follow his example. He said, "Take my yoke upon you. Let me teach you, because I am humble and gentle, and you will find rest for your souls" (Matthew 11:29).

My moment of reflection...

Happiness—Through Righteousness

August 5
Isaiah 55:1-13

It was a hot, sultry day; wind was blowing and the sun was beating down on those who were gathered around Jesus on the mountain side. Their stomachs were growling with hunger and their throats parched with thirst. Then Jesus spoke: "God blesses those who are hungry and thirsty for justice, for they will receive it in full" (Matthew 5:6). These words of Jesus were real to his audience—they knew what it meant to "hunger and thirst!"

Everyone recognizes a good appetite is a treasure; it is a mark of life and the roadway to growth. Hunger and thirst is normal, the mark of a vigorous healthy life. God has placed in every one of us a hunger for himself, yet we often allow our spiritual hunger to go dormant with little taste for the spiritual. So the challenge is clear: "Hunger and thirst after righteousness!"

Before anyone can hunger and thirst after righteousness, he must get rid of his "own" righteousness and accept God's perfect gift of forgiveness and acceptance. As the most demanding of the beatitudes, hungering and thirsting after righteousness is a matter of life and death.

Look at the promise: "They shall be filled!" If a person hungers and thirsts for righteousness that God alone gives, God will fill them until their longings are achieved and soul satisfied. The wealth of heaven is given to the poor and their heart is filled. This is God's gift to everyone who hungers and thirsts for righteousness. Your hunger and thirst for God is a badge of wholeness—a mark of your greatness!

My moment of reflection…

Happiness—Through Mercy

August 6
Luke 10:30-37

Christians are the only genuinely happy people on earth! In the beatitudes our Lord is laying the foundation for Christianity. Jesus said, "God blesses those who are merciful, for they will be shown mercy" (Matthew 5:7). Everyone believes in mercy and most persons would rate themselves as merciful. We give to the poor and spread mercy around freely. But mercy is not something to be dispensed at regular intervals; it is a God-given virtue and a quality of redemption.

When Jesus spoke these words, it was to a callous and pagan world that had little respect for human life. Mercy was never a characteristic of pagan life. In contrast, both Old and New Testaments make numerous references to mercy as a virtue and disposition of the soul. It is primarily a thing of inner life and a gift of God.

The Bible reminds Christians we are recipients of God's mercy. Blessed with God's mercy, believers will be merciful! Our Lord gave us a perfect example of mercy in the parable of the Good Samaritan who not only felt sorry for the victim, but made provision for the wounded traveler. That, says our Lord is mercy! Mercy is the love and life of Christ flowing through the believer!

If you show mercy, you "will be shown mercy!" We need mercy when we sin but also on the Day of Judgment when we stand before Christ to give an account of the deeds done in the flesh. Micah reminds us that the whole duty of man is "to love mercy and to walk humbly with your God" (Micah 6:8).

My moment of reflection…

Happiness—Through Purity

August 7
Philippians 4:1-8

"God blesses those whose hearts are pure, for they will see God" (Matthew 5:8) is one of the greatest statements in the Bible! These words seem ridiculous and nonsense to the man of the world who believes that "happiness" is found in doing whatever makes him feel good! But that philosophy claiming purity is out of date and is the sure road to destruction.

All Biblical writers demand purity of heart and personal holiness! James pleads with believers to "draw close to God...and purify their hearts" (James 4:8). The focus of the Gospel is on the heart because the heart is the fount out of which everything else comes. The heart is the seat of our troubles but we often blame environment, poverty, education and other factors. Jeremiah reminds us the "heart is desperately wicked." The heart must be cleansed before life can be cleansed. Man becomes pure when God takes control of his heart. Purity is a gift of God and totally provided by the grace of God.

The promise given to the pure in heart is "they will see God." Job tells us that he had heard about God but now "I have seen God with my own eyes. I take back everything I said and I sit in dust and ashes to show my repentance" (Job 42:5-6). Job suggests it is not a veil that hides us from God, but our own bulky shape. We block ourselves from God's view! The moment our ego collapses we see Jesus and enter into full knowledge and intimate fellowship with God. It begins when our hearts are pure!

My moment of reflection...

Happiness—Through Peace

August 8
Ephesians 4:17-32

The most sought after and pressing need of man is peace. For twenty centuries "peace" has been knocking at the door of men's hearts and still we have little peace. Jesus, recognizing peace and peacemakers were the great need of his day said, "God blesses those who work for peace, for they will be called the children of God" (Matthew 5:9). As followers of Christ, we live to please God—and that includes being a peacemaker.

The world longs for peace! With less than 300 years of peace in the last 4,000 years, it appears we have failed in attempts to secure peace. Peace is not a dream or removal of strife won at a conference table. Shalom or peace describes intimacy and fellowship with God and our fellow man. To find true and lasting peace in this world you need to find it in Jesus Christ.

Jesus brought peace to others through his death and resurrection and now challenges his followers to remove the causes of strife dividing humanity. Let's be peacemakers who build bridges of understanding and trust between brothers and above all, be peacemakers who reconcile men to God.

The promise given to peacemakers is they "shall be called the children of God." As sons of God we are to repeat what God has done. Once a year we celebrate the birthday of the greatest peacemaker of all, the Prince of Peace. As his last bequest to his disciples he gave them the gift of his own peace: "Peace I leave with you, my peace I give unto you!" Thank God for his gift of peace.

My moment of reflection…

Happiness—Through Persecution

August 9
Matthew 5:10-12

The New Testament is a handbook for the persecuted! It was written to give courage to those who were to undergo persecution. The message of the Gospel is to stand fast in your trials and endure hardness as a good soldier of Christ. Jesus was determined his followers would be trained for a life of spiritual fitness in the face of difficulties. Jesus said "God blesses those who are persecuted because they live for God, for the Kingdom of Heaven is theirs" (Matthew 5:10).

The world and the Christian faith are at war! A believer is a person of faith who seeks to live a holy life which is a condemnation of pagan life. People will always seek to eliminate that which condemns them. Jesus predicts persecution will mark every believer who manifests the graces of spiritual living as portrayed in the beatitudes. Being "persecuted for righteousness" means practicing righteousness; and persecution is blessed when a person is willing to live by faith and be like Jesus.

Jesus gave the persecuted this promise: "for the Kingdom of Heaven is theirs!" While living for Jesus will cause persecution, we will not be forsaken. Because persecution is a demonstration of loyalty and a roadway to larger usefulness, heaven is our gift for the trials and sufferings in life. Jesus closes this beatitude with these words: "Be happy about it! Be very glad! For a great reward awaits you in heaven…" (Matthew 5:12). In suffering and enduring trials here on earth because of righteous living, God is shaping us down here so we will be prepared for heaven! Stand fast, take heart and endure hardness!

My moment of reflection…

Salt of the Earth

August 10
Luke 14:25-35

After a night in prayer, Jesus chose his disciples and lectured them on discipleship. In graphic terms he described the influence of effective believers: "You are like salt for everyone on earth" (Matthew 5:13, CEV).

From ringside seats, the disciples watched fishermen dock their boats and crate their catch. They saw fishermen plunge hands into the salt barrel and throw a handful of salt into the crate. Then he put a layer of fish on the salt, then more salt and another layer of fish until the crate was full. The lesson was obvious: As fish need salt to keep them from rotting, this world needs the influence of Christians in a world of rot and sin! As salt, believers must preserve the good and purify that which is worthwhile.

While salt is a preservative and antiseptic, it is a wonderful flavoring agent. But Jesus issues a warning! If the salt loses its distinctive nature, it loses the preserving power and becomes dull and tasteless. Likewise, Christians through compromise with a contaminated world and through spiritual indifference can lose "saltiness!"

Frank Smith invented potato chips! Without salt on chips his business was very slow. But then he added salt and his business boomed to the point that he had to buy a farm to grow potatoes. Result: the potato chip business has spread all over the world! Without the "salty influence" of Christians, the Christian movement would have died years ago. By the witness of your life and happiness of your heart you can impact others by creating within them an appetite to know the Savior. Just be salt!

My moment of reflection...

Light of the World

August 11
Luke 11:29-36

The Bible opens with God declaring, "Let there be light and there was light" (Genesis 1:3). Centuries later when Jesus came into the world, he shocked everyone declaring, "I am the light of the world" (John 8:12). If that is shocking it is even more amazing to hear him tell the disciples "You are the light of the world" (Matthew 5:14).

The nature of light is amazing: it exposes darkness and serves as a guide warning of dangers. Darkness abounds and is symbolic of evil in the world and the ultimate cause of Christ's death. To combat darkness, Jesus chose his followers to be the life-changing agents in a society dominated by sin and darkness. No one else can take the place of the Christian!

When Jesus left, Christians were given the responsibility of presenting Jesus to the world. Paul challenged believers to shine as lights in the world (Philippians 2:15-16). Like a city on a hill, the Christian's influence cannot be hidden. But Jesus gives believers a warning: "Do not put your light under a bushel" (Matthew 5:15). As Christ-followers we are not fired up to fizzle but for the purpose of shining brightly, so those in darkness may see their good works. Good works are products of faith and glorifies our Father in heaven! Through our witness, God gives every believer the opportunity to glorify him.

Light makes no noise, sound no drums! Light just shines and causes others to see Christ in us. To shine is not optional. Our Lord's command is imperative: "You are the light of the world." So shine brightly today!

My moment of reflection…

Time Marches On

August 12
Acts 20:17-38

While we don't live in the past, it is interesting to look where we were and now where we are. Paul, toward the end of this missionary journey gave a challenge to his friends, whom he probably would not see again. He said: "Be strong with the Lord's mighty power" (Ephesians 6:10).

We are in a battle with the forces of evil! Satan is strong, wise and subtle and we cannot be ignorant of his strategy. As an angel of light, Satan seeks to blind minds to the truth of God's word—his weapons and battle plan are formidable. So Paul makes a strong appeal with his command "be strong in the Lord." This is not an elective—it is a command! We are no match for the devil; we can only overcome the enemy by availing ourselves of God's power. Never underestimate the power of the evil one. Jesus called him a thief who comes to "steal and kill and destroy" (John 10:10).

Leaving his friends, Paul knows they will experience savage attacks of the enemy. Apart from Christ Christians can accomplish nothing—we are like branches severed from the vine. On the other hand, in close fellowship with the Lord we can do whatever we must do. His power has been proven in creation and throughout history—and you know that he is able to do more than all we ask or imagine! So trust his mighty power for all your needs—today and always!

My moment of reflection...

Goodness

August 13
Romans 12:1-21

The apostle Paul had a battle: "When I want to do good I don't. And when I try not to do wrong, I do it anyway" (Romans 7:19). It is no easy task to be good and do good! Jesus commands us to "do good" to those who hate you and Paul reminds us not to get tired of doing what is good (Galatians 6:9).

Goodness is defined as generosity which is undeserved—to be generous! Goodness has to do with a quality of life and quality of relationships. Jesus came to help us be "good!" Goodness originates with God, not with man! The Bible says that Barnabas was a "good man" and "full of goodness." He had a great sense of God's loving care in his life which gave him the ability to be good, gracious and generous toward others—and he was!

Barnabas was good because he majored on looking for good in others. The goodness of his heart searched for that which was potentially good in others. He was a cheerleader! In a time of great need and suffering, he sold a piece of property and gave the money to those who were in need. His act of generosity brought joy into the hearts of others and as such became known as the "Son of Encouragement!" The beauty of his life—his kindness and generosity attracted many to Jesus Christ. By your goodness, you can be a "cheerleader" to someone who needs a "lift" today!

My moment of reflection…

A Word from the Lord

August 14
Jeremiah 37:11-21

Jeremiah had spoken very clearly about trusting in foreign powers—making alliances with hostile nations. After his arrest, he was released and asked a question by King Zedekiah, a weak vacillating unbeliever: "Jeremiah is there any word from the Lord?" Jeremiah told the king that they would be delivered into captivity!

God still speaks: he lives… he's alive…he rules! The God Isaiah saw centuries ago is still "sitting on a throne, high and lifted up" and he still reigns in our world (Isaiah 6). My favorite Christmas song has a powerful phrase: "He rules the world with truth and grace!" He may not rule the world the way we want him to, but he is on the throne. Some theological mavericks suggested that "God is dead." Amid all their confusion, there is one who is not confused. Is there any word from the Lord? There is: "the Lord God omnipotent reigns" (Revelation 19:6).

In Jeremiah's day, people broke God's laws and were carried into captivity. But in spite of captivity and judgment, there was the promise of a remnant! If you will repent, your city shall not be burned and you will live; if not, you will be destroyed! We still have a clear word from God: "You can't ignore 'me' and get away with it. You will always reap what you sow" (Galatians 6:7). It's clear: "For the Lord our God, the Almighty reigns" (Revelation 19:6). That's God's word for today!

My moment of reflection…

Promise of the Ages

August 15
John 14:1-6

Jesus made numerous promises—we could really call him the "Promise Maker!" Perhaps the most anticipated promise that Jesus made was his promise to return to earth: "I am going to prepare a place for you…When everything is ready, I will come and get you, so that you will always be with me where I am" (John 14:2-3).

After his death and resurrection, Jesus told his disciples that "he would return!" As you study his parables, you will note his promised return would be sudden, unexpected like a thief! Without attempting to be speculative, the manner of his coming will be personal, unexpected and visible. Because of the unannounced date, Christians should live each day as if the Lord would return that day! Believing that the Lord will return challenges God's people to live in such a way that they will not be ashamed when he comes.

On March 11, 1942 President Franklin Roosevelt ordered General Douglas MacArthur's departure to Australia. MacArthur said to the people on the Japanese occupied islands, "I shall return." In 1944 the general walked on the Philippine Island of Leyte and announced, "I have returned!" In about AD 33 our Lord said, "I will come again!" Some day he will step out of heaven to earth and say, "I have returned." Not only do we remember the many promises he made—He is the Promise Keeper! The promise of the ages is a wonderful gift—"I will return!"

My moment of reflection…

Think

August 16
Joshua 1:1-9

A little girl was sitting under a tree for quite some time. Her mother said, "Honey, what are you doing?" "Oh Mommy, I was just having a good think!" Do you realize over 10,000 thoughts pass in and out of our minds every day? Thoughts like, "What's for dinner tonight?" "Did Jack really mean what he said?" "Where are those bills I'm supposed to pay?" And so it goes. We not only think about today but for the future as well. In this computer brain is an inventory of everything from A to Z!

Americans spend lot of time in meditation—twice a day, fold your hands, close your eyes and drift off is very appealing for many people. God clearly commanded the process of meditation. To Joshua God said, "Study this Book of the Law continually. Meditate on it day and night so you may be sure to obey all that is written in it" (Joshua 1:8). Most believers understand we are to hear, read, study and memorize the Word. But we are also commanded to "meditate" upon the Word!

Want to start? Here's how! Take a passage of scripture and read it carefully. Ask the Spirit to impress a thought on which you meditate during the day. If you awaken at night, let your mind rest on that thought—share the thought with a friend! "O how I love your law! I think about it all day long" (Psalm 119:97).

My moment of reflection…

Undisciplined Living

August 17
Galatians 6:1-10

Our beloved United States was founded at a time when "rugged individualism" was a highly prized quality by our pioneer fathers. This spirit of individualism was necessary for meeting the challenges of life out on the prairie. Now several centuries later, many of our nation's citizens have opted out for "spineless conformity," attempting to escape life's challenges by escaping to alcoholism, drug addiction or other forms of pleasure seeking activities. Their philosophy may stress individualism in the sense of everyone is "doing his own thing" but moral and spiritual brakes are off—and disaster is in sight!

Billionaire Howard Hughes was a man of mystery during his later years. After he died, it was reported he suffered from various diseases, including decayed teeth and malnutrition. Illness is no respecter of persons but it is amazing that a fabulously wealthy man lacked proper dental care and basic nutrition! Failing to take care of our physical needs will lead to suffering and death. But the same principle applies in the spiritual realm!

We are reaping the tragic results of an undisciplined, permissive philosophy. The consequences of undisciplined living abound—marriage and family life is crumbling, crime is increasing, laziness rampant and spirituality is no longer a priority. What's the answer to our dilemma? One thing is sure: You reap exactly what you sow! Choosing to reject God and his revealed truth will guarantee harsh consequences. On the other hand, a spiritually disciplined life will bring joy and satisfaction—now and forever!

My moment of reflection…

Farming—Divine Style

August 18
Mark 4:1-20

Jesus told a story about a fella who threw seed on different kinds of soil! Some seed fell on good soil, other seed fell on thorny ground, stony ground and on hard ground. This parable is a profound story about life—real life. It's a picture of four responses people have toward spiritual things!

The seed is the Word, the truth of the Bible. The different soils represent people of all ages, interests and backgrounds who respond to spiritual truth. Some listen and reject; others hear, seem to enjoy it but soon spin off when the going gets rough; others get sidetracked as their growth is throttled by life's "thorns." But there are those who hear, believe, grow and become healthy plants in God's field.

Some reject and "bail" when things get tough! Jesus warns about the thorns, which he said are "the cares of this life, wealth and nice things." Thorns are dictators; they know nothing of a life of freedom and victory. Their long, sharp points keep annoying us. They demand first place as they siphon every ounce of interest in spiritual things and reduce one to an ineffective pigmy!

Like farming, spirituality is risky because God calls us to abandon our entire life to God by faith. The exciting news is this: The good soil represents "those who hear and accept God's message and produce a huge harvest—thirty, sixty, or even a hundred times as much as had been planted" (Mark 4:20). Now that's "farming—divine style!"

My moment of reflection…

Signboards

August 19
2 Corinthians 3:1-6

At country crossroads there is usually a tall post with a signboard telling people where the road leads and how far it is to the nearest town. Often strangers driving through the country don't know which way to turn...there is no one to give them personal directions. So they look for the signboard...and there it is. They follow the direction given and soon reach their destination.

Sometimes the signs are wrong! One day a man wanted to go to a town called "Eureka." He saw the signboard which pointed south and said "Eureka seven miles!" So the traveler started off in that direction...but after many miles had the feeling he was on the wrong road. So he stopped at a farmstead to inquire and was told that "Eureka" was miles back the way he had come. The sign he had followed was pointed in the wrong direction! He found out that a recent storm blew the sign down and careless workmen put it up pointing in the wrong direction.

Long ago the apostle Paul said, "Your lives are a letter written in our hearts and everyone can read it" (2 Corinthians 3:2). This is what Paul meant: We are like signboards...people are looking to us for directions as to how to live their lives. If we point the right way, they will go that way too! What a responsibility! Friend, your life might be the only Bible another person may read!

My moment of reflection...

His Workmanship

August 20
Ephesians 1:15-23

The Bible is filled with incidents showing the omnipotence of God and his greatness. But what would you list as the three greatest acts God performed to display His power? Flinging the world into space? The incarnation—God becoming flesh? Walking on water? Stilling the storm? Healing the sick?

Paul taught the Ephesians there are three great demonstrations of God's power in the world: Resurrection of Christ from the dead, seating Christ at the place of honor and putting all things under his feet (Ephesians 2:20-21). Then Paul tells us that God performs the same three great acts in us as He did in Christ, "so God can always point to us as examples of the incredible wealth of his favor and kindness toward us, as shown in all he has done for us through Christ Jesus" (Ephesians 2:7).

Paul quickly adds that this great work of Christ makes us "his workmanship" to the world around us, that they might see in our good works the effect of Christ working in us. Remember the last time you shopped for a new car? The salesperson wanted to show it off...he had it cleaned and highly polished and finely tuned. Then he invited you to put it to the test because he was confident it would stand up under any test! God does his powerful and creative work in our lives so he can show us off as his Workmanship—his masterpiece to the world!

My moment of reflection...

Self-Centered Living

August 21
Philippians 2:12-18

I read a very provocative statement: "Too many people conduct their lives on the cafeteria plan—self-service only!" Most of us can remember times when our interests and desires had priority over Godly interests and desires. In a sense, we become the people Paul was speaking about when he said, "Others care only for themselves and not for what matters to Jesus Christ" (Philippians 2:21). It's clear we must put the brakes on our desires and interests! That's easy to say—but so hard to do!

The only way to slow-down and hopefully stop those self-centered desires is to spend time at the cross. In reflecting about the death of Christ Paul teaches that Jesus died for all so we should not live unto ourselves, but unto him who died and rose again. When Christ died on the cross, he not only paid our penalty for sin but he died to "put to death" our selfish style of living.

A very untidy little girl saw a statue of a beautiful Greek slave girl. Her desire was "to be like" that statue! She washed her face and hands, combed her hair and washed her dress. She became a living image of the statue. If we are going to live the kind of life God expects, we must compare ourselves to the One who died on the cross so that we no longer live unto ourselves but unto him who died for us. The "cafeteria plan" is not an option for any serious believer!

My moment of reflection…

No More Premiums

August 22
John 3:1-17

Some people likened our current "recession" to the great depression of the 30's. But the interesting thing is as soon as prosperity followed those hard days, most people forgot about it. An old timid lady walked into a Minneapolis Insurance office. Taking an old life-insurance policy from her purse she explained she was unable to meet the current premium. After a quick investigation, the agent recognized the policy was very valuable and that it was unwise to stop paying the premiums. She told the agent that the policy belonged to her husband who died three years ago.

They discovered the old lady was telling the truth. What she didn't understand was that she was the beneficiary at his death. The insurance company was obligated to refund the overpaid premiums plus the full amount for which the husband had insured his life. The money due was sufficient to take care of the lady for the rest of her life!

The greatest life insurance policy of all time came due the day Jesus died on the cross! The tragedy is that millions of people continue trying to make payments while all they need to do is accept the immeasurable gift that has already been paid. To become a beneficiary, all we need to do is acknowledge him as the One who died and rose again that we might have forgiveness. Yes, the "premium has been paid"—once and for all. There are no more premiums to pay!

My moment of reflection...

Making a Difference

August 23
Galatians 5:22-23

I know you want to make a difference! There was an old man who carried a can of oil with him everywhere he went. If there was a door that squeaked he poured a little oil on the hinges. If there was a gate hard to open, he oiled the latch. He passed through life lubricating the hard places and making it easier for those who came after him. People called him eccentric and odd—but the old man went on, refilling his can when it was empty and oiling every hard place. He didn't wait until he found a creaky door or a rusty hinge and then go home to get his oil can…he carried it with him!

There are many lives that creak and grate harshly as they live day by day. Nothing seems to go right for them. They need lubricating with the oil of kindness, gentleness or thoughtfulness.

Don't forget to carry your oil can with you! Be ready with the oil helpfulness—it may change someone's day. Someone needs the oil of good cheer and someone is about to run out of courage. Our lives touch others but once and then maybe our ways diverge, never to meet again. Carry your little can of oil! The oil of kindness has worn the sharp, hard edges off of many a hardened life and left it pliable, ready for the redeeming grace of God. So my friend, carry your oil can and spill some today!

My moment of reflection…

Self-Control

August 24
Galatians 5:16-26

From the dawn of human history man sought to make laws to control selfish behavior. But external laws have not controlled his evil inclinations. Solomon likened an undisciplined spirit to a city in a state of collapse: "A person without self-control is as defenseless as a city with broken-down walls" (Proverbs 25:28). Saint Paul urged self-control: "All athletes practice strict self-control" (1 Corinthians 9:25).

Our lives are like rivers—either useful with their energies or destructive with their forces! It all depends on how water is channeled. Meaningful lives can only come from temperate hearts which have passions channeled for good. The key to successful living is correct channeling and proper control. Strong self-discipline—to live by the rules—is critical to self-control. Mastery of self always adds dignity and poise to one's character.

Ultimately, self-control is a work of the Holy Spirit! Self-control is inward, voluntary but exceedingly difficult; it is not a permanent achievement but a "way of life" practiced moment by moment under the guidance of the Holy Spirit. God wants to set us free from the control of destructive forces, power, habits and appetites. Christ came to set us free from this self-destruction. Self-control will only become a reality when we are filled and walk in the Spirit. Without the Holy Spirit, we're like broken-down walls, becoming prey to every kind of enemy. The only way to rise above our natures is the Power of the Holy Spirit!

My moment of reflection...

Jesus—All-sufficient

August 25
Colossians 1:1-23

All of you have put together a puzzle of some kind! It takes time, energy and effort to complete a puzzle; but it's worth it when you finally slip in that "last" piece and the puzzle is complete. What a relief and fulfillment—even joy! But we all know that without that last "key" piece the puzzle is incomplete!

Jesus Christ is the "key piece" to the completion and operation of God's eternal program. Every-thing hinges on him! If he is left out of the picture, it remains a jumble of unrelated pieces. But when he is given his proper place in God's program—be it in creation or revelation—the picture is complete!

When Franklin D. Roosevelt was campaigning for his fourth term as President, campaign orators described him as the "indispensable man," the only one who could carry the nation to a successful conclusion of World War II. The strategy succeeded and FDR was reelected for an unprecedented fourth term. However, death soon exploded the "indispensable man" concept!

The idea of an "indispensable man" is an illusion! Seldom is one man so important in an organization that its success or failure depends solely on him. However, there is one exception: Jesus Christ is the only all-sufficient one and is supreme over all creation. Thank God for the "indispensable man" who calls us his friends, brought us "into the very presence of God" and declared us holy and blameless! Now that's an "indispensable man!"

My moment of reflection...

Buried Talent

August 26
Matthew 25:14-30

Faithful or unfaithful—all of us are stewards and will be all of our lives! We are stewards of our years, the time God has given us. We are stewards of our bodies; we must care for them and use them wisely. We are stewards of all we possess; our possessions belong to God and must be used for his glory. We are stewards of our minds, our abilities and our skills.

Jesus told a story: A man went on a journey and entrusted his possessions to his servants, each according to their ability to invest until he returned. As stewards all that we have is a gift from God; the gift of these possessions is not chance or choice, but according to divine planning! Our skills and talents and opportunities vary from person to person; each must be faithful to what we have been given!

Finally, "their master returned from his trip and called them to give an account of how they had used his money" (Matthew 25:19). There will be an accounting! Our success is not dependent on equality but on individuality; success is measured in terms of faithfulness. The Lord's commendation was not based on brilliance or giftedness of the servants—only faithfulness. In the final analysis on the "day of reckoning" the only words that are important are: "Well done, my good and faithful servant!" Whatever talent you possess, use it today for his glory—don't hide it!

My moment of reflection...

Trophies of Grace

August 27
1 Corinthians 15:1-11

God interrupted Paul's career of persecution with an offer of grace and forgiveness. Paul said "yes" to that offer and never forgot it! Throughout his writings Paul responded with an attitude of gratitude and surrender—giving God the praise and credit for the miracle that changed his life.

John Newton felt deeply about the wonder of God's grace. After his conversion in the early 1700's from a life of slave trading and debauchery, Newton became a great preacher and song writer. Crowds came to hear him preach with power and authority—to see a trophy of God's grace!

John Newton was a trophy of God's grace—but so was Paul. God's grace saved him, disciplined his mind, enriched his life, empowered his ministry and sustained him to the end. He could truthfully say "I am what I am because of the grace of God!" But every Christian can say the same thing—I'm saved, disciplined, enriched, empowered and sustained by God's grace.

Two years before Newton's death when his sight was so dim he no longer could read, a friend joined him for breakfast. Later they read "by the grace of God I am what I am," Newton said, "I am not what I ought to be...not what I wish to be...not what I hope to be; but by the grace of God, I am not what I was once!" God's grace finds "sinners" but leaves "saints"—trophies of his grace!

My moment of reflection...

Victory

August 28
John 19:28-37

In the early days of our country one of the great achievements was laying the tracks for the transcontinental railroad. Finally it happened: In 1869 the East and West were united after great sacrifice. A ceremony was held on the border of Colorado and New Mexico. The governors drove the final spike of gold symbolizing the completion of the railroad, uniting East and West. Crowds cheered and the news spread. There was a simple message sent via telegraph: "It is finished!"

Two thousand years ago on the border between heaven and hell, spikes were driven into the hands and feet of Jesus. When these men had done their evil work, the word was shouted, "It is finished!" At that moment, heaven and earth were joined as God reconciled the world unto himself (2 Corinthians 5:19).

Those who heard Jesus say "It is finished" heard different things! For the soldiers, it was the end of a day's work; for Mary it meant sorrow and grief; to Pilate it meant the threat to his authority was over; to his enemies it meant that this imposter was dead; and to his friends, it meant the end of their hopes! To the Father "It is finished" meant that love triumphed over sin, that life triumphed over death and Jesus has triumphed over Satan. For believers today, it means there is a King who reigns and rules the universe—and most of all, "It is finished" shouts victory for every Christian!

My moment of reflection...

Redemptive Praise

August 29
Psalm 107:1-32

God in his providence watches over his children and his ear is ever open to their cry of distress. God continuously rescued Israel from their numerous bondages—it seems like Israel was always in trouble! He freed them from Egyptian slavery and led them to the land of Canaan. He liberated them from the captivity of the Babylonians. And in the end, God sent Jesus to rescue the entire human race from bondage!

In this Psalm we have four vivid pictures of people needing help: There is the picture of a lost traveler—they were wondering in the wilderness, hungry and thirsty. They couldn't find their way; they were lost! Some were captives; they lived in darkness and were in misery and chains. Others were sick and in their need, they cried out to the Lord. The final portrait is one of sailors in a storm. Death was imminent, they were at their wits end and they found themselves face to face with death! They had only "one" alternative: "Turn to the Lord!"

These people—lost traveler, captives, sick and sailors—all were in bondage; yet all turned to the Lord and found deliverance from their bondage. The psalmist exhorts all of us to render thanks to God for his goodness. It is just not enough to "feel" grateful; we must "say so!" Divine mercies call for human acknowledgment. The redeemed are commanded to rejoice and be glad. Today, if the Lord has redeemed you, then "speak out!" (Psalm 107:2).

My moment of reflection…

Extraordinary Living

August 30
Isaiah 40:28-31

Isaiah paints a picture of a world in a titanic struggle! World forces battle for supremacy. There is political unrest, deplorable social conditions, corrupt government and abuses everywhere. In a religious sense, superstition and low ethical standards had replaced the true worship of Jehovah. The moral fiber was gone! Sound familiar?

Isaiah had deep convictions, clear vision, courage and unusual power in driving home truth. He spent his life trying to get Israel to become acquainted with God! In that setting this preacher of social righteousness says to Israel: "But those who wait on the Lord will find new strength. They will fly high on wings like eagles. They will run and not grow weary. They will walk and not faint" (Isaiah 40:31). Isaiah was trying to help Israel understand that God was acquainted with their misery, that he never grows weak and he sustains the weary. He can be trusted! Why not wait on him?

This extra-ordinary living and life-style is not only for Israel; it is for men and women of every age. Isaiah compares it to the eagle, king of the birds. He pleads: If you will yield your life to God, surrender your will to his, you will renew your strength—and that is extra-ordinary living. The same promise that Jehovah God gave to the children of Israel in the wilderness he gives to us today—"I brought you to myself and carried you on eagle's wings" (Exodus 19:4). Now that's "extra-ordinary living!"

My moment of reflection…

Problems or Possibilities

August 31
Numbers 13:25-33

An advertising brochure of a well-known amusement park said: "is the way you'd like the rest of the world to be all the time...sparkling clean...adventurous—yet safe and comfortable...alive with people of all ages enjoying a good time...full of exciting things to do." But that isn't the real world—it's a make-believe world! Much of life makes hard demands on us. There are times we really don't know what to do—is the issue ahead a problem or possibility?

Twelve spies were given the responsibility of spying out the Promised Land—was it a possibility or a problem? Joshua and Caleb saw the new challenge as an opportunity but the other ten saw the Promised Land as a problem—full of giants! As you face life, you will be faced with two alternatives: problems or possibilities!

We are a "problem-conscious" people! While we cannot ignore problems, we must not over-emphasize them to the point we are paralyzed, filled with fear and end up doing nothing or at worst, retreating! But if we are the people God intended us to be, we must have the vision to see beyond the problem to the possibilities. To see the possibilities we must have a sense of mission, clear vision and dependency on God!

Life presents each of us with problems and possibilities! We can look at the problems and be defeated—or see the possibilities and be victorious! It all depends on your interpretation and "who" is in control!

My moment of reflection...

Faithfulness

September 1
Matthew 25:14-30

Centuries ago King Solomon declared, "Many will say they are loyal friends, but who can find one who is really faithful?" (Proverbs 20:6) Faithfulness has always been a great trait of human character and is desperately needed today. Implied in faithfulness are consistency, loyalty, dependability and trustworthiness. Genuine faith is not only something we believe but something we behave!

One of the favorite expressions of the nature of God is faithfulness! Jeremiah affirmed the reliability of the God of Israel in his statement, "Great is thy faithfulness" (Lamentations 3:23). The testimony of history is that God is solid as marble, more reliable and dependable than the Rock of Gibraltar. Jesus becomes the model and pattern of faithfulness for every believer.

Superior talent or unusual cleverness is not the norm for believers! Faithfulness is demanded: "It is required in stewards that a man be found faithful" (1 Corinthians 4:1-2, KJV). Our world is characterized by a general lack of faithfulness. A societal problem in our culture is that people give the appearance of faithfulness but really are not—they are phony, counterfeit! Our faithfulness must not be occasional or peripheral; it must be exercised out of love!

In the Parable of the Talents only two of the servants were found faithful and entered into the joy of the Lord and were given greater responsibility. Faithfulness is an indispensable mark of every Christian—without it our witness is hypocritical. God help us to behave what we believe today. Be faithful always!

My moment of reflection…

Pleasing God

September 2
Genesis 5:21-31

Some men "tower" above other men in their generation! I suppose there are a number of characteristics that account for that fact. Towering above men in his generation and impressing multitudes in the centuries which followed was Enoch—a remarkable man of faith whose impressive and fascinating testimony has been forever preserved in history.

The Bible says, "When Enoch was 65 years old, his son Methuselah was born...Enoch lived another 300 years in close fellowship with God...Enoch live 365 years in all. He enjoyed a close relationship with God throughout his life" (Genesis 5:21-23). In Hebrews we are told that Enoch "was approved as pleasing to God...it is impossible to please God without faith" (Hebrews 11:5-6).

Enoch did not become great because of his profound scholarship, successful statesmanship, military renown or even philanthropic achievements, but because "he walked with God" and thereby "pleased God." The highest praise that can be bestowed on man is "that he pleased God." For 300 years Enoch walked with God, enjoying the friendship and companionship of God. Because Enoch walked in compliance with God's will and found great delight in God's way, God "took him" to live with him in glory!

Any and every true child of God can do just what Enoch did—walk with God and please him! Make every effort to walk with him today, cost what it may; for there is no greater satisfaction in life than in knowing that we have pleased God!

My moment of reflection...

Forgetfulness

September 3
Philippians 3:7-14

People often complain about their inability to remember—especially names! Those who study the mind tell us that nothing is ever completely forgotten. Things that we have done, said or heard are stored away in the computer of our unconsciousness. Sometimes without any deliberate effort something will provoke the computer to lift into our conscious thought that which happened decades ago. Amazing!

Memory is one of the most valuable faculties that we possess—memory can be a great blessing and a real curse! We need to remember the goodness and faithfulness of God, the kindnesses of others and the truths that make life worth living. But there is an evil side to the coin of memory. Memory can be a devil to defeat! As Christians, it would be wise and profitable for us to forget our past successes, failures and grievances. If you major on your handicaps and allow fear to control the future, you will undoubtedly cloud your memory and negate potential blessings and victories of the future.

The way to forgetfulness is by the pathway of forgiveness! To forgive means to deliberately refuse to retaliate and at the same time restore warm, loving feelings. We must forgive ourselves and others and by so doing, we will have made greater progress toward forgetting things that would hinder and drag us down as we try to walk into an unknown tomorrow with God. Remembering to forget the evil side of memory will make tomorrow a beautiful day!

My moment of reflection…

Dead-end Streets

September 4
Genesis 22:1-19

Most of us have had the "dead-end" street experience! Sometimes it happens because we have not paid attention to the signs or there was no sign. Generally we get on "dead-end" streets because of ignorance or lack of attention! Believers are objects of God's loving care. Upon entrance into the heavenly family, God begins to work in us. We are like shapeless lumps of clay in his hands. With precise movements of a master potter, God molds and fashions until we have been formed into the image of God's dear son!

However, there are times when testing experiences which God permits or initiates appear to us as "dead-end" streets. Such was the case with Abraham and Sarah. Unable to have children, the Lord assured Abraham through his seed all the nations of the earth would be blessed—and the Messiah would come from his genealogical line. Now old and beyond child-bearing years, the Lord worked a miracle—Isaac was born! Then God asked the unthinkable: "Offer your son as a burnt offering!" In Abraham's mind, this looks like a "dead-end" street!

It is not uncommon for a believer to find he is trudging along what appears to be a "dead-end" street—a dreary road of trial and heartache! But then we see God's provision and a happy ending to the trial. God miraculously provides—"a ram in the thicket!" Even on "dead-end" streets God provides! His name is "Jehovah-jireh" which means, "the Lord will provide..." and he has!

My moment of reflection...

Walk Worthily

September 5
Ephesians 4:1-16

It is a privilege to be a Christian—at least that's how Paul viewed Christianity! A little boy asked a woman who sat by a swimming pool, "Do you believe in God?" The woman was stunned, but she replied, "Of course I believe in God." Upon hearing this answer the boy said, "Good, then you can keep my money and my watch while I go swimming!" You see, this little boy felt that belief and behavior belong together—and he was right!

Paul taught that the Christian is a very privileged person—our privileges include the Gospel and a personal relationship with Jesus Christ. Because we have privileges, we have responsibilities; it's always been that way! Abraham was instructed by God to walk before the Lord and "be perfect" (Genesis 17:1). Paul gave Christians this advice: "The way you live will always honor and please the Lord, and you will continually do good, kind things for others" (Colossians 1:10).

You see, the privilege of being Christian carries a heavy responsibility: "To walk worthily!" Believers should live lives consistent and in harmony with God's intention. Our behavior should be evident by our humility, gentleness, patience and love. When those virtues are present in our walk, our behavior confirms our belief! I wonder if some little boy would pick you out and say, "Mister, would you hold my money while I go swimming?" Make every effort today to "walk worthily" of your high calling!

My moment of reflection...

Revival

September 6
2 Chronicles 7:11-22

In Revelation the Son of Man is walking among the churches—he is broken as to what he sees! He utters a strong rebuke: "I know your works—be watchful and strengthen the things that remain, which are ready to die…" Looking at the churches the Lord makes these charges: "You have lost your first love…you are rich…you are worshipping idols…there is complacency…you are lukewarm" (Revelation 2-3). In each case the Lord calls for repentance—for an awakening, for revival!

The psalmist prays for revival: "Restore to me again the joy of your salvation, and make me willing to obey you" (Psalm 51:12). Habakkuk prayed for revival: "I have heard all about you, Lord, and I am filled with awe by the amazing things you have done. In this time of our deep need, begin again to help us, as you did in years gone by" (Habakkuk 3:2).

Looking at our world today and especially at the church, there is simply no question as to whether or not we need revival. Any time when iniquity abounds, when the presence of God is overlooked, when material things are most important, when there is little separation, that is the time for renewal and revival! God has not changed—his promises are still true! "If my people…will humble themselves and pray and seek my face and turn from their wicked ways, I will hear from heaven and will forgive their sins and heal their land" (2 Chronicles 7:14).

My moment of reflection…

Work

September 7
Proverbs 6:1-11

Kemmons Wilson, founder of Holiday Inns never graduated from high school. But in spite of the fact at Mr. Wilson didn't get a diploma, he was asked back to give the commencement address. He began his talk by saying, "I don't know why I'm here. I never got a degree and I've only worked half-days my entire life. I guess my advice to you is to do the same. Work half-days every day…and it doesn't matter which half—the first twelve hours or the second twelve hours!"

The Bible says, "Take a lesson from the ants, you lazy bones. Learn from their ways and be wise!" (Proverbs 6:6) Why? Because ants are industrious, providing for the future. God places a high value on work and faithful workers!

In spite of the lazy streak in most of us, work is not a dirty word! Work is essential in God's economy and it is integral to our human role in creation. God is a worker and we are never more Godly than when we are working. Man was made for work; he was put in the garden to "till and keep the garden." Before humanity botched creation with disobedience we had the responsibility of working at our daily task—not just for ourselves but working for others and for God's glory! John Kennedy said "our work is to make God's work truly our own!" Whatever ones calling, work heartily as for the Lord! Thank God for work and faithful workers!

My moment of reflection…

Word of the Cross

September 8
1 Corinthians 1:18-25

On the horizons of history, there are many mountain peaks that remind us of special events! Noah and his family landed on Mt. Ararat after the flood. Mt. Moriah was where Abraham offered his son Isaac as a sacrifice. God's people received the Law at Mt. Sinai and Jesus ascended into heaven from Mount of Olives! But towering above every mountain is Mount Calvary where Jesus was crucified. No mountain towers so high in its influence over the hearts and minds of men as Mt. Calvary.

Paul told the Corinthians the message of the cross is foolishness to those who are on the road to destruction but to those who are saved, it is "the very power of God" (1 Corinthians 1:18). The Gospel is essentially the story of the cross and God's word to man—a story that has never lost its power! The cross is God's supreme declaration of man's guilt and helplessness but at the same time, an incredible picture of God's justice and love.

A little boy was lost in the London fog. A policeman sought to assist him: "Is there any familiar building or monument that is near your home?" A light came over the boy's face as he said, "If you take me to the 'Cross' I think I can find my way home from there!" The cross continues to guide all those who are lost—it is still the power of God! Thank God for the cross!

My moment of reflection...

Personal Worship

September 9
Psalm 15:1-5

The Bible says that one day "at the name of Jesus every knee will bow...and every tongue will confess that Jesus Christ is Lord, to the glory of God the Father" (Philippians 2:10-11). What we are doing now here on earth ought to be a time of preparation for what we will do continuously in glory. Repeatedly in the book of Psalms, we are invited to give thanks and worship the Lord.

We live in a very unholy and profane age where little reverence is given to God! This does not hurt God because he is self-existent and has no need for our worship. But it is our loss to neglect worshipping God. If our hearts and spirits are as they should be, then worship will be the life-long exercise of our lives, resulting in hearts more pure and lives more worthy.

Worship is not the execution of a set of mechanical motions or reading of ready-made prayers or the chanting of litanies or the singing of traditional tunes. These may all be done without a scrap of worship in them as is frequently the case. Worship must never be haphazard and careless. Worship is the complete surrender and submission of oneself to God—the awakening of our conscience by his holiness. Calling his own soul on the carpet, David says, "Praise the Lord, I tell myself; with my whole heart, I will praise his Holy name" (Psalm 103:1). May it ever be so!

My moment of reflection...

The Master Designer

September 10
Psalm 139:1-24

The Bible leaves no question as to your value in the sight of God! After speaking about God's omnipresence and omniscience, David talks about man, God's crowning creation: "You made all the delicate, inner parts of my body...thank you for making me so wonderfully complex. Your workmanship is marvelous" (Psalm 139:13-14). Paul says essentially the same thing: "For we are God's masterpiece...so that we can do the good things he planned for us long ago" (Ephesians 2:10).

The whole world is a testimony to the "Master Designer." In an olive wood factory in Israel, I was shown piles of olive wood curing in the sun—some for five years! Then with an imaginative mind and skillful hands, woodworkers made such attractive products. God is like that—he takes a human being, battered and scarred with sin and he makes a beautiful life! Designed with perfection, we chose to depart from the design of God.

With an impossible product to work with—dead, disobedient, depraved, doomed—the Master Designer begins his work to make his masterpiece! It happens because of his grace and by his power. Now he wants to "show off" his product created to "do good things he planned for us to do!" God made us for great things! If you want to see some of God's great work—look at a believer! See what he was and now what he is—only God could do a work like that! God alone is the Master Designer!

My moment of reflection...

In God We Trust

September 11
Psalm 46

God has richly blessed our wonderful country but we often take for granted the many freedoms we enjoy daily. But on that fateful day of September 11, 2001, we came face to face with terrorism as it destroyed the Twin Towers in New York City. Our nation will never be the same; we were changed in the face of such a horrific act of violence that brought pain, death and destruction to so many. We may never understand the depth of chaos and pain that followed in many people's lives that day.

The events of September 11 remind us that as Americans we are vulnerable and not invincible as we thought we were. No matter how superior our military, our system of government or way of life—we are no longer isolated from evil acts of destruction. When suffering, pain and sin surround us we get discouraged and overwhelmed. But God is in control even when all else is in chaos! Our nation's motto, "In God we trust" has always been the roadmap for healing, peace and restoration in our lives—and still is!

Whatever happened on this day or whatever will happen tomorrow, we can have confidence in God because "he is our refuge and strength!" Nothing escapes his watchful eye; just as his eye is on the sparrow, so he watches over us and becomes our refuge in times of storm. When "my heart is overwhelmed, lead me to the towering rock of safety, for you are my safe refuge, a fortress where my enemies cannot reach me" (Psalm 61:2-3).

My moment of reflection…

Making the Difference

September 12
Ephesians 2:11-22

What do you say to a divided, troubled world? What do you say to nations plagued with war and poverty? What do you say to people in Syria, Afghanistan or Ukraine? What hope can we really offer these people?

In 1938 the British Prime Minister Chamberlain said, "Peace in our time! Peace with honor!" Yet one year later, Hitler invaded Poland and the great peace mission had failed…in fact, most peace missions fail. Between 1500 Bc and 850 Bc there were over 7,500 "covenants" agreed upon by various nations with the hope of bringing peace; but no "covenant" lasted longer than two years. The only "covenant" that has lasted is the one made by God, sealed with the blood of Jesus Christ. Without Christ, people are separated and alienated; they are outsiders. But because of the work of Jesus, outsiders become insiders and strangers become citizens of the Kingdom: "You are no longer strangers and foreigners…you are members of God family…and the cornerstone is Christ Jesus" (Ephesians 2:19-20).

A man sought membership in a hunting club. The members did not respect him because he failed to obey the rules of sportsmanship. One outstanding community leader who was a member of the club interceded on his behalf. He promised the club that he would take full responsibility for the applicant. The man was admitted on the character and strength of another man! Jesus does make a difference—what a privilege to be part of God's eternal program!

My moment of reflection…

Slothfulness

September 13
2 Thessalonians 3:6-10

One of the great problems of our culture is laziness—slothfulness! We use many words to describe the attitude of slothfulness: idleness, apathy, indifference, goofing off, procrastination, laziness. The sloth is a lethargic animal with course hair; it builds no nest, sleeps eighteen hours a day and wakes very slowly. The sloth is so inactive that green algae grow in its hair. It has low intelligence and travels very slowly!

Slothfulness permeates everything these days: schoolwork, the work-place, home, friendships and Christianity. The only area immune from slothfulness is our leisure! Laziness is soundly condemned in the Bible: "The desires of lazy people will be their ruin, for their hands refuse to work" (Proverbs 21:25). Paul says, "Whoever does not work should not eat" (2 Thessalonians 2:10). Jews glorified work and as a trained Rabbi, Paul worked hard!

God does not intend for a person to be idle but to labor! Solomon says the ant has no commander, overseer or ruler but still knows to work. It works hard in summer in order to enjoy the fruits of its labor in winter (Proverbs 6). Every Christian should do his best at all times. We should labor as though God were our employer—to do less is wrong! Laziness is a neglect of duty and a violation of Christian living. Christians should be better workmen than anyone else! "Work with enthusiasm, as though you were working for the Lord" (Ephesians 6:7).

My moment of reflection…

Dress the Part

September 14
Colossians 3:1-11

There are a lot of professions that can be identified by the kind of uniform or clothes a person wears. It isn't hard to detect a soldier, bus driver, baseball player, policeman or postman—in each of these professions the worker "dresses" the part…they must "look the part!" People dress according to their role in life.

If you are a Christian you must "dress the part." A new man should wear new clothes—spiritual garb. When you become a believer there are some clothes that go along with that new image. Believers must clothe themselves with new garments: garments of mercy, kindness, humility, gentleness and patience. We often read stories about people who are very wealthy but dress like bums. Some Christians hang on to the old garments. But when we give our hearts to Christ, he redeems us; the old man died and you were born again a new man. And the new man doesn't want to wear the old man's clothes—that's the idea. Not old clothes but the new robe!

Let's understand that the old life is gone; it has been condemned, crucified. A new life has begun. Practices that were normal to the old man are now abnormal—they just don't fit, they are incongruent! Now that you are a new man, dress the part, act like one! Because you possess eternal life, there ought to be an external manifestation of your new life—so friend, "dress the part!"

My moment of reflection…

New Men Dress the Part

September 15
Colossians 3:12-17

Chrysostom, the early church father said that "animals that went into Noah's ark went out exactly the same way." The crow went in a crow and came out a crow! But those who enter into Christ go in one thing but come out something else totally transformed. Why? Because conversion to Christ is transformational—that is, inner change demands equally a dramatic change on the outside.

In our back yard we have a Pin Oak tree. In autumn when other trees shed their leaves, the Pin Oak doesn't. Their leaves remain intact all winter. But when spring comes and the sap begins to ascend, the old leaves are literally "pushed" off by the rising tide of new life. So it is in the Christian: the dead leaves of the old life are pushed off by the rising tide of eternal life!

Peter gives a fantastic picture of the transformational life: "But you are not like that, for you are a chosen people...a kingdom of priests, God's holy nation, his very own possession. This is so you can show others the goodness of God, for he called you out of the darkness into his wonderful light" (1 Peter 2:9). God is looking for a new life-style, expecting us to put on new clothes because we no longer walk or act or live the "old life." So since you are a new man, don't put on the old garments any more—"New men dress the part!"

My moment of reflection...

New Man—New Performance

September 16
Colossians 3:12-17

In the history of penology of the Roman Empire there was a custom in some places that if you murdered someone, the punishment was to strap the dead body of the victim to the killer! It wouldn't take long to have an effect on you! That was the way killers were punished. Paul may have had that in mind—if you are a new man, put off the old "dead" man and clothe yourself with a new life-style!

Since God chose you to be his, adopt a performance that is consistent with your new life; leave behind old habits, shed the old leaves, take that dead body off your back and throw away those filthy garments of your former life—and do it now! Righteous behavior must match your righteous position!

God says this about the new man: "God chose you to be holy people whom he loves" (Colossians 3:12). The new man is chosen, sovereignly selected by God for performance that is consistent with the new nature—his workmanship! The new man is to be holy, set-apart for the Lord. If the new man doesn't live a holy life, he is violating his calling, living in violation of the total intention of God. Finally, the new man is loved by God—we are objects of divine love and affection. As believers, God declares that we are chosen, holy and loved by God; therefore, we must "put on" a performance that is consistent with our calling!

My moment of reflection...

Our Speech

September 17
Colossians 4:1-6

Our words and speech are very important—they tell a story! When you move from one area of the country to another, you lose your "old" accent and develop a new accent which identifies your new location. When one becomes a "new man" they should begin to lose the accent of the world and "put on" language which is consistent with a new life-style. Your mouth ought to match your new life. New creatures demand a new accent even as they lose the accent of the world.

Consistency of life is followed by consistency of speech! Paul says, "Let your conversation be gracious" so you know how to respond to people (Colossians 4:6). We know that the "old man" speaks with lust, envy, swearing, gossip and destruction. But the new man speaks with grace—speech that is wholesome, kind, sensible, truthful, loving and thoughtful—speech seasoned with salt. Salt makes food delightful and palatable. The presence of grace and salt in a believer's speech will produce the ability to respond appropriately. Your speech and mouth is so important—you must speak the truth!

The ungodly say: "We will lie to our hearts' content. Our lips are our own—who can stop us?" (Psalm 12:4). In contrast, the "new man" pleads, "Take control of what I say, O Lord, and keep my lips sealed" (Psalm 141:3). You are a new man—out of your new life-style there needs to issue a new speech!

My moment of reflection…

Teamwork

September 18
Colossians 4:7-18

Friends are critical to meaningful and joyful living! By their loyalty, love, sympathy, helpfulness and encouragement we can accomplish much more than if we did not have their support. Nobody can survive without support—no one has!

Moses was fighting a battle with a foreign enemy. As long as he held his arms outstretched Israel won; but when his arms got tired and he let them down, Israel lost. So Aaron and Hur supported Moses and Israel won the battle. With a little help from his friends, Israel won a great victory. Any person can accomplish much more with help from his teammates!

Solomon teaches us "as iron sharpens iron, a friend sharpens a friend" (Proverbs 27:17). Our friends increase our effectiveness! "Two people can accomplish more than twice as much as one; they get a better return for their labor. If one person falls, the other can reach out and help. But people who are alone when they fall are in real trouble" (Ecclesiastes 4:9-10).

At home, at work or in ministry, we need people around us with a sympathetic heart; they don't have to be upfront people—just people who care! Thank God for people who stick with you when the going gets tough—that's greatness! In prison Paul says "thanks" to all those who have helped him. As others help you in various ways, remember to say "thanks" and do your part. Remember you are part of the team—don't let the captain down!

My moment of reflection…

The Eleventh Commandment

September 19
John 13:31-35

World history has been greatly affected by two events taking place in separate rooms—separated by thousands of miles and hundreds of years. One room was in London where Karl Marx wrote "Das Kapital." The other room was in Jerusalem where Jesus ate the Passover with his disciples. About to go to the cross, he gave his disciples a badge they would need to wear—a sign they were his disciples: "I am giving you a new commandment: love each other just as I have loved you, you should love each other. Your love for one another will prove to the world that you are my disciples" (John 13:34-35).

I call this the "eleventh commandment!" They had just observed the Passover meal together; Judas has left the group to betray Jesus. Alone with the "eleven" disciples, Jesus said, "Now is the time for the Son of Man to be glorified!" Then he added he was going away and the disciples would be alone in the world. In this context he gave them the "eleventh" commandment: "by this all men will know that you are my disciples if you have love for one another."

Moses...David...Isaiah...Micah...Habakkuk all gave commandments—guidelines defining the heart of the Hebrew faith! But Jesus said, "Love one another!" He went about his entire life... doing good, loving, touching the poor, rich, lame, blind and needy. Those of us who follow him must do the same—it's called "The Eleventh Commandment!"

My moment of reflection...

Born to Die

September 20
Matthew 20:17-28

The purpose of his life was clear: "I...came here not to be served but to serve others, and to give my life as a ransom for many" (Matthew 20:28). Jesus was really saying, "I was born to die!" The motive of his life was clear: He came do the will of God, to be a giver rather than a getter, to serve others rather than be served and to make people happy rather than seek his own personal happiness.

His whole life was unusual—born of a virgin and lived a perfect life. The impact he made upon the world was profound. His death was unusual—he died, not as a martyr or as a good example, but as our Savior. He lived a life of self-denial in order to be a channel of God's love to us. He measured greatness in terms of doing things for others! He suggested that the way to greatness was through service.

The epitaph on the tomb of General Chinese Gordon in St. Paul's Cathedral reads as follows: "Who at all times and everywhere gave his strength to the weak, his substance to the poor, his sympathy to the suffering and his heart to God." This is true greatness in the eyes of Christ! His whole life was one of serving. Yes, Jesus was "born to die" but he rose again to provide eternal life for all who would put their trust in him.

My moment of reflection...

Discipline

September 21
1 Peter 4:1-7

We know his words: "If any of you wants to be my follower, you must put aside your selfish ambition, shoulder your cross daily, and follow me" (Luke 9:23). Jesus is talking about the discipline of one's life. An athlete disciplines himself to be in top condition physically. In the Olympics every marathon runner is disciplined to run twenty-six miles in any kind of weather, refuses to be distracted by crowds and commits to run his style of race!

A disciplined person is one who lives by a pattern of behavior that expresses the control he has gained! A disciplined Christian is one who expresses a control in his life that is gained by becoming obedient to Christ and who lives by a pattern of behavior that is empowered by the Holy Spirit.

When Peter urges us to be disciplined and earnest, he is pleading with us to be "in one's right mind, in control of himself!" Christians must keep their heads and not get carried away by self-indulgence or excitement; preserving mental alertness in times of temptation and stress. We discipline ourselves with a particular mindset— "the mind of Christ!" We live a disciplined life in the light of the impending consummation: "The end of the world is coming soon" (1 Peter 4:7). Since the end of all things is at hand, we must bring all of life under Christ's control and live by his pattern of behavior if we are to be prepared for his return!

My moment of reflection…

Worry-Free Living

September 22
Luke 10:38-42

A flyer said, "So far today God, I've done all right! I haven't gossiped, lost my temper, haven't been grumpy or selfish. But in a few minutes, I'm going to get out of bed and then I'm going to need a lot of help!" Worry is a problem we face every day. We worry over health concerns, about the economy, about our children—it can overwhelm us if we allow it. But you don't have to let worry win the day!

Jesus warns us about worry! He was visiting friends Mary and Martha. He told Martha, "Martha, you are worried and upset about many things…Mary has chosen to spend time with me." Martha is yelling at Mary for spending time with Jesus instead of helping with housework—she is stressed out, filled with worry. Jesus said "Listen, worry is unnecessary, unreasonable and unproductive—it doesn't work, it's useless, it just makes you miserable." It doesn't change the past or alter the future!

Worry actually says to God, "God, I know you can keep the sun in orbit, sustain all life on earth, answer prayers all over the world and you have been in control in the past…but I don't believe you can take care of the problem I'm going through now!" Here's the answer to worry-free living: "Trust in the Lord with all your heart; do not depend on your own understanding. Seek his will in all you do, and he will direct your paths" (Proverbs 3:5-6).

My moment of reflection…

Fruitfulness

September 23
Luke 13:1-9

There was a man who had a fig tree. Again and again he came looking for fruit but found none! So he told the gardener to cut the tree down so it would not take up space. But the gardener asked permission to work with it a little longer—if in the next year it did not bear fruit, then it could be cut down.

In this story, our Lord speaks about the penalty of being useless and fruitless. As the owner and sustainer of all creation, God has the right to expect an appropriate return. But even God has a limitation to his patience: "Finally, he said to his gardener, 'I've waited three years, and there hasn't been a single fig! Cut it down. It's taking up space we can use for something else'" (Luke 13:7). But the gardener pleads with the owner to give him more time: "Give me another year; I will give the tree special attention and plenty of fertilizer. If we don't get figs next year then I will cut it down!"

We must all admit that there have been times when we were not very productive as "fig trees" in God's vineyard. But we rejoice in the fact that God is so kind, giving us a "second" chance. As our creator, owner and sustainer let's respond to the working of God's Spirit in our hearts and cooperate with the Father that we might be productive plants in his garden rather than barren plants!

My moment of reflection…

Confession

September 24
Luke 3:3-10

When we sin and confess any sin, the Lord will forgive our sin and "remember it no more...will bury it in the deepest sea." History has a long record of what men do with their sins. In some instances the whole world has been affected by what some men have done with their sins. In every instance this decision has affected more than simply the one who sinned!

We know what Adam did with his sin! Confronted with personal sin, Adam thought of nothing else than to try to hide his sin from God—it's the natural thing to do. It's so foolish and childish, yet we do it—but it never works! Some men boast of their sin while others deny sin. Little children will instinctively be tempted to deny that "they did it!" We never quite outgrow this characteristic of our childhood. Others use the "bandwagon psychology" to share their sin—since everybody's doing it they pressure others to join in too!

Solomon gives us the only answer to handling sin: "People who cover over their sins will not prosper. But if they confess and forsake them, they will receive mercy" (Proverbs 28:13). The wise man agrees with Jesus that the only honorable and wise choice for you to make is to confess your sin to God and claim his wonderful promise of forgiveness (1 John 1:9). Then live each day with the knowledge that his Holy Spirit is within you to keep you from falling again!

My moment of reflection...

Spiritual Sight

September 25
Luke 4:14-21

An ophthalmologist is a person who specializes in the treatment of eyes—to prevent diseases of the eyes and to improve the ability of his patients to see, often by surgery. To restore sight to a blind person opens up a new world, new avenues of usefulness and new avenues of delight for the blind!

Thank God for the ability to see! Erasmus said, "In the country of the blind the one-eyed man is king!" With over half million blind people in America, our hearts go out to those who miss the beauty of sight. Some are mentally blind because of a closed mind or prejudice. But spiritual blindness is the most critical blindness in the world. Jesus said, "An evil eye shuts out the light and plunges you into darkness...how deep that darkness will be" (Matthew 6:23). To live in spiritual darkness is the worst fate imaginable! The most devilish work of Satan is that he blindfolds the minds of men lest the glorious Gospel of Christ should shine into their hearts.

But Christ has come so that "the blind will see!" The psalmist prayed that God would "open his eyes to see the wonderful truths in God's law" (Psalm 119:18). It is true—there are none so blind as those who will not see! Each of us needs to take a seat by the roadside that leads from Jericho to Jerusalem and as Jesus passes by pray, "Lord, that our eyes may be opened!"

My moment of reflection...

Radiant Living

September 26
Luke 15:1-10

Young and old alike are challenged and puzzled by the will of God. Paul repeatedly shared three aspects of God's will for the believer: "Rejoice always, pray constantly and give thanks in all circumstances "for this is God's will for you who belong to Christ Jesus" (1 Thessalonians 5:15-18). This trilogy—joy, prayer, thanks— must be a daily, intentional experience in the life of every believer!

Joy is the key to radiant living and the birthmark of every member of the body of Christ. In the New Testament we encounter joy or rejoicing more than 130 times. It wasn't doctrine exactness or organizational structure that characterized the early church; it was the atmosphere of joy and love. The dynamic witness and power of the early church was their joy "in the Lord." Until joy becomes an essential and deliberate part of our religious exercises, we are not going to be very attractive to saints or sinners!

The primary color surrounding our Lord's birth was joy— everyone was joyful except Herod! When a lost coin is recovered or a lost son is found, friends and neighbors come together for a party, celebration and a time of rejoicing. Reconciliation is always a time for joy! Joy does not come, nor is it cultivated by favorable winds. It is a gift of God, an integral component of God's will for every believer. "Rejoicing in the Lord always" is God's permanent answer for radiant living!

My moment of reflection…

Intercession

September 27
John 17:1-26

Loneliness is a significant problem in spite of our growing population and social media. Loneliness is that feeling inside that nobody cares, that you "don't count" and if you were missing nobody would really miss you! The wonderful message of the Gospel is that the Father cares for us—and he proves it by making intercession for us and our needs. Because he make intercession for us we need not feel alone or afraid!

Paul tells us that Jesus who is at the right hand of the Father is "pleading for us" (Romans 8:34). In heaven, Jesus serves as our Advocate and our High Priest. So in times of loneliness, temptation and failure, he carries our burdens and through intercession, he helps us succeed. The Holy Spirit does the same: "The Holy Spirit prays for us with groaning's that cannot be expressed in words" (Romans 8:26). Here is a beautiful picture: The Holy Spirit intercedes for us on earth and Jesus Christ intercedes for us in heaven!

As believers, we should care and intercede for others—our family, friends and the lost! Intercession is a tremendous privilege that you should exercise every day. Don't ever say to someone, "well, the least I can do is pray for you!" No, the "most" you can do is pray because intercession has great power and is a sacred privilege! Someone you know has a great need and may be lonely—Intercede on their behalf today!

My moment of reflection...

Urgency

September 28
John 9:1-12

Today, many of you are in a hurry: You have places to go, people to see and important things to do! "Hurry! Hurry!" is the watchword of the day. It seems like there is a sense of urgency all around us—eat faster, travel faster, learn faster and sell faster.

God's commands are throbbing with urgency as well. Jesus lived an urgent and busy life. His ministry was so compelling that he crowded into three and one-half years work that could have graced a century. People think because "God is without beginning or end" (Psalm 90:2), he has no concern for the passage of time. They read Peter's statement, "A day is like a thousand years to the Lord, and a thousand years is like a day" (2 Peter 3:8). Likewise, the New Testament is an urgent book, filled with phrases as "Go quickly and tell his disciples" and "I come quickly." God's work is urgent and his love demands haste!

By our lack of urgency, we let missed opportunities to reap God's harvest fall to the ground. Jesus urges us to be diligent in his business because "there is little time left before the night falls and all work comes to an end" (John 9:4). We need a clear vision of God, of a God who is in a hurry because there is so little time left. God help us today to realize the King's business requires urgency—and the heartbeat of God sets the tempo!

My moment of reflection...

God Always Provides

September 29
Exodus 16:1-9

Sometimes life is colored with discouragement and despair! In the Exodus struggle, the Children of Israel gained insight about the nature and character of God. They learned that: God cares—he heard their cries; God delivers—he delivered them from Egypt and across the Red Sea; and God provides—provided care in the wilderness!

God provided for Israel day and night—pillar of fire by night and cloud by day. There was no absence of God's presence. He promised to be with them and never relented on that promise—or any other! God provided for them in the common problems of life. The logistics of moving 2 million people is almost unthinkable. Yet, God provided—water and manna and quail. He gives to us what we cannot get in any other way and gives these things as we need them. God provides for each situation but does not give in advance, lest we fail to live by faith and dependence upon him. In the critical pressures of life God provides, holds our hand and gives us the needed strength. We call this the "providence of God!"

God's timing is unpredictable but absolutely dependable! He loves and cares for his children and promises that valleys of despair and discouragement are going to bloom again—that's God's prescription for our predicament. God provides in unique and unusual ways as well as in common and expected ways. By faith, trust God who will provide in love—he always has!

My moment of reflection…

Confronted by God

September 30
Exodus 3:1-22

A man traveled to Europe, excited to visit the shrines in England. He went to Aldergate where John Wesley's heart was strangely warmed, to Whittenberg and to Rome where Martin Luther's encounter took place. He was disappointed; he had expected to be inspired, but these were just buildings and towns. As he thought about his disappointment, he realized these shrines were just ordinary places, marking the place where a man made a decision concerning God's will for himself—a time when someone turned his life over to God.

It was a great day for Moses at Mt. Horeb when he saw a burning bush that was not consumed. It was just like any other bush but for Moses it was a life-changing experience; it was there he accepted the commission to lead the Hebrew people out of slavery to the Promised Land. Any place that faith comes alive becomes a holy place!

The key to this whole "burning bush" experience was Moses' obedience! St. Augustine was obedient to the voice he heard in the garden—he read Romans and trusted Christ! But the big question is this: Where do we get the courage to be obedient? It comes from the presence of God. God promised Moses, "I will be with you" (Exodus 3:12, CEV). God may not confront us through such a dramatic experience as a burning bush. But God confronts each one of us—somewhere, somehow, sometime! What's needed? Faith and obedience!

My moment of reflection…

Giving your Best

October 1
Luke 14:25-35

The national news carried a story about a six-year old boy who needed a kidney transplant. His one kidney had been removed and the remaining organ was not functioning. The only donor whose tissue would match was the boy's twin brother. But there was a donor problem! At issue was an impending court decision as to whether the donor brother was old enough to understand what he was doing. The interview with the boy revealed that not only did he know what his decision meant, but his willingness to sacrifice was based on man's greatest motive—love!

When asked about the impending operation, the boy said he was going to give his brother his "right" kidney. When asked why his "right" kidney, the lad replied, "Because I'm right handed, my right kidney must be the strongest. I want to give my brother the "best one." Love demands our best! No great sacrifice is needed when we give rummage items to friends in need. Contributing spare time to the Lord's work represents no service beyond the call of duty.

David was commanded to build an altar. Araunah offered to give David some land on which to build the altar and oxen for the burnt offering; but David insisted on payment. His heart reflected his love for God when he said, "I cannot present burnt offerings to the Lord my God that have cost me nothing" (2 Samuel 24:24). May our giving reflect our love and sacrifice as well!

My moment of reflection...

Sacrifice

October 2
Psalm 51:1-19

Two wealthy Christians, a lawyer and a businessman were traveling around the world. While traveling through Korea, they saw a field by the side of the road; in the field was a boy pulling a crude plow while an old gray haired man held the plow handles and guided it through the rice paddy. The lawyer was amused and took a photo of the scene. "That's a curious sight," he said to the missionary who was their interpreter and guide.

"Yes," was the reply, "that is the family of Chi Noui. When their church building was built, they were eager to give something, but had no money! So they sold the only ox they had and gave the money to the church. This spring they are pulling the plow by themselves."

The men were silent for several moments, reflecting on the scene. Finally the businessman said, "That must have been real sacrifice." "They did not call it that," said the missionary. "They thought it was fortunate they had an ox to sell!"

Arriving home, the lawyer took the picture to his pastor and told him of the incident. "I want to double my offering for missions," he said, "and give me some 'plow' work to do. I have never known what sacrifice for the Lord really means. I am ashamed to say that I have never given anything to him that really cost me something!" That's probably true for many of us. God help us to repeat the story!

My moment of reflection...

It's Who You Know!

October 3
John 8:1-11

The popular philosophy "It's who you know" has been around for a long time and is growing in intensity. It goes something like this: In order to get what you want and need in life—what you've got to have—you must associate with and know the right people!

I read about a woman who radically espoused this particular viewpoint, to the degree that she let it be known it was her intention to marry four men in her lifetime: a banker, a movie star, a preacher and finally an undertaker...in that order. When asked why, she simply said, "Isn't it obvious...One for the money, two for the show, three to get ready, and four to go!"

Though the story may be highly questionable, there's still some truth in it. Really now, who you know effects how you go through this journey of life and even beyond. Or to say it another way: First you make friends...then they make you!

The Bible talks about being friends with God. Imagine what that means as a Christian! Talk about having friends in high places. What a privilege to be known and loved by God, our Heavenly Father. What a pleasure to share this treasure with our community of friends. Pray today that God will inspire and motivate us to enlarge our circle of friends in ever increasing ways so Christ might use us to befriend the world where we live for him! Bottom line— It's really who you know, isn't it?

My moment of reflection...

Remember...

October 4
1 Thessalonians 1:1-10

If someone was describing you to a friend, what kind of things would they mention or "what" do people remember most about you? You might know what they would say or maybe you don't! But this is certain: you can know what they should say. Paul had some great memories of his friends: "We think of your faithful work, your loving deeds, and your continual anticipation of the return of our Lord" (1 Thessalonians 1:3). What a memory—their faith, love and hope!

Paul's friends at Thessalonica were folks characterized by action, not apathy or idleness. Their "work of faith" really means the work faith produces—the help they gave to those in need. Paul remembered their "labor" of love, a work that spared no sacrifice. Their lives were expressions of kindness and care they gave to strangers. Paul also remembered them because of their "patience of hope," a phrase that refers to their hope in the Lord and his return.

When people think about you, what do they remember? This is certain: our lives either helps or hinders! A business man gave his employees this charge: "Remember, my reputation is in your hands." In a very real sense, Christ's reputation is in your hand! What others think about him is often determined by what they think of you! What a responsibility—but what a privilege! May our work and service and hope cause others to be filled with positive and pleasant memories!

My moment of reflection...

Thriving or Surviving

October 5
Luke 10:38-42

In our busy lives we often find ourselves in the "surviving" rather than the "thriving" mode! In the story, Jesus takes time to visit some good friends. He puts high value on relationships and spending time with people. In his visit with Mary and Martha we see Jesus reinforcing the importance of relationships.

Martha was a doer; she was concerned about all the things on her to-do list. She was "distracted with much serving!" Like many of us, we get over-extended and over-committed and take on too much and get distracted. We find ourselves in the "survival" mode and forget what's most important. Mary on the other hand was more concerned about relationships; she was more concerned being with Jesus than worrying about all the details of his visit. She wanted to sit at his feet to listen, learn and show her love for the Master.

We can learn from both of them! Work has to get done, but there is a priority that demands our attention: spending time with Jesus—then doing our work! Mary was enjoying his presence while Martha was preparing dinner. We need Mary's heart and Martha's hands—worship then work!

Spending time alone with Jesus each day needs to be our priority if we are going to "thrive" and not just "survive!" David prayed, "You will show me the way of life, granting me the joy of your presence and the pleasures of living with you forever" (Psalm 16:11). Start "thriving" today!

My moment of reflection…

Share the Load

October 6
Ephesians 4:1-16

One of the great rewards of ministry is learning to work and serve along-side some truly amazing people. Seeing team members work together to discover their gifting is most gratifying. Look at this scriptural picture: "Under his direction, the whole body is fitted together perfectly. As each part does its own special work, it helps the other parts grow so that the whole body is healthy and growing and full of love" (Ephesians 4:16).

Team approach to ministry has many advantages. When you surround yourself with others who have different gifts and talents much can be accomplished. Sitting down to pray, plan and dream together brings endless ministry possibilities. In the process we build relationships, experience excitement and may learn patience as well. It is a wonderful opportunity to affirm and grow close friendships.

Learning to lean on each other is not always an easy task! After praying, pooling resources and delegating responsibilities, it's time to trust each other and God for the outcomes. Failing to delegate, we take away the joy of letting others do the tasks that they do well and remove God's blessing from them and their ministry.

Sharing the load is the biblical plan: "Plans go wrong for lack of advice; many counselors bring success" (Proverbs 15:22). Nothing is more rewarding than to work with a ministry team! Don't be afraid to trust God for what he wants to accomplish through your team as you share the load in growing the Kingdom!

My moment of reflection...

My Dad Can Fix It

October 7
Matthew 6:25-34

Memory is a phenomenal gift! Do events from your childhood ever pop into your mind? Looking through some old photos recently, I was reminded of a phrase I used as a small child: "My dad can fix it!"

As I remember, no matter what was broken or how difficult the problem was, I would always answer, "my dad can fix it!" There was no doubt in my mind that my father could overcome any obstacle. I just knew my father could fix it.

Wouldn't it be wonderful if each of us could have that same confidence in our Heavenly Father? Since all things were made by our Father's omnipotent hand, is there anything too difficult for our God? Can he not do the impossible? When storms arrive and trials are heavy, can we not say, "My Father can take care of it?"

God lead Israel out of bondage, took care of them and supplied all their needs. Yet they complained and fretted! We resemble our forefathers: He supplies our needs but we worry, complain about the small things and forget to thank God for the wonderful blessings he sends us. He cares for the sparrow that falls to the ground—is he not more concerned about your needs? God wants to be Lord of our lives so he can mold us to his perfect will. My Father knows my heart and what is best for me. Yes, my "Father can fix it"—How about yours?

My moment of reflection…

OCTOBER

Free to Fail

October 8
Psalm 51

Nowhere on earth are people more accustomed to success than in America. Courses abound in the fine art of making "success a habit." But have you ever heard of a course of study that instructs one in the art of "failure?" Because all of us fail, it is imperative that we learn how to fail "successfully." History is filled with accounts of failure: Ponce de Leon failed in his search for the Fountain of Youth; the Mayflower was headed for Virginia and landed at Plymouth Rock by mistake; the first attempt of the Wright Brothers to fly their glider failed. No one enjoys failing—but all of us do!

Ever watch a child learning to walk? He totters, falls down, but gets up and staggers triumphantly into his mother's arms. But as soon as that child enters school, he discovers that "failure" is a no-no! A proper understanding of failure is critical to adjustments in life and to the world in which we live. Sometimes, there is more success in failure than in success itself!

Freedom to fail...what a delightful freedom! Just don't make failure your life-style and get up each time you stumble. The Bible is full of stories of folks who failed before they succeeded. David failed again and again but was called "a man after God's own heart." So friends, take heart when you stumble because the weakest of us reach the pearly gates only by the mercy and grace of a loving Father!

My moment of reflection...

Cart or the Horse

October 9
Psalm 95

You remember the saying, "Don't put the cart before the horse!" A man took much pride in always looking dignified. His horse was so beautiful that whenever he rode into town, people would stare admiringly at the lovely animal. And that made him feel proud!

At an auction, he bought an old buggy that needed a lot of work; but he planned to make it the best looking buggy in the country. He worked day and night on the buggy, carefully sanding and repainting it. After months of hard work, the man came out of the shed pushing his cart which was an eloquent piece of art.

That afternoon he decided to ride into town to show off his buggy. He went out to the barn to get his horse—but his horse was dead. In his weeks of work on the buggy he had forgotten to feed his horse! What's more important, a cart or a horse? Obviously, the horse, but he forgot that and put his cart first; now he couldn't even get to town!

As Christians, many times we make the same mistake! Service and ministry are wonderful—but we must remember our first call is to gather at the temple for worship. Jesus taught his disciples to "make the Kingdom of God" your primary concern (Matthew 6:33). We have busy schedules, but must not neglect our time of worship. Remember: If the horse dies, it doesn't matter how pretty the cart is!

My moment of reflection...

Community

October 10
Colossians 2:1-10

People in our world often feel isolated and alone—that was never God's intention! God created a unique and loving community called the church. In establishing his kingdom, one of the first things Jesus did was to choose twelve disciples, thereby creating community. Throughout his ministry, Jesus emphasized transformed lives working together in harmony, creating community.

We were not created to do life alone! Paul's goal for the Colossian believers was that they become a dynamic community, a body of believers devoted and committed to one another. He prayed that this group would be knit together by love and encouraged to experience the fullness of Christ. In community we find friends to encourage us and support us in our common struggles. We are to love each other as Christ loves us and we work together in unity toward a common goal—fullness in Christ!

Community calls for tolerance and concern for each other. Our mandate is to be gentle, ready to forgive, never hold grudges and let love guide your life (Colossians 3:13-14). Community demands humility, gentleness and patience with one another: "Bearing with one another in love...make every effort to keep the unity of the Spirit" (Ephesians 4:2-3, NIV).

In community, our challenge is to "think of ways to encourage one another to outbursts of love and good deeds...encourage and warn each other" (Hebrews 10:24, 25). Somewhere, someone is longing for community—for someone to come along-side them and show them you care! Be creative and encourage someone today!

My moment of reflection...

Just Judging

October 11
Romans 2:1-4

Since I grew up on the farm, I enjoy humorous farm stories! A hog farmer refused to have anything to do with church because, as he said, "All I ever see is a bunch of hypocrites who attend." It's really hard to convince "judgers" otherwise! But the pastor came up with an idea. One day he went to buy a hog from the farmer. After looking at the entire herd, the preacher pointed to a sickly little runt and said, "I want that one!" The farmer protested vigorously, "you don't want that one. He's the scrawniest runt of the herd. Look, over here are some fine pigs." "That's fine," said the pastor, "I want the runt!"

After the purchase was completed, the farmer asked why the preacher purchased the "runt" of the herd. "Now that the runt is mine, I'm going to haul this pig all over the country and tell everyone that that is the kind of pigs you raise." "That's not fair. I raise an occasional runt but that doesn't ruin my whole stock" protested the farmer. "I'm only following your example of condemning a whole church because of the stunted spirituality of a few members," said the pastor.

Paul wrote, "What terrible people you have been talking about! But you are just as bad, and you have no excuse! When you say they are wicked and should be punished, you are condemning yourself, for you do these very same things" (Romans 2:1). Stop judging!

My moment of reflection...

Patience—God Is At Work

October 12
James 1:1-8

A Norwegian family lived in a cottage on cliffs overlooking the sea. Each morning the wife saw her husband and son off as they rowed their boat into the fog to earn their living fishing. One day a storm arose and their little boat was about to capsize. It seemed certain that they would drown. The storm was so intense that the fishermen could not tell whether they were rowing out to sea or back to shore—they had lost all perspective in the storm!

Suddenly, there was a glow in the distance. Blindly, they followed the light. They were overcome with joy when they found that the glow was from the cliffs above the sea. When they arrived on shore, the fisherman's wife met them, weeping uncontrollably. Lightning had struck their cottage and it burned to the ground. In anger she blamed God, but her husband said, "That fire seems like a tragedy to you, but to us it was a blessing from God—it saved our lives!

James wrote, "Whenever trouble comes your way, let it be an opportunity for joy. For when your faith is tested, your endurance has a chance to grow...when your endurance is fully developed, you will be strong in character and ready for anything" (James 1:2-4). God uses our heartaches and hurts for greater good. Our trials may be difficult, but beyond the trial God is working all things for our good and his glory" (Romans 8:28).

My moment of reflection...

Press On for the Prize

October 13
Corinthians 9:24-27

The most dramatic scene in sports is the last lap of the marathoner's 26-mile race. As the fatigued runner approaches the finish line, the crowd cheers him on! Straining every muscle, the runner "hits" the tape to receive the prize before the cheering crowd. Paul compared the grueling marathon to the Christian life; he challenged believers not only to enter the race of faith, but to go "all out" and run as to win. God wants winners!

You can't win the race with halfhearted effort! Runners must have a strong will to win and be deeply committed to make whatever sacrifice is necessary. Victory depends on the athlete's rigorous training—exercising mastery over life, foregoing pleasures all for the sake of winning. The marathon course was clearly marked and the runner needed to stay on course, his eyes always on the goal.

After the race, every runner was brought to stand before a raised platform that supported a throne-like seat for the judge. As each marathoner would pass before the judge, they would be crowned, passed over, or disqualified. The same is true for every believer: "We must all stand before Christ to be judged. We will each receive whatever we deserve for the good or evil we have done in our bodies" (2 Corinthians 5:10). Every step of the Christian's life has eternal importance. Let's run with great anticipation of that moment when we will stand before Christ our Judge!

My moment of reflection…

Persistence

October 14
Galatians 6:1-10

Many of us have "left" too soon! We have turned away too soon from that which we desperately hoped to see come to fruition. Simon Peter heard Jesus say one day, "Come, follow me" and he did enthusiastically. Things went well for a time; then things began to slip. There were angry opponents, Gethsemane, the betrayal, the arrest and trial. Peter saw the handwriting on the wall. While the fisherman followed at a distance, he denied Christ three times and soon Jesus was dead. It seemed to Peter that the curtain had come down with a thud...and he ran!

But he left too soon! Three days later and he would have seen the resurrection! In his despair, disappointment and disillusionment, what he thought was the end was not the end! President Calvin Coolidge said that nothing in the world can take the place of persistence. For him, persistence and determination were omnipotent! His message: Stick to the fight when you're hardest hit because it is when things go wrong that you must not quit!

Do not leave too soon! What may seem to you to be the end may be only the prologue to the beginning. If you don't leave too soon, you too may see God act in your life in ways that you have never dreamed possible. Paul said, "So don't get tired of doing what is good. Don't get discouraged and give up, for we will reap a harvest of blessing at the appropriate time" (Galatians 6:9).

My moment of reflection…

Always Thankful

October 15
Colossians 1:12-14

When writing a letter, Paul always seems to be thankful! We know he had some "bad" days, yet we see his heart full of thanksgiving and hear his voice of praise. I wonder if we understand how "thanks" fits into our lives! God spoke through the psalmist with such clarity: "The only sacrifice I want is for you to be thankful" (Psalm 50:14). True thanksgiving pleases the Lord—whether we talk, write, sing, play or pray we are to praise the Lord. Thanksgiving is to make up a major part of our life!

The heart of the Father is that we give thanks for "all things" (Ephesians 5:20). Our praise is to be practiced privately and publicly. But thanks for what? You see most of the time we are grateful for food, friends and the many necessities of life—but there is much more that commands our thanks! Paul is urging us to understand that the primary point of thanksgiving is the work of Christ—"Be thankful for his unspeakable gift" (2 Corinthians 9:15).

That "unspeakable gift" is how Paul describes "our inheritance!" On the basis of Christ's death you were qualified for an inheritance—totally a matter of sovereign grace! This inheritance is fantastic, eternal and does not fade away. You don't have to work or wait for it—it is something you have, to be enjoyed right now! When we contemplate our inheritance and his completed work, no wonder Paul is "always" filled with thanksgiving! And so should we!

My moment of reflection...

Reconciliation

October 16
Romans 5:1-11

During a presidential campaign in Ohio, one of the candidates stopped in a small town for a political speech. A thirteen-year-old girl picked up a sign that someone had dropped which said, "Bring us together again!" That's the cry of hearts today—reconciliation!

The Bible begins with a record of perfect harmony—heaven and earth working together in joyful cooperation. But then sin enters into the picture and there is trouble, big trouble—division, dissention, death and separation. Man runs from God and hides; he is separated from God. And then man kills his brother and is separated from humanity—so the consequence of sin is great. We need reconciliation to God and to man! Then the answer: Jesus comes to bring that needed reconciliation and hope. He came as our mediator, bringing two sides together for agreement! God did not need to be reconciled to man; it was man who needed to be reconciled to God.

Reconciliation is not a temporary truce—it is permanent! So because of the life, death and resurrection of Jesus, we have reconciliation—that is, peace with God, no longer enemies but friends. It means that God has accepted us and that we have access to God at any time. We can pray and intercede for others because of his mediation. And the best news of all is we have security! Nothing can change our relationship to Jesus Christ. All that we've needed he has provided: security, sufficiency, victory!

My moment of reflection…

Encouraging One Another

October 17
Hebrews 10:23-25

Paul emphatically says that God gives encouragement to his children: "May God, who gives this patience and encouragement, help you live in complete harmony" (Romans 15:5). God encourages us with the scriptures and by His Spirit who is our present indwelling Encourager. Encouragement is real—every person needs encouragement sooner or later!

If you are busy in your work or personal ministry, you need words of encouragement! Anyone in authority needs to encourage those under their leadership. An employer needs to encourage his employees and parents need to encourage their children. A husband needs to encourage his wife by a word, a touch, a smile or a hug. When we encourage, our hands are strengthened for our work. When we face a new challenge or are about to finish a task, we are particularly vulnerable to discouragement! Ezra had been confronted with the challenge of building the Temple at Jerusalem. Adversaries were hindering the work. But he received encouragement from an unexpected source—the king of Assyria! The Lord had prompted the king to encourage Israel during this difficult time (Ezra 6).

Someone you know today is facing a challenge or finishing a task! It may be an older person completing life or someone struggling with sickness or a student about to finished school. Your sensitive word and loving spirit may motivate someone not to give up but succeed. Encouragement is a privilege to receive—a blessing to give! Be an encourager today!

My moment of reflection…

Encouragement through Intervention

October 18
2 Timothy 1:3-12

Timothy was discouraged shedding tears over difficulties he faced in ministry. Paul came to his rescue by encouraging him, reminding him of his godly heritage; he encouraged Timothy by teaching him fear is not from God, but that he gives power, love and a disciplined life. Certainly God provides encouragement through friends, his word, and the Holy Spirit! But there is a unique encouragement that comes by divine intervention!

Paul and Silas were beaten by prison guards and thrown into prison where they were guarded securely. It's safe to assume they needed encouragement! But they were not feeling sorry for themselves— they were praying and singing hymns of praise to God. They were being encouraged when suddenly a great earthquake shook the prison, open doors, and set prisoners free. God intervened! Or there was the time when Jesus was asleep during a storm on the Sea of Galilee. The disciples cried out, "Don't you care?" Yes, he cared! He commanded the storm to cease and their hearts to be stilled.

Through divine intervention, God is able to do beyond all that we could ask or think. Jesus is adequate to meet our every need— even our greatest discouragement and fear. Jesus really does care. He is the Good Shepherd, not a hireling merely tending the sheep in a perfunctory way. In fact, he gives the ultimate encouragement: "I lay down my life for the sheep" (John 10:15). Be encouraged with his presence and power!

My moment of reflection…

Meekness

October 19
Numbers 12:1-16

God is not content with us as we are! Jesus came not only to save us but to enrich, enlarge and improve our lives. He is seeking to change our thought processes and choices so as to reproduce within us the character of Jesus Christ (Romans 12:2). For many, meekness refers to a weak, spineless person with no fortitude and poor self-image! That's not the biblical definition of meekness—it was not true of Moses, Paul, or Jesus!

Meekness is an inward grace of the soul that is exercised chiefly toward God. Meekness is not weakness! Christ was meek but not weak. He was meek because He had the infinite resources of God at his disposal. To be meek is to be completely open to the suggestions and corrections of God and instantly responsive to his wishes. Meekness is listed as part of the spiritual wardrobe of a follower of Jesus: "put on meekness" (Colossians 3:12).

The Bible says "Moses was very meek" above all the men on the earth (Numbers 12:1-3). Yet we know from history that Moses didn't whimper nor was his faith shattered but strengthened when he did not see "eye to eye" with God. Moses responded like the psalmist, "His way is perfect!" Meekness is to be completely open, to have a teachable mind and to be instantly responsive to God's Will. God help us with meekness so we can see ourselves as tools in God's hand, to be used for his glory!

My moment of reflection…

Riches

October 20
Ephesians 1:1-14

Hetty Green was known as "America's Greatest Miser." When she died in 1916, she left an estate valued at one hundred million dollars—a lot of money in 1916! Hetty Green was so miserly that she ate cold oatmeal because it was too expensive to heat water to warm it. Her son had a severe leg injury, but because she waited too long for medical care, his leg had to be amputated. In every way, Hetty Green was a strange lady—one who obviously did not understand wealth and riches!

In the New Testament, the book of Ephesians is a book about riches and the inheritance we have in Christ. Paul uses some illustrations to speak of our wealth: "the riches of his grace... the unsearchable riches of Christ...and the riches of his glory!" As believers, all the fullness of Christ is ours! That is an amazing thought! There are enough resources in glory to cover all our past debts, all our present liabilities and all our future needs—and still not diminish our account.

So because we trust in Christ, we have what he has—we possess what he possesses. All his riches are at our disposal. Peter calls it "a priceless inheritance...kept in heaven for you, pure and undefiled, beyond the reach of change and decay" (1 Peter 1:4). All we possess as believers is ours because we are in Christ. Without him we're poor and destitute. But in Christ we're rich beyond our wildest imagination!

My moment of reflection...

Personal Significance

October 21
Ephesians 1:3-14

In our culture, people are looking for self-worth, value, and acceptance! They want to be "somebody" and have a meaningful identity in a world deprived of purpose. There are many seminars telling folks how to be successful, how to be number one and how to get "on top of the pile!" Some even trace their roots, searching for someone important in their lineage to give them a sense of identity and importance. But in the end, all these things are just psychological gloss—giving them a false sense of worth!

Self-worth and significance with a corresponding joy and meaning comes when a person understands their position in Christ. Without Jesus, people have no eternal value—they are like the chaff which the wind drives away. Our value and identity come because we are in Christ. When we understand as believers we were chosen before the foundations of the world, the only conclusion is—"I am somebody…my life has meaning and purpose!" You are so important to Jesus that the whole story of redemption was simply to reach you and draw you into fellowship with God forever. That's how important you are to Christ!

This is both exciting and humbling: Nobody ever became a Christian as a surprise to God. It was all planned—long, long ago! So don't struggle with a sense of self-worth—you are worthy in Christ. And don't ever struggle with a sense of inadequacy or sufficiency—he has given you all things richly to enjoy!

My moment of reflection…

Walking in Wisdom

October 22
Ephesians 5:15-20

No question about it—we live in a world full of fools! Everyone born into the world comes in with congenital foolishness—also known as the "sin nature." Solomon, the wise man, says "a youngster's heart is filled with foolishness, but discipline will drive it away" (Proverbs 22:15). Normally, when we think of a fool, we think of someone who acts or speaks irresponsibly. However, the Bible defines a fool as one who exists apart from God!

A fool lives as if there is no God—they deny God with words and actions. David said, "Only fools say in their hearts, 'There is no God'" (Psalm 14:1). No man can live without a god. It isn't a question of "does" he worship, it's a question of "whom" does he worship. If a person doesn't worship the true God, he will worship a false god—who inevitably will be himself! Since a fool makes his rules, he justifies his behavior; so in the end he eliminates sin along with its consequences. A fool lives as if there is no God and justifies his actions.

God reaches out of heaven and offers to take men out of a kingdom of fools into a kingdom of the wise. Salvation is the only cure for foolishness! If you are a Christian, you have wisdom. You're no longer a fool, you're wise. And on that basis, Paul says, "Walk as wise—not as unwise. Live according to the wisdom you possess!"

My moment of reflection...

Truthfulness

October 23
Ephesians 6:10-20

The Christian life is war—we must learn that lesson sooner rather than later! Satan is our enemy and he is real! Satan was so real to Martin Luther that he almost took on a physical appearance. One day Luther was so angry at Satan that he picked up an inkwell from his desk and threw it at him. It broke and splattered all over the wall. The stain remained for years, reminding believers of how vivid evil was in Luther's life.

Since believers and Satan are on a collision course, we must understand Satan's strategy! He undermines the character of God—he wants you to doubt God! He wants you to think God is a liar but Satan tells the truth. Satan wants you to doubt God's power, grace, mercy and love. Part of his strategy is to confuse believers with false doctrine. He causes division, hinders our service and makes us "worldly."

Because Satan is a liar and the father of lies, we must know truth and follow truth and be committed to truthfulness. Paul teaches us to let "truth be like a belt around your waist" (Ephesians 6:14, CEV). When our minds are renewed by the Word of God and we know the truth, we can live committed, victorious lives. We must be satisfied with nothing less than excellence—committed to truthfulness if we are going to be victorious over our enemy, the devil! Never, never give up or give in to evil—always follow truth!

My moment of reflection…

God Is in Control

October 24
Psalm 73:1-28

It's hard to understand why evil men prosper while good men fail! The psalmist captures our feelings: "For I envied the proud when I saw them prosper despite their wickedness" (Psalm 73:3). The greatest saints in the Bible had their struggles with God, trying to understand what he was doing in their lives and in the world. Why do bad things happen to good people like Job or Jeremiah?

To understand this dilemma, we are reminded that God is good. Looking back we discover that God is good—he always has been and always will be! But looking around, Asaph was envious of the prosperity and popularity of his neighbors. It appeared they had no need for God. So Asaph examined his own heart. His conclusion was his purity wasn't bringing him any special blessings from God—the wicked were prospering while he was being plagued. In spite of his hurt, Asaph went to the temple to present his case. He made this discovery: "outlook determines outcome!" He saw the truth about the prosperity of the wicked—and it all made sense!

Conclusion: God was with him, even held his hand and promised to guide him with his counsel! Did the situation in the world change? No, but Asaph changed! Don't be envious or critical of God. Just find out what good things God wants to do for his people—and let him work! God's justice is sometimes slow, but it is always true!

My moment of reflection…

Dream Big Dreams

October 25
Ephesians 3:14-21

Henrietta Mears, a pioneer in Christian leadership, faced big challenges when she arrived at Hollywood Presbyterian Church in 1928. Regardless of the challenge, she was never afraid to dream big dreams! From writing simple Bible school lessons to building wonderful camping facilities, she influenced many students to become great leaders of her day. She was not afraid to look for what could be instead of looking at what was! Her mantra was "there is no magic in small plans!"

When we get a clear vision of God and his mighty power, the clearer our vision of what God might want to accomplish through us. The more we get to know God the more wisdom we receive as to how to carry out dreams he gives us. He has unlimited resources from which he will empower us by his Spirit to do his work. This gives us confidence to make big plans—to dream big dreams! He tells us in his word that "his love for us is so great we will never understand or see the end of it…nothing is impossible for him… he is able to do immeasurably more than all you can ask, think or even dream…he is the creator, the wonderful counselor, the mighty God…he never grows tired or weary."

When we remind ourselves of the greatness of God, abide in his word and faithfully act on his promises, we can not only dream big dreams but we see them come to pass! Keep dreaming!

My moment of reflection…

Grace of Sufficiency

October 26
2 Corinthians 12:1-10

The world considers trouble to be a terrible intruder into life! Sometimes trouble keeps us down; yet, on the other hand, problems can make us strong. Paul experienced a "thorn" in the flesh; but his weakness made him strong—it didn't keep him down but he gained strength out of his weakness. Grace is the key to life—God's activity for us and "in" us!

Years earlier, Paul was given a divine revelation no man ever had. He was caught up to the third heaven into the very presence of God. While he said nothing about this experience, God gave him a "thorn in the flesh" to keep him from exalting himself, to keep him from pride. Some people blame God, become bitter or give up when faced with challenges. Paul prayed—begged the Lord to remove this "thorn" from his life—three times! But the answer: "My gracious favor is all you need. My power works best in your weakness" (2 Corinthians 12:9). Through the "grace" of a thorn, God was perfecting Paul.

A storekeeper said to a little girl who was eagerly looking at a jar of candy. "Take some…take a whole handful!" She hesitated a moment and replied, "Will you please give it to me? Your hand is bigger than mine!" God's hand is bigger than yours! Let him give you his best rather than continue to insist on what you want most! If you have thorns in your life today, remember roses come tomorrow!

My moment of reflection…

Grace of Serving

October 27
Romans 15:14-19

The grace of God is like a diamond—it has many facets of beauty! God's grace is the most profound divine revelation given to man—difficult to comprehend. Jesus was full of grace and truth and he went about "doing good." His whole life was given to ministry and service. He exhibited the grace of serving!

One of the facets of grace is service. We were selected and saved so that we might serve Jesus and others. Only the grace of God can make an effective worker out of an individual. Paul said, "How thankful I am to Christ...for considering me trustworthy and appointing me to serve him" (1 Timothy 1:12). It was God's grace that enabled Paul to do the work of the kingdom—serving God and mankind! And by his grace we have been called to serve Christ by serving others!

God gives us grace to serve Jesus by serving one another! In the seventeenth century Thomas Hobson rented horses at Cambridge, England. He had a rule that any person who rented a horse must take the one standing nearest the stable door. No matter "who" you were—that was his rule! It didn't take long for "Hobson's choice," which was really no choice at all, to become a familiar phrase. For the Christian, serving is a "Hobson's choice." We really don't have a choice about "whether" we will serve. Our only choice is about what kind of server we will be!

My moment of reflection...

God Isn't Dead

October 28
Psalm 115:1-18

Men of every generation ask, "Where is your God? Why doesn't he do something? Does your God really care?" We live in a spirit of unbelief when our culture challenges us to prove our God is alive and real! Israel was weak and weary, trying to rebound from captivity and regain their former glory! They needed a "word" from God to assure them that God was alive, on the throne and in control!

So the psalmist shouts, "God is alive—glorify him!" In contrast to the false idols, the living God has power, makes promises and is worthy of our praise. He is "Emmanuel...God with us" in every situation (Matthew 1:23). This God of Israel helps us, therefore we should trust him! How prone we are to forget the mercies of God. Spurgeon used to say that we write our blessings in the sand but engrave our trials in marble! God blesses us—he is mindful of his people, never forget us! Because of all he has done for his children, the psalmist reminds us again that "God is worthy—praise him!" The dead body in the grave cannot give thanks; but you can!

Because God is alive—praise becomes the thermometer of our spiritual life. For years we saw plaques that read "prayer changes things;" but now we see "praise changes things!" If your heart is warm and appreciative of God's blessings, praise him and bless God wherever you are—and never forget, God is alive!

My moment of reflection...

Choices

October 29
Matthew 12:1-21

In the Alpine Mountains of Switzerland, there is a place where a visitor can throw a piece of wood in one direction and it will float to the Black Sea. If you throw it in another direction, it will end up in the North Sea; or in another direction, it will go to the Mediterranean Sea. Although these pieces of wood are thrown from the same place, they will eventually reach three different seas, miles apart. Destination is determined by direction! Life is like that: What we will be tomorrow is determined by choices we make today.

Jesus made choices that determined his character and life! Jesus willingly raised Lazarus and healed the man with the withered arm. But there is another side to the ministry of Jesus. He refused to be impatient with sinners: "He will not crush those who are weak, or quench the smallest hope" (Matthew 12:20). He refuses to discourage those who are weary—Jesus is the great encourager! He strengthens—does not tear down! He cheers—does not chide!

Jesus refuses to enter where uninvited. Holman Hunt's painting of Christ is deeply moving. He pictures the Savior knocking at the vine-covered door; there is no knob on the outside of the door—it must be opened from within. In the corner written in Latin are these words, "O do not pass me by." Jesus pleads with us to receive him—but he never enters where he is not invited! It's your choice!

My moment of reflection...

Effective Service

October 30
Zechariah 4:1-14

A little boy climbed to the top of a big barn. He was having a wonderful time, looking down when suddenly he slipped—he could see he was going to be hurt if he fell on the rocks below. So he quickly prayed, "Dear God, don't let me fall...please don't let me fall." Just then his pants got caught on a nail! He looked up and said, "Never mind, God, I got hung up on a nail!

We make the same mistake! Like the young boy, we feel more certain of being held by a nail than by being helped by God. Lots of us make a habit of depending on our own strength rather than seeking and calling on God. We forget that Jesus said, "For apart from me you can do nothing" (John 15:5). We haven't learned the principle which meant so much to Paul: "I can do everything with the help of Christ who gives me the strength I need" (Philippians 4:13).

We keep making the same mistake over and over—we try to do the work of God in our own strength. If we desire fruitful and effective service, then we must operate on this principle: The work of God can only be done through the power of God—by his Spirit! When we serve in the power of His Spirit, we will finish our God-given assignments rejoicing, knowing that we have had the privilege of assisting the Lord of the whole earth!

My moment of reflection...

Grace of Growing

October 31
2 Peter 3:17-18

A woman in India was making a pilgrimage to a place where she heard God was to be seen. Someone asked her what she wanted from this laborious journey. She answered with a light in her eye, "Vision of him…Vision of him!" Throughout history, man's desire has been for a full revelation of God. Job voiced this universal longing, "If only I knew where to find God" (Job 23:3).

Growing Christians render the most fruitful service. Static Christianity is a growing problem among believers—believers acting the same year after year without any evidence of spiritual growth. They continue as spiritual infants and never seem to mature spiritually. Spiritual growth is always a struggle; it is never easy or automatic. There are obstacles to overcome and handicaps to be conquered.

Growth comes as a result of divine work in our lives. God began a good work in you and he will keep on performing until the end. But we must do our part—accepting his promises and provision. So Peter pleads with us to reject stagnation in our spiritual walk. His lament was they were still infants, living carnal lives. So his command is clear: "But grow in the special favor and knowledge of our Lord and Savior" (2 Peter 3:18). As we grow by God's grace and provision, we can serve effectively and fruitfully! Christianity's great problem is not deep waters, but shallow pools—the bottlenecks of God's unappropriated power!

My moment of reflection…

It All Belongs to God

November 1
Psalm 24:1-10

In November, our devotional focus will be giving thanks to our creator and sustainer of the universe! America has achieved greatness because of her dependence on God and his grace. As creator, God loves his world. It's his world—it all belongs to him!

Christianity makes it clear that "the earth is the Lord's, and everything in it. The world and all its people belong to him" (Psalm 24:1). The ancient Hebrews and apostles John and Paul believed God made the world and that he gives life to all men and breath to all things. We sing the "Doxology" in which we are admonished to "Praise God from whom all blessings flow!" When we do, we are proclaiming God's ownership! We cannot own it or create it; it belongs to God and he holds the title.

Jesus told a parable to emphasize his ownership. A land owner went away and left the responsibility of the vineyard to workers. But the tenants did not send the owner his share of the crop; so the owner sent servants to collect the rent. When their attempts failed, the owner sent his son to collect the rent but the workers killed him. The owner returned with a large force, killed the evil workers and gave the vineyard to others.

It's a great privilege to live in God's wonderful world. We must never forget it is his world! We have no right to take that which belongs to him—we are just tenants, only stewards! So as you celebrate the Thanksgiving season, remember this is God's world and "It all belongs to him!"

My moment of reflection…

How Big Is Your God?

November 2
Philippians 4:10-23

Sitting in a dark Roman prison cell is an aged man named Paul. He had done so much for the kingdom and was now in captivity awaiting possible execution. By himself, separated from friends who knew and loved him dearly, he was deprived of earning a living. But in his poverty, Paul was remembered generously by devoted friends at Philippi. They too were poor but in their poverty they sent a gift to Paul. This gift awakened a spirit of thanksgiving and gratitude in Paul. Their thoughtfulness revived him, their love encouraged and comforted him.

In response to their generosity, Paul writes a letter thanking them for their love and concern and assured them of his contentment even within prison walls. In his thank-you note, he tells them that "this same God who takes care of me will supply all your needs from his glorious riches" (Philippians 4:19).

The trouble with many people is their God is "too small!" In his letter, Paul reveals that his God is a "big" God. For Paul, the words "my God" meant that he was great enough to cover his entire life. Unless your God is that big, then he is too small!

The Bible is filled with promise after promise. In fact, there are over eight thousand promises in God's word and our Father will keep everyone! While God has not promised to give us all we want, he has assured us that our needs will be met from his great storehouse of unlimited supply. Remember his promise: "God will supply all your needs from his glorious riches!"

My moment of reflection...

Wise Investments

November 3
Matthew 6:19-24

As we contemplate Thanksgiving, we are reminded of our possessions. Many of us have been quite successful as indicated by all our "stuff." But by our standards, Jesus achieved few of the status symbols that we consider important. The only status symbol he achieved was a cross on which he suffered a lonely death. While some people think of Jesus as one who is concerned only with spiritual matters, he has a relevant message that impacts all of life.

As heaven's wonderful teacher, Jesus has a word concerning investments and our relationship to the material world. He warns us against the peril of letting material things over-shadow the abundant life. As our investment counselor Jesus instructs us to "store our treasures in heaven" (Matthew 6:20). Earthly treasures have a way of controlling our affections and attitudes! Millionaire Charles Schwab said his happiest days were when he had a modest income and lived in a cottage with his wife. We store up treasures in heaven by living a life in loving obedience to Christ, by being salt of the earth.

A tourist was visiting a famous art gallery. He noticed a woman on her knees scrubbing the floor. He turned to her and commented there were so many beautiful paintings to which she replied, "I suppose so, if you have time to look up!" Therein is the tragedy! We become so engrossed in our treasures that we don't take time or have the inclination to look up! This Thanksgiving season make sure you "look up" and give thanks for what you have and continue to make wise investments!

My moment of reflection…

Blessed...To Be a Blessing

November 4
Psalm 103:1-32

Our Father is generous and gracious to his children; he provides so many blessings for his family. We must never forget we are responsible to God for our stewardship of his provisions. It is not optional; it is required in stewards that "a manager must be faithful" (1 Corinthians 4:2).

If God is going to load me up from his storehouse of blessings, then I want to be a "blesser!" I'm convinced that one of the reasons God prospers certain people with resources is because he knows they will in turn prosper his people. I can feel good about "emptying my barn" if I remember who filled it to begin with. King David, a man after God's own heart, needed a little prodding regarding his own thinking. Perhaps, that is the reason why he wrote, "Praise the Lord...and never forget the good things he does for me" (Psalm 103:2).

In a position of abundance and surplus, David engages in "self-talk" about his need to thank the Lord. Why does God fill your life with good things? Is it so you can go out to your warehouse and count all the inventory? No, he doesn't want you to worry about what you have "in stock!" The Giver wants you to concern yourself with the "outflow" and leave the "inflow" to him. In fact, when your cupboard is empty you are most ready for God's provision. When the pantry is empty and you are at the bottom of the barrel, even then you can encourage others! Indeed, you are blessed to be a "blesser!" Bless someone today!

My moment of reflection...

Generosity—Mark of Maturity

November 5
Luke 12:13-34

Thanksgiving reminds us of gratitude—Christmas of giving! What a marvelous season of the year! A child becomes an adult when he stops taking, stops begging and learns how to give. A sense of responsibility for others is a mark of emotional and spiritual maturity. Gratitude and giving is not one of mankind's natural virtues.

When we move from the habit of taking to the habit of giving we are becoming accountable. Generous givers have learned that all they have is a gift from God and some-day will give an account for the way they have managed God's gifts. Jesus instructed the rich fool that "real life is not measured by how much we own" (Luke 12:15), but how we use what we have been given. As members of God's family, we have an obligation to share and care for one another while remembering that we give not to win God's grace but because his grace has won us!

The importance of generosity is not what the giving does for the recipient, but what it does for the giver. Reflecting on the faithfulness and goodness of God, we are moved to be "doers" of the word by giving cheerfully, not reluctantly or in response to pressure. Paul reminds us that our generosity and "good deeds will never be forgotten" (2 Corinthians 9:9) and that God will generously provide all you need with plenty left over to share with others. Recently I heard a missionary say, "You are never more like God than when you give!" What a testimony to the gift of generosity!

My moment of reflection…

Gratitude

November 6
Psalm 95:1-7

According to the United States Bureau of Standards, a dense fog covering seven city blocks to a depth of 100 feet is composed of less than one glass of water—sixty billion tiny droplets. Yet when those minute particles of water settle over a city or the countryside, they can almost blot out everything from sight.

Sadly, many Christians live in a fog! They allow a cupful of troubles to cloud their vision and dampen their spirit. Worry, turmoil and defeat strangle their thinking and their attitudes; their lives are being choked by "the cares of this life" (Matthew 13:22) and they sense that life is hopeless. The real tragedy is that fog robs so many of a thankful spirit!

A little boy said that "salt is what always spoils the potatoes when it is left out." How true. Potatoes without proper seasoning are tasteless! In like fashion, gratitude is what spoils life when it is left out! A thankful spirit enables folks to praise God even when circumstances are difficult. Paul cautions believers to "always be full of joy in the Lord...and thank him for all he has done" (Philippians 4:4, 6).

Alexander Whyte, the great Scottish preacher often began his prayers with an expression of gratitude. One cold, miserable day his parishioners wondered how he would open his prayer. True to form and habit he said, "We thank Thee, O Lord, that it is not always like this!" No Christian should ever live in "the fog!" Because we are children of the King, let's determine to always live in the Sonshine!

My moment of reflection...

Time to Say Thanks

November 7
2 Corinthians 2:12-17

November is the season for us to say thanks for acts of kindness others have done for us. I read a sign recently which read: "Fall has returned and so has Thanksgiving and pumpkin pie!" Thanksgiving has many implications, especially for the Christian. The tenor of our times has influenced our thinking. Very little of the current news produces joy or causes one to be thankful.

Depression, terrorism, hunger, war, crime, corruption, dishonesty, unemployment, earthquakes, floods, the list goes on! The apostle Paul was jailed, beaten, arrested, imprisoned, and finally executed. Before his death he gave this word: "Always be full of joy in the Lord. I say it again—rejoice" (Philippians 4:4).

For Christians, Thanksgiving is not so much a national holiday as it is a "daily" affair! We must realize that it is "God...who leads us along in Christ's triumphal procession" (2 Corinthians 2:14). If I know the Lord and am committed to his Lordship, I can be assured that he will be with me always, helping me even when my circumstances are difficult and I cannot see the way before me. Bad news will fade away and become insignificant as we think about reasons to be thankful. By faith, we focus on the eternal: "We don't look at the troubles we can see right now; rather, we look forward to what we have not yet seen...joys to come will last forever" (2 Corinthians 4:18). Thanksgiving starts with a "Thankful Heart!"

My moment of reflection…

Draw Near to God

November 8
James 4:7-10

In the Christian life, we have great and precious promises! We have the peace of God, which surpasses all understanding. We have unconditional love of the Father, and we have the Holy Spirit who is sent to be our comfort and guide. Yet we have this yearning to be close to God. We want more of God in our lives…we want to overcome sin…we want to live Godly lives! So how do we "come near to God?"

James commands believers to "Draw close to God, and God will draw close to you" (James 4:8). On many occasions in Paul's writings he commands us to "learn to be thankful!" He told his friends to "be thankful" and "be watchful and thankful!" No matter what our situation is, no matter what is going on around us, we are exhorted to be thankful. No choice! Even in our pain! So how do we "come" close to the Lord?

We draw close to God by having an attitude of thanksgiving— by looking at the glass as half full, by believing that what we have coming is greater than what we have now, knowing that what we have is temporary compared to what we will have in heaven is eternal. A thanksgiving mindset thinks of God and his abundant blessings; that "mindset" shows appreciation to God and others for "all the things he has done for us!" "Drawing near to God" is the perfect way to express our Thanksgiving to God!

My moment of reflection…

Thanks

November 9
Psalm 136:1-26

One evening during the depression of the thirties, businessmen were talking about banks closing and people out of work. It was a gloomy conversation!

One man said, "There sure isn't much to be thankful for."

After listening to one sad story after another, one man said, "I am grateful for Mrs. Jones!" He went on to explain that she was his teacher who went out of her way to introduce him to great books.

Someone asked, "Did you ever thank her?"

He admitted he never did, but that evening he wrote his former teacher a letter of thanks. A few weeks later, a reply came from the aged woman.

> My Dear Eddie
>
> I want you to know what your note meant to me. I'm an old lady now in my eighties, living alone in a small home, lonely like the last leaf on a tree…I taught school for fifty years and in all that time yours is the first letter of appreciation I have ever received. It came on a cold morning and it cheered my lonely heart as nothing has cheered me in years.

November is the time for all of us to say thanks, to remember the kindnesses that others have done for us. Let me encourage you to write a note of thanks this month to someone who has blessed your life. It might just make someone's day—and the Lord will be pleased. "It's a good thing to give thanks…"

My moment of reflection…

Giving is a Risk

November 10
2 Corinthians 9:1-15

Wandering in the desert, near death from thirst, a man saw shade trees in the distance. But at the trees there was no water or bubbling spring; instead, the man found a pump. Beside the pump was a small jar of water and a note which explained the water was for "priming the pump" and not for drinking! He faced a dilemma: drink the water or prime the pump! If the note was accurate, by priming the pump he would have plenty of water to drink. What should he do?

This parable demonstrates that giving is a very important issue for believers! We become Christians by giving up confidence in ourselves and trusting God. In order to grow in faith we give time for worship, fellowship and giving to those in need. In fact, everything we do as believers is an act of giving and thanksgiving!

It's obvious the whole idea of "giving" is more than the gifts we share with others. God wants every part of us, to get close to us and mold us into the image of Jesus. But there is a risk—to find your life, you must lose your life! There is a pump out there somewhere and God has given you just enough water to prime that pump. But you have a choice—satisfy your own thirst or provide water for all who are thirsty! Giving is a risk you can't afford not to take!

My moment of reflection...

Opening the Floodgates

November 11
Luke 6:37-38

Solomon teaches that "it is possible to give freely and become more wealthy, but those who are stingy will lose everything. The generous prosper and are satisfied; those who refresh others will themselves be refreshed" (Proverbs 11:24-25).

A truth expressed in the parable of the pump is this: only as we give do we prepare ourselves to receive! The man in the parable would never experience an abundance of water until he was willing to part with the small amount he had for priming the pump. We open "floodgates" only as we are willing to cheerfully give to others. Here is the divine "cycle" of giving: we must give, which enables us to receive, so that we can give again! Jesus said, "If you give, you will receive. Your gift will return to you in full measure, pressed down, shaken together...and running over. Whatever measure you use in giving—large or small—it will be used to measure what is given back to you" (Luke 6:38).

Don't give in order to receive—that short circuits the cycle! We give in order to receive so that we can give again. If we keep our small jar of water, it will soon be gone, leaving us with nothing! But in pouring it out—priming the pump—an unlimited abundance of water is released to us and others. Express your thanksgiving by "opening the floodgates" to a thirsty world—and you will be satisfied over and over again!

My moment of reflection...

Giving Is a Risk

November 12
Psalm 126:1-6

We take risks all the time—especially when we give! "Those who plant in tears will harvest with shouts of joy. They weep as they go to plant their seed, but they sing as they return with the harvest" (Psalm 126:5-6). You take a "risk" when you commit your last grain to the ground, but the reward comes when the seed you have sown returns "many-fold" at harvest time!

The thirsty desert wanderer was at the crossroads: maybe the parchment note is a lie or the pump gasket is worn out—then what? Pouring out the last bit of water means risking his life! It happens all the time in life: when we give our love to someone we risk rejection! We give money in a sacrificial way without knowing if we will have unexpected expenses. But that is what Christianity is all about—about putting our faith on the line when we decide to give. It is in the risk of giving that God shows himself to be true and faithful to his every promise.

So thirsty, wandering in the desert we find this old pump with a small glass of water and a note! Its decision time—what should we do? We can't cling to our little jar of water, no matter how thirsty we are. We are going to have to risk it all—pour it out! This Thanksgiving, take a risk and pour out the water and watch the pump work!

My moment of reflection…

Thanksgiving Heretics

November 13
Habakkuk 3:17-19

Habakkuk was a prominent citizen of Jerusalem! Tyranny and strife and lawlessness were everywhere and the prophet was perplexed: Why does God allow injustice to reign on the earth? Confused, Habakkuk says to God, "How long, O Lord, must I call for help? But you do not listen" (Habakkuk 1:2). But look at his attitude: "Even though the fig trees have no blossoms, and there are no grapes on the vine; even though the olive crop fails, and the fields lie empty...though the flocks die in the fields, and the cattle barns are empty, yet I will rejoice in the Lord" (Habakkuk 3:17-18).

Habakkuk says when everything goes wrong, yet there is reason for Thanksgiving! Thanksgiving heretics are folks who observe the feast of thanksgiving but give no thanks. Their tables are full of things to eat and the day filled with feasting—but will lack thanks. Thanksgiving heretics feel there is nothing for which to give thanks—it calls for gratitude! Any person who rejoices in his abundance with no thought of those who are hungry and homeless and wrongly treated are Thanksgiving heretics!

America is an oasis of plenty in a world of want! Many of the world's people will spend Thanksgiving uprooted from their homes, hungry and suffering. God will not accept folded hands of thanks unless they are also offered as outstretched hands of help to those in need. Truly thankful people not only put stress on "thanks" but also on "giving."

My moment of reflection...

Melody of Love

November 14
Psalm 116:1-19

In this Psalm we have the picture of a man who comes to the temple for worship. He had suffered a severe illness and been in the very jaws of death—but God was gracious to deliver him. Having been delivered, he is in the temple to offer a sacrifice of Thanksgiving. He's not alone—friends and neighbors are there too, rejoicing in his deliverance!

This psalm is a testimony, a glorious shout of Thanksgiving—his gratitude prompts him to do something for the One he loves. He loves the Lord because God heard his cry and saw his need (Psalm 116:2). God heard and answered his prayer and offered him grace! When death seemed certain, God came and rescued him! No wonder he shouted, "I love the Lord!"

Love is always a duet—a melody! There must be a human reaction to a divine action! He declares that he will walk with the Lord and offer a sacrifice of Thanksgiving. In his illness he had made a vow to God. He promised to pay his vows in the presence of God's people in the temple. He is filled with gratitude and gratitude always moves toward balancing the books. Looking up in thanksgiving must be accompanied by paying up in honesty. So in gratitude and thanksgiving for all that God has done for us, let's join the psalmist in offering our sacrifice of Thanksgiving to express our thanks for his mercy and grace!

My moment of reflection…

Praise the Lord

November 15
Psalm 117:1-2

There is an old Jewish legend which says after God created the world, he called the angels and asked them what they thought of his world. One of them said, "One thing is lacking: the sound of praise to the Creator." So God created music and it was heard in the whisper of the wind and in the song of the birds. Down through the ages the gift of music has proven a blessing to multitudes. Other religions may have chants but only Christianity has music!

At every great event in the Bible, music was the vehicle used to express thanksgiving. When Moses crossed the Red Sea or Solomon dedicated the temple or when Jesus was born, praise and worship was an expression of thanksgiving for God's gifts. When we praise God, we remind ourselves of God's goodness, greatness, generosity and faithfulness. Satan will come with the subtle suggestion that God is not good, that God does not love us or that God cannot be trusted. But in our praises, we are strengthened and reminded that God is "for us!"

When noted agnostic Robert Ingersoll died, the printed funeral program said, "There will be no singing…no hymns, anthems or spiritual songs." Without God or redemption agnostics have no hope—they have nothing to sing about! But we do! Today as you count your blessings and enjoy the goodness of God—do not remain silent. Give voice to your gratitude which brings his blessings to you.

My moment of reflection…

Thanksgiving in America

November 16
Psalm 111

The Pilgrims endured a bitter two-month journey from England to Plymouth Rock. When they landed, they gathered for a prayer service before building shelter for the harsh New England winter. Nearly half of their number died in 1620, but in the providence of God, Indians taught the colonists about fishing, hunting and planting, ensuring their survival. Thanks to their Indian neighbors, they reaped a bountiful harvest. As an expression of their "thanks" to God, they held a three-day feast to thank God for saving their lives during the severe winter. This meal is thought of today as the first Thanksgiving!

In the years to come during the fall, the governors of each New England colony declared a day of Thanksgiving so that people could thank God for supplying their needs. Later in 1789, President George Washington issued a declaration "that we may all unite to render unto him our sincere and humble thanks for his kind care and protection."

Thanksgiving is the perfect time to understand the Judeo-Christian history of our nation. Our forefathers were not uneasy about openly thanking God for his blessings or beseeching him in times of trouble and need. There are so many who wish to ignore or rewrite our history as our nation further embraces secularism. I am so thankful for America and for the God of history who shed his grace on us, beginning with the landing of the colonists at Plymouth Rock nearly 400 years ago. May we never cease to give thanks for our country and to pray for our continued freedom as our forefathers intended.

My moment of reflection...

Thank you...Thank you

November 17
Psalm 147

Recently, I heard a lively Gospel chorus that focused on three words, "thank you, Lord!" For some reason, this tune and these words lingered in my mind—I just couldn't forget them. As the chorus continued, the lyrics thanked the Lord for one joyful blessing after another. We are to thank the Lord for everything that we are...that we can be...that we can do...that we can hear...that we can see! It was a wonderful reminder of many things that are so easily taken for granted.

The joys of summer and beauty of fall are a memory, yet our smile of gratitude is not diminished. The change of season in no way dims the light of God's faithful provision. In spite of our highs and lows, in contrast to our drifting moods and shifting needs, God remains the same. How thankful I am for that! Like the great Welsh hymn declares, "We blossom and flourish as leaves on the tree, and wither and perish—but naught changeth Thee!"

Our thankfulness not only reaches up to God, it also reaches out to friends and family members who make life so rich and fulfilling. We especially appreciate the faithfulness of loved ones for their prayers, caring and encouragement. And so as Thanksgiving Day approaches, please know that our list of things for which we say "Thank you, thank you, thank you, thank you Lord" includes you! "Sing out your thanks to the Lord; sing praises to our God" (Psalm 147:7).

My moment of reflection...

Common Courtesy

November 18
Psalm 95:1-11

Common courtesy requires an expression of thanks to the giver of every gift! In addition to courtesy, every Christian should be moved by the goodness of God to cultivate this quality at all times. It is alarming to see how bold the spirit of ingratitude can be in the human spirit. A little boy was given an apple by a neighbor. When the youngster failed to say "thanks" his mother prompted him, "Son, what do you say?" Handing the apple to the neighbor, the boy said "peel it!" This societal attitude today creeps into the lives of God's people! Tragic!

Lack of gratitude is blind to the mercies and blessings of God; but the heart open to God finds a constant display of his goodness which draws forth our praise. Paul stated it this way: "always give thanks for everything" (Ephesians 5:20). In the Psalms, joy always comes out of a sense of gratitude. Behind the words of thanksgiving we do not see luxuriant fields or flocks or bursting barns. The spirit of thanksgiving does not come from things but rather from a "big" idea of God—"Know that the Lord is God...we are his...enter his gates with thanksgiving" (Psalm 100:3-4).

Real joy comes out of thanksgiving...and thanksgiving comes out of faith—faith in one who is in and behind this world, who is behind life! Remove thanksgiving—someone to thank and you remove joy! Thanksgiving is not only our Christian privilege—it is "common courtesy!"

My moment of reflection…

Thanksgiving Memories

November 19
Psalm 100

The apostle John warned followers of Christ of the danger of forgetting God and following substitute gods: "Dear children, keep away from anything that might take God's place in your hearts" (1 John 5:21). Every Christian needs to be instructed again and again that the "Lord he is God" and as God, he is the basis for blessing and thanksgiving. Idolatry cancels thanksgiving!

Idolatry is the failure to let God be God! Moses warned the children of Israel the peril of forgetting that God is God. Moses said, "Beware that in your plenty you do not forget the Lord your God and disobey His commandments" (Deuteronomy 8:11). He further instructed Israel to utilize their memory at all times: "Always remember that it is the Lord your God who gives you power to become rich" (Deut. 8:18). Even the psalmist charged himself with the responsibility of remembering: "Never forget how kind he has been" (Psalm 103:2, CEV).

Every plague the Egyptians faced was a picture of God's superiority to all other gods. The current spirit of our world does not encourage us to remember God or the gifts he gives to his children. God is presented as obsolete, belonging to another era. But as you travel through the corridors of biblical history you are commanded to remember the Lord your God who has given you all things richly to enjoy! Indeed, it is the memories of the past that opens the gates of praise and makes Thanksgiving unforgettable!

My moment of reflection…

Faithfulness

November 20
1 Corinthians 6:19-20

A very wealthy CEO of a large corporation visited the home of one of his employees. Looking at their guest, a young boy greeted the guest with this question: "Why did you make yourself that way?" "What do you mean?" asked the company leader. The lad replied, "Mother said you were a self-made man!" While that's a common view, God said "he made us and we are his…the sheep of his pasture" (Psalm 100:3).

The Corinthian Christians either forgot or were uninformed that they belonged to the Lord, that he was their owner. They did not belong to themselves! Why do we forget that the Lord is God? Perhaps we have an immature and incomplete concept of God or we've allowed Satan to misrepresent the nature and character of God. Elijah and his contest with false prophets at Mount Carmel made it unmistakably clear that "the Lord is God" (1 Kings 18:39).

The psalmist declared that God is our Creator and our bountiful and faithful benefactor whose unfailing love continues forever. His mercy is from everlasting to everlasting and he is faithful throughout all generations. You can trust him; there is no fluctuation or change in his character and in his benevolent purpose. Because his faithfulness extends to each generation, we choose to give thanks and bless his name. As his people and the sheep of his pasture, "Let us come before him with thanksgiving. Let us sing him psalms of praise" (Psalm 95:2).

My moment of reflection…

Thanksgiving Heroes

November 21
Psalm 150

Throughout history there have been champions of freedom who had a dramatic influence on the rise of freedom in America... heroes that we need to honor every Thanksgiving. We salute men like William Bradford, George Washington, Abraham Lincoln and Franklin Roosevelt.

Governor Bradford came to America on the Mayflower with his wife Dorothy, who drowned on December 7, 1620, while the ship was anchored in the harbor. Despite the anguish of losing his wife, Gov. Bradford wrote the following proclamation: "Inasmuch as the great Father has given us this year an abundant harvest of Indian corn, wheat, peas, beans, squashes, and has made the forests to abound with game and the sea with fish, and inasmuch as he has protected us...spared us from pestilence and disease... granted us freedom to worship God according to the dictates of our own conscience...I proclaim November 29, 1623, as a day of thanksgiving to Almighty God for all his blessings."

As we celebrate Thanksgiving this year, nearly 400 years after Gov. Bradford's first proclamation, we see an aggressive assault on Judeo-Christian values that served as a foundation for our nation. It is imperative that we defend Thanksgiving and other God-inspired celebrations that define our nation against those ugly forces that wish to drive us into secular oblivion.

Our praise this Thanksgiving should be natural and spontaneous, a delight rather than a duty. Our hearts should sing for joy. Indeed, "Let every living creature praise the Lord" (Psalm 150:6, CEV).

My moment of reflection...

Gratitude or Grumbling

November 22
Luke 17:11-19

Being grateful is a choice! It is not an emotion guided by our circumstances. Jesus had just healed ten lepers; and the story indicates that he was not pleased with their response since only one returned to give thanks. It is not surprising that God let the Israelites wander in the wilderness for forty years because they grumbled and complained? Paul now challenges us to "always be joyful...always be thankful" because this is God's will (1 Thessalonians 6:16).

Paul's challenge seems to be a tall order; it's difficult to see the good in every circumstance. It goes against our natural instincts. Mopping the floor is not necessarily a happy task! We can grumble about the dirt and all the people that made it so messy and the fact that we are left to clean up the mess. However, we could view the task in a positive way and be thankful for the home we have, for the strength to do the work and for a family to clean up after! Choosing gratitude can change our perspective on the simplest of tasks and transform them into praise and gratitude, experiencing God's peace and presence.

To get you focused, find something to be thankful for that starts with each letter of the alphabet. You see, it's all about choosing to focus on God's wonderful provision for the present, trusting him for our future and realizing his blessings of the past. For me and my house, we choose "gratitude!"

My moment of reflection...

The Habit of Giving Thanks

November 23
1 Thessalonians 5:1-28

We have some good habits and some bad habits! We are what we are because of the habits we have developed over the years. Paul writes, "no matter what happens, always be thankful, for this is God's will for you who belong to Christ Jesus" (1 Thessalonians 5:18). We tend to be thankful when reminded of our blessings, but when the reminders are not present or when they are too common our giving of thanks is forgotten.

Thanksgiving is not to be based on feelings but a command to be obeyed! Paul teaches that thanksgiving is a habit to be learned and cultivated rather than some spontaneous and accidental thing. In the story of the ten lepers (Luke 17) only one returned to give thanks for his healing. We are not born thankful—we must learn thanksgiving and praise!

When we learn "thanksgiving" we tend to be people of joy even in difficult times. The expression of joy and gratitude brings joy to the heart of our heavenly Father. Life can be beautiful if we look for the flowers! Consciously we must determine that we are going to be grateful, again and again until it becomes an automatic expression of life.

Gratitude is an experience—not just a theory! Paul suffered in prison but he was never without gratitude. For Paul and us, thanks and gratitude helps us over the mountains of life and turns defeat into victory. Gratitude and thanksgiving grows as it is given away. May the "habit of thanks" flourish in your life this Thanksgiving season!

My moment of reflection...

The Grace of Gratitude

November 24
Psalm 95:1-11

When Robinson Crusoe was wrecked on a lonely island he evaluated his situation. He concluded that even in one's misery and misfortunate one could find something for which to be thankful. Living in affluence, we seem to be long on demands and but short on thanksgivings. Following the spiritual journey of Paul there is no scarcity of praise. On a missionary journey or in prison, wherever he went he appeared in the "garment of praise." It seems that praise was woven into the fabric of his life and he longed for that pattern for his friends.

Paul was not privileged with affluence or possessions of material things and yet he was filled with joy and cheerfulness. He experienced the affliction of a "thorn" and the bitterness of persecution. On the other hand, when Paul took inventory of his life he had so many things that brought gratitude: daily bread, people of faith, deliverance from temptation, memory of friends, kindness from strangers and most of all the unspeakable gift of Jesus.

For Paul, gratitude is a matter of humility and duty, not a matter of emotion. The full measure and meaning of gratitude does not come in an instant. As believers, we are called to "abound with thanksgiving" so our lives would over-flow with joy and thankfulness. Gratitude exalts God but ingratitude is an insult to the Almighty.

During this Thanksgiving season, count your blessings and try to enumerate the things for which you should be grateful. When you do, you will pleasantly discover that gratitude is God's design for all creation. Thanksgiving and gratitude is the Christian's mandate!

My moment of reflection...

Blessings and Thanksgiving

November 25
Psalm 50:1-23

As I think about Thanksgiving, my mind focuses on all the blessings that have come my way from the gracious hand of God. One of my favorite Gospel songs at Thanksgiving is "Count your many blessings, name them one by one!" Indeed, while there have been disappointments and losses and some setbacks this past year, our blessings have been so numerous that it would take hours to inventory them "one by one."

The word "thanksgiving" has a subject and an object! What we are thankful for is the subject and the One to whom we are thankful is the object. People are often worthy objects and we should give thanks to one another for their kindness and goodness. But the supreme object of our thanks is the Lord! While we are to be thankful for his benefits, we must be thankful for him!

In 1618, Martin Rinkart became a pastor in his native Germany. Soon thereafter, the "Thirty Year War" erupted. Near the end of the war, pestilence and devastating famine swept the land. Out of this crucible of war, famine and pestilence, he revealed a heart fixed on God, not the problems of his beloved country when he wrote, "Now thank we all Our God."

This Thanksgiving season let your attitude "ring" with gladness. Praise the Lord for what he has done and then ask him to use you to further his cause with a godly and thankful spirit. The psalmist spoke for the Lord when he said, "Giving of thanks is a sacrifice that truly honors me…" (Psalm 50:23).

My moment of reflection…

Choose Thanksgiving

November 26
Psalm 92

One of the American Thanksgivings recorded in the mid 1600's was much different than the first which was primarily a celebration of thanksgiving. Because of severe drought and hard times it became not only a time of thanks but prayer and fasting. Desperate for rain, the pilgrims set aside a day to pray for rain. A gentle rain began to fall as they were praying and a spontaneous time of great thanksgiving erupted! It was not until 1863 that Abraham Lincoln declared a national day of thanksgiving, hoping it would bring unity to the nation.

Choosing thankfulness can actually make us healthier! Recent research has shown that being thankful improves our physical and emotional health, even though we may stuff ourselves at the dinner table. Holding on to feelings of thankfulness boosts our immune system and increases blood supply to our heart. A daily exercise of keeping a gratitude journal can increase our alertness, enthusiasm, energy and improve our sleep. People who describe themselves as feeling grateful tend to suffer less stress and depression.

God takes great pleasure in receiving our thanks and praise. He not only longs for our expressions of love and gratefulness, he wants to hear our sorrows and the desires of our hearts. God knows that when we focus on our blessings, it's easier to keep our problems and concerns in the right perspective. "It is good to give thanks to the Lord…You are exalted in the heavens, You, O Lord, continue forever!" (Psalm 92:1, 8).

My moment of reflection…

Giving Thanks

November 27
1 Thessalonians 5:12-22

Jesus stood in the middle of 5000 hungry men, women and children with only one sack lunch. What was he to do? How do you feed that many starving people? He could have panicked or complained to his Father! Instead, he looked up and "gave thanks."

A cargo ship loaded with 276 people was caught in a raging storm. They were at their "wits" end! For two weeks they had been tossed about and it seemed inevitable that they would die. It was a terrifying situation! But one passenger, the apostle Paul stood up, faced the scared passengers, "took bread and gave thanks to God."

Nearly half of the pilgrims that came to America died during the preceding winter. These folks were thousands of miles from family and food was low. But in spite of their hardships, they knelt to thank God for their blessings!

Thanksgiving! What a wonderful time of the year; better yet, what a wonderful way to live! Thanksgiving should be at the very heart of every authentic Christian. The Word of God instructs us that whatever happens "to be thankful, for this is God's will for you" (1 Thessalonians 5:16). So when life is painful and the road seems dark or when we seem to be unable to understand what is taking place, we can still give thanks. God is to be trusted—he is still in control. He is Lord and he will bless us! Let us rejoice and give thanks!

My moment of reflection…

My Cup Runs Over

November 28
Psalm 23:1-6

George Herbert, the beloved English Poet prayed, "Thou hast given so much to me! Give one thing more—a grateful heart!" That's a prayer everyone needs to pray not only at Thanksgiving, but every day of the year. When reading the songs and psalms of King David, it seems he is always saying "thanks" to the Lord—especially it is true in Psalm 23. David looks back over his life and can't help himself—he shouts "My cup runs over!"

Our greed and pride blind us to a thousand mercies that are ours for the asking. It seems like we have so many wants that have not been met. But is this really true? David reminds us, "I have everything I need...you prepare a feast for me" (Psalm 23:1, 5). Even in our valleys and shadows there is a presence to sustain and a strength that causes us to go on: "I will not be afraid...your rod and staff protect and comfort me" (Psalm 23:4). Like David, Paul found God's provision sufficient when he reported that "God's grace is sufficient!"

David's cup was running over—running over with love, care, comfort and assurance that he would dwell "in the house of the Lord forever" (Psalm 23:6). What do you do with a full cup? David said he would offer unto the Lord a sacrifice of Thanksgiving! I hope that your Thanksgiving celebration includes a "sacrifice of praise" for a cup that runs over!

My moment of reflection...

It's Thanksgiving Time

November 29
Psalm 105:37-45

The last time they sang was the day they crossed the Red Sea! But now Israel is at a well singing this song: "Spring up, O well! Yes, sing about it! Sing of this well, which princes dug" (Numbers 21:17). Israel had been traveling in the desert and they were famished with thirst. God told Moses to gather the people together and he would give them water. And sure enough—out of "a rock" water flowed! Praise still opens the fountain in the desert while murmuring only brings judgment. Nothing honors and pleases God as our praise. Martin Luther said when he couldn't pray, he would sing! While the devil is a grumbler, a believer should be a living doxology!

Four times Jesus "gave thanks" to his Father. He gave thanks for daily bread at the feeding of the five thousand. He gave thanks for trials. He gave thanks for prayer at the gravesite of his friend Lazarus. His last recorded occasion for prayer was giving thanks for the privilege of providing salvation. Four times Jesus is recorded giving thanks—can we do any less?

The calendar says, "It's Thanksgiving time!" But what does your heart say? Have you learned to praise him in advance for the things you have not yet received? Let Thanksgiving be more than a social holiday or family reunion. Let it be a celebration of love, a sacrifice of praise to him who crowns the year with his goodness.

My moment of reflection...

Most Wonderful Time of the Year

November 30
Luke 2:8-20

We are approaching a joyful season that some have called "The most wonderful time of the year!" Indeed, Christmas is a time full of wonder and amazement as we consider the incredible event of God becoming flesh. Those who witnessed our Lord's spectacular arrival were filled with wonder and amazement and joy!

The miracles of the Christmas Story continue to fill us with wonder and awe. Mary was surprised by the unbelievable news that she would give birth to the Son of God. Joseph was troubled with his angelic encounter but was obedient to the command to take Mary as his wife. The shepherds were frightened with the angelic news of the Savior's birth but found their way to the manger to worship the new born King. And the wise men were filled with awe as they found the baby and gave him costly gifts. Though an ancient story, the birth of Jesus still fills our hearts with joy and wonder!

As we leave the Thanksgiving Season we may dread the preparations and activities that zap our energy as we face Christmas. Finding the perfect gift, baking cookies, decorating, sending cards and attending programs can distort the real meaning of Christmas. Hopefully, the fatigue, materialism and hurried lifestyle will not rob us of the joy and beauty of the season. So as we give gifts, sing of his glorious birth, gather for worship and enjoy celebrations with family and friends lets' focus our attention on Jesus whose wonderful love truly makes this "The most wonderful time of the year!"

My moment of reflection…

Signs of Christmas

December 1
Luke 2:1-12

Traveling the Upper Midwest states, you may be surprised to see billboards, encouraging you to visit a drug store in Wall, South Dakota. It seems strange to see advertisements so far in the distance, but the billboards become more frequent the closer the traveler gets to the little town of Wall, S.D. By the time you reach the drug store, most travelers are too curious not to stop.

It's December now and we are approaching the wonderful season of Christmas. The Bible gives us many signs, telling about the coming of Christ. To make sure we are prepared for his birth, Genesis 3:15 gives us the first "billboard" sign of our Lord's birth: "From now on, you and the woman will be enemies, and your offspring and her offspring will be enemies. He will crush your head, and you will strike his heel." That sign was given 4000 years before the event took place. The prophets gave us more signs of the Messiah's arrival, until about 400 years before his birth, when the signs suddenly stopped!

On Christmas Eve, an angel appeared and gave the final sign: "The Savior—yes, the Messiah, the Lord—has been born tonight in Bethlehem, the city of David. And this is how you will recognize him: You will find a baby lying in a manger, wrapped snugly in strips of cloth" (Luke 2:11-12). Gifts, cards and cookies are secular signs that something is "in the air!" But the true meaning of Christmas is hope, joy, peace and love—those are the real signs that tell you, it's soon going to be Christmas.

My moment of reflection...

God Became Man...

December 2
John 1:1-14

One summer day a gifted scientist was walking in his backyard thinking on what lies behind the observable facts of the universe. "There must be a Higher Being," he thought, "some kind of God." But he couldn't really conceive of how a sovereign God who created the universe could be known by man. How can little, insignificant man understand God? Just then his shadow fell across an ant hill, and the ants quickly began to scurry underground to safety. Watching their flight, he suddenly realized, "the only way I could ever tell them that I mean no harm would be for me to become one of them...an ant!"

Because God wanted to communicate to us and because he wanted us to understand his feelings and thoughts, he sent someone who could communicate with us on the human level. God wanted to tell us he loved us, but we couldn't possibly understand him. He was so anxious to communicate with us that he decided to do something that literally shook the universe: at Christmas time, God decided to become man without ceasing to be God!

God took the form of a human being, made in our likeness so he could communicate with us on our level! Christ was born so he could lift man to the divine level. At Christmas, we are not simply celebrating the birth of an exemplary human being, but rather the coming of God into our midst. He became "Emmanuel...God with us" (Matthew. 1:23).

Christmas for God meant great sacrifice! For us, Christmas means joy unspeakable! Thanks to God for his unspeakable gift. Merry Christmas!

My moment of reflection...

Sending the Very Best

December 3
John 3:1-17

Network news carried a story of a 6-year old boy who needed a kidney transplant. One kidney had already been removed, and now the remaining organ was not functioning. The only donor whose tissue would match was the boy's twin brother. At issue was an impending court decision as to whether the donor brother was old enough to understand what he was doing. The court interview with the boy revealed that not only did he know what his decision meant, but his willingness to sacrifice was based on man's greatest motive—love!

When a reporter asked the young lad about the operation, the young boy said he was going to give his brother his right kidney. Amused, the reporter asked, "why the right kidney?" "Because I'm right handed," the lad replied, "so my right kidney must be the strongest. I want to give my brother the best one!"

Love demands our very best! Giving rummage sale items to friends in need require no great sacrifice. Sending missionaries our left-overs is not a true representation of love. Or contributing one's spare time to the Lord's work represents no service beyond the call of duty. God sent his very best! He didn't send some run-down angel to pay for the price of our redemption. He sent his very best—his only begotten Son! So today, because of his love, we have eternal life.

Christmas music, evergreens, colored lights and gifts galore are all part of Christmas, but not the "Heart of Christmas." So the Father gave Jesus, his very best—Jesus Christ the Lord!

My moment of reflection…

Glory of the Incarnation

December 4
Philippians 2:1-11

We have seen pictures of Jesus, but really don't know what he looked like! However, the Bible gives us some clues to his appearance. The prophet Isaiah tells us "there was nothing beautiful or majestic about his appearance, nothing to attract us to him" (Isaiah 53:2). Paul wrote that Jesus "took the humble position of a slave and appeared in human form" (Philippians 2:7). Jesus appeared very ordinary, in a way you and I might describe as common.

When Jesus took human form his appearance changed. He no longer "looked" like God; He looked human in every way: he hurt, laughed and cried! He had a family and boyhood friends and eventually grew up choosing the work of a carpenter. While He was God, he wore none of the items associated with royalty. Think of it: "The Word (Jesus) became flesh" and tented among us! Since he was one of us, people could come near him. Little children loved him, fishermen felt comfortable in his presence and sick people longed for his touch. In every way, he was human, one like us!

Ultimately, he came to die for us! At his Father's bidding, Christ willingly came to earth to release us from the death-grip of sin. His accomplished mission of becoming flesh is the story of Christmas. From the throne room to the manger to the cross, Christ became flesh so we might pass from bondage to freedom, from death to life. Paul captures the gift of Christmas: "Thank God for his Son—a gift too wonderful for words" (2 Corinthians 9:15). Merry Christmas!

My moment of reflection...

In the Fullness of Time

December 5
Galatians 4:1-7

Christmas is just a few days away and folks are finishing their shopping. We don't know the exact date of our Lord's birth! December 25 was the date of the Roman feast of Saturnalia, when worshippers of the false god Saturn gave themselves to all forms of sin. It was, however, a season of goodwill when friends gave gifts to one another. Refusing to participate in this pagan event, Christians used the day to celebrate the birth of Jesus.

Whatever the actual date of Christ's birth, we are certain of one thing: the events surrounding his Advent were timed with precision. The Bible says, "When the right time came, God sent his Son, born of a woman...so that he could adopt us as his very own children" (Galatians 4:4-5). Every event surrounding Christmas took place at exactly the right time and "in the fullness of time."

At the proper stroke of the divine clock, an expectant teenager stopped at a crowded inn, a star appeared and angels sang to a bunch of frightened shepherds. Every event of Christmas was perfectly synchronized. Nothing happened too early or too late!

Like Mary and Martha, we fear God showing up late in the critical events of life. We call and he doesn't seem to hear; we think God has forgotten us...that he is late. But Christmas assures us he always comes "in the fullness of time." And best of all, as his birth was "on time," His second coming will also be "on time"— Christmas announces as he came to Bethlehem on time, he will come again—on time!

My moment of reflection...

Advent...a Time for Joy

December 6
Philippians 4:4-9

Advent—what a marvelous season of the year! It is a time of joy and expectancy as we prepare for the birth of Jesus. However, because of holiday stress joy often turns to gloom and we lose our enthusiasm for the season. Paul wrote, "Always be full of joy in the Lord. I say it again, rejoice" (Philippians 4:4). This verse is a strong command to gladness...and must be embraced by followers of Jesus. Our hearts may ache with the struggles of life, but we still have joy. Joy is the celebration of walking in the gift of God's presence, our Emmanuel, the God who is always present and with us!

In A.D. 200, Cyprian, Bishop of Carthage wrote to a friend about the joy of early Christians. In his letter he listed some of the cruelties of man: selfishness, armies fighting, men murdered in the coliseum to please applauding crowds and other sinful practices. But in spite of their troubles and persecution, believers were masters of their soul and filled with joy! That is the hallmark of faith—always full of joy!

Our feelings go up and down and our attitudes may be suspect at times, but joy runs deep that nothing can take it away! This Advent season is a time for joy and gladness—especially for the Christ Follower. Someone needs a good dose of joy and happiness today, and you are just the person to give it! Thanks for being a happy and joyful witness for Jesus who is the reason for our joy and the "reason for the season."

My moment of reflection...

Christmas Is People

December 7
Luke 2:1-12

We spend lots of time in crowded malls looking for the "right" gift, decorating and planning for that special meal with family and friends. Christmas is people; in fact, without people there would be little meaning to Christmas. Think of the people we focus our attention on at Christmas: shepherds watching their flocks, wise men with gifts, Joseph and Mary rejoicing in the birth of Jesus and crowds in Bethlehem. Often Christ gets lost in the shuffle!

Billy was writing a letter to God asking for a baby sister. "Dear God, I've been a very good boy…" He stopped, "No, God will never believe that." So he started again, "Dear God, most of the time I've been a good boy;" but he stopped again. "God won't buy that either—this will never work." An idea came to him! He went to the bathroom, grabbed a big towel, spread it out on the living room floor. Then he went to the mantle and brought down the statue of the Madonna. He wrapped the statute carefully and started to write again. "Dear God, I've got your mother. If you ever want to see her again…" Talk about leverage!

If Christmas means anything it means God is leveraging his love toward all of us. As you reflect on the people of Christmas, on gifts, on decorations and meals, make sure you don't forget the One in the manger! "God loved the people of this world so much that he gave his only Son, so that everyone who has faith in him will have eternal life and never really die" (John 3:16, CEV).

My moment of reflection…

Hope of the Wise Men

December 8
Matthew 2:1-12

Hope is a powerful word—at least it was to the Wise Men. The very sound of the word lifts your spirit when you are down and the future looks dark! Hope keeps you going and something to cling to when you have lost your way. It's the sparkle inside your soul that announces tomorrow things will be better. But the problem with hope is that its focus is based on uncertainty—and in a moment things can change that dash our dreams. Hope is one of the strongest motivators of the soul—it kept the Wise Men going for about two years!

In the Bible hope is never a wish but an absolute certainty. With Bible hope you can hope for something with utter confidence it will happen. That's the kind of hope the Wise Men had in the Nativity Story. For the Wise Men, hope was based upon what God had promised. And since God is faithful to his word, he always fulfills his promises; therefore, we can look forward with absolute hope!

When the Wise Men traveled to Bethlehem, they were hoping to find a King, someone who would bring an end to injustice, someone who would bring everlasting joy and peace to the world. In the fullness of time, Jesus was born and about two years later, the Wise Men arrived in Bethlehem. It was not a wish that brought them to Jerusalem to worship King Jesus, but a certainty, an absolute hope. As you re-read the Christmas story, remember that God is the source of all hope and Jesus is the fulfillment of hope!

My moment of reflection…

Wise Men Still Seek Him

December 9
Matthew 2:1-2

During the reign of King Herod, "Wise Men from the East came to Jerusalem and said, 'Where is the child born to be king of the Jews? We saw his star in the east...'" (Matthew 2:1-2, CEV). While our knowledge of the Wise Men is based on speculation, we know they sensed God's leading in their lives. Like O.T. patriarchs, these men had an understanding of the times. They probably came from Persia or Babylon and may have been introduced to the scriptures by Daniel. Perhaps, hope was born through the influence of Daniel that one day 'Someone' would be born who would save his people.

These Magi were looking for the Messiah! They traveled for months across a desert to search for the king. Because of their hope, God sent a supernatural signal confirming the arrival of Jesus—a star! Indeed, the whole narrative of the birth of Christ was accompanied by supernatural phenomena. However it happened, this we know: God did it! And so their "hope" led them on a long journey to Jerusalem.

Not only did they use their personal resources for the journey, they had expensive gifts with them—gold, frankincense and myrrh to honor the new-born king. We live in a culture when many people don't have time for the birth of Jesus. But "wise men" today like the wise men of old know there is a God in heaven who requires an accountability of all men and that he is the answer to the deepest needs of the human heart. Remember this Christmas: Wise men still seek him!

My moment of reflection...

Wise Men Still Worship Him

December 10
Matthew 2:1-11

It was not curiosity that sent the wise men on a long journey to Jerusalem to seek the promised Messiah. Rather, by faith they came seeking the one, born King of the Jews that they might worship him. Matthew spoke of the purpose of their trip: "We saw his star in the east and have come to worship him…When the men went into the house and saw the child with Mary, his mother, they knelt down and worshiped him…" (Matthew 2:2, 11, CEV).

The Magi didn't set out for a leisurely walk and just happened to show up in Jerusalem. No, they came in hope and confidence with the purpose of worshiping the Christ. All humanity worships someone or something! Tragically, much of modern Christianity does not know how to worship. Worship involves praising God, hearing his Word and giving gifts to God.

The Wise Men sacrificed their own comfort to find the King and worship him. It was a spontaneous and willing expression of devotion: "they fell down and worshipped him." Their worship was surrender to his authority and acknowledgement of his right to rule their lives. In worship, they presented gifts of gold, frankincense and myrrh. But perhaps the greatest treasure they were giving was themselves. They came to give—not to get! God wants our heart and attention, not just expensive gifts. The Magi were willing to leave their comfort zone and follow the Christ. David captures the intent of their giving when he wrote, "I can't offer the Lord my God a sacrifice that I got for nothing" (2 Samuel 24:24, CEV). How about you?

My moment of reflection…

Wise Men Still Listen

December 11
Matthew 2:9-11

The Wise Men followed God's guidance and listened carefully to God's warnings! When the Magi arrived in Jerusalem to worship the new King, Herod was troubled because Jesus was competition—a threat to his throne...He was worried! When they found the baby in Bethlehem's stable, they "were warned in a dream not to return to Herod, and they went back home by another road" (Matthew 2:12, CEV).

King Herod was a vicious, cruel ruler who killed everyone around him who threatened his position, including several sons, wife, mother-in-law and a number of court officers. So when the Wise Men asked him where the new king was to be born, he was very disturbed because he didn't want any rival for the throne. Seven centuries earlier Micah gave the answer: "In Bethlehem," just a few miles away! We know Herod's intention, "Kill the baby!"

But remember, the Magi were "wise men." They heard God's warning and knew this warning superseded the request of this cruel king; they knew the value of listening to God's Word: "Don't go back to Herod!" Solomon wrote, "Pay attention, my children! Follow my advice, and you will be happy. Listen carefully to my instructions, and you will be wise" (Proverbs 8:32-33, CEV). Wise men not only seek and worship him they listen carefully to his voice!

Like the Wise Men, giving God first place in life is a prerequisite to receiving his wisdom. If you need wisdom this Christmas, if you want to know what God wants you to do—ask him, and he will gladly tell you! Wise Men still listen!

My moment of reflection…

Wise Men Are Changed People

December 12
Matthew 2:1-12

A "wise man's" journey is a "journey of change." Look at the final instructions given to the Magi after their encounter with the King: "They were warned in a dream not to return to Herod, and they went back home by another road" (Matthew 2:12, CEV).

After the wise men had worshipped Jesus, they could not return the same way they had come! That is still true today! Once you've met the Savior, you will never be the same. An encounter with God changes things—it changes you! It has always been that way. Jacob wrestled with God and never walked the same. Isaiah stepped into the presence of God, saw his sinfulness and was changed—never to be the same. And Job after he questioned God about his suffering said that he talked too much; but now he was ready to listen!

Likewise, the Magi were changed...they left Bethlehem different than when they came. You can't come in contact with Jesus and remain the same...there will be change—change in attitude, in behavior and in conduct. Finding new direction in life comes as a result of finding the King!

Gift certificates are great because they eliminate restrictions and give the option to choose. It does not say "good for one tie or sweater." At Christmas, we need to say to the King, "You know better than anyone else, better that I do...You Choose!" He will always make the right choice as he did for the Wise Men. Seek him today...listen carefully to his warnings and be wise in the way you walk!

My moment of reflection...

A Giant Step for God

December 13
John 1:1-18

On July 20, 1969, Neil Armstrong became the first man to put his foot on another world. His first statement was, "One small step for man—one giant step for mankind." Another giant step for humanity occurred at Bethlehem when the Lord of Glory stepped out of heaven and came to earth to communicate love and grace to the world.

Since the dawn of history, God sought to communicate with man. He tried nature as a form of communication, but it often failed. God placed a conscience in man, but it too was unreliable. He gave prophets, personal witnesses and the Holy Scriptures, yet man was unable or unwilling to understand. When all else failed, God sent his Son to reveal God to man. The best way to know and understand a person is to hear him speak, see him act, see what makes him angry and what makes him glad. In short, the best way to know a person is to live with him! So God took a giant step and came as "Emmanuel—God with us!"

God becoming flesh is the greatest giant step recorded in history! We know a deed is more powerful than a declaration! So in the incarnation, Jesus was reflecting the nature and character of God and declaring that he knows us and loves us as none other. Reading the Christmas Story and reflecting on his ministry, the immediate conclusion is, "Jesus is more than a man—he is the Son of God." Praise God that Jesus was willing to take that "Giant Step" and become our Savior. Merry Christmas!

My moment of reflection…

Dedication Is an Expensive Gift

December 14
Luke 2:41-52

A person's greatness can be measured by their degree of dedication—a willingness to be a servant! Jesus was dedicated to do his Father's will and at the same time willing to serve humanity. At the onset of his ministry, Jesus determined to do his Father's business. When Mary and Joseph found their son in the temple, Jesus said, "Why did you have to look for me? Didn't you know that I would be in my Father's house?" (Luke 2:49, CEV). When tempted in the wilderness, Jesus chose to obey the Father. All through life, Jesus was committed to doing his Father's will!

Jesus announced his ministry intention in a temple sermon at Nazareth: "The Spirit of the Lord is upon me, for he has appointed me to preach Good News to the poor. He has sent me to proclaim that captives will be released, that the blind will see, that the downtrodden will be freed from their oppressors" (Luke 4:18).

Ultimately, His dedication was expressed by his death. Some thought this masterful teacher and miracle worker had been silenced forever. But God raised him from the dead and exalted him in glory. This very moment he is Lord who reigns over the affairs of history. Because of his dedication, God exalted his Son as a testimony of his obedience to do the Father's will and his ministry to all creation. Christmas is not merely a beautiful story or a manger scene or a star in the sky. Christmas is Christ living in me and it happened because of a gift—a very expensive gift!

My moment of reflection...

Most Valuable Gift Ever Given

December 15
Isaiah 53:1-12

Paul understood the meaning of Christmas when he wrote: "You know that our Lord Jesus Christ was kind enough to give up all his riches and become poor, so that you could become rich" (2 Corinthians 8:9, CEV). The baby born in a stable was rich, but became poor so you could be rich! Amazing!

Jesus was the possessor of heaven and earth and all creation because he created all things! As heir of all things, he was rich—rich in glory, power and authority. Yet, he became poor! Think of those words. He disrobed Himself of glory and covered himself with the flesh of our humanity. Born in a manger, raised in the poor community of Nazareth, he didn't have a place to lay his head. He was unable to pay taxes without the performance of a miracle. When he died, he was buried in another man's grave. As the Eternal God, he was rich in power, position, and possessions…He had it all, but became poor! His ultimate experience of poverty was when he was made sin for us on the cross…that's when Christ became the poorest of the poor!

Here's the good news: He became poor so you could become rich! His humiliation and poverty were for the purpose of introducing us to the riches of heaven. This suggests we were poor, totally bankrupt before we met Christ. On a Christmas night long ago, the most valuable gift ever given was for "all people." "This very day in King David's hometown a Savior was born for you. He is Christ the Lord" (Luke 2:11, CEV).

My moment of reflection…

Jesus...Our Wonderful Counselor

December 16
Isaiah 9:2-7

The Prophet Isaiah lived in troubled times! Everywhere you looked were gathering clouds of darkness and despair. Soon his beloved nation would be taken into captivity—cities destroyed, vineyards uprooted, land would lie in waste and only a remnant would remain...how sad!

Despite that devastating picture, Isaiah saw a prophetic bright spot—hope! In the midst of this destruction, the Lord said, "The people who walk in darkness will see a great light—a light that will shine on all who live in the land where death casts its shadow" (Isaiah 9:2). What was the promised light that would shine in the darkness? The answer: "For a child is born to us, a son is given to us. And the government will rest on his shoulders. These will be his royal titles: Wonderful Counselor..." (Isaiah 9:6a).

The Hebrew word for counselor means to guide, to direct and to give counsel. From time to time, people need a trusted counselor who can listen to problems, sympathize and give hope. Seven hundred years before Christ's miraculous birth Isaiah declared a Savior would be born to serve as our Counselor. Satan advised Adam and Eve to disobey the command of God; this was counseling to sin. But God's Christmas gift to men everywhere is the divine Counselor who came to restore order from chaos, to sweep away evil and forgive sin. We are so blessed to have a competent Counselor who instructs us, inspires us, and influences us. This Christmas, the Wonderful Counselor gives us light: "We have seen a great light..." and now we have hope!

My moment of reflection...

Jesus…Our Mighty God

December 17
Hebrews 1:1-12

With prophetic insight, Isaiah looked forward to the promised Messiah. Seven hundred years before his birth, Isaiah wrote, "For a child is born to us, a son is given to us. And the government will rest on his shoulders. These will be his royal titles: Wonderful Counselor, Mighty God…" (Isaiah 9:6a).

Men stand in awe of those who possess power and authority! No one is greater in power and authority and influence than Jesus. The wonder and might of the new born King begins with his miraculous conception and birth. But ultimately, a man's greatness is measured by works and deeds, especially acts of love and mercy. This "Mighty God" knows the thoughts of our hearts, creates what he pleases, raises the dead, able to forgive sin and can say things only God can say. His life was filled with acts of mercy and power—power that no one can explain in the human realm!

When we think of might and power, we think of overcoming a difficult task that has innumerable and seemingly insurmountable odds. Yet, Jesus was an over-comer in every instance—temptation, sin, sorrow, the cross and the grave! He left no great art or wealth or armies—just twelve disciples! Yet, today he has millions of followers, found in every country in the world. Isaiah was right when he declared the coming King to be the "Mighty God."

As we prepare for that Holy Night, let's make him our Wonderful Counselor and recognize him as the Mighty God who has eternally invaded history and spoken to us by his Son!

My moment of reflection…

Jesus...Our Everlasting Father

December 18
John 1:1-14

When presenting the Messiah, Isaiah called him the "Everlasting Father." In a world needing protection and safety, Isaiah wrote, "For a child is born to us, a son is given to us. And the government will rest on his shoulders. These will be his royal titles: Wonderful Counselor, Mighty God, Everlasting Father..." (Isaiah 9:6).

In Eastern Culture men were often given a name which signified some quality or characteristic for which they were famous—father of wisdom or the father of folly! "Everlasting Father" speaks of the coming Savior as "The Father of Eternity," our Father forever! It is a title referring to Christ's Lordship over eternity. As the everlasting Provider and Protector, by virtue of his divine character, he will never vacate His office.

We are bound by time and make plans—yet there comes a day when our plans will come to an end. In contrast, the Everlasting Father is not bound by time because he himself controls time... he is the same yesterday, today and forever, totally immune to the limitations of time. As our Everlasting Father he alone provides eternal life for all who call upon him.

The Savior we worship at Christmas did not come into existence at his birth in Bethlehem. He always was! At his birth, the eternal God was clothing himself in the garments of human flesh that men might more perfectly understand the nature and character of God and rest in his care. The Pharisees thought when Jesus died His influence would quickly die and his name soon forgotten. But they forgot he was the "Everlasting Father!"

My moment of reflection...

Jesus…Our Prince of Peace

December 19
Ephesians 2:1-22

Isaiah's world was full of greed, hatred and conflict! God let the prophet put on prophetic glasses to catch a glimpse of the One bringing peace to all men. "For a child is born to us, a son is given to us. And the government will rest on his shoulders. These will be his royal titles: Wonderful Counselor, Mighty God, Everlasting Father, Prince of Peace" (Isaiah 9:6).

The Angels sang about peace and the world cries for peace. The peace the Messiah brought was not the abolishment of war on earth, but the reconciling of God to man and then man to God! Man originally gave glory to God and walked with him. But sin disrupted this perfect harmony and man cannot find his way back to God by himself. So God sent his Son to make a way of return—to bring peace.

Peace is a Christmas gift from God that all creation needs and can only be found in Christ. Peace is the blessing he died to purchase and the blessing he longs to give. The singing of Christmas carols and receiving Christmas cards with the vague wish that you may have peace is impossible. The good news is this: Abiding in Jesus, staying close to him is how and where peace can be found. Paul reminds us that he is our Peace. Not only did Isaiah present the coming Savior as our Prince of Peace, he told us about the gift he gives: "You will keep in perfect peace all who trust in you, whose thoughts are fixed on you" (Isaiah 26:3).

My moment of reflection…

Peace While Fearful

December 20
Matthew 1:18-25

Our world is filled with fearful people! Man is the only creature whose existence is plagued by fear. People are afraid of the loss of health, loss of business and afraid of death. Fear is nothing new—it has plagued mankind since the beginning! But 2000 years ago, the answer to fear was announced to the world—Jesus was born and with his birth came the assurance that God was in control.

Joseph was engaged to be married to Mary; he was happy, looking forward to a wonderful life. But before they were married, he was told Mary was pregnant. Filled with fear...what should he do? Considering options, an angel appeared with this message: "do not be afraid to go ahead with your marriage to Mary. For the child within her has been conceived by the Holy Spirit...You are to name him Jesus, for he will save his people from their sins" (Matthew 1:20-21). Suddenly Joseph had his answer—he would not put Mary away. His fear vanished because God's plan brought peace in the presence of fear.

Mary was frightened! She did not understand the angel's message that she would become pregnant and have a baby named Jesus. As she listened, her fear was dispelled. In faith she replied, "I am the Lord's servant, and I am willing to accept whatever he wants. May everything you have said come true" (Luke 1:30-38).

Facing fear Joseph and Mary found peace as they placed their future in God's hands. Christmas reminds us Jesus came to dispel fear and give us peace as we trust him today and forever!

My moment of reflection...

Promises, Promises…

December 21
Isaiah 49:1-18

God's promises always come true—his Word is absolute truth! God promised a very unique person would step onto the stage of human history. Centuries before the babe's arrival, God gave some amazing details!

Place of his Coming: Bethlehem! "But you, O Bethlehem Ephrathah, are only a small village in Judah. Yet a ruler of Israel will come from you" (Micah 5:2).

Peculiarity of his Coming: Virgin Birth! "The Lord Himself will choose the sign. Look! The virgin will conceive a child! She will give birth to a son and will call him Immanuel" (Isaiah 7:14).

Purpose of his Coming: Redemption! "I will make you a light to the Gentiles, and you will bring my salvation to the ends of the earth" (Isaiah 49:6).

Position at his Coming: King of Kings! "For a child is born to us, a son is given to us. And the government will rest on his shoulders" (Isaiah 9:6).

Because God keeps his word, in due time, Jesus was born—born in Bethlehem of a virgin. The virgin birth was a sign to identify and confirm that Jesus was God the Son. The world was in darkness and sin had entered history, mankind needed redemption. So a child was born, who one day would receive glory and honor and blessing as the King of Kings. Jesus came in the midst of darkness and we find light that is irrepressible, in the midst of sorrow we have joy unspeakable, and in the midst of death there is life eternal—all because God keeps his promises!

My moment of reflection…

Good News of Christmas: You Are Important

December 22
Luke 2:8-14

Christmas means different things to people! To the merchant it is the busiest time of the year and for many it is a time for fun and parties. Christmas isn't our birthday—it's the Lord's birthday...a time to remember and celebrate his birth.

God announced the birth of his Son to shepherds: "For God so loved the world that he gave his only Son" (John 3:16). Shepherds lived in the fields with their animals. They were not influential, respected, had little prestige. Yet, God came to them and said, "I have good news for you, which will make everyone happy. This very day in King David's hometown a Savior was born for you" (Luke 2:10-11, CEV).

By the announcement of Christ's birth, God was saying, "I know you and you are important to me, no matter how insignificant you may think you are!" God uses people the world often overlooks. When God selected a mother for His Son, he went to an insignificant village called Nazareth and found a peasant girl. She didn't have designer clothes or a sophisticated education. But she was pure and God selected her to be the mother of his only begotten Son!

Years later Jesus said his Father cares about sparrows and lilies. And if God cares about shepherds, he cares about you. We all need to hear that! All of us have known rejection and feelings of being left out. But Christmas comes, the Light shines and God says, "I made the announcement to shepherds and I make it to you: "Unto you a Savior is born!"

My moment of reflection...

Christmas Wisdom

December 23
1 Corinthians 1:18-31

Some look at the miracle of Christmas and declare, "That's foolishness!" But the Bible teaches the "foolish plan of God is far wiser than the wisest of human plans, and God's weakness is far stronger than the greatest of human strength" (1 Corinthians 1:25).

Sitting around a hillside campfire, the shepherds must have wondered if life was really worthwhile. They must have asked each other if watching sheep makes any difference. But consider this: When God announced to the shepherds that Jesus was born, he was saying, "Listen, your life is worthwhile. It is my gift to you. Live every moment because your life—every life—matters to me!" It is impossible to live and not influence someone in some way. We are always influencing someone, for good or evil. I wonder if anyone in Bethlehem on the day of our Lord's birth asked, "Anything exciting happen today?" Maybe someone said, "Oh, I heard some woman gave birth in a stable" and somebody else responded, "but nothing exciting ever happens around here." Nothing except a baby was born and that baby changed the world!

Those insignificant shepherds were men of faith! They believed in the Messiah and probably prayed over and over, "Let the Messiah come…let him come today!" When God gave the announcement of Jesus' birth, God was saying, "Your faith matters and you matter, it is not foolishness. I am he who keeps my word. The Messiah has come—I have kept my promise."

Life counts, life matters…your life and mine! Lives of shepherds and lives of kings, they are all important to God.

My moment of reflection…

Gift of a Lifetime...Indescribable

December 24
John 3:16-17

Soon, we will gather as families and open our gifts! We've spent lots of time choosing the right gift. While those gifts may be expensive and beautiful, the thought behind the gift is love; it was given to you by someone very special. Paul was reminding his friends the nature of God's gift to them—the gift was staggering, indescribable! He cannot find words to describe it. He simply says, "Thank God for his Son—a gift too wonderful for words" (2 Corinthians 9:15).

What words would you use to describe Jesus? How do you describe a baby born of a virgin? How do you describe God in the flesh, walking on earth, reaching out to masses of people? How do you describe a God who is all-powerful? Isaiah called him Emmanuel, "God with us!" How do you describe him? Paul says we can't...words are inadequate! The greatest minds and most extensive vocabularies cannot adequately describe Jesus.

God gives a gift, not because he feels obligated but because his love is so overwhelming. It is a gift of grace. There are no words to describe God's grace towards us in Jesus. So to help us come to grips with his gift in the fullness of time God sent forth his Son as a baby. Indescribable! Yes, but the good news is you don't have to describe him to accept him. So make your journey to the manger with the shepherds. Take him into your heart and receive him as God's indescribable gift for you—the Gift of a Lifetime!

My moment of reflection...

Immanuel—Jesus With Us!

December 25
Isaiah 7:10-16

God sent prophets and personal witnesses to reveal Jesus to us! Through long and painful centuries God was seeking to communicate with men. Yet, man was unwilling to understand. So Christ came as Immanuel: "Look! The virgin will conceive a child! She will give birth to a son and will call Him Immanuel—God is with us" (Isaiah 7:14).

Isaiah uses the title "Immanuel" to help us understand the nature of the promised King—that he is God! But there is more: Not only is he God, he is God with us! He is not a god who is distant and unconcerned. He is "with" us. Often you will find that wonderful promise, "I am with you." That promise was given to Moses and Joshua and Matthew introduces his Gospel by telling us that "God is with us" and ended the book on the same note: "I am with you always, even to the end of the earth." Jesus is God and he is with us in every area of life—in trials, service, sorrows, and death. Immanuel means there is One who knows exactly how we feel and we never have to feel alone.

In our journey to Christmas, we have heard many sounds—good news that God is for us, he is over us and he is with us. But there is more: Because of Christmas, God can live in us and can work through us. At one time we were strangers! But now God and man are partners—the God who seemed so distant is actually here with us. Merry Christmas!

My moment of reflection…

Opposition to the King

December 26
Matthew 2:1-21

Not everyone honors the newborn king! Sometimes, we forget that even at his birth, there was a movement afoot to get rid of Jesus. For more than forty years, King Herod ruled with absolute authority and power. If he suspected anyone a rival to his throne, they were promptly eliminated. When informed a "newborn King" had arrived, Herod was troubled and all of Jerusalem, for the people knew the steps Herod would take to eliminate this child.

While there was great rejoicing in many hearts when Jesus was born, Herod sought his destruction. There are many like Herod today. They become involved in all the activities of the season, but they oppose all the season stands for. Herod was disturbed and troubled when he heard the birth announcement because he was not willing to let baby Jesus become king. He wanted control. Herod was deceitful with the wise men when he asked them to report back to him so he too could worship the king! Herod's real plan was to kill his competition like he did before. When they failed to inform Herod, his true nature was exposed. His hatred and wrath was exposed by killing babies two years and under! Herod stands as a terrible illustration of what men will do to get rid of Jesus! We still have Herod's around this Christmas!

Christ, born to be King of all men, experienced opposition all of his life, ending in his crucifixion! Jesus, born a King, died a King, but lives as a King! Even though men oppose him today, he is still on the throne!

My moment of reflection…

Love Was Born at Christmas

December 27
I John 4:7-17

The foundational truth of our faith is "God is love!" When Jesus was born love entered into history in a unique way. John wrote, "God showed how much he loved us by sending his only Son into the world so that we might have eternal life through him. This is real love. It is not that we loved God, but that he loved us and sent his Son as a sacrifice to take away our sins" (1 John 4:9-10).

The angels announced to the shepherds, "Jesus was born for you!" That's the message of Christmas! An angel appeared to Joseph, telling him not to be afraid to take Mary as his wife, that their baby would be called Jesus who will save his people from their sins. The angel's message was simple: Good news of great joy for all the people! When shepherds saw the baby, they told others. No one told them it was their duty to tell others. They were so amazed at what they had seen they wanted others to see this "Gift of Christmas." And the result of their action, many of us have come to understand the real meaning of Christmas.

I have six grandchildren—I love each one of them with a love that is unique to each of them. If I, a fallible human being, can love like that, how much more God must love every one of us. His love includes every human being who ever draws breath. So it's clear: Love was born at Christmas—and he never wants us to forget it!

My moment of reflection...

Christmas Is Over...Now What?

December 28
Luke 2:1-20

The celebration of Christmas is over! We have enjoyed the activities of the season: presents, decorations, cards, music, dinners, family and friends. For believers, we have honored the Christ, born as our Savior. But now that Christmas is over, how do we respond to his coming? Perhaps we can take our clue from the characters of the Christmas Story.

The "Shepherds told everyone what had happened and what the angels said to them about this child" (Luke 2:17). Like the shepherds, we are to make Jesus known and help people understand that the baby came as our Savior. The shepherds were amazed at the Christmas Story—they meditated and thought about the events! Here is a baby born to die, a King born in a stable; yet he was God in the flesh. Mary pondered the events in her heart; that is, she thought deeply what this birth really meant. It's easy to become so busy that we don't spend time in contemplation. The shepherds also answered the "now what" by glorifying and praising God. That should be our response! Because he has come, we celebrate his birth by engaging in prayer, in praise and public worship all through the year.

The celebrations are over! We've taken down the tree, packed the decorations and the parties are over. But we must never forget that Jesus is our celebration. He always is the honored One. He is our King. Now that December 25 is past, let's honor him by our witness and worship of Jesus, the Lord of lords and King of kings!

My moment of reflection...

Wisdom for the Journey

December 29
Proverbs 3:1-4

Christmas is over! Some are exhausted, disappointed with their gifts and others are worried about the next credit card statement...but for most this season has been a wonderful experience of revisiting our Savior's birth. Now our focus is on the New Year. Facing the New Year, we must admit that "what's gone is gone!" No matter how we like to relive the past, it's over...gone. But thank God for new beginnings.

God wants you to have a satisfying life. But how do we get it? We need wisdom for living in the New Year. Solomon gives us great advice: "Never let loyalty and kindness get away from you! Wear them like a necklace; write them deep within your heart" (Proverbs 3:3). Solomon teaches that love and loyalty must be the guiding lights in our lives—in everything we do. They are foundational for success! Solomon pleads with us never to let love and faithfulness leave us! Paul tells us that "love is the most excellent way." It is love that enables us to be like Jesus. Love is forgiveness...it doesn't keep score...it is about giving and helping.

Faithfulness and loyalty is a conscious response to a God who has revealed himself. Remember Abraham? His story illustrates that faithfulness must be exercised in everyday living. For Abraham it meant trusting God daily and ready to follow the commands of God. Of course, we won't always get it right. It's like learning to ski: If you're not falling down, you're not learning to ski." Our prayer for the journey should be, "Faithful to the end!" That's wisdom!

My moment of reflection...

More Wisdom for the Journey

December 30
Proverbs 3:5-6

Demands are made on us; we are bombarded by the secular influences of our world. Solomon gives us more wisdom for the journey: "Trust in the Lord with all your heart; do not depend on your own understanding. Seek his will in all you do, and he will direct your path" (Proverbs 3:5-6).

When Eskimos travel through northern Alaska, they are often in danger because there are few natural landmarks and permanent roads. In snowstorms, trails are hard to follow and freezing to death is a threat. To help travelers, trails are marked with tripods bearing reflective tape. By following the tripods, travelers find their way. Likewise, life is made up of choices and often we have no idea what choice to make. The wise believer learns to spot God's tripods! Our part in the journey is to have confidence in God...to trust in the Lord, to be cautious regarding our understanding and realize his plan is best!

Look at God's part in the journey: "he will direct your path!" His guidance is personal, practical and perfect; it is infallible and trustworthy. Patiently, he leads step by step! God isn't looking for better methods but for surrendered hearts, people who search the scriptures and see prayer as laying hold of God. The philosophy of our day is, "if it feels good, do it." But there is "higher" wisdom in life for the journey: "Trust in the Lord with all your heart; do not depend on your own understanding. Seek his will in all you do, and he will direct your path." Now that's wisdom!

My moment of reflection...

Thank God and Take Courage

December 31
Acts 28:11-16

It's always a solemn moment to approach the end of an era. This is true regarding a student graduating or an employee coming to the end of a relationship. It's also true as we face times of saying "goodbye" or as we approach the end of a year. As we come to the end of the year, let's "look back" and thank God for what he has done. But at the same time, we need to "look forward" with faith for what God will do.

Paul was at a turning point in his life! His life was marked by significant service for the Kingdom. There were experiences that could have caused him discouragement and despair and depression. He had been imprisoned in Caesarea and now was headed to Rome to face Caesar's Court. He was exhausted and faced uncertainty. Believers heard that Paul was on his way to Rome; so they went to meet their friend.

Paul's reaction to this reception is noteworthy: "When Paul saw them, he thanked God and was encouraged" (Acts 28:15, CEV). While Paul was encouraged when he saw these dear friends who had come to support him, his actions provide us with a pattern for releasing the old year and face the coming year. The only way to victoriously embrace the New Year is by "thanking God and taking courage." God has not reversed his promises or his provisions. He is still the Light of the world, the Way, the Truth and the Life. As we close one year and begin a new one, let's "Thank God and take courage!"

My moment of reflection...

A Final Note

Our journey has come to an end! In our yearlong walk, we have seen Jesus demonstrate his power and presence in remarkable ways. Throughout the life and ministry of Jesus, through stories from people's lives, we have been taught and encouraged. This gives us hope that God can work in our lives also! Thanks for letting me share my life with you; it's been a pleasure and a joy.

As we say farewell, my hope is that you have learned some new skills in risking faith and trusting God, perhaps even gained some wisdom for your daily journey. *Moments with the Master* is a practical guide to help believers cope with life's problems and experience the joys of walking close to Jesus. D. L. Moody said that "the Bible was not given to increase our knowledge, but to change our lives!" It is my prayer that our *moments* together have taught you that the Master not only deeply loves and cares for you, but that he can and will use you in a significant way as you continue to spend *moments with the Master.*

Blessings…grace and peace!